Cora's Heart

A CYPRESS HOLLOW YARN

RACHAEL HERRON

Publisher's Note: This is a work of fiction. Names, characters, places, and incidents are a product of the author's imagination. Locales and public names are sometimes used for atmospheric purposes. Any resemblance to actual people, living or dead, or to businesses, companies, events, institutions, or locales is completely coincidental.

Cora's Heart/ Rachael Herron. -- 1st ed.
ISBN 978-1-940785-00-4

Also by Rachael Herron

Fiction:

How to Knit a Love Song
How to Knit a Heart Back Home
Wishes & Stitches

Memoir:

A Life in Stitches

DEDICATION

For my sisters Christy Herron and Bethany Herron,
who inspire me with their bravery, always.

ACKNOWLEDGMENTS

Thanks to A.J. Larrieu for knowing before I did who Cora was supposed to be, and to Cari Luna for her belief, which gets me through the hard days. Thanks to Sophie Littlefield and Juliet Blackwell for the plotting lunches and inappropriate gossip, and to all my PensFatales, without whom I couldn't imagine my writing life. Thanks to Todd Thomas for his wealth of rodeo info, and Mel Vassey for checking my veterinarian facts. Any error belongs entirely to me. Thanks to Martha Flynn who always, *always* knows where the emergency exits are located, and to Kira Dulaney who saved the day again. And as always, thanks and love to Lala Hulse for plotting the original idea with me while in line for chicken sandwiches at Bakesale Betty's in Oakland, the city we both adore.

CHAPTER ONE

Danger lurks in every ball of cashmere. – Eliza Carpenter

Cora sat on an overturned apple basket in front of her storage shed, her legs splayed out, the heels of her old blue cowboy boots resting in the dirt. The fire engine had driven away minutes before, Jake Keller waving his arm cheerfully out the window as they went. Of course he was cheerful. They'd gotten to fight a fire and isn't that what firefighters lived for?

The worst part was that it was a *ridiculous* fire. It was a teeny-tiny blaze, entirely the result of her own stupidity. Cora couldn't begin to imagine how people in town would talk. Or, more appropriately, how they would laugh. When Cade MacArthur's old shack burned down a few years ago, the valley had rocked with explosions as propane bottles blew through the outer walls, which in turn ignited a grass fire that blazed up the hill. It had been the lead story in the *Cypress Hollow Independent*, with color pictures on the front page. And when Phyllis Gill's chimney caught on fire and spread into her attic and then down into her yarn room, the whole town had taken up a collection to replenish her stash. Skeins from almost every family had flooded in until Phyllis begged them to stop, saying that she'd reached the limit of the amount of yarn she'd be able to knit before she died.

Compared to those, the little fire at Cora's shed hadn't rated more than one engine using the water it carried on board. She herself had missed it all. She had been across the yard in the house, making a sandwich. She'd heard a siren but it had shut off so abruptly that Cora had assumed Buddy Hansen was practicing on the engine again – all the volunteer firefighters loved whooping the siren as often as they could get away with it.

After she'd finished pressing her sandwich together, using tomatoes from the garden and her homemade mozzarella, and cutting it diagonally with her sharpest knife, Cora had put it onto a chipped china plate and had wandered out of the house into the sunshine. She would eat it in the storage shed, as she often did. Fall was finally settling into the valley – leaves bursting into scarlet, the scent of wood fires in the air. It was her favorite time of year. Although the smoke smelled stronger now than it had when she'd gone inside . . .

It had taken a moment for her eyes to register the fire engine parked, lights flashing, in front of the shed. Water. They were streaming water. Into her *shed*.

She dropped the sandwich, the plate shattering on a flagstone, and ran.

It was over when she got there.

In the time it took to make lunch, everything she'd worked toward for the last three years was gone.

It was a tiny fire, comparably. The entire shed wasn't more than a hundred square feet total. But it had been chock-full – lower shelves held whatever she was growing that was in season (recently figs and small persimmons), the higher ones stacked three jars deep with her canned goods – cucumbers and chilies and apricot jams. Heck, she'd even made the shelves that had held her washed and carded merino fiber. She had learned to use the electric saw without cutting off any fingers, learned just how many thwacks it took with the hammer to get the nails in and flush to the board. The shed was more than storage – it was her workshop. Her larder. She did most of her spinning and dyeing inside it. It held everything she sold at her stand at the Cypress Hollow weekly farmers market. All her soap and candles. All the seeds, the dried herbs . . .

The walls hadn't burned. They were only blackened. But everything else she'd had inside the shed was either burned or ruined by smoke or water.

"We were on our way to the training tower up the valley," said Jake Keller. "Saw the smoke. It was just dumb luck we were here. Coulda been worse."

"But how . . . ?" Cora wasn't able to finish the sentence.

"Best guess, one of those candles," one of the firefighters said.

"Oh," she said in a small voice. Earlier, while she'd been sorting heirloom squash seeds, she'd lit one of last year's rosemary-lemon candles, wanting the scent to mix with the wood smoke coming from up the valley.

It was all her fault.

"Accidents happen," Jake said. He had a piece of paper for her to sign, and then asked if he could call anyone for her or take her anywhere. The men wanted to help. She could see it in their eyes. But she shook her head, unable to say anything else. Then they were gone, leaving Cora sitting on the apple basket, staring across the road, over the low dune, out to the ocean.

The waves continued beating the shore as if nothing had happened. A thin white plume of smoke showed from up in the valley, rising to meet the lazy clouds that drifted east. She should have heard the siren. Maybe she could have done something . . .

Oh. Her heart dropped. Her favorite spinning wheel, the one Logan had bought her the year before he died, had been in the shed. Slowly, she turned. If she stood at the edge, in the wide puddle of mud the firefighters had left behind, she could peer over the charred table. There it was, the Ashford Joy tipped flat in the dirt. One treadle was destroyed, burnt through, and the other was separated from the body as if a firefighter in heavy boots had kicked it out of his way.

Gone. How quickly things were taken. She'd almost forgotten that.

A black Mercedes rolled smoothly over the ruts in the dirt road. Of course. This was exactly what she needed now; a visit from Louisa, her mother-in-law's twin. Cora looked up to see if any clouds were gathering overhead, because the next thing in line was, of course, to be hit by lightning.

"Valentine called me." Louisa climbed out of the car, the door thunking solidly behind her. "She said she got a text about a fire and I was on my way back home. She wanted me to check on you." She looked over Cora's shoulder to gaze at the wreckage behind her. "I see she wasn't exaggerating. Well, at least you're insured."

Insurance. Yet another thing Cora hadn't gotten around to. The house, of course, was insured. But the shed . . . A sudden mix of nausea and grief rolled through her and she was glad she'd stayed seated. But she'd be damned if she let Louisa read the emotion on her face. "Of course. Insurance. Yes."

Why couldn't her mother-in-law, Valentine, have been the one to come check on her? Valentine would have pressed her hands and then kissed her cheek while smoothing her hair. She would have come equipped with a dog or two, good for hugging, and she would have let Cora cry into one of her huge handkerchiefs embroidered with watering cans that Valentine always had tucked into a pocket, fresh, ready to be used. Valentine believed in really giving a good *blow* into a handkerchief. "That's why God made washing machines, sweet cheeks." Valentine was the best thing she'd gotten from being married to Logan.

And in the stack of presents Cora had received from her marriage, Louisa was the one gift she wished she could give back. She was all prickles and sharp points, the polar opposite of her short,

"I'll be fine, really, Louisa." As soon as she was in bed, covers over her head. "It's nice of you to ask, though."

"Oh, not because of *this*. Don't be silly. We're celebrating the prodigal son's return."

Of course it wasn't for Cora. How could she have thought for a moment that it was about her? "Pardon?"

"Mac is back." Pride lit Louisa's voice and made her sound almost human. "He's home." She opened her car door and spoke over the roof. "And can you bake some bread? You'll have time, right? Since you don't have to do anything out here in your . . . workspace?"

Louisa's son. Logan's cousin. *Mac.*

Lightning. Cora had expected it from the sky, but it had come from her mother-in-law instead.

CHAPTER TWO

It's old-fashioned what we do. Fiber to yarn? Yarn to clothing? Yes, old-fashioned and, to my mind, always, always in style. – E.C.

Mac rested his palm flat against the door of the biggest bedroom in the old house. Behind that door, his grandfather had died, years ago. He'd died with his boots on, literally, his cracked leather Ariats kicked up, a thin paperback Western lying on the bed next to him, as if it had fallen out of his hand when he fell asleep. Only he hadn't woken up again.

It didn't feel right that the house was Mac's. What was *he* supposed to do with it? He'd never lived in it, had never wanted to. Mac didn't believe in ghosts, but if anyone had a spirit big enough to come back and haunt someone, it would be his grandfather. That man had had a pair of lungs unrivaled by an angry bull trying to avoid castration.

Mac had been in this house hundreds of times. Maybe thousands. But even though he'd owned it for years, it had never really been his. The dark wood-paneled walls and lighter colored slat floors still smelled of the Pine-Sol his grandfather cleaned everything with, and faintly, as if it were almost just a memory, Mac caught the scent of cigar smoke, bittersweet and ghostly.

The smaller bedroom's door stood halfway open as his aunt worked. The way she worked – enthusiastically, cheerily – made the guilt even worse.

"The thing about you, Aunt Valentine, is that you're too nice," said Mac. He watched her take down another curtain. She flapped it as the late afternoon sun sent a shaft of light bouncing across the wooden floor. "You don't have to do all this."

"I did a good clean a few months ago, but these are dirty. You can't have dusty curtains on your first night back in the house."

It was so *Valentine*. She had practically made a religion of taking care of other people, and now it was pathological. She couldn't have stopped if she wanted to. If the curtains hadn't been dusty, his aunt would have found something else to do for him: mopping under the bed, maybe, or replacing the contact paper in the pantry. Mac knew she came in at least once a year to clear away the dust and spiders in the old place – she sent him an email every time she did it. *Your grandfather's house is spit-shiny, ready for you to move back anytime you want. Don't even bother calling! Just show up!*

But except to bury his father and grandfather, he never showed up.

Valentine dropped the curtains on the bed and said, "What this room needs is fresh air." She struggled with the window, hitting it with the edge of her hand.

"No, let me. Don't hurt yourself." Mac ignored Valentine's protestations and moved her gently to the side. Then he fought with the sill for a moment, shaking it until it squawked like a startled chicken.

"Oh, thank you!"

Mac smiled at her as he pushed the window upward. Then he leaned out. Below him, a low hill sloped down to a copse of syca-more trees. To the north he could see his mother's land where she and Valentine lived, and to the south he could just see the edge of Cora's property.

Cora.

Out there, next to the fence line, the old path ran through the dry grass. Did they still use it, walking back and forth? He'd trampled that path innumerable times as a kid, he and Logan tumbling between the properties like puppies, always on the verge of getting in trouble, knocking down hornets' nests – and running like hell – or doing equally stupid and pointless things like hunting garter snakes and gophers, or throwing rocks into the creek, startling the crawdads. No wonder he'd become a vet. It was probably his moral obligation after he'd disturbed all that wildlife for so many years.

"Your mother is thrilled, you know. It'll be wonderful to have you back home, Mac."

He could tell she was working her hardest to keep her excitement in check. She pressed her hands together, grinned, and then did a tiny dance-like move, her feet shuffling quickly, happily.

"Oh, you're *home*. Finally home. I can't believe it."

Mac grimaced. *Don't get too excited.* It did feel okay, opening up the house, taking the covers off the old furniture, rediscovering the view of the surf from the smaller bedroom. It felt like the house wanted it, somehow. But he couldn't rest in that feeling. The whole point was not to. "I'm not staying. It's just business. I told her that . . ."

"This is where we all end up eventually," said Aunt Valentine, making it sound easy. Predestined. As if he hadn't screwed everything up all those years ago. "Your mother knows this is the land we come back to, even if we leave for a while. Daddy saw to that."

In the seventies, Mac's grandfather Henry Millet had won a whack of money in a long-shot bet on a horse with a forelock blaze like his first Irish pony, and in what could be argued his only sensible move, he bought the four parcels of coastal land. He'd built houses for his family as they needed them – a bungalow for his daughter Valentine, and a bigger house for his more demanding daughter Louisa, Mac's mother. There was an old farm house on the land that got passed around, according to who needed it most. Mac had inherited the old foreman's house where his grandfather had insisted on living until he died.

They'd buried him up on the ridge, near where Mac's father lay.

God. Dad. It brought it all back, being here, gazing up that hill. His father, stuck in bed with hypertension, uncontrolled blood pressure, and congestive heart failure from smoking for thirty years, had been told to stay home with his oxygen and wait for the new medications to start working. He should have been eating healthily. Sleeping a lot. Watching *The Price Is Right*.

Instead, Mac's mother had driven him the seventy miles to the casino so they could both stay up all night, drinking and smoking and eating Christ knew what, and by dawn, his father had suffered a massive heart attack that killed him before the ambulance pulled up to the hospital.

Both his parents were gamblers like his grandfather had been. And like so many times before, they'd taken a chance that day that everything would be okay.

It hadn't been. Now they were both on the ridge. Mac assumed Logan was up there now, too. He wouldn't know. But he'd find out.

With a thump, Mac pried up another window, satisfied with the pure force it took to break the seal that had formed with years of closure.

"You could live anywhere, you know." It wasn't what he wanted to say, but at least it was a start. "Land doesn't make a family."

"What?" Valentine said. "Oh, no, this is where we belong. On our land. Just like Daddy planned."

"He never planned a damn thing that didn't involve a dime bet," said Mac, but as Valentine shook a rag with a *tsk* in his direction, a smile tugged the corners of his mouth.

Mac had never taken possession of the house, had never spent a night in it, not even when he'd received it legally in the will. He would have given it away, but no one else had needed it. Not his mother, not Aunt Valentine, who didn't even live in her own house but with her sister . . . Not Cora.

And Mac had been happy being away, living his life. He'd gone to school and made his own way, ending up in the best job he could imagine. He loved what he did, and he counted his boss one of his best friends.

But in the end, all those roads had just led stubbornly back here, hadn't they? He should have seen it coming. Yeah, fine, he was back. But who knew for how long? Mac felt a pang of guilt that twanged like a sore tooth. All of this was to help the family. They'd know that soon enough, and hopefully they'd understand.

CHAPTER THREE

Relax your eyes. Quiet your fingers. If you clutch the knitting until your neck hurts, the sweater will pick up on the tension and worry about its warmth while you sleep. Trust the yarn, and your clever, talented hands. – E.C.

Cora didn't want to knock. Her fingers refused to curl, staying stubbornly at her side. It was stupid to feel this way but she couldn't help it. Here on Louisa's porch was the last place she wanted to be. She'd rather be in Siberia. They needed sweaters there, after all. Or maybe prison would be preferable. She could knit in prison, right? Or offloading trucks at the dump? That would be interesting, and she'd be able to salvage a few things: old dressers, beat up furniture that just needed a new coat of paint. Nice people went to the dump. Sure.

Push the doorbell. Push it. She coached herself into a smile, feeling her cheeks rise. *Push the doorbell.*

"God*damn* it," she muttered.

"Problem?" The low voice came from her right.

Mac sat on the porch swing in the dark. She hadn't even noticed him. *Awesome.* He leaned forward, and the moonlight touched the brim of his cowboy hat. McGibboney Cross Wildwood. Named after his father's favorite racehorse, he'd always been Mac for short. She couldn't see his eyes, and for that Cora was grateful. Had he been watching the whole time? Oh! Had he seen . . .?

"Did you really drop the bread?"

"Um," she said.

"And then wrap it back up in that dishtowel?"

"I wasn't going to serve it."

"Yeah you were." Mac's voice was amused.

Might as well admit it. "Yeah, I was." Cora had brushed it off and held it up to the moonlight, trying to see if the dirt was obvious. She'd spent hours making the loaf, stubbornly refusing to start the shed clean up. It had relaxed her to make it, folding its softness and beating it down so that it could rise back up again on the warmth on top of the stove. She'd baked it in her Dutch oven so the crust would be crispy, never leaving the stove once while it was on. And she couldn't help but be proud and happy that this, this evidence of caring, had cost about a dollar to make.

And then to have the loaf hit the ground like that . . . "Three second rule."

"I won't tell if you won't," he said, standing. He was taller than she remembered.

As if she remembered him well. Of course she didn't. Why, then, did she have this stupid flush rising to her cheeks? Why, then, did she suddenly remember the time after his father had died, when they'd all been out riding in the hills? It had to have been then – it had been one of the only two times Mac made it home during her marriage. Cora had ridden off alone, annoyed with something Logan had been saying or doing, and Mac had found her suddenly, unexpectedly, as she splashed her feet in the creek. He'd been so far above her on his horse, and the way his eucalyptus-bark eyes had met hers for those two or three seconds, made her know that he still felt the same way he had when he'd left. And she knew she'd telegraphed back to him something that she shouldn't have. A look – you couldn't just stop a look, not if it happened when you weren't expecting it.

She'd been younger. Stupid. For all she knew, he didn't remember that moment. He'd probably never thought of it again.

He probably never thought about what he'd asked her the day of her wedding.

God, she hoped that was true.

Mac hugged her. Cora kept her face carefully still. Had he always been so broad? Had her head only ever reached the top of his shoulder blade? She could have sworn she came up to his nose. "It's good to see you," she said formally, pulling back.

"We gonna stand out here all night?"

"Okay," she said. "Fine by me."

"Don't want to face the dragon?"

"Who does? I've already seen her today," said Cora. "Twice in one day is . . ."

"Totally unfair. Take it from someone who knows."

Cora grimaced. "I'm sorry. I shouldn't say that about your mother."

He shrugged. "I know it's hard to believe but one on one, she's not that bad." His smile was the same, still wide, still a little crooked, as if his head were tilted even when he held it straight. Cora hadn't looked into those light brown eyes yet. She wouldn't meet his gaze, wouldn't figure out if that brown was still flecked with bits of green. If she was lucky, she could avoid looking at him forever.

"That's what you always said. I've still never seen it."

"I'll be right here," said Mac. "Ready for battle?"

Cora nodded.

Inside the house, candles were tastefully lit. They were the pricey kind, Cora noticed, not the ones Cora had made for Louisa – she had never seen those on display. These came from the candle store in the mall in Half-Moon Bay. Ten bucks a pop, at least. If Cora had one of them, she'd hoard it carefully, burning it only on special occasions, instead of the way Louisa did – five grouped together, barely noticeable under the two chandeliers.

The foyer was impressive at a glance – heavy velvet curtains running floor to ceiling over the windows that faced the ocean. Louisa had always favored dark, expensive furniture: an enormous dining table that had taken six men to carry up the steps. But since her sister Valentine had moved in with her last year when her arthritis started acting up, Louisa's house had changed, and Cora thought it was for the better. The intricate china cabinet's beveled glass gleamed, but a dust bunny as large as one of Cora's own Angora rabbits lurked underneath. Two black cats were draped over the back of the rose-print sofa, and a calico watched them carefully from the low damask-covered divan. Beneath the cloying smell of gardenia, the scent of dog fur lingered in the air, and Cora heard the clicks of many small nails on the hardwood floor from the kitchen – that meant that Valentine was in there, surrounded by the four tiny, happy dachshunds who were always dancing around her feet.

Since Valentine had come, the house was *lived* in. That was true despite Louisa's almost constant complaints about the housekeeping.

"Darling," said Louisa as she came forward, lifting her smooth cheek for Mac to kiss. "You're home."

Louisa's voice was remarkable, even for the emotion Cora could see beneath Louisa's cool surface. This was her dream – her son home at last, no one even dead to warrant it. But Cora saw the grin that threatened to break through the surface (no wrinkles! Mustn't smile!), and it was nice to watch.

Until Louisa spoiled it. As usual.

"Don't let Cora near the flame. She's not very good with fire, and she's already burned down one building today. Maybe I should snuff them all out."

Oh, no. The candles weren't what needed to be snuffed, thought Cora.

Valentine emerged from the kitchen and placed a hand on her bosom. She leaned forward. Her forehead and nose were bright pink, signaling she'd already had a glass of wine or two. "I was so worried about you."

"It's fine, it's all fine."

"It was just her old shed," said Louisa with a shrug. "I was there right after it happened. Not a big deal at all."

Oooh. It *was* a big deal, a huge deal. Louisa knew that, which was why she dismissed it. Cora marrying her precious nephew Logan when she was eighteen had made it impossible for Louisa to trust her, or at least, that's what Louisa had said to anyone who wasn't Cora. The words got back to Cora, though. *A girl from who-knows-where. And what about her parents? They could have been drug addicts. Or hippies! And for her to land in town and trap one of our boys. It just goes to show.* God, that was fifteen years ago now. Only Louisa could hold a grudge that long. Luckily, her new aunt-in-law's words had also filtered back to her mother-in-law: Valentine told everyone that Louisa was just plain wrong, that Cora was a darling girl, and she was happy to have her in the family. *Eliza Carpenter loves her. Anyone Eliza cares about is a good egg.*

"Sounds scary, though," said Mac. He stood easily in the room, as if he belonged there, which, of course, he did. Fifteen years of trying to fit in with this family, Cora still felt as if she were a guest, someone who had to be careful not to spill anything. Cora's face flushed red and she thought again of dropping the bread with him watching her brush it off. She never looked good in front of this side of the family, did she?

"I lost almost all my product," said Cora. *So yeah, it was scary, and it was a big deal.*

"How did it start?" asked Valentine. "Are you okay? I knew I should have come over. I'd have brought Lottie, and she helps everything." She stroked her smallest dachshund, then picked her up and tucked her under her arm. The three other dogs darted and weaved through her feet as she walked from the foyer into the dining room.

"I'm fine. It was a candle." Cora cast a pointed look around the candlelit room. "I know never to leave one unattended." For a brief second, Cora allowed herself the luxury of hoping that Louisa forgot about one tonight. Just one. Then she reined herself in. That wasn't fair, and she wouldn't, actually, wish that on her worst enemy, which Louisa wasn't. Louisa was . . . annoying. She couldn't help it. From what her twin sister Valentine said, Louisa had come out of the womb with a complaint about the hospital lighting. "It was good of Louisa to check on me." The generosity of the words felt right. She could give her that.

And indeed, Louisa straightened and looked pleased. "Oh, I didn't do that much," she said.

Anything, Cora corrected in her head. *You didn't do anything.*

Valentine dropped into a chair at the table, tucking tiny Lottie under the tablecloth. The dogs scattered, chasing each other into the kitchen. "But Cora's poor shed. With all your lovely things inside, right?"

"We'll have to do something to help." Louisa smiled vaguely in Cora's direction.

"Of course. Oh, I know!" said Valentine. She clapped her hands and the dogs came skittering back at top speed. "A bake sale! I love a good bake sale! And once they know, people are going to want a way to help. But what can we do to help now? Just so you know, I'm not taking a dime for any of my pies you've been selling at the booth."

"I can't accept them for free. That's the whole point, that you make money, too."

"Piffle," said Valentine. "What else can we do?"

Cora grimaced. "I can't think of a thing, honestly. I have a little savings, and I should be getting paid soon for that big pickle order I did for Garlic Universe in Gilroy." She was counting on that money, and it was already a month late. She'd need to call and nag them again tomorrow. "I'll be able to live on that while I make more of . . . everything." The idea was exhausting.

"Did you lose *all* the yarn?"

Cora nodded as she pulled out her chair. "I can wash the stuff that didn't get charred or burned, but the smoke damage is pretty strong. I don't think washing is going to take it out. I'll need to make more candles – most of them melted."

Valentine's big eyes widened even more than usual. "The knitted items?"

"Gone. Closest to the candle."

Valentine covered her mouth with a plump hand. "Oh, *no.*"

Cora leaned forward and patted her other hand. Val's reaction was gratifying somehow, and made Cora feel stronger. "It's okay. It's all okay." Then she reached into her bag at her feet. "See? I have a half-made sweater right here – it was in the living room of the house. It's a test pattern for Abigail, and speaking of which, I should be knitting."

As Cora made neat stitches, concentrating on economy of motion—something that never failed to please her—she was conscious of Mac watching her. His eyes followed her fingers, and she dropped a stitch that normally she never would have.

Louisa moved back and forth between the kitchen and the dining room, carrying trays of steaming food – roast beef and rolls and a gorgeous green salad dotted with goat cheese and cranberries. While Louisa's back was turned, Valentine dropped bits of cheese on the floor for the dogs to vacuum up. She said, "That's awful. The garments were your highest price points."

"Yep," said Cora. She priced the sweaters, bulky and fast-knitted as they were, at a hundred and fifty dollars, and tourists clamored to buy them, thrilled to purchase a hand-knit in Cypress Hollow knitted by someone who had actually been friends with the legendary knitter Eliza Carpenter. To Valentine, Cora called it fleecing the tourists, and she'd felt bad about it for a while until Valentine pointed out that she was still only making about seven bucks an hour, all told, with spinning and knitting time taken into consideration. "All gone."

"The scarves and hats, too?"

"Burnt like my morning toast."

Valentine put a hand to the base of her throat. "Not the cashmere."

Cora closed her eyes. "Let's not talk about it."

"That's the good stuff, right?" said Mac, who had pulled up a chair opposite Cora. She'd been trying to ignore the way he was listening to her, but it was difficult. It had been a long time since she'd had to ignore Mac Wildwood.

Cora nodded again, briefly. "I have two cashmere goats."

"You're kidding. How many pets do you have?"

Cora looked at Mac. "I have no *pets*. I have animals that work, that can be productive. Six goats, five Angora rabbits, and four Cormo sheep. Not to mention the chickens, which I just use for eggs."

"So you take their fiber, and their eggs, but no using them for meat? What, are you chicken?" He grinned.

Cora's back straightened. "I know how to kill one." She did, she'd studied it and had made three pages of notes in her *What-If* book. "But I'm not *that* broke."

Mac poked at his mashed potatoes as if something lurked beneath. "You manage to pay the bills with your little farm?"

Oooh, he got under her skin. "You have a problem with that?"

Valentine held up her napkin and waved it. "Darlings . . ."

"I make enough to get by," said Cora, hating that she was automatically defending herself. She didn't owe him this. She owed him nothing. "Just because you're some fancy veterinarian, probably raking in money hand over paw, doesn't mean you get to judge me. Why are you here, anyway? Doesn't your job need you? Please don't tell me you're planning on staying."

"Why not?" His voice was light. "Don't y'all need another horse doctor in town?"

Was he serious? Cora swore as she dropped a stitch.

Good God. What would she do if he *stayed*?

CHAPTER FOUR

Simplicity is deceptively difficult to achieve. – E.C.

Cora stared at him. Mac had almost forgotten that direct gaze of hers, how nervous it had always made him. He buttered his bread slowly, deliberately. "I mean, all this ranch land? Gotta be call for a couple of vets, not just one."

"Well," Cora said, "most of us here in town still remember how you missed the shot when you were putting Logan's horse down."

Damn. Mac had also forgotten how she could toss him from amused to pissed in less than a heartbeat. "Someone had to shoot her. And Logan couldn't, God knew. The second shot was true."

"He had nightmares for years about that horse."

"Logan couldn't bear to do anything difficult. He never could." He watched Cora flinch as it struck the nerve he'd aimed for.

Valentine tried to help. "Now, honey, bronc riding wasn't easy, and Logan—"

But Cora struck back. "You'd know, wouldn't you, Mac? Logan died, and you never said goodbye. You never came, even though I'd called to tell you it was the last chance you had. Tell me, who was squeamish then?"

It hurt as much as if she'd reached across the table and slapped him with all her might. And she was right. That was the worst part.

"Logan knew Mac loved him," Aunt Valentine said in a low voice. "You have to know that, Mac."

It made it worse that she defended him.

"You could come home for your father. Your grandfather. Why couldn't you come home for my husband?" Cora asked.

Mac opened his mouth, but nothing came out. What was the right answer? His mother, thank God, chose that moment to bring out the last platter, heaped with roasted root vegetables. "Look at this balsamic glaze. Oh, Mac, you're going to love this."

He cleared his throat and looked at the tablecloth. "All home-made, right, Ma?"

"Oh, you know me," Louisa said breezily. And he did. The food was catered, as usual. Louisa wouldn't make anything from scratch, any more than he could forgive himself for failing Logan – and Cora – when it mattered most.

Seemingly oblivious to the tension in the room, Louisa went on, "How long will you stay, son?"

"As long as I can," he said carefully.

"What does that mean, exactly?" Aunt Valentine leaned forward so that her bosom hung precariously over her mashed potatoes. From her lap, Lottie licked her elbow.

"I can't tell yet," said Mac. "I wish I could."

Valentine said in a small voice, "I'm so glad you're here. But we would have liked to see you more. You know that, right?"

Mac couldn't help feeling defensive. "I've seen you every year. And I call Mom every week."

"That's right," said Louisa proudly. "He does."

"But I never talk to you," said his aunt, almost apologetically. "And we only saw you because we came to see you. Cora, here, she never saw you at all. It would be nice if you could stay. Just a little while, at least. For your family."

Was that a quiver in her voice? Oh, crap, he could take anything but that. Mac took a deep breath. "I think that sounds nice, I do. I missed all of you." He didn't meet Cora's eyes. "I'm not guaranteeing anything. But there might be something happening soon that will help all of you. Us."

Cora rolled her eyes. "You were working for Bay Gate Downs, right? Track vet?"

"Racetrack practitioner, yeah." He hadn't worked there for two years, not since he started working for his friend Royal full-time. But he'd kind of forgotten to keep the family apprised.

Her voice held a challenge. "Jim Younger's the vet in town, and I hadn't heard he was looking for help."

"You know everything that goes on in Cypress Hollow?"

"Not everything," said Cora. "But most of it. I run the farmers market, so I hear a lot."

"Don't you just have a booth there?"

"I do. I love it." Maybe she forgot she was mad at him, maybe she let her guard down, but her blue eyes now sparkled in the candle-light. Mac had forgotten that trick of theirs. She went on, "But I also manage it, rent the space, collect the money for the Chamber of Commerce. I started it in town two years ago when we realized there was nothing like it for thirty miles, which was ridiculous given where we live, surrounded by farms."

"And you're so *good* at it," said Aunt Valentine around a mouthful of green beans.

Cora pushed her plate away and pulled her knitting up out of her lap. She held the needles firmly. Determinedly.

"Always knitting," said Louisa, and Mac was embarrassed by her dismissive tone.

"A girl's gotta eat." Cora's voice was straightforward, and didn't seem to be seeking sympathy as she clicked away sturdily. "But anyway, I'd know if Jim was looking for a new employee. So are you thinking about setting up your own practice? I'm not sure how Cypress Hollow would take to that. You might not remember but we're pretty loyal 'round here."

Cora's right hand floated, pulling up the yarn and letting it drop. Her fingers moved slowly, beautifully, and at the same time, seemed to move at the speed of light, slipping stitches from one needle to the other. Mac felt hypnotized.

"That's amazing," he said, and immediately wanted to swallow the words. He felt like a child distracted by a pinwheel. Cora frowned and looked at her hands as if she didn't recognize them.

"We don't mean to push," started Aunt Valentine. "Oh, what am I saying? We mean to. Tell us."

"I have a couple of ideas."

Louisa smiled and straightened, looking proud. "Cora, you can have your sheep tended to by the resident veterinarian. Oh, and Abigail MacArthur even has alpacas. Those things must need shots or something, right?"

Cora's needles gave small, resolute clicks. "So you *are* setting up a private practice, then."

"I suppose that's what you'd call what I do." It wasn't the truth. Not the whole truth, anyway. "Keeping my options open."

Her eyes narrowed. She wasn't buying it. He should have known. Cora had always been able to read him. Ever since she'd arrived, flame-haired and sixteen years old, she'd had the ability to look at him and know exactly when he was about to get himself in trouble. The fact that she could tell he was going to cut his next class and hightail it to the stables never stopped him from doing it. In fact, it had always been that much more exciting, wondering if she'd show up, looking for a ride. She'd ask in that shy, quick, nervous way she used to have, pretending the answer didn't matter, but he could tell it did, so much. His horse, Two-Pack, had loved her more than he'd loved Mac, he thought. Half the time, Logan was with them, doing roping tricks to try to impress her, but the other half, Mac had her to himself. Those had been the best times. The times he didn't forget.

"You're not telling us something. And it's an important something."

Yep, she still had it. Mac shrugged. "Guess you'll know soon enough."

Aunt Valentine said. "Oh, I love surprises!"

"I hate them." His mother's mouth twisted tightly.

Cora surprised him by laughing. She turned the work and started back the way she'd come. "He'll tell us when he's ready."

Goddammit, she was still amazing. That mop of hair stuck up wildly and randomly all over her head, the burnt red of the iodine he carried in his bag. Her mouth was too big, and she still had that long, thin scar running parallel to her nose, the one she'd gotten when she'd tripped over a piece of driftwood and smacked her face on the rocks in the cave at Moonglass Beach. The shyness she used to have seemed all the way gone. She held herself relaxed, confidently. Her body was just that much wider and softer in all the places his past girlfriends prided themselves on being tiny. She was, he thought, perfectly proportioned. The way a real woman should be.

She was the prettiest girl he'd ever seen.

Mac felt that stab again, the one that had once been so familiar to him – the jolt of jealousy, that she wasn't his, that she would never be, that Logan won her, that he was in second place, again. And since it was the most ludicrous, petty, *small* feeling he could possibly imagine having, he berated himself like he always had. *Idiot. Get over it.*

"This bread," Mac said, holding his piece toward Cora. "It's got a little something . . . extra to the crust, doesn't it?"

Cora quirked her mouth to the left and then said, "Of course. Love is always the extra ingredient."

CHAPTER FIVE

*If you think it's not going to fit, it probably isn't. You can go two ways:
continue knitting and give it to someone else, or throw it in the corner to
think about its sins. Sadly, I usually use the latter method. But my corner nest
is very, very well padded and good for naps. – E.C.*

Something was very wrong with Mavis. When Cora had gone
out to check the sheep before she started the spinning she
needed to do, she'd noticed that she was one animal short.
That wasn't necessarily a problem. She only had four sheep, and
Mavis was a diva who blatantly defied the sheep-stay-together rule.
She liked to wander on her own, so much so that early one morning
when Cora was fixing her coffee, she'd been surprised to see Mavis
warming herself in front of the old stove, the kitchen door standing
open. Sometimes she didn't come in to the feed pen at night, preferring to stay snacking on the grassy slope above the house, and since
they hadn't had any predator problems in the last couple of years,
Cora let her roam at will.

Tonight she looked around one more time before checking the pasture. And there was Mavis, hiding in the dark interior of the barn, standing awkwardly, legs braced apart. "Mavis, come on," Cora said. She flipped the light switch and the bare bulb overhead blazed to life. Mavis bleated, but when she tried to move she only took one stiff-legged step and then stopped, panting.

"What's wrong?" Cora moved closer, and Mavis, usually prone to joyful darting, stayed still, her mouth open, her eyes dull.

Cora touched her head softly, then her nose. Mavis breathed heavily. In the moonlight, Cora could see that the sheep's left side was distended. "Dammit."

Usually she had to decide if she could handle the problem herself or if she'd have to call Tony Fazule, the large-animal vet in Half-Moon Bay. She thought of her *What-If* notebook up at the house, the book she filled with her worries. She'd written carefully, *What if a sheep gets sick?* Her answer to herself had been *Study until you know enough of the symptoms to diagnose whether or not you need to call a vet.* So she'd studied. She knew the anatomy of a sheep – she knew, basically, what happened at the front end, and at the hind, and most of the parts in between.

Bloat. It wasn't something she'd had to deal with much since she tried to keep the sheep off the meadows when the damp was still on the grass, but tonight had been so foggy that she would bet Mavis had eaten the alfalfa when it was wet. Bloat could kill and quickly, Cora knew, and she was out of Bloat Guard.

Jim Younger, the town vet, wasn't an option – he was on vacation. She could call Tony Fazule. He'd be here in an hour, if he was available and drove fast.

But tonight Cora had one more option.

She could call Mac.

But – what if he thought she *needed* him? It wasn't like that. She didn't. But she needed a vet, any vet, and she needed one now. She took out her phone and dialed while her stomach knotted in protest.

"Cora?" His voice sounded surprised, and she didn't blame him. How many years had it been since she'd called him? Five years ago, the night she'd called him to tell him to come see Logan one last time.

"I have a sick sheep. I think it's bloat."

"You've had a hell of a day, haven't you?"

She sighed. "So far, yeah, it's sucked. Can you just come?" The words felt heavier in her mouth than rocks.

"I'll be right there."

And he was. She thought he might walk since their properties adjoined each other, but instead, through the trees, she saw the car lights bouncing down his driveway, turning on the main road, then driving up her rutted path. He drove a beat-up older SUV, which surprised her. Cora would have guessed that by now he would have bought himself something new, something trendy and expensive.

Mac got out and nodded at her. Then he opened the back and pulled out a large bag. "This whole car is full. I could do field surgery on an unexpected army of sick yaks."

"An army of sick yaks *would* be unexpected. You look like a country vet driving that old thing," she said.

"That's the point."

"Ah, so it's planned. I should have known. Like your outfit?"

He smoothed down his flannel shirt under his beat-up green jacket. "You're lucky I pulled on jeans instead of coming over in my boxers."

Cora had a sudden unwanted image of him hurrying through a bedroom, pulling up his jeans with one hand, reaching for his car keys with the other . . . *Damn.*

She spun. "Anyway. She's over here." The sooner he treated Mavis, the sooner he'd be driving away, back toward where he belonged. She held the flashlight behind her so he wouldn't trip. She didn't need its illumination. Cora knew this land, this path. She could run it blindfolded. She knew where each little ditch ran, where the rains had pushed rivulets through the sandy clay. She knew how many steps it took from her front door to get to the pasture gate, and she could undo the latch without glancing down. Home.

Mac wouldn't know anything about that.

From behind her, she heard his footfall stumble and a muffled curse. Things sounded louder than normal to her in the crisp night air. Or was her hearing amplified because it was Mac behind her?

"Sorry, you want to hold the light?"

"I'm fine."

"I know you work mostly with horses now, and this is . . . Anyway, here she is." Cora led him into the barn.

Mavis still stood, but she looked as if she wouldn't be up much longer. Her sides, even more distended, heaved, and she didn't seem to care that a strange man was approaching her.

"Oh, you're not feeling good, are you, honey?" Mac's voice was so warm and soft Cora almost didn't recognize it. He leaned forward, moving smoothly to his knees. In a matter of moments, Mavis had her eyes closed and was swaying as he palpated her stomach. "Good girl, such a beautiful girl," Mac murmured as he kept his movements slow and easy.

Cora stood as close as she could. "What about Bloat Guard? That's worked in the past."

Mac didn't look up at her. His hands moved over Mavis lightly. "She's beyond that. We'd risk rupturing a lung from the pressure. I'm going to use the stomach tube instead."

"Will she be okay?" Crap, her voice was shaking as much as Mavis's legs. Mavis had been her first sheep, and her favorite. Something about the way Mavis never did anything the right 'sheep' way had always pleased Cora deeply.

Mac said, "Can you hold her for me? She needs to stay standing, and I'm not sure how much longer she'll be able to do that."

He hadn't answered her question. Cora held Mavis as Mac did something that the sheep should have thoroughly hated. But Mavis hardly seemed to notice. When she did open her eyes now, they were blank, as if Mavis had checked out.

"Come on, baby girl," Mac muttered. He was using his whole body, twisting the tube, using his thighs to help hold the sheep while his torso moved as much as Mavis's didn't. In the thin yellow light of the bare bulb that hung overhead, he had broken a sweat. Cora felt a wave of nausea roll through her as she realized how much pain Mavis was in. "Hang on, Mavis," she said under her breath. "If anyone can do it, you can."

The other three sheep were in their pen, watching nervously, their hooves scratching on the wooden floor underneath the bed of straw. The goats moved restlessly, blinking sideways at them. Thank God it wasn't them again – Fred and Ethel had gotten sick six months ago, and it had almost drained her bank account getting them well.

Cora held tight, the scent of lanolin and dung and hay filling her nose. *Please,* she wanted to say, but didn't. Mac looked up at her and their eyes met for one long second. Too long. The contact made Cora's heart stutter, and she remembered – in that second – what she'd been trying to forget for a long time.

Cora broke the gaze, her eyes dropping to the sheep. Imagination, that's all it was.

Then Mavis made a burping noise, a kind of stuttered moan, and the pen filled with a foul green odor.

"Whoa." Cora took several steps back.

Mac removed the tube, sinking down on his heels. "That should help. You can let her go."

As Cora released Mavis, the sheep folded to the ground.

"Oh . . ."

"She'll be okay," Mac said.

"Are you sure?" Mavis didn't *look* okay. Mavis looked miserable. But she was breathing more deeply, more regularly. She belched again. Mac gave a bark of laughter. "Eructation is a great sign. Good job, Mavey-baby." He reached out and gave the sheep a scratch on the top of her head. Mavis sighed redolently and leaned into his hand. "She acts more like a dog, huh?"

Cora felt relief flow through her. "She's always been like that. Not normal."

"I don't expect any animal you have would be normal."

Mac twisted as if his lower back hurt and then looked over his shoulder. He peered into the barn, turning his head around and then twisting the other way so he could see all the way around. The light was dim, but Cora knew one thing: her barn was as well-maintained as her animals.

"You have help here?"

"Gee, thanks."

He held up his hands. "I'm only asking."

"No. I don't have the money for help. This is mine. All mine." She couldn't keep the pride out of her voice.

Mac nodded. "It looks great. And . . ." he raised his head and sniffed. "Besides that awful smell coming from our girl here, it smells good in here."

She smiled. "Right? I read once that Martha Stewart demands that her barns smell as disinfected as a kitchen so she can have impromptu dinners there whenever she wants."

Mac's eyebrows raised. "I'm horrified."

"Me, too. Can you imagine if it smelled like air freshener out here? Cool Linen? Spring Rain? If it didn't smell like hay and dust and dirt?"

"Just good clean poop."

"Yes. Exactly. People don't get that." Cora sat on a small bench she'd built into the pen's wall two years ago.

"May I?" He gestured at the other end of the bench.

She nodded. "Of course."

"This is nice," Mac said, touching the wood. "It's sanded and everything. Benches in barns have put more than one splinter in my ass over the years." He paused. "Did Logan build this?"

"No."

Logan had never been good with tools, and Cora knew Mac knew that, too. Logan had ridden horses. That had been his one true talent, and holy hell, he'd been amazing at it. It was what she'd loved about Logan back then, the way he looked up on a bronc that was trying its level best to unseat him. Eventually he'd get down from the saddle (or get thrown from it), and he'd always stand up the same way, slow and long, hooking one thumb into his belt loop, pushing down his sunglasses to send her an insouciant grin, ready to ride into the ring again as soon as the buzzer sounded. Mac had seen him in the saddle as often as Cora had. More, since they'd grown up together. But Mac had always been in the stables, with the animals, moving around and under them, while Logan soaked up the rodeo glory.

Mac was still examining the wood. "Who did, then? They're newish, right?"

He couldn't imagine that she'd done it? It hadn't even crossed his mind? Had she really been *that* helpless then? "They're mine. I breed the girls every year with Charlie Foscalina's ram. When they lamb, I like a place to sit and wait for the births. And afterward, I can rest here and watch them do the sproinging."

"Damn."

"You don't have to sound so surprised."

"But I am. You were such a . . ."

"A what?" What *had* Mac thought she was, so long ago? Just some random foster kid? Some nobody? No, that wasn't right, not the way he used to look at her. She would like to think he'd thought she was a friend, but then he'd left and had never looked back.

"You were such a girl."

She was as surprised as if he'd burst into song. "Okay, *that* was the last thing I thought you'd say."

Mac stretched his long legs out, his brown cowboy boots broken in and scuffed at the sole. "What did you expect?"

She paused. And then she surprised herself by telling him the truth. "That you thought I was just a kid from nowhere."

He tilted his head, and the overhead light lit the long plane of his cheekbone. His jaw was all stubble. He'd probably have half a beard by morning.

"You were from here."

"No, I wasn't."

"You were in all the ways that counted."

"Oh." Cora felt warmed. Then she looked down at her ratty jeans, at the old homespun Aran she'd made ten years ago that she'd thrown on after she'd called him. "But just a girl? Please. I don't even know the last time I used lipstick."

He shook his head. "I didn't say just a girl. I said such a girl."

She frowned. "What do you mean?" Was he teasing her? Because if anything, Cora was closer to a tomboy now than she'd ever been. She wore overalls, not dresses. She used lanolin on her lips, not lip gloss. Her manicures consisted of pushing Bag Balm into her cuticles before bed.

Mac didn't answer. He moved instead back to Mavis. The sheep was lying down now, her eyes closed, her breath even. "You're better, aren't you, love?" His voice was a dark rumble, and Mavis looked like she'd purr if she could. Listening to Mac's soothing tone, Cora wouldn't blame her . . .

She stood, slapping her hands together. Both Mac and Mavis jumped. "All right. Thank you. How can I pay you for this visit?"

Mac ducked his head and kept his gaze on the sheep. "Don't worry about it."

"Don't be ridiculous. I owe you for your time."

Mac collected his gear, throwing it in his bag. His motions were hurried. "We can work it out some other time."

"Fine," said Cora. "But we *will* work it out."

He nodded and brushed past her. Just the shoulder of his jacket touched her as he passed, and Cora caught her breath.

Back at the car, he stashed his gear in the back without meeting her eyes. "Goodnight, Cora." He opened the driver's door and stopped. Then, without getting in, he slammed it shut again. Looking past her, he focused on something over her shoulder.

"No more horses, then?"

"Logan was the one who raised bucking stock. Not me."

"Did he ever make any money on that?"

She twisted her fingers into her belt loop. "Nope. Never went into banking like he said he would, either." Logan had let Cora down, over and over again. Not that she'd tell Mac that. "He worked part-time loping horses out at the fairgrounds. At least that was semi-steady cash."

Mac nodded, thinking. "You still use that old bomb shelter?"

She hadn't expected him to remember that. "It's my favorite place on the property." Inside it she kept a cot, stores of fresh water and enough canned food to last weeks. She'd made it more than just habitable. She'd made it a *cozy* little bomb shelter, as oxymoronic as that was. Just in case.

Mac said, "I used to hide in there when Logan and I played hide and seek. He was scared of it, so he never found me."

After Logan died, I slept in it. Sometimes I still hide there. The words were loud in her head.

Mac's stride was long and he was in front of her almost before she could register his motion. "I'm sorry."

This was the time, then. This was when Cora said, with acid in her voice, all the words she'd planned: *You're sorry you left your cousin to die by himself? You're sorry you never said goodbye to a man who loved you like a brother? You're sorry you'll never get a chance to redo the one thing that mattered the most?*

Instead she just said, "Sorry for what, Mac?"

"I'm sorry I let you both down." He kept his eyes low, focused somewhere at their feet. "I can never forgive myself, and I can never make it right." His voice thickened. "I did it all completely wrong, and I'll never be able to tell you how sorry I am. But I swear, Cora, I'd like to *try* to tell you."

She opened her mouth to speak but had no idea what she wanted to say.

Mac nodded, sharply, and turned. The car door slammed, and he was gone, leaving Cora standing alone in the moonlight.

Don't be ridiculous. Don't be stupid.

She folded her lips firmly. Chores. The rest of them. And then there was spinning to do. A lot of it. Nothing was going to get done if she didn't do it herself.

Don't think of him. Don't.

As she closed the barn door, she wished that for once, she'd listen to herself.

CHAPTER SIX

Home is where you make most of your knitting (and your life) mistakes.
The right pillow and the right shoulder on which to rest can ease the fixing. –
E.C.

The idea came to Cora while she was lying in bed that night, unable to sleep, determinedly blocking the image of Mac taking care of her favorite sheep from her mind. *Money.* She needed a creative way – another one – to bring in more money.

Okay. So what was she good at?

Skipping stones across the creek probably wouldn't pull in any vast income. Nor would reading L. M. Montgomery novels in the bathtub.

She was already making things – candles, yarn, clothes. Sometimes it felt like she was making *all* the things, but the percentage brought back in was low per item. It hadn't mattered that much, though. Her bank account, never robust, had never been totally threadbare. Not until recently.

It should be something that used her brain rather than her hands, not something that would cost almost as much to make as to sell.

Once she'd had what she thought had been a genius idea: she made a series of videos detailing what went into a self-sustainable lifestyle. She had one on how to grow high-yield vegetables in a small space. She'd racked up a lot of views on the canning video – she showed her favorite trick for peeling tomatoes – but by far her most popular video was the one about her 'bug-out bag', the bag she'd grab if she had to in case of tsunami or earthquake or other unnamed terrifying disaster. She sat in front of the camera with the backpack and removed one by one the flashlight, extra batteries, tiny hand-cranked radio, water purifying tablets, toilet paper and small trowel (*very important,* she'd said to the camera, keeping her face straight, because after all it *was* important), local and state map, list of emergency phone numbers, dried granola bars she'd made her-self, can opener (with bonus corkscrew! In case your shelter had wine, and this was California, after all, you had to be able to open the bottle).The video had so many hits that she'd been able to put an ad at the bottom of it. But even so, the video made only a few dollars a month. She wasn't going to get rich that way.

Cora stared at the moonlight illuminating the back of the curtain. She could write. She knew that. She'd written for the paper in high school, and it had been her favorite class, even though Trixie Fletch-er had been the editor. But the thing that had been true in high school was still true today: Cora and Trixie were not pals. The one time she'd gotten up the courage to ask Trixie if she needed any help with the book review column at the paper, she'd been assured that Trixie most certainly did *not.* It had taken days to recover from the deep purple blush of shame.

Nowadays, beside the odd article for *Spin-Off* or *Mother Earth News,* her writing was usually contained to the *What-If* book. Maybe looking at it would help. She flipped on the bedside lamp and pulled the book from the nightstand drawer. The cover was battered leather, scratched and scraped, worn from being handled for so long. A thin, knitted bookmark marked the entry she'd last been working on. But *What If A Boat Sinks* wasn't what she was worried about tonight. Cora flipped the pages, the scent of paper and ink pleasing her, as it always had.

Eliza Carpenter gave her the blank book many years ago, the first week that Cora lived with her that last year of high school. She'd said, "You worry so much. Too much, Cora." At the time, Cora had been seventeen with a brain that never stopped racing, while it seemed Eliza had a secret well of peace that she dipped into regularly. Cora desperately wanted to know how to be more like Eliza.

She had been Cora's first real friend in Cypress Hollow. Before Logan and Mac, before anyone at the stables, Cora had been placed at Windward Group Home. She hadn't understood why the system – which hadn't paid any attention to her for so long – would suddenly send her off to the middle of nowhere, a tiny coastal town full of people who would most likely stare and point and whisper as she walked around. The group home itself could hardly be called that – it only had four other kids, and they'd all been there so long it seemed like they belonged there, like some kind of weird little family. The four of them, Janice and Shirelle and Leona and one lone boy, Marquis, sat on the front porch and spat into the oleander bushes, playing poker using made-up rules and eucalyptus buds for chips.

High school in Cypress Hollow, Cora knew, would probably be brutal. Everyone would know everyone, and she'd be the loser just like she'd always been. Alone.

Then, as she'd been putting her notebooks away on the one bookshelf in the bare room, making sure her two favorite purple pens were secreted away behind them, a woman had knocked gently at her partially open door. "May I come in? I've been trying to give you some time to unpack, but I'm always so impatient. I'm Eliza Carpenter. I come every Tuesday to teach knitting."

Cora had been attracted to the needles at once, even though she'd been shy of Eliza– she'd seemed so happy, so content in her own skin. Everything Cora wasn't. Maybe the key was in the yarn, Cora had thought. She had loved the way the stitches slipped, one by one, from Eliza's left needle to the right one. She'd adored how Eliza looked right into her eyes when she praised her neat, economical stitches. She'd loved how knitting had a *point* – it wasn't just a craft girls did while passing time. You got something out of it. Something useful. It was a practical art.

Then later, when Eliza had taken her out of Windward, that first week of living on Eliza's ranch, Cora kept pinching herself in joy while at the same time, she tried to stay out of the way. She teetered on worry's sharp edge: Was she underfoot? Should she try to be more present? Would Eliza like her more if she vacuumed every day? Or was it better to assist more outside, with the sheep? Eliza would never keep her if she wasn't useful, if she didn't add value to the property. Cora didn't know much, but she knew running a sheep ranch was hard work, and she was going to make it easier for Eliza, no matter what.

After they'd spent the morning repairing a broken fence (Cora had unspooled the barbed wire, not complaining when she cut her palm) and the afternoon making Eliza's famous raspberry scones (Cora had done the mixing by hand, ignoring the sweat that soaked her T-shirt), Eliza had held the blank book between her square, capable hands and said, "Even on my darkest nights, I never worried as much as you do on a good day. But you know the difference between you and me?"

Cora couldn't have begun to list all the differences that rested between them.

"There *is* no difference. At heart, we're exactly the same, and *that's* why we feel like we know each other so well," Eliza had said triumphantly.

As she'd handed Cora the leather book, Eliza said, "You just need a place to store your worries."

"What?"

"Write them down. Every single one." Eliza opened to the first page and wrote *What if . . . ?* "Fill in the blank."

Cora was skeptical. "But that won't fix anything."

"Of course not. You have to write the fix, too."

So it had started. That night, Cora wrote *What if Eliza sends me back?* After a long, long time of thinking, she carefully wrote, *If no one wants me, then I will take care of myself. I will* always *take care of myself.* It was simple. Too easy. She knew she wouldn't be able to do it, not just like that. But she'd slept better that night than she had in years, her mind still and dreamless.

In the morning, when she'd woken in the cupola in Eliza's little cottage, surrounded by windows that looked down on rolling green hills and acres of wooded land, she didn't bother to pinch herself. If it was a dream, she had never wanted to wake up.

Eliza had been her answer to so many What-ifs.

But of course, Cora had learned over the years that there were always more questions, and every one solved meant another two to write down.

<<>>

Now the old leather book fell open to a well-thumbed page: *What if I run out of money?* She'd written the question a few months after Logan died five years before, when she'd spent all the insurance money on first his funeral, then paying off his truck, and finally to fix the roof that had almost blown right off in a spring windstorm.

There were answers listed, so many of them, but the problem was that none was just right. *Stop eating anything store bought.* She was already pretty much doing that. *Give up having coffee with friends.* Cora couldn't remember the last time she'd bought a cup of coffee she didn't make herself at home. *Sell the engagement ring.* She'd done that last year – it was too bad it turned out to be cubic zirconia. She hadn't allowed herself to be mad at Logan. It was too late for all that. *Run away to Bali.* That was just silly. She'd never leave home, not for any reason.

For one brief moment, she pictured Mac asleep in his grandfather's house. If she stood and pulled back the curtain on the north side of the bedroom, she'd be able to see the roof he was sleeping under.

It would be a ridiculous thing to do. *Think about the money. Think about saving yourself.* She read the pages again and thought about getting up to find a pen.

But even without an answer, holding the notebook calmed her. She yawned. The moon had tucked itself behind a cloud, and its light no longer filtered through the thin curtain. Cora barely noticed when the book slipped from her hands, and sleep rolled over her like the ocean waves outside the window.

CHAPTER SEVEN

I've been called crazy, and if you knit as much as I do, you will be too. I like to nod my head seriously, as if considering the accusation, then cross my eyes and say loudly, 'the right double-left-leaning decrease will save the world.' They run away quickly, and I can knit in peace again. – E.C.

Thursday morning, Mac stood on the sidewalk, staring at the sign. *Cypress Hollow Animal Shelter.* Maybe if he stayed in place long enough, he'd be able to talk himself out of pushing open the door. He should walk down the street, over to the farmers market. See if he could find Cora, maybe. Just to see what she was up to.

What he *shouldn't* do was to open the door of the animal shelter. Not if he knew what was good for him.

"Dammit." He shoved his hands into his pockets and jingled the change he found. "Nope. No way, Jose."

He pulled out a penny. Heads he went inside. Tails he went to find Cora. He flipped it into the air as high as he could, but he missed catching it as it fell, and it rolled into the gutter and through the drain grate. "Oh. That's just great." Then he laughed at his own pun.

A passing woman approximately the age of the sun gave him a wary look. She walked carefully past, putting the city trashcan between him and herself. Mac couldn't help himself – he laughed harder, and the old woman scuttled even faster. He was immediately ashamed of himself for scaring her.

"Top o' the mornin' to ya," he called out by way of apology in his worst fake Irish brogue, the accent he usually only affected after several pints of beer while watching soccer with Royal in the racetrack's main bar.

Royal. The whole reason he was here. This was all Royal's idea, and if anyone knew how crazy Royal's ideas were, it was Mac.

And if Royal were here, he'd say, "No way in hell you're going through that door. You've got things to do."

And Mac would undoubtedly say, "Screw you – try stopping me." Mac could almost hear Royal's bellow of laughter.

So he should back away. He *did* have things to do. He should walk the two blocks to Tillie's and see if Shirley still worked there like she had when he was in high school. He'd eat scrambled eggs and watch the waves break across the street.

Hell, it wasn't like Mac needed a dog. He needed a dog like a horse needed an oil change. He was nowhere near getting over losing his last two dogs who had committed the unforgivable sin of dying last year. Spartacus, his tiny black teacup poodle, had thought he ruled the universe with his mighty yap, and sometimes he even convinced Mac that it was true. Mac had found him as a three-pound puppy on the sidewalk in Oakland, covered in mangy sores. The owners who'd left him without shelter in the front yard didn't answer when he knocked on their door, just peeked at Mac from behind a bed sheet hung over the window. The third time he passed the house and saw the puppy lying shivering on his side, eyes dull, Mac had simply reached over the fence and picked the puppy up, holding its trembling, dirty body against his shirt. He knocked one last time. The eyes peeked. Mac had held the dog up so they could see exactly what he was doing. The sheet dropped into place and the light inside went out. So he'd stolen Spartacus, and hadn't felt badly about it for one hot second.

His other dog, Petaluma, had been the sweetest, dumbest creature in the world. A huge brindled Great Dane, she'd weighed a hundred and fifty pounds and had reminded Mac of a fur-covered container ship. She'd believed she belonged nowhere but in Mac's lap and had no apparent concept of her enormity. Rescued from a shelter he'd "accidentally" visited while on a work trip to LA, he'd had to exchange his rental car for a full-sized cargo van in order to bring her home. That whole trip, six hours up the I5 through the Central Valley, Petaluma had kept her gigantic head on his thigh, as if trying to express her gratefulness for escaping the stress of the shelter. She'd drooled the whole way, too, until his pant leg was soaked past his knee. He'd just turned the heater on and kept one hand on her ears.

Both had died of osteosarcoma only two weeks apart, a bitter coincidence. So, no. No new dog for him.

The door of the shelter opened, and a woman with thinning blonde hair and a grey, shapeless dress stepped out. "Help you with something?"

"Sorry?" Mac was caught off-guard.

"You've been staring at the door for ten minutes. Are you a terrorist? You don't look like one."

He scratched his head. "A terrorist?"

"We got a bomb threat three years ago."

"You're an *animal* shelter."

"I'm aware of that, sir. We're a kill shelter, though, and that don't rest well with the PETA-types coming in from the city."

A kill shelter. Great. Mac could resist a no-kill place, a shelter he could leave with confidence that all the animals would eventually be placed, but a shelter where they killed those who weren't adopted after a certain amount of time?

It was sort of his obligation to go inside. Yeah. That penny had probably landed heads up in the sewer.

The woman introduced herself as Cindi and said she had a lot of things to do, and to holler if he needed help. He could use the leashes on the walls to take any of the dogs out to run if he wanted to see what they were like. "Mind what the cards on the cages say, though. The volunteers know their personalities better than anyone else. If the card says the animal's a biter, you'll get bit."

People were stupid. Insensitive to the point of cruelty. The majority of dogs left at shelters were around a year old, right at the age where they started chewing chairs and destroying sofas. What did people think? That they were going to bring home these precious little cuties, and that they'd learn (somehow, magically) how to sit and stay and look adorable on command? Hell, no. They were animals. They took cues from their owners, and if the owners were idiots, you got unmanageable animals that ended up in places like this, behind bars, barking themselves hoarse, alone and miserable.

Mac went through the door, cursing himself as he did so.

Just looking. That's all he was doing. A bossy-looking Jack Russell yapped up at him, spinning and jumping in place. A volunteer's card, handwritten by someone named Jonas, said, "This guy will give you a workout even after he's had his run on the beach. Lively house recommended." A shaggy dog with dreadlocks looked up mournfully and then rested his head back onto his paws. A note said, "This one's person died a few months ago. He needs nothing but kibble and a new love." It was signed Cora. Mac looked closer at the handwriting. Was it . . . ? Sure looked like it. But how could someone with no pets volunteer at a shelter? Huh. For a moment he put his fingers through the wire fence separating him from the old dog.

But no, a creature that sad-looking would get adopted for sure.

Keep walking, he told himself. *You're just looking.* The room smelled of wet concrete and antiseptic and the sharp tang of urine. No matter how clean a shelter was, no matter how well it was run, you couldn't get rid of that acrid scent. It was pushed into the walls and stained the floors, the smell of desperation and frantic hope.

He kept his eye out for other cards written by Cora. One hung on the cage of a chocolate lab. "Ideal family dog, wants to copilot your minivan and act as extra couch cushions for your kids." Another was on the front of a cage holding a mournful basset hound. "This guy is heavier and faster than he looks. If you lost a tennis ball last year in the bushes, he'll find it for you today. He has a job to do, and he'd love to do it with you."

Cora, if it was the Cora he knew, did a good job with the cards. If he were looking for a dog, which he wasn't, she'd get him with these. Maybe.

And then he came across the bedraggled mutt at the end of the hall.

"Hiya, girl."

The orange and white mix looked like a beagle shoved into a pit bull costume. Her jaw was wide and when she raised it, her bite looked off-center, as if her jaw had been broken at some point. Her ears had been cropped. On her front leg was something that appeared suspiciously like a cigarette burn, and a part of her back was marred by another hot item – a motorcycle's tailpipe, maybe? The hair would never grow back there, he knew. Mac's blood sped in his veins. He'd like to take a heated lighter to the person who would treat an animal this way.

The card was also by Cora. "This little love needs someone to watch over her before her timidity takes over her sweetness. She is a scared little darling. Confession: I'd keep this one if I could. *Caution:* Aggressiveness not fully tested. Please ask at desk for help in handling."

The front desk woman, Cindi, squeezed past him carrying a length of hose. "Don't bother with that one. You'd be taking too big a chance on her. I wouldn't risk it."

Well, now. Nothing Mac liked better than a challenge.

"Look, I'm a vet. You can shoot straight with me. Do you mean she hasn't been tested for disease? Or that she hasn't had her shots? Or do you actually mean she's going to rip my face off if I open the cage?"

Cindi's lips twitched, but she didn't quite smile. "I think your face will be safe. It's your arms, legs, hands, and feet I might be concerned about."

"I'm pretty good at dodging teeth."

"She lunged at me when she got brought in here."

"Well, you were the one putting her in the cage, right? I wouldn't like that, either. How did she come in?"

Cindi said, "A guy found her in the street. He carried her eight blocks in his arms because he didn't have a leash."

"Didn't lunge at him?"

"I guess not." Cindi shifted the hose, draping it over her shoulder, and didn't say anything else. She watched him as if he were the one who might need shots.

The silence lengthened. He wasn't going to break it. She would have to.

"So," Cindi said, finally. "You want to take her for a walk?"

Mac nodded.

Cindi flapped a hand. "Fine. Leashes in the hallway. Put a cage muzzle on her."

"Where can I take her?"

She looked at him. "Might be her last walk, right? Take her wherever you want to take her. Just leave your driver's license on the counter so I know you're not some sicko. Although if you're really a vet you might want to think twice about coming back here – our vet is on vacation and he barely has time to come in when he's in town. I might just make you stay."

"I'll bear that in mind."

It wasn't hard to get the dog ready to go. In fact, she seemed grateful for anything that Mac did to her. He snapped a prong collar on and she didn't seem to notice. As he sat on the bench, she leaned against his legs. As he slipped the muzzle over her nose, she rubbed the top of her head against his arm.

"Come on," said Mac. "Let's get out of here."

Once outside, they could cross the road and go up and over the dunes, coming down to the hard-packed sand. She was pulling that way, in fact, and when she saw two seagulls squabbling over someone's dropped muffin, she pulled harder, dropping low into her stance, making a chirping noise in the back of her throat.

"Nope. None of that." The beach would be difficult. Too much open space, too many birds. A dog like this wanted to run – he could feel the desire straining through her compact musculature. "What about just a walk, then? A regular old sidewalk walk."

She looked up at him as if he were God. Her tail wagged and thwapped against the mailbox so hard he worried she might break it, and then she leaned on his legs again, as if she were helping to prop him up.

Cora could use a dog like this, an animal that had no purpose but to give and receive love. Would encouraging her that way be too heavy-handed? Sure. Mac would be taking a chance, telling her what she might want to do.

But he'd always liked the long shot.

CHAPTER EIGHT

By letting a teenager abscond with your best needles, you're guaranteeing the future of our race. – E.C.

After Cora had arranged her booth at the farmers market, spreading out her wares to make it look like she had more than just the three bins of product she'd had in her car, a young woman wearing a camouflage T-shirt and cargo pants entered the booth with a scowl as dark as her dyed black hair. She looked familiar, but Cora couldn't place her. Someone's kid, going through a rough patch. Poor kid. Cora remembered well what that felt like. The girl skulked toward the batts of fiber, and then looked at the skeins of yarn. She poked a soap bar with one finger and picked up a lemon candle, frowning as she held it to her nose.

If Cora hadn't miscarried Logan's child, that little girl would have been about this girl's age.

It was unimaginable.

"Let me know if I can help you with anything," said Cora, keeping her eyes carefully on the lace panel of the sweater she was knitting.

The girl shrugged and turned as if to leave. But at the front of the stall, she turned back and said, "What is this stuff?" She pointed to the unspun roving and batts. "It's not, like, yarn. Every other place in this whole town sells yarn. But that's different."

Cora smiled and stayed still, not wanting to scare the girl off. "It's pre-yarn. Fiber from my sheep."

"You have sheep?" The girl didn't meet her eyes.

Olivia Fletcher – that's who she was. Trixie Fletcher's daughter.

Well, crap. But it looked like the apple *did* fall far from this particular tree. Trixie was tall and thin, with beautiful long, straight, red hair. Her daughter, on the other hand, was much shorter, with black messy curls. It looked as if she'd cut her own hair with a pair of blunt scissors – the edges were ragged and asymmetrical. Her nails were bitten down to the quick, rough and reddened as if she chewed the skin, too. Something about the girl reminded Cora, strangely, of herself. Had she looked this bad when she'd first come to Cypress Hollow? How had Logan seen past that? Why had Mac befriended her?

Cora struggled to remember what they'd been talking about. "Sheep. Yeah. I have four of them."

"Do you just cut it off them?" Olivia poked at another pale gray batt.

Cora wanted to laugh, but she didn't want Olivia to think she'd said anything wrong. "No, the wool that comes off them is pretty gross, actually. Full of VM."

"Huh?"

"Vegetable matter. It's all the stuff they walk through and lie in while they're in the fields, hay, and dead bugs, and stickers, and poop."

"It's *shit?*" Olivia pulled her finger back.

"Oh, yeah, lots of it. To get all that junk out, you have to wash the fiber carefully so you don't felt it. Otherwise you get dreadlocks, all matted up. Then you have to comb it so it looks pretty and perfect like that."

Olivia sighed and touched the batt again. "It's so soft I can barely feel it."

"I love that about it. Here," Cora reached forward and pulled out a few staple-lengths. "Hold this in the palm of your hand."

Olivia looked skeptical but held out her hand.

"Just let it sit there. Close your eyes. Yes, like that. Now, wait." Cora gave it a second, then said, "Do you feel your hand heating up underneath it?"

Olivia's eyes flew open. "Yes!"

"Isn't that neat? It feels like the wool is generating heat, doesn't it?"

"Is it?"

"It's just using the heat of your hand, trapping it, and then returning it to you."

"Wow." Olivia stared into her palm, and then at the batt. "How much does it cost?"

"Sixteen dollars for that much."

"Oh, fuck." The word fell naturally from the girl's mouth, and her shoulders hunched forward. "Okay." She took a step away.

"Wait," said Cora. "You should have it." Quickly, she put the batt in a clear plastic bag and shut it with a twist-tie. She placed it in Olivia's hands.

Olivia frowned harder and shook her head. "I don't need this. I don't even know what to fucking *do* with it. What are you supposed to do with fluff?"

Cora perched herself on the edge of her stool. She chose her words carefully. "You're Trixie Fletcher's daughter?"

A curt nod was her only answer.

"Olivia, right?"

Another nod.

"I'm Cora. I've known your mom since high school." *No love lost.* Hopefully Olivia wouldn't ask her mother about her. "I've seen her spinning a couple of times with the yarn store crowd, so I know she has a drop spindle somewhere in the house."

"So . . ."

"So go find it. Figure out what to do with it. Google it, or if you can't figure it out, come back here."

"I'm not into yarn like all the other damn crazies in this dumb town," said Olivia, but she already had the bag open and was stroking the fiber inside again.

"What are you into, then?"

"Horses." The word came quickly, but a second after Olivia spoke, she looked furious, as if she'd just overheard someone else telling a secret about her.

"Horses, huh?"

Instead of answering, Olivia touched the edge of one of the votive candle holders that Cora had made out of old china. "Are these tea cups?"

"Yep," said Cora.

"They don't match."

"That's what I like about them." Cora thought for a moment. "Did you know Eliza Carpenter?"

Olivia rolled her eyes. "No."

"But you know who she is?"

"How could I live here and not know who she is? She wrote all those knitting books my mom loves. I swear she sleeps with one under her pillow sometimes."

Cora laughed. "Patron saint of the purl stitch, they call her. She was a friend of mine. We had tea together as often as we could. She bought me my first tea set. I guess I make those to honor her, in my own way."

Olivia said slowly, "Do you have any?"

"Any . . . tea?"

"No, horses." Olivia sounded exasperated, as if Cora should have followed her conversational backward leap.

"Me? No. Just the sheep and goats. I had a llama once to help with the sheep, but she died, and I was too sad to get another one. My friend Stark, though, she has horses. You've been to the public stables, right? That's where she works."

Olivia shook her head.

"Do you know about them?"

Another shake.

"Oh, you're kidding. You have to go."

"I've heard of it. But we're on a budget. Whatever."

Cora grinned. "That's the best part. It's run by the city. It's out at the end of Mines Road, you know, where the bus barn is? Just past that, in the hills, where the last bus stop is. They have these programs that bring in groups of kids from the city who've never been in the country, who've never touched a large animal before. And they teach autistic kids to ride. They have a whole volunteer program, actually. I work with the kids from the Windward group home and they love it." She paused. "Volunteers also get to ride."

If Cora hadn't witnessed the change, she wouldn't have thought it likely to happen, not to this kid, but as she spoke, she watched Olivia's eyes go from downcast to interested. As if Olivia were moving from shade into sunlight, her countenance cleared, her chin lifted even higher, and she blinked, hard.

"I want to go."

"You *should* go."

"Can you go with me?"

Startled, Cora said, "Me?"

"You know the person who works there."

"I can call her for you—"

"I could catch the bus after school out there. I could just meet you. Whenever's good for you. Does Wednesday work? Can you go with me?"

Because Olivia looked so hopeful, her eyes bright but still with that stubborn cloud of loneliness that clung to her clothes like a damp smell, and because there was nothing in the world harder than asking for something that was important, Cora had no other choice but to say, "Okay."

CHAPTER NINE

You don't have to decide anything today. If it's too difficult today, put it down. Walk away. Pet a cat. Soak in sunshine. Be patient with yourself. –
E.C.

The dog pulled Mac hard as she saw a retriever on the board-walk across the street. "Whoa there." She was stronger than she looked, sturdily built even though she was small. Solid. Kind of like . . . Kind of like Cora herself, that way. Right down to the dark orange-red hair.

No wonder he liked this dog.

Farther down the street, at the intersection where Tillie's stood, he saw people and motion. Tents and awnings were set up, and the scent of sweet, fried breads mixed with something darker, barbecued ribs and hamburgers, met his nose. The dog's nose went into hyper drive, as well. She set it low to the ground and pulled against the leash harder. The plastic cage of the muzzle skittered on the side-walk and thumped into a wooden bumper placed around a newly planted tree.

Mac's senses went on alert like they hadn't since he was a teenager. He felt that same way as back then, spending all his free time watching for Cora, and if he could have put *his* nose against the sidewalk to pick up if she were anywhere close, he would have considered doing it.

He tugged the leash. "Come on, Clementine." The name fell from Mac's mouth. He had no idea where it had come from, but she seemed to respond to it, walking alongside him instead of pulling as she'd been doing.

The market was in full swing as they entered between the two tents on the end. Dozens of people filled the streets, environmentally friendly shopping bags hanging from their arms. One man had a basket of baguettes so fresh they were still steaming. A long line snaked from a stand that advertised handmade truffles, and an equally long queue stood patiently in front of the lumpia stand. It was like being at the track except the clients were whole families instead of couples, and everyone was laughing.

Was this stupid? Looking for her like this? He wasn't really *that* concerned with finding Cora. Nope. He was just back in town, enjoying the sights and smells on a gorgeous, crisp, clear fall day. That was all. Just out for a friendly walk with a poor dog that needed walking. No big deal.

And then he saw the sign.

Handmade by Cora. It was small and wooden, hanging from the white awning. Inside the tent-like structure, she'd created a space that was so . . . .her. Dark-stained shelves held what looked like different colors of puffs of what must be fiber. Maybe. He wasn't quite sure – it also might have been cotton candy. Colorful jars lined the lower shelves. Cora stood behind the counter wearing overalls over the same thick, creamy sweater she'd worn last night in the barn. Her cheeks were red as if they were windburned, and she was laughing at something a man in a firefighter's uniform was saying. Mac's step faltered just as Clementine jumped toward him, startled by a small child's sudden scream of laughter.

A leashed border collie trotted past them going the opposite direction, growling under its breath at Clementine. The dog pressed farther into Mac's calf, cowed, her back hunched. The border collie lunged with a strangled bark. The woman holding the leash said, "Control your dog!"

Fantastic. Now he looked irresponsible. "It's not my dog that's the problem," he called, but the woman didn't care, and was gone in the crowd already.

"Mac?" Cora looked at him, down at Clementine, and then back at him. "Was that a dog fight?"

"No!"

"It sounded like it was."

"Have I ever lied to you?"

Cora gave him a suspicious look. "Not as far as I know." She pulled up her overall strap from where it had slipped down one shoulder. "What are you–" She cut herself off. "Is that a shelter dog?"

"Um . . ."

"It is! It's Salt!" She went down onto her knees and grabbed the dog's ears.

"Careful," he started, but the animal had already launched itself at Cora. For a split second, Mac's heart stopped, even though he knew the muzzle was secure. Another second later, he realized that the dog was too busy tying itself into knots of happiness to be any kind of threat.

"Oh, she's the sweetest thing, isn't she?" The dog pushed her body against Cora so hard that Cora tipped and ended up sitting fully on the ground. Cora laughed.

God, he'd missed the sound of her laugh.

The firefighter tapped Cora on the shoulder and said, "Just think about it. I'll get you an account. We can set it up together. I'll answer all the questions for you."

She laughed again. "I don't think so, Jake. But feel free to keep bugging me."

"Will do." With a polite nod to Mac, he left.

"That guy is short, huh?" Mac straightened his back.

"Who, Jake?"

"Are you dating him?" The idiotic words were out before he could stop them.

Cora gave a nervous, startled laugh. "No."

"But you're going to set something up together?"

Crossing her arms, Cora leaned back, gazing at him. "If you must know, and I'm not sure why I'm telling you, he lost his wife to cancer, but met someone not long ago. Now that he's all love-happy, he wants to get me on a young widow-widower's dating site."

Whatever reaction he displayed would be wrong. He could only lose, no matter what he said – Mac had at least a few brain cells left, and he knew this. So he just nodded.

"And you have Salt!" said Cora, her attention back on the dog. "So you two met. Isn't she the best?"

"What kind of a name is that?" said Mac.

She shrugged. "I like salt. It's useful. In food, in cleaning, in weed-killing."

"No way."

"What do you call her, then?" Cora's bright blue eyes sparkled up at him. She had a smudge of something, dirt or soot, on her cheek next to the old scar next to her nose. Her hair stood straight up in one spot. If she wasn't so damn beautiful, she'd look ridiculous.

Almost as ridiculous as the dog, who was practically standing on her head now, twisting herself into positions that would have been impossible for most living creatures.

"Clementine," Mac said.

"Why?"

"Because she's sweet and orange-colored. It fits." And it was true: the dog was a round ball of happy, wiggling and wriggling itself up and down Cora's side.

Cora laughed again. "I suppose it's better than Salt."

"So you named her," said Mac.

She shrugged. "I name them all. I just don't write my names for them on the cards."

"I thought you said you had no pets. Just the working animals."

"I don't."

"How can you volunteer there, then?"

"Easy."

"You don't take any of them home?"

"Nope." She scratched the end of the dog's nose with her short nails.

"Never?"

She shook her head.

"Not even one little kitten?"

"*Nyet.*" Her hands rubbed the spot between Clementine's ears, and the dog groaned and leaned against her harder.

"One tiny three-legged puppy with big eyes, who has no mother. The one that's gonna get put down tomorrow if you don't save her."

Cora pulled an ear one more time and then stood, brushing off her hands. "The animal population is already too overcrowded. It would be ridiculous of me to think that my saving one dog would make any kind of difference in this world."

Mac blinked.

"Just realistic." She stepped back into her stall and reached into a small red tin in the shape of the London Bridge. "Can I?" She held up a dog treat.

"Yeah, sure. You're going to have to get it past her muzzle, though."

"I hate that she's wearing that."

Mac said, "Cindi told me to."

"I still hate it." She broke the biscuit in half and pushed it carefully between the slots. Clementine's tongue caught it and she chomped happily. "So, you're adopting her?"

"No," he said. "I'd never take your dog from you."

She laughed again. "Oh, stop."

"Why not?"

"I don't need a dog."

"Adopting a pet isn't about need. It's about want."

Cora crossed her arms and looked down at the mutt. "She wouldn't even be a good herder."

"She's a good cuddler, though. I bet you already know that."

"Yeah, sure. You should adopt her then. I have to help a customer . . ." Her eyes didn't meet his as she went to assist a woman who was looking for olallieberry jam.

Mac moved carefully in the stand, making sure he kept the dog from getting underfoot. He watched as Cora sold the jam, and then a skein of yarn to another of the browsing women. As people continuously called into the stand as they passed, Cora acknowledged all of them with a smile or a wave while continuing to focus on whichever customer was in front of her.

She was damned good at this.

After three sales, the stand was empty again except for the two of them and the dog. "So this is your place."

"Yeah . . . Sorry about that. I'm not that good at multi-tasking," she said, and then cleared her throat. "It's overrated. Better to do one thing at a time right? Anyway. Yes. This is my place. Not that much to see, huh?" She looked sad, and Mac hated himself for reminding her of the fire.

"No, it's awesome."

She moved her hand, as if to brush off his compliment. "Whatever. It's okay. I have almost no stock, just what was left in my kitchen and my car."

"But you'll get more of . . ." He looked at the yarn, and the candles, and the canned goods. Everything here was made by her, wasn't it? "More of whatever all this stuff is. You'll make more."

"Yeah," she said. "Of course."

But in that moment, he heard it. The same fear he'd heard in voices at the track for years, a mixture of bravado and confidence that people injected into their voices when they kept betting on the same horse, sure that today would be the payoff.

Cora was scared.

CHAPTER TEN

Many a friendship is cemented over a dropped stitch. – E.C.

She wanted Mac out of her stall. There should have been nothing wrong with him being there – an old acquaintance, come
to say hello. Browsing. The problem was that while Mac
looked at her little soaps decorated with thin carvings, trails of
whimsy she'd added to each one, her cheeks flushed harder. When
he picked up a bath bomb and held it to his nose, she wanted to
yank it out of his hand.

She wouldn't be made fun of.

"So, anyway," Cora said, brushing off her hands and stepping toward him in the hopes that he would take a step back, and then
again, and eventually out. "Thanks for saying hello."

But Mac didn't step backward.

They were as close as they'd been that day so long ago. Only
inches separated them. The memory flooded her, and Cora reached
back to touch the low shelf she'd built by hand. Instead of concentrating on the plane of his jaw, instead of noticing where the stubble

was already starting, instead of wondering if his eyes were more coffee or more whisky colored, she thought about the hours she'd spent choosing the wood for the shelf, the time she'd spent cutting and hammering and sanding, making sure the lines were true and strong while still making certain they would fit in her car for easy transport. She dug her fingernails into the wood and held on.

"I should go," he said, and in the echo of those three words, Cora knew he remembered the day of her wedding, too.

From behind him, a welcome voice said, "Hey, there."

Mac moved to the side, and his eyes fell to the dog at his feet.

"Abigail," she said. "Come on in. This is Mac. Mac, Abigail." Cora congratulated herself on the casualness of her voice.

"Nice to meet you." Abigail stuck out her hand and Mac shook it.

"Okay, then." Mac smiled. "I was just leaving. With Cora's little friend here."

Trying to hide her relief, Cora said, "Take good care of her. You should keep her."

He shook his head and grinned in response and was gone, the dog tagging at his heels.

Abigail moved behind the counter and plopped down on the three-legged stool Cora kept in the booth. From her bag she withdrew a paper-clipped pattern.

"Here's the next part of the sweater. I think this is the neckline I want. Funnel-neck, see? Thank you again for doing this for me. Are you liking the way the lace is knitting up on the side panels?"

"It's gorgeous. Never a problem." Test knitting Abigail's patterns was easy money, and then Cora got to sell the finished product after it was photographed. Though this sweater she might keep – it was delicate and sturdy at the same time, a shaped sweater with a lace panel that ran up the sides and sleeves.

"I think I'm going to call it Side Impact. Now the important question. What was *that*?" Abigail leaned back, watching Mac push into the crowd.

"That was Mac."

"That's the only part I got," said Abigail, folding her legs underneath her. Cora never had gotten the hang of that, especially not on a stool. "But *what* was that?"

Turning her back to Abigail, she took a pile of Corriedale two-ply and untwisted the skein so that she could retwist it into a smoother, more perfect one.

"That was a piece of my past that I didn't think I'd ever run into again."

"Tell me," said Abigail.

"I can't."

"You have to."

"Why?"

"Because remember last year when I told you about that guy I fell in love with when I was in high school? The science teacher who was married? The one I thought was my soul mate?"

"Of course I remember," said Cora, her back still turned. "You cut all your hair off because he told you he liked girls with short hair."

"And then I showed up on his doorstep–"

"And his wife answered the door."

"It was *terrible*. My heart was completely broken. Do you remember what you said when I told you that story?"

Cora shook her head. "Not a clue. Something dumb, I'm sure."

"You said that unrequited love was like trying to breathe underwater."

"Oh." Cora did remember that.

"I didn't get it then but later I remembered the time when I was swimming as a little girl, when I just knew that I was a mermaid, and that I could breathe water through my invisible gills. I went under, opened my mouth, and almost drowned myself. And yeah, it felt exactly the same."

If Cora opened her mouth, would a bubble drift to the top of the tent?

"And don't say a thing about that to Cade. He doesn't know I had the hots for my teacher, and he'd tease me daily if he knew." Abigail dangled her sandal from the end of her toe and didn't take her eyes off Cora. "So you were right. Everyone tries breathing underwater at least once. But even though you know all about my past, I know almost nothing about yours. We knit together, you help me out, yes, but I want the dirt, honey. Give me some, okay?"

"My shed burned yesterday . . ."

Abigail nodded. "I heard the news. And while regrettable, that's also not what I want. I want the story of you trying to breathe underwater in that very wide river who just walked away."

"Don't you have patterns or something to sell at your own booth?"

"Lucy's helping me out today."

Cora rolled her eyes, and then sold raspberry jelly to three tourists who were thrilled to meet the manufacturer. Abigail sat patiently, spinning using the Forrester spindle she always carried in her purse.

After Cora had rung up the women and sent them happily on their way, she said, "I wish you weren't so smart."

"No, you don't. You like my brains." Abigail smiled.

"You're always *right*, too. It's incredibly annoying."

"Cade agrees. So. Tell me about this Mac person."

"He's my cousin."

"Oh." Abigail's mouth was a perfect O, a moue of distress. "I guess I got that one wrong . . ."

"Okay, cousin-in-law. Or something. No blood relation. He's Logan's cousin, Louisa Wildwood's son."

"Sucks to be him."

"Right? It's hard enough to be even peripherally related to her."

Abigail tilted her head to the side. "So tell me what you're trying not to tell me."

Cora sighed. "It's really nothing. It's in fact less than nothing." She picked up a bag of prepared Cormo she'd gotten from a sheep rancher a few miles past the MacArthur ranch. "See this? You know how this bag is mostly empty? There's more air in here than fiber, right? That's the story. All air. No substance." Cora felt pleased with her analogy.

Abigail, though, didn't seem to think much of it. She held up her spindle and gave a tug on the fine yarn she was spinning. "Strength. See that? Just a few fibers, twisted enough times, are strong enough not to break."

"Beaten at my own game."

"I'm not giving up until you tell me why the atmosphere in here was so . . . charged when I got here. I could hear the crackle in the air."

Cora twisted her head around before she spoke, making sure no one was within audible range. Abigail looked even more interested, if such a thing were possible. "Fine. I'll tell you." She glanced over her shoulder again. The coast was clear. "He almost kissed me once."

Abigail slumped backward. "That's it?"

"He was going to be my cousin!"

"Cousin-in-law."

Cora continued, "He was going to become my cousin-in-law that exact day. The day of our wedding."

"Well, that's a little more interesting." Abigail smiled and spun her spindle against her thigh.

Covering her eyes with her hands, Cora said, "It was awful. I still haven't forgiven myself for it."

"I must be missing something," said Abigail. "You're trying to forgive yourself for a *non*-kiss? That's kind of like forgiving myself for not having extramarital sex with Channing Tatum, right?"

"It was more than that. He came into the house where I was getting ready. I had the dress on and everything. Logan's mother, Valentine, had been doing my hair, and Eliza was steam-blocking my shawl, but I'd finally chased them out of the room for the last time." Cora took a breath, feeling suddenly nervous again, as if the wedding had been mere hours ago, instead of years. "There was a knock at the door and I thought it was them, coming back for something they forgot. I opened it . . ." Cora trailed off.

When she'd opened that door, Mac had been standing there, fiddling with his bow tie, which hung loose and crooked.

If she'd never opened the door, if what had happened next had never occurred, would her life have been at all different? If he hadn't asked what he had?

"Can you help me?" he'd asked Cora.

CHAPTER ELEVEN

*Take a chance. Risk your heart. Knit in the dark. Dance on the beach by
moonlight with no music but your heartbeat. – E.C.*

I can't do this damn thing, and Logan's too busy preening to help
me. Can you help . . ." He'd looked up, his gaze moving slowly
up her dress, to her breasts, to her neck, to her mouth where his
look lingered, and finally to her eyes. She sucked in her breath and
hoped he wasn't judging the size of her waistline, which, after all,
was partially why the wedding was happening so quickly. At five
months, she still barely showed.

Cora struggled to find something light to say, but the air was
heavy with a feeling that hadn't been there before she'd opened the
door. "Yeah," she said. "Sure. Come here."

She raised her hands to the tie, the silk warm in her fingers
where Mac had been holding it. "It's not difficult," she said, conscious of how close her face was to his. God, why was she so hot?
Sweat broke at her hairline. "It's just fiddly. It's the knitter in me.
Everything like this is easy."

But it wasn't. For the first time ever, she had trouble fixing a bow tie. Her fingers were clumsy, and the silk slipped, refusing to stay where she placed it. "Dammit," she muttered. At least he couldn't see her fingers, which were shaking. And if he did, if he called her on it, she could at least blame it on the fact that she was getting married.

Married.

In thirty minutes.

Cora dared a glance up. Mac's eyes were closed, and his lips were moving the slightest bit, as if he were saying words he didn't want her to hear.

"What?" she said.

"Married," he said, so low she almost missed it. His breath was warm on her cheek, and the word jolted her, even though it was the one word that kept reverberating in her mind. *Married.* Soon she'd be married to Logan.

Logan who'd begged her to help him too, the week before they graduated. They'd been dating for two months then. *We don't want to be virgins forever, right? We love each other like friends. Can't we just do it together and get it over with? You know you can trust me. You can lean on me. You know I adore you. And you're sexy as hell. Come on, Cora. Be a pal.* She'd laughed at him – even then, as young as he was, he was becoming the bronc ridin' rodeo star he wanted to be, and he had to shake girls off with a stick. She'd told him that, and he'd said, *That's the problem. No one but you knows I'm a virgin. Help a guy out.*

Then she'd thought about Mac, who'd been dating Trixie the same length of time, since the Spring Fling Dance two months before. She'd heard the gossip in the hall, that Trixie had bagged Mac Wildwood. Cora kissed Logan with all the passion she could muster.

Logan had trusted her to help him. It had felt so good to be the one leaned upon. And she knew he was dependable. Reliable. Solid. So, because it wasn't really a hardship, losing her virginity to the gorgeous boy she knew was her friend, and because in sex, just like in most of life, Logan was innocently clueless, she had done it to help him. It didn't hurt that she was curious about what it would be like.

It had been fine, that one time with Logan. A fun romp with a friend on a blanket in the back of his truck parked at the beach, the stars so close she could almost touch them.

But she'd gotten knocked up. It had just taken that once. Three months later, when she'd told him, Logan had paled. Then he'd insisted on marrying her, and because Cora wanted to keep the baby no matter how it had happened, and because yes, she did love Logan in her way, she'd agreed. She would help Logan in his career by taking care of his house and his baby, and she could trust him to take care of her. They could rely on each other.

It was a win-win. It was smart. It was right. They would make each other happy. Most likely.

Why, then, did she never shake like this when she was close to Logan? But maybe it was *because* she loved Logan that she was calm and steady in his presence. Wasn't that what love gave you? Self-possession?

It was the absolute opposite of how she felt in front of Mac.

"Married," Cora echoed. "Yes. I'm getting married." Her fingers still fiddled with the tie and she kept her eyes on the silk. Just keep looking at the tie, she told herself. "Dammit. Oh, shit, I mean dammit about the tie, not the . . . not the getting married . . . *Shit*."

Cora looked up one more time. She couldn't help it.

His eyes were on her lips, and the look on his face . . . She'd never seen a man look how he looked at that moment. Everything Mac had ever wanted or desired was right there, clear in his eyes. She'd seen him in every light, in every mood. Cora had thought she knew him.

In that moment, she realized she'd never known one single thing that mattered.

His gaze moved from her lips to her eyes, and she saw it there again.

Cora's heart said something, deep inside her, that she couldn't hear. She wouldn't hear it. It was impossible. She was *pregnant* in her *wedding* dress, for chrissakes.

Mac's head tilted down. With one breath, one tiny motion, she would be in his arms, her mouth on his. Her lips moved, formed to meet his. And Cora knew true desire for the first time in her life. She'd never felt this, this heat of longing, the feeling that if she didn't kiss Mac that world would crumble around her, leaving only dust at her feet.

"Don't do it." Again, his voice was almost inaudible.

"What?"

Louder, he said, "Marry me."

A gasp was her only answer.

"Trust me. Lean on me." Mac said. "Marry me instead."

For one second her vision went blindingly white. And for that unreal moment, Cora wanted to do it. To chuck everything she thought she'd figured out right out the window and run away with this man who made her feel like someone she didn't recognize. Like someone who would take a risk. A gamble so big that everything might be lost.

It was exactly what she'd sworn she'd never do. She wasn't a gambler like that. Logan was reliable, right? Sure. Good old Logan.

Cora tightened the knot on Mac's tie as much as she could. It wasn't going anywhere. But she was. Cora took the crucial step backward, and it did exactly what she hoped it would – it broke the spell.

"Jesus," said Mac.

"You're right. It wasn't easy. There's something about that fabric." Cora's voice was thin and shaky, even to her own ears.

"I should go," he said. "I'm sorry . . ."

"Don't," said Cora. "There's nothing to be sorry for. It's my wedding!" She smiled as brightly as she could. "I'll see you down there."

"Yes." His hands opened at his sides as if he were giving her an invisible gift. "Congratulations, Cora."

He'd left, and she'd closed the door. Then she'd burst into tears, which she'd blamed on emotion and excitement when Valentine and Eliza had come tumbling back in with flowers to twist into her hair.

<<>>

Now, in the farmers market stall, it all came rushing back to her. Abigail's eyes were bright with curiosity. "You opened the door and he was standing there and *what happened?*"

"I tied his damn tie. And there were a few seconds where maybe we almost kissed. We could have. That is, we could have if we were both total assholes, which, thank god, neither of us were, and so we didn't, and I'd pretty much forgotten about it totally until he came back." A lie. "I bet he doesn't remember it either. Stupid weird wedding day jitters. That's all it was."

"Huh. If you say so."

Cora nodded and thumped the top of the counter. "I do."

"Are you going to be okay, Cora?"

"Fine. I'm going to be just fine. Now. Tell me what shade of Polwarth I should spin next."

"Come up to the ranch soon. I miss you. I feel like we haven't just hung out in so long. I only see you when I'm bringing you patterns, or you're giving me the sweaters to photograph. It can't be all business all the time, can it?"

Cora frowned. "Might be like that for a while."

"I won't accept that," said Abigail. "Come next week just to knit. I'll wear out the kids before you get there so maybe they'll nap."

That was the difference between them – Abigail knitted for relaxation, but Cora knitted for money. The more she knitted, the faster she went, the more she could make. It must be nice just to sit and knit, with nothing more pressing on the agenda than chatting.

"Okay."

Abigail eyebrows remained raised. Well, Cora wouldn't believe her if their places were exchanged, either.

She smiled as cheerfully as she could as two women came in, poked at the yarn, and left taking their cash with them, saying they had too much stash already. The bottom of the bank account was going to be visible if this kept up.

It was time for the treasure hunt, much as she hated to admit it to herself. Later, she told herself. Tonight. When she'd had a chance to recover the breath she'd first lost fifteen years before.

CHAPTER TWELVE

Startitis is a symptom of an impeding crisis of confidence in what you already hold on the needles. That said, it's delicious to cast on with abandon. – E.C.

At home that night, Cora sat at the kitchen table and clutched her least favorite teacup – it certainly wasn't the right time for a favorite, not in this mood – while she thought. She shut the laptop and pushed it away from her. She'd called the pickle shop in Gilroy and had gotten a fast busy tone, like the phone wasn't connected. Their website was down. If they'd gone out of business . . . No, completely impossible. She'd try again tomorrow. They owed her, and she needed that money yesterday.

Now, Cora finished reading the list she hadn't gone all the way through the day before. *What if I run out of money?*

Under the ridiculous *Run away to Bali* suggestion were more brainstorming results.

Spin and sell wool. Check. She was already doing that.

Raise vegetables and sell them. That, too, she was all over, both canned and fresh, thanks to the farmers market.

Go to Louisa and ask for a loan. Written next to that, in smaller print, was a note that said, *when pigs fly.* That was still out of the question. Louisa may be the only one in the family with money, but Cora couldn't and wouldn't ever ask.

Dig up the coffee can. It was the last item on the list, two full pages after her first set of brainstorming ideas. She needed to see the words on the page, and there they were. In her own handwriting.

The coffee can full of cash. She'd hoped she'd never have to use it. But Cora hadn't planned on losing her shed to fire the same year she'd almost lost two goats, Fred and Ethel, and had to pay gobs of money to Tony Fazule to save them. Then there had been the root ball that had grown right through the bathroom pipe which had cost thousands, bringing her savings balance down to numbers she could count in her head.

<<>>

The coffee can had been Logan's idea – he'd buried it when they'd first gotten married. He'd been fixing the house with his grandfather, ripping up the roof and the flooring. In the kitchen, directly underneath where they'd ended up placing the dining table, he'd buried a coffee can full of money in the dirt under the new floorboards. He'd never told her exactly how much was in the can, but from the way he'd talked, it had been a considerable amount. "In case we ever have to run off to Mexico, baby. This'll be our starter fund. It's our panic account." With a gambler in the family, there was no such thing as a savings account, and both his mother and grandmother had come up with alternate methods to put away money. Logan's father had never married Valentine, but Skully had been around long enough to let them down over and over again while he was growing up. You couldn't sock cash away with the intention of not touching it, not if you needed it for that night's stake, Logan told her. So the coffee can had come into play. Logan's mother had hidden her cans by the creek. As a child, not finding Valentine in the empty house when he woke in the night sometimes, he'd spy her outside, adding to or taking from the 'bank' of the river.

After he'd fixed the kitchen floor, Logan had said, "Don't excavate the coffee can. Not unless you really need it, not unless I'm not around." When he'd said that, they hadn't even known about the brain tumor.

They'd only ever talked about the can once while he was sick. She'd been in their bedroom, which had become his sickroom, knitting. Logan said, "This is what you wanted, isn't it?"

She'd felt the color leave her face. "What?"

He'd laughed. "Not for me to get sick. I know that. But a home, this was all you ever wanted."

"Oh. Yes."

His voice was still husky from the last intubation. "Since the day you moved to Cypress Hollow when you were just a teenager, this was what you needed. Eliza gave it to you for a while. Then I got to. I may not have been the best husband, but I tried, baby. We didn't plan it well, but it turned out okay, didn't it?"

It hadn't been okay. He'd never been what she needed. Not at all. And ending like this – it meant he never would be. She couldn't bear it.

He went on. "I worry about you and money. What will you do?"

"Don't." She'd stood, tidying the items on the tray next to him.

"You never talk about it."

"Why would I?" The last thing she wanted to talk about with her husband was what she'd do after he was gone. Somehow, her deep-seated need to plan things evaporated when it came to Logan. Whatever came afterward – she wouldn't, couldn't deal with it until she had to.

"We have to think about it," he said.

"I don't. And neither do you. You never know what's going to happen."

"I'm not getting better. And you need a way to make money."

"What about your coffee can?" She'd meant it to be funny, a lighthearted joke, since she'd always teased him about his savings plan, but the look that had crossed his face – a combination of pain and regret – made her want to take the words back. "I can do anything, you know that. People love my jam. I'm spinning more than I ever have, way more than I need to knit. I can sell that. If anything happened, I'd be fine. But you *are* getting better so this is stupid."

Logan shook his head. "You'll have to *do* something. Instead of just take care of me. You've been taking care of me since we got married, since way before I got sick."

Cora felt a sharp flash of anger jolt through her. Of course she had been. It was her job.

"I'm going to make you some eggs." She left their bedroom, the room that had become Logan's sick room, furious that he wasn't even trying.

<<>>

Now, as Cora stared into the blackness outside, ignoring her reflection, she knew she should have talked to him about it. Just one more regret. If she'd ever really tried to tell the truth to Logan, she wouldn't have known where to start. And then where would she have stopped? It had been better to do as she had: she kept smiling, kept making things, kept kissing him, kept telling him everything was going to be okay, even when it was finally evident to her that it wasn't.

At the very end, the day before he died, she'd brought her spinning wheel – the Joy, the one he'd surprised her with at Christmas – into the bedroom, and she'd treadled evenly, keeping time to his breathing. He said the sound of the wheel helped him sleep. When he opened his eyes, he watched the wheel with a faint smile. "Beautiful," he'd said.

"I love the way it sounds. You couldn't have given me anything nicer," Cora said.

"Not the wheel." It was all he said, and his eyes closed shortly after that as he dropped into a restless sleep. She'd cried then, the tears she tried so hard to never let him see dropping into the batt of fiber resting on her lap.

The memory of it still hurt. They'd done so many things wrong. They'd lost the baby, the reason they'd gotten married at eighteen. Logan had stayed so very Logan right to the end – careless, carefree, ready with a rope and a laugh, never becoming the ant she believed he could be. Always the grasshopper. But in the ten years they had together, they'd built a real something. Not a marriage based on love, no. They'd never had romance. But God knew a bronc rider needed someone to bandage his wounds on a regular basis. It had worked out. And Cora still missed him.

Restless now, she stood and turned on the front floodlight, erasing her image from the window.

How was she supposed to know for sure that this was the right time? Should she wait until she spent the *very* last dime in the bank account? Until she used up all the canned goods? Until PG&E shut off her power?

No, the time was now.

Cora dragged out her tool box from the pantry where she kept it under the food dehydrator. The right choice of hammer was no small matter. Not the tack or the sledge. The dead-blow hammer was more than she'd need for this job, maybe more than she'd ever need for any job, but she'd loved the heft of it in the hardware store. The simple curved claw, then, was the right hammer for tearing up her kitchen floor. Combined with the slim pry bar, they should be enough.

She moved the table, pulling hard on the heavy oak. It protested as it scraped the floor. Except for when she moved it to mop, the table had stood in that spot as long as she'd lived there. Cora pushed until it was against the wall and then stacked the matching chairs on top of it.

Two tries, that's all it took. It was surprising, actually, how easy it was to pry up the first board, and then the next. The wood was soft, almost pliant, like the house wanted her to find the can. One board broke, and for that she was sorry – it was going to be hard to fix that later.

When she had a big enough hole, she realized that while she'd seen Logan put the can in the ground, and while she'd imagined it would be easy to find the same place, she had no idea where it was precisely. They hadn't marked it, and over the years, the dirt had shifted and settled three feet beneath the beams.

This might take a while.

She got her favorite shovel from the tool shed in the back (the red one with the yellow anchors she'd painted up the handle), shimmied her way into the hole, and started digging.

Cora worked as hard as she could, but she didn't find anything in the first spot she tried. She widened her hole. An hour and a half later, the edge of the kitchen floor at the level of her shoulders, she hadn't found anything but an old metal fitting and two thick glass medicine bottles.

"This is why most houses have a crawl space," she muttered to herself. "Jesus, what did you do, come and get it after you died?"

"I'd ask who you're talking to, but I'm scared of what you might say." The voice came from behind her.

"Holy crap!" Cora spun in the dirt, and almost fell over in the hole. "Mac!"

He stood at the open door with the shelter dog, who pulled against the leash, straining hard toward her.

She didn't want him here. He should leave and take the dog with him.

And at the same time, Cora had never been so glad to see someone in all her life.

CHAPTER THIRTEEN

A few stitches a day keeps the worries at bay. (And that whole apple/doctor thing is probably a good idea, too.) – E.C.

Cora was covered in dirt. From a stripe across her cheekbone where she'd probably wiped the back of her hand to the brown, dirty circles at her knees, she looked like she'd been grave digging. Inside her own house.

"I knocked, but you were so busy deconstructing your kitchen you didn't hear me. Do you have a permit for what you're doing there? Because if you're redoing the floors, I think you're doing it wrong."

"I'm looking for something. What are you doing?"

"Bringing Clementine to say hello." He gestured at the dog as she pulled against the leash, trying to join Cora in the hole. "She might be able to help."

Cora straightened, her hands at the small of her back. "You adopted Salt."

"Cindi said I should keep her overnight. I'm just borrowing her until you realize she's supposed to be yours."

"Not gonna happen." Cora leaned against the splintered wood. Something skittered at her feet in the dirt, and while he saw her jerk, she didn't jump out.

And just like that, Mac remembered the first time he'd seen Cora in the school's quad on a rainy afternoon. Her hair had drawn his eye – long and tangled and red as a Mustang's tail; she'd been impossible to ignore as she tried to push past Billy Thunker, who held her by the shoulders, making smart comments to his friends about her boobs.

"Let me *go*." Her voice had been embarrassed, her face white with fury.

The boys laughed harder, and Mac moved toward them. This new girl was going to need help. Billy was a jackass of titanic proportions. He went after everyone regardless of gender or size – most of the school feared him, and because of that, most also hated him, with the exception of his small, socially stunted posse. He'd never troubled Mac, maybe because their dads gambled together, but there was a first for everything. Mac would rescue the girl, kick Billy's ass, and then figure out where the heck she'd come from. New faces were rare in Cypress Hollow, especially one as pretty as hers.

Billy said, "You think you're something, huh? At least wherever it is you came from they knew how to grow 'em." He released her and pantomimed Cora's already generous curves with his hands, adding a hip thrust for emphasis. His friends doubled over, howling with laughter.

"I think you're nothing." Her small hands were clenched into fists at her sides and her tattered purple backpack had slipped off her shoulder.

Billy puffed out his chest and said, "You know what I think? I think you're some dumb slut who probably *likes* it when guys talk about her tits. That how you ended up at Windward? Huh? Mommy like to drink too much, lost you to the system, huh, baby? Or did Daddy touch you in the wrong places?"

Mac, only feet away, yelled, "Hey, asshole," but no one noticed him – not Billy, not the girl, not the crowd that had formed around them.

Then Billy was on the ground, taking the beating that Mac wanted to give him. But it was Logan on top of him. Logan who'd come out of nowhere, Logan landing the punch that broke Billy's nose, the punch that must have felt so damn good.

Cora had hunched her shoulders and escaped, scurrying through the crowd, hiding away the tears that fell from her cheeks. She'd jostled his shoulder as she'd run past him. Jesus, he'd wanted, even then, at sixteen, to take her in his arms and make it all okay. Mac had fallen in love with the new girl at that moment, and now, looking at the adult version of her, covered in dirt and cobwebs, panting with the exertion of whatever the hell it was she was doing, he knew that had never changed.

Shit.

Cora held out her hand and the dog wriggled forward on the end of the leash, licking her fingers. "She's a sweetie. I'm glad she found you. You're good with animals." She blushed. "Of course you are. That's what you do, right? You're a vet. You have to be good with them."

"Whatever." He brushed off her words lightly. "So you're looking for the coffee can?"

She gaped. "How did you know about that?"

"Everyone in this family has a coffee can. I keep mine in a safe deposit box, but the principle is the same."

"Fine, yes. You're right."

"Times that hard?"

"Did I fail to mention the fire?"

He knelt on the floor at the edge of the hole. Clementine sat obediently next to him. "Savings?"

"Gone wherever it is money goes. Emergencies. Rainy days." Cora pushed her hair out of her eyes but it looked like she only managed to get dirt in them instead. "Ow. Crap."

Mac moved to the sink. "Stop. You need a wet cloth or something. There's dirt on your hands."

"You think?" she said but she waited while he dampened a paper towel and handed it to her. "Thank you."

"You want help there?"

Cora looked down. "It's really a one-person job, I think. Not much room."

"Then give me a shot. I'm fresh."

"I can do it by myself."

"Come on, Cora. When did you get so stubborn?"

Cora's eyes narrowed, then she turned her back to him and bent at the waist, digging as hard as she could again. The shovel slipped in her hands, and the sweat dripping down her face gave away her tiredness.

Fine. Mac pulled out a wooden chair and sat. He watched.

"Don't mind me," she called. "Make yourself comfortable."

"Okay, then."

The chair creaked as he leaned back. Why didn't she just turn around and ask him to leave? Tell him it was time to go?

Instead, Mac watched as Cora dug harder, using all her weight to rock the spade back and forth, tearing up the ground underneath her house. It was *killing* him to sit still. To watch as he did nothing. In another minute, maybe she'd give in. Hell, in another minute he'd take the shovel away from her, no matter what she said. She was strong, yes. But he was stronger, could get this done faster . . .

The blade of the shovel gave a *chunk* as it hit something solid.

"Hey, now," said Mac, leaning forward. "I think you got it."

"Really?" said Cora. "Thank God you're here. How would I have known?" But she grinned as she dropped to her knees. Using a small trowel, she scooped away the dirt at her feet.

"Is it the can?" He knelt on the floorboards, Cora below him.

"Give me a minute. Sheesh."

Then there it was, under the trowel's blade, the old metal of the can dull and tarnished although the plastic lid, untouched by sun, was still bright green.

"Do you want help?"

"*Will you back off?*" Cora shook her head. "I'm sorry. But I've got this, okay?"

"Fine," said Mac. "Yeah."

She rocked the can until it came all the way free and brushed it off with her filthy hands. Clutching it, she glanced at him, and his heart did that strange knock inside his chest again.

Reaching out to her, he offered his hands. "Here," he said.

But Cora shook her head and placed the can on the floor. She jumped up as if she were exiting a swimming pool, pushing up on her arms, twisting her hips at the last moment to sit on the splintered edge of the planks. "I'm up." She stood. "Now."

"Do it."

Cora paused.

Was this a thing she should do in private? This was hers and Logan's. He had no right to watch this. "You wanna take it upstairs? Light a candle or something?"

"What? No," she said, but she was hesitant.

Mac said, "You want me to go?"

"No, it's fine." A beat. "It's nice that you're here. You and Logan . . . were more than cousins. You were like brothers. He'd want you here."

It felt good, suddenly, that he was in this torn-up kitchen with her. Somehow, it was right. He'd fix the floor for her when they were done. He wouldn't ask, either – he'd just do it.

"Okay," he said. A simple word. The right one.

Cora reached for the can. "It's light. So it's not gold coins," she said, shaking it. "I know that much."

"I'm dying here. Open it."

So Cora did. She took off the plastic lid and stared inside. Then she looked harder, holding it under the kitchen overhead light.

A note. It held nothing but a single piece of paper, folded twice over.

CHAPTER FOURTEEN

Knitting is like a make-believe play language that actually works.
– E.C.

Cora frowned and pulled out the note. Maybe it was a game Logan had been playing. He'd always liked to make up scavenger hunts for her, sending her to the pasture and back to the fridge and then out to the barn to find something as simple as a bouquet of daisies he'd found in the field.

"That's it?"

"No, it's something. It's from him." Cora automatically went on the defense, just like she always had when it came to Logan.

Mac sat back, waiting.

Cora unfolded the piece of paper, and there it was: his handwriting, dark against the faint blue lines.

Dearest Cora,

If you're reading this, I apologize. I'm only writing this note in case something awful happens like I kick the bucket before I get a chance to refill the nest egg. I'm borrowing the money to put on a horse that can't lose. I'll be able to repay the coffee can five times over. But if I get hit by a bus or bucked one time too many at least you'll know I'm sorry.

You're my girl,

L

Cora pressed her lips firmly together. The tears that pricked at the back of her lids weren't sad tears – they were furious ones, hot and painful. A clod of dirt startled her by tumbling down into the hole she'd dug.

"What?" Mac's voice was quiet in the small room.

At her feet, Clementine leaned into her calf, and she didn't push the dog away. Silently, she handed him the note.

Mac read it. Then he said, "Bastard. I wish he was alive so I could kick his ass."

"Don't –" But it came out half-heartedly. Cora corrected her tone. "He wasn't a bastard."

"Technically he was, since Uncle Skully never got around to marrying Valentine before he skivved off and died. And sometimes Logan was just a freaking jerk." Mac handed the note back to her. "You know that."

Cora read it again. No money. There was no money. Nothing put away, nothing to fall back on. Cora had managed this long, and the thing that had kept her going some cold nights was the thought that she could someday, if she really needed it, dig up the coffee can. In her head, it was capitalized. The Coffee Can.

Empty. Logan had blown it at the races.

Of course.

Any money they'd ever had in the bank account had been in there because she'd earned it, because she'd put it there. He hadn't even been as bad as some in his family – he wasn't like his father, Skully, who hadn't been able to pass an Indian casino without taking out another mortgage, leaving Valentine to scramble once again. But if Logan had been actively controlling himself in the betting, then he'd blow their money on more bucking stock. *This mare is gonna be our golden ticket, this is the one,* he'd say to her, never listening when she said they had all the horses they could afford to feed. And when Logan would notice they didn't have enough in the bank to stake his next bet, he'd sell that new mare without a backward glance. He assured Cora over and over again that he'd take that management class, really start his breeding business, of course he would. As soon as they were a little more comfortable.

When they'd had to sell Logan's last horse to pay the property taxes a year before he died, he'd blamed Cora for not having a real job. The work she did a hundred hours a week, the work that brought in actual *money:* the knitting and the spinning and the gardening, the articles that she managed to sell here and there, none of it meant anything to him. After one bad fight that lasted three days during which she'd told him she'd get a nine-to-five job the same day he gave up riding broncs, she'd thought long and hard about leaving him. He hadn't turned out to be the man she'd thought he was, the man she'd thought he *could* be, if he just tried a little harder. Maybe the belief she'd placed in him hadn't been fair.

But then Logan had gotten sick so fast. He'd been thrown for the millionth time and took a little longer getting up. They'd thought he had a concussion, but something showed on the MRI that the doctor at the small local hospital couldn't name. The brain tumor grew the way Logan rode – fast and aggressively. Almost as quickly, he'd died. The years she'd spent expecting the call from the rodeo grounds that he'd been hurt, paralyzed, killed, were for nothing. Not one minute of that wasted time prepared her for losing him to something attacking him from the inside.

Maybe they hadn't had a "normal" marriage, but who had one of those, anyway? She'd loved him as best she could, picking up the pieces, one by one, trying desperately to hold them all in hands that seemed too small some days.

She shouldn't have relied on the coffee can. Cora knew better than that. But Logan had told her she could, and dammit, she'd trusted him. And he'd let her down. Again.

"I'm an idiot. He was just like all the men in your family." She bent to scratch the dog's head, carefully not making eye contact with Mac.

"Not all the men," Mac quietly corrected.

"Fine. So you're the only one who doesn't gamble. Your grandfather did. Your father did. Logan's father did. Logan did. Now they're all dead – do you see a pattern here?" She tried to keep her voice level. "Or at least you don't admit you gamble. Who knows what the real truth is?"

"Never. I never would."

"Do I need to remind you that you're a *racetrack* veterinarian?"

"Not anymore. Private practice now." Mac leaned forward, his face serious. "No matter what Logan did, he should have taken care of you. That was his job."

"No," she said. It was important that he understand this. "I thought that at first, yeah. I thought he would do that. But it was never his *job* to take care of me, and even though the bank account was slim, we still had our farm, our home, and this, our secret treasure trove. It felt good that he'd left me something, even though he didn't need to." She tapped the side of the can. "I shouldn't have gotten my hopes up. It's all my fault. Again."

Mac came toward her. As he reached out, Cora flinched.

"I'm okay," she said. She moved backward, remembering the hole just in time. "I'll be fine."

"You're not fine."

"I'm like a cat. I always land on my feet," she said lightly, looking at the floorboards. "Or maybe I'm like Clementine-also-known-as-Salt here, finding a sucker right out of the gate to take care of her." The dog looked up at her in what appeared to be blind devotion. Cora did *not* need this. "Now, really, I have to put my house back together again. How the *hell* did Logan get the can out and back and fix the floor without my noticing? He must have worked his ass off. For once."

"I can help."

She met Mac's eyes. "You can go."

"You don't want me here."

That was the crazy part. She really, really did. She hadn't wanted someone here so much since . . . she couldn't remember. But he couldn't stay.

"Please go." The words weren't easy to say. But then again, she didn't do things that were easy. Cora did the things that had to be done. And he had to go, because she had a sneaking suspicion that she was going to cry soon, and no way in hell would she allow Mac to witness it. "Now," she added.

"Okay," he said. "All right." He clicked his tongue once toward Clementine who wagged her tail.

But he didn't move.

"So?" she asked.

He shook himself like she'd caught him in the rain. "I have no idea what I'm doing," he admitted. "I'm sorry. I should go." The same words, again, that he'd said so long ago, the morning of her wedding.

But still he didn't make a motion. It felt as if something were tethering Cora in the spot where she stood, an invisible rope, with him holding one end, her the other. The only thing moving was Cora's heart which jumped around inside her chest so much she thought he might be able to hear it.

Then with one large and sudden step, Mac closed the distance between them. Toe to toe, his eyes met hers, and in them she saw her own emotions reflected back – trepidation, resistance. Fear. She read the apology in his eyes as he lifted his hand and placed it on her cheek. Then his head lowered, his body curving and bending to claim her mouth for the first time.

The touch of his lips, infinitely softer than she would have imagined, made her head swim. Cora's hand went to his elbow, and she held him there, not sure if she was trying to remove his hand from her cheek or if she wanted to press it there forever. At first the kiss was slow. Sweet. Mac's lips barely touched hers, and Cora had to sway forward to keep him with her. And she did.

Then the kiss heated. His tongue met hers, tentatively at first, and then with more force, a pressure that she matched and raised. She lifted her other hand so that now she clung to both his arms, and then her fingers went higher, touching the side of his jaw, reveling in the rough stubble under her fingertips. It had been so long since she'd kissed a man . . . No, it was more than that. It was this man making her dizzy, *this* one.

He whispered words against her mouth that she didn't understand, and his lips felt superheated. The heat reminded her of something, and as she drew him further into her mouth she searched her brain – what was it, what was this like? Why was this small bell ringing in her mind?

Oh, *God.* His lips were as hot as Logan's had been when he'd been sick, when the tumor messed with his hypothalamus, screwing up his body temperature, sending him into a fever nothing could bring down.

Cora gasped and pulled away. It was only when Mac bucked forward and he wrapped his arms around her that she realized she'd almost fallen backwards into the hole in the floor.

"Careful," he said, and there was a breathless laugh in his voice.

"That was – no," she started, twisting herself out of his grasp. She rubbed the skin on her upper arms. From so hot, she went to freezing in an instant. "I can't believe –"

"I'm sorry," Mac said, releasing her. He scraped his jawline with the heel of his hand. His lips still gleamed wet. "Jesus, Cora."

"You apologize now? And you apologized the other day. I was almost ready to accept it, too. But this, this is the *worst* thing you could have possibly done."

"I know."

"That wasn't fair." It was the cry of a child, and Cora felt seventeen again. How she'd wished for this, then. Before Logan. "We can't *do* that to him."

Mac's eyes were twin pools of shocked despair. Without saying another word, he spun on his cowboy boots and crashed out the kitchen door, out into the darkness. Heavy silence landed in the room.

She sat, heavily, on the floor and stared into the empty pit she'd dug for herself. Tears threatened, hot and insistent. "Shit."

I will not cry. Crying would make what they'd done to Logan even worse than it already was. Only Logan deserved this kind of tears, and she'd long ago learned how to shut it off.

CHAPTER FIFTEEN

When in doubt, knit. – E.C.

Three days passed without a glimpse of Cora.

He'd kissed Logan's wife. There was nothing Cora could have said to him, yelled at him, beat him over the head with, that would make him feel worse than he already did. Way to fuck it all up, right from the get-go.

He worried that staying on the property next to hers might automatically mean another meeting, but it was as if she'd closed herself into the hole she'd dug in her kitchen floor and disappeared. Deliberately, he pushed the thought of her out of his mind. He'd always been good at doing that – God knew he should be, he'd been practicing for years. He returned Clementine to the shelter, telling Cindi he hoped she'd find a nice home, trying not to think of what a dog could mean for someone like Cora. The dog had such a lonely, hollow look in her eyes when he left her behind. It was the same loneliness he'd seen in Cora's eyes – she needed a pet. Something to really love, to hold.

But that wasn't his place. Not after he'd screwed it so far up he couldn't see down.

Maybe not seeing Cora was for the best, anyway. Mac had plans, and they were plans that she didn't need to know about. Not yet, anyway. And the best place to talk over plans in Cypress Hollow had always been Tillie's.

In high school, his group of friends had congregated at the diner late at night to discuss the next day's hijinks. Old Bill (who looked no older than he had then) had closed at ten o'clock back in the day, but if he liked the kids in question, he'd stay open late after football games and serve them chocolate milkshakes and plain cheese quesadillas. Nothing else – you couldn't talk him into even a single French-fry. But the quesadillas were fried crispy, ropy with mozzarella and set next to giant sides of sour cream, and the milkshakes were so thick you could hardly shove the straw down, let alone suck it up. Those shakes had taken time and patience, and deliciousness was the reward.

<<>>

Mac watched Old Bill, slowly wiping the counter next to the register with what looked like the same red cloth he'd used back then. He chatted with Pete Wegman and Jessie Sunol about the possible cold rain they had coming their way, and Mac knew that none of them really cared, not anymore. The ranchers didn't really ranch – they were too old now. Their sons and grandsons had taken over, leaving them to reminisce. But the weather had always been what they talked about since creatures started crawling out of the muck, and long after Mac was gone he hoped that they'd still be there, perched temporarily on their stools before they headed to the side room to their permanent tables.

Shirley – still Shirley! – came up to his booth, pad in hand. "Coffee?"

"I remember you used to have those chocolate milkshakes that could choke a horse. You still got those?"

She peeked over her reading glasses. "We have 'em, yeah." Then she looked at the red cat clock hanging on the wall, its black tail swishing away the seconds. "It's nine in the morning, though. You sure that's what you want?"

Mac said, "Yep. And a cheese quesadilla."

Was that a small smile he saw on her face? "Good enough," Shirley said. "Coffee, too?"

"Why not?" He turned over the upside-down coffee mug so she could expertly pour exactly the right amount without a drop spilled. It was good to be back.

Outside the window, he saw the black Rolls as it pulled into the open spot in front of the diner, and it looked like everyone else saw it, too. Pedestrians paused on the sidewalk, and one guy stopped backing out so he could gawk. It was true, Cypress Hollow got its fair share of tourists in fancy vehicles, but a Rolls Royce, all long lines and sleek paint, didn't come along often. Even though he knew better, Mac almost expected a chauffeur wearing white gloves to glide out of the driver's seat.

Instead, Royal got out, flushed and rumpled as usual. Today he wore black mirrored sunglasses, a knit beanie that looked as if he'd had it rolled in his back pocket before putting it on, two T-shirts – a long sleeved one under a short sleeved one – and jeans with holes at the knees. He looked like Mark Zuckerberg after a rave.

Royal stomped through the diner, greeting Old Bill as if he were a long-lost friend. Bill looked startled, but then gripped the hand-shake offered to him. Royal worked the whole room this way, press-ing hands and cracking jokes that made people laugh in spite of their surprise, before making his way to Mac's booth.

"Yo, man. I *missed* you," said Royal as he sat. Then he leaned for-ward, his elbows on the table, not noticing until Mac pointed it out that the cuff of his long sleeved T-shirt was trailing in Mac's coffee. "Oh, sorry about that." He shook the moisture off, wiping the rest on his jeans. "So tell me. How's small town life treating you?"

Mac said, "Fine."

"Tell me more." Royal, as usual, was bossy. Demanding. But as well as being his employer, Royal was his friend. Mac felt something he hadn't even known he'd been worrying about slip away.

"Slow, I guess," Mac said.

"You've only been here for what, five days?"

"I feel like I should have done more. I should be already setting things up and I haven't started."

Royal shook his head and patted Mac's hand paternally. "You're here to smooth the road, not pave it. You can leave that part to me. I'm the steamroller. You're the face. Now, how does it feel to be back home?"

Royal was good at getting people to not only trust him but to tell him things – it was how he'd gotten so far in business. Though only in his early forties, he'd amassed a huge fortune, raking in money in the dot-com boom, then plundering the housing market. He'd gotten out right before the bubble burst. Now he did something with solar energy, but Mac knew him through horses. Royal's true passion was raising thoroughbreds – every moment he didn't spend making money, he spent in his barns. They'd met at Bay Gate Downs when one of Royal's stabled horses had failed a CO_2 test (a faulty read, or the horse would have been scratched and the trainer possibly ousted for illegally enhanced performance). Mac and Royal had taken instantly to each other. Royal had worked hard to woo Mac away from the track with a high salary and promises of breeding winners, but in all honesty, Mac had been ready to leave. Racetracks were drying up, down to about eighty from the couple hundred that had been in business when Mac had started practicing. In ten years, there'd only be a handful of tracks left. Most people were separated from the country, from horses, two or three generations away from living on the land. They watched TV and ate at drive-throughs. Dirt and animals and farms didn't exist in people's minds anymore, and racetracks were part of that dying life. Hell, most of the bets placed at

Bay Gate Downs came in through the twenty-four satellite casinos that played the races. The stands didn't even fill up anymore.

The chance paid off. He loved working for Royal, being with the same horses every day. There were two hundred of them, enough to keep him busy as they came in and out from track stables, always some mare to breed or deliver, or a foal with its first hot foot. Didn't stop him from missing the roar of the crowds, though.

Royal was still waiting for him to answer how it felt to be home. His expression was patient, as if he had all the time in the world.

Mac had a sudden urge to tell him about Cora, about the way she looked digging in that hole she'd made in her kitchen, the look she'd worn when she'd opened the coffee can to find Logan had left her exactly nothing. Instead, he said, "There's . . ."

"A woman." Royal said, triumphant. "I knew it!"

"Whatever," said Mac. "It doesn't matter."

"Did you tell me about her?"

"No. No way."

"Who is she?"

"No one. I'm sorry it came up." And he was.

Royal leaned back, and put one finger alongside his nose, exactly as Santa would have done if Santa looked like a Los Angeles surfer. "More and more interesting. Is this the one that got away?"

Mac twisted in his seat. Royal was just guessing, but he was too close to the truth for comfort. "You think about women too much."

"They're why we *live*," said Royal, and his eyes focused dreamily on the backside of Abigail MacArthur.

"Watch it. I hear she's married to a very tall sheep rancher."

Royal straightened. "Right. But dude, this town is full of real women. You know how rarely I see those? I see blondes with enhancements they'll still be paying off when the warrantees run out. Although who am I kidding? I like an enhancement as much as the next man. But the women here wear jeans like they mean it. I could fall in love here." He paused. "I already know it wouldn't be mutual, but that's okay. I could deal with unrequited. Unrequited with maybe some touching. You think?"

"Women in Cypress Hollow want relationships to go with the touching."

Royal sighed happily. "This is the perfect town."

Mac knew this about his friend: he loved three things – love, money, and horses. Love always came first, even ahead of the horses. He fell for women left and right, and he was always looking for The One. It was too bad most of them were after the wallet in his back pocket.

Royal said, "So what, you haven't said a word to your family yet?"

"I haven't found the right time." Sure, he could have brought it up that night when everyone was together at dinner. He should have. But he hadn't.

"Did you at least talk to your mom?"

Mac shook his head.

"But they do need the money, right? You still think they'll go for it?"

Mac said, "My Aunt Valentine is perennially scratching her pennies together. My mom is better off, with some investments she made when my dad died. Cora doesn't work a real job, just pulls money in with sheer grit, I think."

Shirley interrupted them with another coffee refill.

Royal smiled. "Hello, ma'am. You know, this place is pretty –" he pointed to the ocean, the waves breaking on the sand just across the main street " – but you're the one I can't take my eyes off."

Mac snorted.

Shirley just raised her eyebrows. "You ever get anywhere with that line, little boy?"

"Never used it before. You inspire me."

Mac watched her soften before his very eyes. She laughed. "I've got a man my own age, twenty-five years older than you."—

"Is he a good man?"

Mac felt himself sink into the booth.

But Shirley smiled and said, "Yeah. He's good."

"I'm glad he is, because if he were a bad man, I'd be forced to track him down and make him regret the error of his ways."

"Oh, you'd do that, would you?" Shirley looked ten years younger than she had thirty seconds before.

"It would be my honor and my duty."

Shirley swung to look at Mac. "He always talk like this?"

"Yes, ma'am."

"There ought to be a law." But she was pink and pleased as she took Royal's order, and Mac knew that the eggs would come to Royal perfectly cooked.

"So, back to you," said Royal. "How can I help?"

"Are you here to scope out the land or to bully me into moving faster?"

"I'd never bully you." Royal's eyebrows flew upward in affront. "As if. I just like to keep an eye on the people I care about. You should know that. But yeah, I want to see the land. Now, who's the girl?"

"Not telling you."

"She's the wife of your cousin, the loser who died."

Mac's mouth dropped open. He glanced around to see if anyone could have heard Royal's words. "How did –"

Royal popped his knuckles in satisfaction. "I pay people to find these things out."

"But –"

Royal laughed. "I'm teasing you, bro. When he died, you remember I took you out and got you so hammered you wanted to throw away your paycheck on video ponies?"

"I don't gamble." *Not on anything that costs money.*

"And you crawled up your front steps on all fours, pretending to be a tiger?"

"What I remember about that night was the pain I felt the next morning. I don't think I'd ever been that hungover in my life."

"*In vino veritas,* brother. That's all I'm going to say."

It was so Royal, to know a secret for so long, *Mac's* secret, and never say a word, but just save it until he could use it. "You do that to all your friends? Get them drunk and learn their secrets?"

Royal looked into his coffee cup as if there were a fifty dollar bill at the bottom that he could find if he just peered hard enough. "Nah. You're my only friend."

Mac laughed. "You've got a million friends."

"No, I've got a million dollars. Lots of millions. That means I have millions of people who call me a friend but don't know my birthday."

"New Year's Day."

"Everyone thinks I'm just throwing a New Year's party," said Royal.

"But you never tell them. And you never let me tell them."

Royal blinked. "They should know. People should ask about their friends. That's what friends are for."

"What's going on with you?"

"You're only asking because I just said that. And because I pay you."

Mac frowned at Royal. "No. You asshole."

"That's better. I'm fine." Royal thumped Mac on the shoulder. "Quit being so sensitive."

Mac leaned back in the booth and smiled. It was good to have a friend, even one who knew more secrets than he should.

CHAPTER SIXTEEN

Once I dreamed the perfect sweater. I couldn't remember its design when I woke, but I'll spend the rest of my life trying. And isn't that a worthy goal? –
E.C.

In front of Tillie's Diner, Cora swerved into a parking space three spots down from Mac's truck. The turn of the wheel had been almost involuntary – she'd had no plans to stop anywhere but at the feed store for beet pulp for the goats, and now here she was. Stalking Mac Wildwood. She'd had better moments.

Cora pulled her sunshade down in case Mac looked outside and saw her. Because, of course, there he was, sitting large as life and twice as handsome in the booth next to the last long window of the cafe. The way the sun was slanted meant that she could see him well through the glass, from the top of his head, the slope of his nose, his green flannel shirt, all the way to the tops of his jeans-clad thighs. At that point the wood of the outside wall cut off her view, but Cora had a clear image in her mind of his long legs, his scuffed cowboy boots . . . She touched her bottom lip, remembering the feel of his kiss.

That unforgivable kiss.

Cora saw two other patrons look out and squint as the sun bounced off the glass on the cars lined up outside. Hopefully, if Mac glanced out, he wouldn't be able to see her at all. Why was she watching him? What on earth would she gain from it? She waited for her blood to heat in anger, and it did, but it was a slow burn, much slower than it should have been. She told herself to put the car in reverse, but her hand refused to follow her brain's direction.

When the Rolls Royce had rolled up, she'd stared along with everyone else. A guy who looked like he would be selling used Playstations at the games store got out, the only person in the car. And then, jaw-droppingly, he'd gone in and sat with Mac. They'd done that classic guy hand-clasp-shoulder-bump that women never, ever did. They looked comfortable with each other. It was weird. Okay, maybe if the guy had pulled up in a Honda, Cora wouldn't be as instantly curious, but a Rolls? In Cypress Hollow?

Mac was up to something. She knew he was. And her gut told her that the scruffy man was involved.

There were two ways of proceeding. Cora could get out, write down the Rolls's license plate number, and call John Moss at the police department. He owed her – he'd brought her his wife's favorite sweater, a forty-year-old Norgie, and Cora had fixed all the worn spots, closing the holes almost invisibly. He'd wanted to pay her, but Cora hadn't accepted. She could call in that debt now. He could run the plate, give her a name, and Google would tell her the rest.

That would be the way she normally did things. Non-confrontational. Research from home. Be angry about that kiss, alone, at home.

But it was awfully complicated. And it would be easy for Mac to look outside and see her jotting down numbers.

So Cora chose the second, more foreign option.

She walked into Tillie's, ignoring the feeling that she was making a mistake. Maybe Mac *didn't* have anything planned. Maybe she should just trust him. She nodded at Old Bill who nodded back, then she jumped as Toots Harrison held out a catalog for her to look at.

"You have to look at my new nipple clamps!" said Toots, who was showing a beet-faced Pete Wegman a glossy magazine filled with products that Pete had most likely never seen anywhere in real life before.

"Okay, sure, I will, later," said Cora. She didn't exactly need sex toys, thank you very much, but Toots was sweet and harmless, and it never hurt to support local businesses.

Mac hadn't seen her yet. He was laughing at the man with him, his eyes closed, his wide shoulders shaking.

She wished briefly, fervently, that she'd said something that made Mac react like that. Like he had when they were riding through the woods as teenagers. She'd always been able to hear that laugh for what felt like miles, as if she had some kind of special hearing, tuned to exactly that register.

It didn't take Mac even a full second to see her – his eyes lit happily, the laughter still spread on his lips, and Cora felt something warm and sweet move inside her.

Oh, that wasn't fair. That look wasn't right. He couldn't just pull that on her.

"Hey," he said. "Fancy meeting you here."

Cora smiled. Politely. She hoped her voice wouldn't shake. "I came in because I saw your car parked outside, and then I saw the fancy car drive up. And . . ." *What the hell am I doing?* "I want to know what you're up to." Her gaze encompassed Mac's friend who looked even scruffier close up. Six or seven holes gaped in his top T-shirt – which boasted a dinosaur that was eating a pink Barbie while burping bubbles – and the long-sleeved black T-shirt he wore under that one looked almost as ratty. The man grinned at her, and she could see how he might be considered cute if he shaved all that facial fuzz away.

"You going to introduce me to her, Mac?" said the man. "This is the one, right?"

Mac's smile left his face as suddenly as it had arrived. "Shut up. And by that I mean, Cora, this is Royal Berring. Royal, this is Cora Sylvan. Don't believe a word he tells you. He lies."

"You didn't lie about her, brother," said Royal. "She *is* gorgeous."

"Jesus Christ," mumbled Mac.

Cora felt the wood floor beneath her shake like the rubber mats of the high school gym during a basketball game. Was that . . . no. That wasn't a flush on Mac's cheeks, was it? So there *was* something going on, and it had to do with her. She knew it.

"So . . . you're just . . ."

"We're just drinking coffee." Royal held up his cup. "Waiting for some eggs. And for you, apparently. I wasn't told that's what we were doing, but I approve, now that I know about it."

Cora popped her hip his direction. "Please scooch."

Royal obliged, scooting toward the window so Cora could sit. Thankfully, her voice was still steady when she said, "What are you really doing here, Mac?"

Pulling his ear lobe, he said, "Visiting family. Finally."

"Why now? What changed, suddenly? I don't get it. I doubt your mom gets it." Cora pressed her lips together and then said, "You've never been able to lie to me. That's not the real reason."

Mac looked startled.

"It's true. Remember when you tried to convince me that Mr. Pederston had another wife and family in another state? Or that Jamie Stockton was the first test tube baby?" Mac had told good whoppers, but she'd never fallen for a single one. He'd been a stammering fool, so young and thin and ridiculous, tugging his ear while he lied.

"So what do *you* think we're up to?" Royal's voice was amused.

She didn't spare him a glance, keeping her eyes on Mac. "I don't know. But I don't trust him. Or you, for that matter."

"You didn't mention she was such a scrapper," said Royal.

"She doesn't like me much," said Mac. His voice was genial, though, and Cora wanted to slug him.

"You haven't given me reason to like you. Not for years and years."

Shirley came up at her elbow and said, "Coffee, Cora?"

"No," she said shortly, and immediately regretted her tone. "Sorry. Maybe some water?"

Shirley gave her a long look and then said, "Sure, honey."

Royal watched her walk away. "That woman knows the way the world works."

Mac snapped, "She's twenty-five years older than you. Don't be an ass."

"So, Cora," said Royal, cheerily undaunted, "what's our Mac done to you to piss you off like this? Because if I don't miss my guess, you're considering spitting in his coffee just for the fun of it."

Cora didn't need to tell him. Royal was a stranger. But, then again, he was a stranger who appeared to be very much Mac's friend. And Mac's friend deserved to know the truth about him. "You really want to know?"

"I do," said Royal.

Mac sat up straighter. "Now wait a minute –"

"He never came home. My husband, his cousin, the man he was as close to as a brother, died. It was quick as these things go, I'm told, but we all knew he was going, and the one good thing about that was that we had time to say our farewells. Mac never came to say goodbye." Cora didn't think about the kiss, the betrayal of it. She couldn't. "And even more than that, he just abandoned us. The whole family, what was left of it."

She turned to Mac, steeling herself. "If you couldn't come back for the funeral, couldn't you have come back later? I don't understand." There it was, the weak shake in her voice she'd been dreading. Cora hated it.

"I said I was sorry," Mac said roughly. The skin under his eyes was white. "I thought you accepted that."

"I heard you. I accepted your apology. But it hurts, especially since I still don't understand it."

"I can't just – it's not that easy. But I should have come, I know that. At least to help you."

"To *help* me? You think *that's* what I needed? God, Mac. That's not what this is about. I didn't want help. *I* was fine. He wasn't. And now you're suddenly back here –"

"Working for me," said Royal.

"Awesome," said Cora thinly. That explained it. Kind of. She should have known Mac wasn't here by choice. "And you're in . . ."

"I do a lot of things for work but horses are what I love. Racing thoroughbreds. And Mac here makes good guesses."

"Oh." Cora sat back in the booth, feeling a spring poke her in the shoulder. "So the same as the rest of your family then. You're gambling, Mac?" She wouldn't have guessed she could have felt this disappointed in him.

There was a full, long pause as Mac slowly lifted his eyes from the table and met hers. "After where I came from?"

Cora shrugged and looked out the window. A small child raced past the glass, chased by a woman with outstretched arms.

"Fine," said Mac. "Think whatever you want."

"I've never been able to talk our boy into putting a dime on the horses," said Royal. "And believe me, I've tried. He's my vet. I just meant he makes good guesses when it comes to buying and breeding, that's all."

"You have horses."

"I do. Mac works for me exclusively."

"You must have a lot of them, to employ a vet full-time."

"Two hundred or so."

"Two *hundred*?" Cora said.

Royal shrugged. "I'm an all or nothing kind of guy. I like horses."

Cora stabbed the napkin in front of her with the butter knife. "So neither of you is going to tell me the full truth?'"

"She's a suspicious one, isn't she?" Royal nudged Cora with his shoulder. "I'm one of the good guys, gorgeous."

Cora knocked his shoulder back, harder, so that he bumped into the glass. Over his laughter, she said, "Flattery will literally get you nowhere."

Mac said, "Easy, Cora. It's not a big deal." He was still pale, though, and he wiped his hand over his mouth and jaw. That mouth . . . those lips that she'd . . .

And with that, Cora lost what little thread she'd held on her anger up till that point. "It *is* a big deal. You're up to something, and I swear to God, I'll keep working at it until I figure it out." She stood and faced them, shoving her hands into the back pockets of her jeans so they wouldn't see them shaking.

"What if it turns out to be good?" asked Royal. "What if Mac has your best interests at heart?"

"I'll tell you the truth." Cora paused. "I don't think he does. I don't think he ever has."

Mac looked stricken, blue veins standing out on his neck. And while it was exactly what she'd wanted, Cora felt sick. She'd made him look like that.

But dammit, all of this was his fault in the first place. *He* was the one who had let her – no, Logan – down. He was the one who had kissed *her.* As Mac's mouth opened to speak, Cora turned, and without another word she walked out of Tillie's. She managed to keep her composure, walking slowly and with purpose. She felt Mac's eyes follow her, even after she'd pulled out of her parking space and laid rubber peeling out. She didn't know any more than she did before.

She'd only made things worse.

CHAPTER SEVENTEEN

Knit the current trends, certainly. Why not knit a novelty yarn tank top at least once? But don't forget the warmth of an Aran's cables, the uniqueness of a Gansey's design, or the delight of a Norgie's peeries. These are our touchstones, our common language, our shared knowledge. –E.C.

On Wednesday, Cora found Olivia waiting at the stables as she'd said she would be. She wore thick, black combat boots that were already covered in country dust, and her hair had more twisted green strands than it had the week before.

"How long have you been waiting? Does the bus run pretty often?" Cora asked, shoving her keys into her overall pocket.

"You don't want to know." Olivia shuffled her feet and twisted her face as if she were itching her nose without touching it.

"What, did you hitchhike or something?"

Olivia's face scrunched even further.

"Oh," said Cora. "I was kidding."

Olivia shrugged. "People feel sorry for a kid."

"Or they *kidnap* them and chop them into little tiny pieces and leave those bloody bits alongside the highway."

Olivia's eyes widened. "Shit."

"I grew up in foster homes. You want to know something? At least once a month, one kid I knew in the system disappeared."

"Really?"

"Yes." They were taken out of the system by family members, usually, sometimes turning up again with little fanfare a month or three later. "They were all murdered."

"Bullshit."

The girl had a mouth on her, but her last curse was weak. Unconvinced. "Okay," admitted Cora. "Only most of them were. Don't do that again, okay? Will you call me when you need a ride?"

"You sound like my mom."

"Easy, tiger. I wouldn't go *that* far." Cora thought about Trixie and her breathy laugh. No *way* did she sound like her. "Come on, this way. I'll introduce you to Stark."

Stark was the manager, a thin woman who went solely by her last name. Only forty or so, her face was deeply lined by too much sun over the years. She wore sunglasses all the time, even indoors, which, with the addition of her long leather swing coat, gave her a science fiction look, as if she were as likely to pull a ray gun as a curry comb.

Olivia looked star-struck and stayed quiet as Stark led the way to the red barn with its tired-looking roof.

"Got a couple of Windward kids here now, Cora. Bill and Ted. Like the excellent adventure, only if they don't quit goofing off, I'm gonna adventure them right out. They spilled a gallon of paint all over the west drive earlier."

Cora smiled. Bill and Ted, brothers who'd been placed at Windward last month were two of her favorites. Twelve and thirteen, they were all thumbs and elbows, eager to help but clueless as to how much havoc they left in their 'helpful' wake.

"I'll talk to them."

Stark shrugged. "They're okay." Still moving quickly ahead, she glanced over her shoulder at Olivia. "What is it exactly you're looking to do?"

A pause. "I dunno," said Olivia.

"She might like to volunteer," said Cora.

"We have a lot of work that needs doin', all the time. But I already have volunteers. What is it *you* want to do?"

Olivia said nothing, keeping her eyes on the ground.

Stark stopped and turned, midstride, startling Cora and making Olivia stumble to a halt. "Know what? I get you. I *was* you."

Olivia looked startled, and turned her head to catch Cora's eye.

Stark went on, "I don't know if you got friends, but I know I didn't. No offense, but I dressed funny, too. Know what I had? Horses. They were all I cared about, still are. And I think you've got some of that in you, if I don't miss my guess, which I rarely do. But if you want to get on board this train, you gotta buy a ticket, Olivia."

"What –"

Stark turned again and continued forward without looking to see if Olivia followed her.

Appearing lost and even younger than she was, Olivia whispered to Cora, "I *want* to. Buy a ticket, I mean."

Without thinking, Cora said, "I think this might be the best thing you've ever done."

It was as if she'd flipped some kind of internal switch in the girl. Olivia went from slouched to upright, from glowering to glowing. She chased after Stark. "Wait! Can I come twice a week? After school? I already know how to ride – I won riding lessons once, or I mean, my mom did and she gave them to me. It's been a long time, but I'll remember, I know I will."

Stark said something that Cora couldn't catch. She'd been like that once, trailing hopefully after Mac and Logan, wanting to get to ride one of their horses, wishing for . . . something she'd never been able to name, not even now.

Olivia peppered Stark with questions. "I could come help more often, if you needed someone. What about every day? Do you have any volunteers who come every day? Can I ride one of the horses, maybe? I mean, when the groups are done riding at the end of the day?"

Stark nodded. "You can ride now, if you want."

The look on Olivia's face reminded Cora of what she'd felt like the first time she'd seen Eliza steek a sweater, using sharp scissors to cut it up the middle. Awestruck. "Yes," Olivia said. "Please."

They went into the next stall together, Stark and Olivia, and Cora leaned outside as Stark talked her through the way to saddle the sorrel.

That day so long ago, Eliza had held up the new cardigan triumphantly. "There. Like magic, isn't it?" She'd poured another cup of tea for Cora, remembering how she took it, every time, which made Cora feel more loved than anything else she could remember in her life. "Now let me show you how I did that, so you'll know, too."

Cora had bloomed under Eliza's smile.

Now Stark had Olivia up on the horse named Purple Rain. They moved together out to the ring, walking at first, then easing into a slow canter.

Cora leaned forward against a fence post, threading her fingers through the wire as she watched Olivia ride. Stark stood next to her, one hip jutted out, her eyes intent on Olivia.

"I might be wrong," said Cora, "but she's good. Right? She said she's only had one set of lessons before."

Stark smiled. "The first time I rode, I knew it was what I was meant to do. That girl's the same as me. She was born to ride." She looked sideways at Cora and then back at Olivia. "She new in town?"

Cora shook her head. "Her mom is Trixie Fletcher, with the *Independent*."

"Oh shit, seriously? I know that one. She came here once to write something about the kids, and she asked for a wet wipe to clean the horse germs off her hands when we went into the office." Stark spit into the dirt unselfconsciously. "Can't stand a woman like that."

"Who can?" said Cora.

They watched Olivia, her face alight with joy, canter and prance on Purple Rain until the sun dropped and the air cooled. A strip of pink lit the sky at the tops of the trees and a finger of fog traced its way into the valley.

Trixie Fletcher. There was a time when Cora had been able to stand her. There had been a moment, at least, when she'd thought Trixie was going to be a friend. During high school, Trixie had been part of the crowd Mac and Logan had run with, the crowd that sometimes stopped by the barns on their way to somewhere more fun. Cora would be currying a horse, keeping her head behind its flank as she listened to the kids yell friendly abuse at each other, so comfortable with each other. How did they all *learn* that?

<<>>

Mac and Logan had idly been teaching her poker using pennies, letting her keep them when she won, which wasn't often. One afternoon, just as they'd sat down to play, Trixie joined them. She'd been on her way home, but she wanted to play poker, she said, and Cora had been astonished when Trixie smiled at her the same way she did Misty Barrigan. The look was friendly. It seemed accepting.

Louisa came onto the porch then, and yelled at the boys to finish taking the leaves to the bonfire pile. Cora was left sitting with Trixie at the picnic table under the vast, spreading oak. Cora shuffled the cards, trying to get them to move smoothly, like Mac did, but she was all thumbs.

"Let me show you," said Trixie. She expertly slid the pack from Cora's finger and shuffled, creating a waterfall of cards that feathered together on the table top. "See? It's easy."

Cora nodded. "Do it again?"

"Hey, which one do you like?"

Did Trixie really want to know her favorite card? Jack of Spades, if she had to pick, but . . .

Trixie smiled again, that inclusive grin that made Cora want to lean closer to her. She studied the fall of Trixie's hair, wishing fervently that her hair was as smooth, as straight. The light that fell through the oak leaves dappled Trixie's skin, highlighting her porcelain skin. Cora could practically feel her freckles getting bigger.

"Of the guys, silly. Which one are you after?"

"Neither!" Cora pulled her arms off the table and held her elbows. "Are you joking?"

"Because at school, you're always staring at Mac. But I think it's Logan that really likes you."

Cora felt wobbly, standing on territory she had no idea how to navigate. This was what girls who were friends talked about, right? But the boys would be back any moment, and she would *die* if they heard this . . .

"And you're *always* here, doing something for them. There must be one you're crushing on."

Mac, Mac, Mac . . . "No, neither of them," she lied again. "No way."

Trixie let the cards ripple through her fingers again, a soft whirring sound matching their motion. "Well, I think Logan is cuter. More exciting, you know? The way he rides? But Mac is taller. He looks older, and I heard he was able to buy beer for the last beach party. And he's freakin' hot. Those eyes, you know? All sleepy-sexy."

It felt wrong to talk about them like this, and at the same time Cora was desperate to hear more.

Trixie went on, "Becca Raddison says Mac was the *best* kisser."

Cora, who had never been kissed, felt her stomach twist unfamiliarly.

"They didn't do anything else, though. I bet I could get him to do more."

What more?

Trixie's eyes reminded Cora of a well-fed cat. "Logan likes you better, anyway. So you don't mind if I go for Mac?"

Cora *did* mind. Oh, she minded so much. "Logan doesn't like me."

"Don't be stupid. He can't stop staring at you." Trixie's voice had changed – Cora didn't understand it. Why did she sound angry about what Logan was doing if she wanted to date Mac? Cora was missing great chunks of subtext, and she knew it, but she didn't know how to keep up. She continued, "He asked you to the Spring Fling dance, right?"

Cora felt dumb surprise. How did Trixie know that? "I said no. I don't need to go to some dumb dance." In reality, Cora hadn't wanted to ask Eliza for the money for a dress. "Why? Do you want to date Logan?"

"Date? Oh, little girl. I want more than a date from a guy. But Mac will do," said Trixie, licking her gloss-slicked lips.

Mac would do? Cora wanted to take the cards out of her hands and throw them, she wanted to push Trixie across the yard to the main road and tell her to keep going, that she didn't belong in their little club. That she couldn't ruin the threesome Cora and the boys had become. But instead, Cora clutched a penny so hard it indented her palm.

"Yeah, I like Logan," she lied. "You're right."

When the boys rejoined them, Cora asked, "Is it too late to change my answer to yes?"

He'd whooped, and thrown his hat into the air.

"If I was a Scan-tron test, then it would be too late. But I'm *Logan*, baby." He'd put his strong, muscled arms around her and lifted her off the ground, spinning her in a circle right there. She'd laughed out loud as she looked up, suddenly dizzyingly happy.

Mac was so busy teaching Trixie a card trick, he'd hardly seemed to notice.

<<>>

That day, along with the game, Cora had lost something else, something she couldn't name. But it felt precious. She didn't know how to get it back. And she and Trixie had most definitely *not* become friends.

Cora shook herself, coming back to the present. Trixie's daughter was right here in front of her, the horse dancing smoothly underneath her.

"Can you take a picture of me?" called Olivia. "Before I have to put her away?"

Cora snapped a shot with her phone. She'd email it to Olivia tonight.

Olivia beamed at Cora, and Cora grinned back.

Oh, this, at least, was just right. Everyone needed a passion. A calling. Eliza had taught her that so well. Cora felt Eliza's ghost next to her, a pale, unseen shadow, illuminated only by her imagination. She would have approved of Olivia's joy.

CHAPTER EIGHTEEN

Happiness is a cardigan that matches your eyes. – E.C.

Mac finished running the table by smacking the eight ball into the corner pocket right where he'd called it. "And *that's* the way you do it, my friend."

"I can't believe you just did that," said Royal, shaking his head. "I've never seen you play like that."

"You mean I've been waiting for years to hustle you," said Mac, feeling ridiculously satisfied by how much fun he'd just had, watching Royal's face get redder and redder every time Mac sank a ball. "I don't believe in spanking a man at his own table, and we've only ever played together at yours."

"So for years you've just been letting me win."

"Think about it, you rarely actually beat me." Mac leaned his cue stick against the table and dug three more quarters out of his pocket. "I'm just a little more considerate when it's your table."

"Shit. So you've been soft-hustling me?"

"Learned from the best," said Mac.

That, at least, puffed out Royal's chest, as Mac had known it would. "It's true. I'm the best."

"Just keep telling yourself that," said Mac. He put the quarters in the slot and pumped them into the table. The *shoonk* of the balls as they dropped and rolled for the next game was a friendly sound and for just a moment, Mac was happy to be exactly where he was, back in his home town, around people who'd known him before he'd had to shave.

Looking for the same girl he'd been looking for back then.

Well, that was awkward.

Mac shook his head as if he could shake the thoughts of Cora out of it, but even so, he scanned the incoming crowd for the twelfth time, looking for that red hair of hers. Tonight the Rite Spot wasn't so much a bar as it was turning into a gathering place. Down the street, at the center the new doctors had opened, the community had held some kind of a fundraiser for Windward Group Home. Mac had stopped by on his way to meet Royal, but had only gotten a few feet inside before he'd had to fend off questions from six different people about what he was doing back in town. He'd received a hug from a tall, skinny blonde woman he hardly recognized but thought maybe he'd gone to high school with and had finally written a check he could barely afford to buy his way out of the place in a hurry. As he'd pushed open the side door, though, he'd caught sight of Cora, just for a split second. She was at the front of the room by the dais where a teenager was getting ready to sing a song with his guitar. She'd been laughing at something the boy'd said, and Mac felt compassion for the red flush that started at the base of the boy's neck. Any guy would feel like that, if Cora turned those blue eyes of hers on his. God, when he was the kid's age, he hadn't been able to think of much else but kissing her. Of course, Logan had beaten him to the punch, as usual.

He'd watched her for another moment, thinking of the video he'd found last month on YouTube. He and Royal had already hatched their plan, and Mac had known he'd see Cora soon. Fine, that would be fine. It would have to be, right? He'd googled her, unable to stop himself, and then stared in shock as he heard her voice again for the first time in years. And God bless it, the image of her had still made him feel exactly the same way.

Intoxicated.

Infatuated.

Okay, more than infatuated. Way more.

Goddammit.

In the video, she'd described item by item what to pack in an emergency bag. He'd been fascinated by the way her mouth moved, how she laughed about the corkscrew and the way she blushed when she held up a ziplock full of sanitary supplies. He'd watched it three times before he realized that doing so was creepy as hell. He wasn't a stalker. And he wasn't going to become one, thanks very much. But that last little lilt in her voice as she'd signed off, the cute way she'd leaned forward with a grin to shut down the camera – it got him.

At the fundraiser, he'd been in grave danger of staring at her the same way he had the video on his MacBook. As if he might never see her again.

Jesus, get a grip.

Mac had made it out of the center without Cora seeing him, and he'd met Royal at the bar, shaking off the intense longing by smacking the cue ball with ferocity, slaking his thirst with cold beer.

The problem was that Cypress Hollow was, always would be, a small town. When the fundraising concert finished, a crowd of people started squeezing their way in to the Rite Spot, and they were still coming. Just as much coffee was ordered as alcohol. Jesus, couldn't they do that at Lucy's bookstore or something? Anywhere but here. At any minute, Cora might push her way through that old-fashioned swinging bar door. After realizing *that*, Mac couldn't sink another shot to save his life.

"I know you're full of crap, Mac. You trying to make me feel better? You feel sorry for me now?" Royal shook his head and smacked the side pocket, calling his next shot. "'Cause I know you'd never play pity pool with me. I mean, you'd never do it *again*."

"Guess you'll never know, huh?" It wasn't pity pool, though. Mac couldn't keep his attention on the game for more than the twenty seconds it took for him to line up each crap shot.

A flame of red hair caught his eye – no. It wasn't her. The redhead was too tall, too thin. Cora had curves on her, real girl-shaped curves. Without having her in front of him, Mac could conjure in his mind exactly where Cora's breasts curved out, and where her waist dipped in. Cora looked like a real woman.

Whereas the redhead, the one that had just come through the door, just looked skinny. Pretty, but not interesting like Cora. The woman smiled at him and waved, and with a jolt Mac realized he knew her. Knew her well. He'd been thinking about Cora so hard he'd almost looked right through her.

Trixie Fletcher. He hadn't seen her in the last fifteen years, but her long green cat eyes were the same as always. Somehow, she'd grown into her looks, which had been spectacular even at eighteen. She smiled at Jonas, the bartender. How her gaze managed to be friendly and predatory at the same time baffled Mac, but then again, he'd dated her for a short time in high school and had never understood it even then.

"Holy hell. Who . . . ?" Royal's mouth hung open for one ludicrous second.

"You're actually gaping, you know that? You look like an idiot."

Royal snapped his mouth shut. "Introduce me."

"In a minute," Mac turned around to take his shot. Missed it, chunking the felt with his cue tip. Again.

"You're fired if you don't introduce me this second."

Mac took a sip of his beer and tried to ignore the fact that Trixie was coming toward them. "Screw you," he said out of the corner of his mouth.

She was upon them then: one long arm wrapping around his neck, cool lips pressing against his for one short second, just long enough to remind him that they had a history. "Mac," she purred. "I heard you were back."

He untangled himself from her arm and took a step backward.

"Aren't you going to introduce me to your friend?" Trixie leaned against the pool table and picked up Mac's cue stick, running her fingers up its length.

"Do I have to?"

"Jesus, Mac," Royal said, stepping in front of him. "I apologize for my friend, but you obviously know him, and you know what a jack-ass he can be. Me, I'm the opposite. Nicest guy you'll probably ever meet."

"Trixie Fletcher," she said, holding out her hand. "Editor of the *Cypress Hollow Independent*."

"Royal Berring. In charge of nothing but horses and this guy right here."

"Oh, you're Mac's boss?" Trixie's smile increased.

"Yeah?" Royal squinted at Mac. "It's kinda like breaking a stubborn bronc. But he makes good jokes and every once in a while buys the beers, so I guess he's all right with me."

Mac scowled. "If anyone's the problem, it's you."

"Ow." Royal put his fist to his chest. "You see how he treats his superior? I'm wounded. To the core."

Trixie laughed, a tinkling sound. God, that brought back late nights, Trixie leaning against him, her hand stuck in his pocket, Mac's mind stuck on Cora.

The same Cora who was standing now just behind Trixie. She looked surprised, and then, worse: she looked irritated. How could Mac have confused Trixie's red hair at the door of the Rite Spot with

Cora's? Trix's was obviously out of the bottle, always had been, while Cora's was all natural sun and flame. Just like the color on Trixie's lips was glossy, while Cora's shone a natural pink. He watched as she bit one, and forgot that he should say something. He wanted to watch her, and remember – again – about how her lips had tasted.

"Excuse me," she said, her voice slightly hoarse, as if she'd used it too much at the benefit. "Can I get by?"

Trixie turned and said, "Oh, look. It's just like old times, isn't it, Mac?" Her eyes glinted. Mac didn't trust her any more than a three-year-old filly.

"Good times, yeah." Cora tried to brush past them, but Royal was too quick for her.

"No," said Royal. "Stay a minute, can't you? I'm pretty sure I didn't help anything last Sunday at the diner. I'm back in town again to make it right. Can I buy you a beer?"

"No, thanks." Cora jammed a hand into her hair. And that, in turn, made her look even sexier. Lord, if he had his hands in that wild tangle . . . Mac wanted to speak, but found his mouth suddenly too dry to form words.

"Come on." Royal slid his pool stick onto the green felt. "Open table," he said. "Someone else play. I feel like drinking, not playing pool. Cora, want to do a shot? Barkeep! Line us all up with tequila!"

Jonas grinned and set out four shot glasses.

"Do I *look* twenty-one?" Cora asked. But there it was, in her voice, that hint of amusement that every single woman had in response to Royal's playful innocence.

"No one could accuse you of that." Trixie said and opened her eyes guilelessly.

"I suppose none of us look that young, I guess," said Cora. "But you were always the oldest of the group, right, Trixie?"

Mac laughed while Trixie shot him a glare.

"It was sixth grade, and you didn't even live here when I was held back," said Trixie. The jukebox cut off abruptly as if someone had kicked out the plug, so her voice was loud in the sudden quiet. "So, tell us. Did you have a family then, or had you already been ditched?"

CHAPTER NINETEEN

*Not following the pattern will not bring the knitting police. Those officers
are all tipsy on red wine, anyway, discussing with slurred words the most
appropriate bind-offs for sturdy blue cardigans. Do not fear them.*
— E.C.

Well, Cora supposed she had that coming. She had, after
all, just made the snark about Trixie being older, which
had been uncalled for and uncharitable. It had been *fun*
to say, even though she regretted it, so she took a deep breath and
said lightly, "Yep. I'd been ditched by then, a couple of times, actually. But I didn't move to Cypress Hollow until I was sixteen, so no
one here knew me until I was in the deepest, ugliest throes of my
teenaged angst."

Trixie looked vaguely disappointed that she hadn't gotten a bigger reaction. She turned back to Royal. "So what brings a man like
you to town?"

Royal, as friendly as he was, looked as if he wasn't prepared for the bright glow of Trixie's attention. "I run horses. I'm always looking for, you know . . . more. You know?"

"I don't," Trixie said, leaning toward him, stroking her finger around the rim of her empty shot glass. "Tell me."

"You know, the next big business move."

Mac said warningly, "Royal . . ."

"It's okay," said Trixie. "I may be a reporter, but if you say something's off the record, I can keep a secret with the best of them."

Cora didn't believe her, and the look on Mac's face said he tended toward the same conclusion.

But it was obvious Royal was sinking under her spell. "Wouldn't Mac's little town be just the right place to raise horses? Climate's perfect, only a couple hours either direction from Bay Gate Downs and Golden Gate Fields . . . I need the right amount of land, because I won't do anything smaller than I think is appropriate. People get into trouble that way. Do it right. Do it big, I always say."

"Not much land for sale," said Cora. "Most the folks around here have lived on their parcels all their lives. There's a piece down closer to Pescadero, but I hear it has drainage issues."

Trixie raised a perfectly shaped eyebrow. "Launching a commercial thoroughbred venture? That would bring some attention to our little one-horse town, as it were."

Grinning, Royal signaled Jonas to pour them all another shot. "I'm a good businessman. And a good dreamer."

"Do your dreams often come true?"

Cora watched Royal's Adam's apple bob up and down. He cleared his throat.

"Usually. Financially, yes."

Mac, leaning over the green, mumbled, "Sometimes people hate you for that."

"I know, brother." Royal held out the tequila. "Bottoms up!"

Trixie laughed again and joined him in tossing back the shot.

Instead of draining the alcohol that had somehow refilled her shot glass, Cora clutched it. How long did she have to stand here, pretending to be social? Listening to Trixie flirt? High school was rushing back to her, all those teenaged feelings of inadequacy. Standing in the hall, smelling the rust in her locker, pretending she couldn't hear everyone talking about who was doing what on the weekend.

Now she turned her back on Trixie and Royal while she watched Mac finish putting the balls in perfect order. He corralled them inside the rack, threading his fingers into the space at the end, and then spinning it up and off so that not a ball moved. The muscles along the back of his neck – who *had* those? Cora could swear she'd never noticed neck muscles on a man alive before, and now she couldn't take her eyes off them. He looked up. *Caught.*

"Your dog's still waiting for you at the shelter," he said.

Cora jumped. "My dog? Your dog. I can't believe you took her back there."

"She was just on loan. Clementine should be yours."

"No pets for me. She wouldn't even make a good guard dog. Did you see the way she shakes?"

"She's waiting. Pining, I tell you. In the meantime, you want to play?" Mac patted the edge of the pool table.

"Me? No."

"Give it a shot." Mac waggled the rack at her and then slipped it into the slot at the end of the table. "Come on. How bad can it be?"

Cora looked over her shoulder as if there were someone watching her, as if someone might talk her out of it. And maybe they should. But the only people behind her were Jonas and his sister Lucy, and they were talking to each other. Trixie and Royal had taken seats at the crowded bar and were paying them no attention. "I guess it couldn't be that bad."

But it was.

Playing pool with Mac was excruciating. He was good, as always, and even though Cora knew he had miles more practice than she did, the game brought out a competitive streak that felt foreign. She lined up her shots carefully, studying the angle the ball would take and when it failed to drop into the right pocket, she stepped back in abject disappointment. The worst part was that she knew Mac could tell, and he was adjusting his game to her.

"I hate it that you're going easy on me," she said when he sunk the cue ball. She dug it out of the pocket and placed it on the felt. "Just do what you always do."

"I usually play with Royal. He's not very good. Does that help?"

"No." Her stick glanced off the cue ball with a sharp crack. "Shit."

"Chalk," he said helpfully.

"I *know*." But she didn't. She'd completely forgotten that. Cora rubbed the chalk on the tip of her stick and lined it up again, leaning forward over the table. Thank god she was wearing a regular black t-shirt and not the V-neck she'd thought of putting on for the benefit.

He stood at the other end of the table and said softly, "It's just a game, *Corazón*."

Oh, God. She hadn't been called that in years.

Heart.

Not even Logan had ever called her that – it had been Mac's way of teasing her in high school. Cora wasn't short for anything, and she'd hated how girly it had sounded. Mac said it suited her since she wore her heart on her sleeve, which made her hate it even more. She *didn't* show her heart. To anyone, really. She was proud of that.

She risked a glance at him. His eyes were quiet, his arms folded. He didn't look like he was teasing.

Taking a deep breath, she made her shot on the exhale, like Logan had taught her so long ago. It worked – her aim was true and steady, and her combo shot sunk two of her balls, leaving her next shot obvious, long green on the seven.

"Nicely done."

"Thanks." The heat of anger had left her body. She wasn't sure what had done it – maybe it was the fact that he hadn't even glanced at Trixie once.

Ridiculous. That would mean she was still – what? Jealous? Cora shot a look to where Trixie was still flirting with Royal. Trixie tossed her long hair over her shoulder as she made whatever point she was making by opening her arms expansively and then touching his hand.

Then Trixie looked at Cora, and to Cora's vast surprise, Trixie smiled. It was an open, genuine-looking smile, and it threw Cora completely. She had no idea what to do in response other than smile back. The surprise was so great that she missed what Mac was saying.

"I'm sorry, what?"

He followed her gaze. Trixie had turned back to Royal who was, improbably, flexing so that she could feel his muscle. "Oh. Uh-oh."

"Yeah," said Cora. "How tough is he? Can he handle her?" She tended to doubt it, given the few moments she'd spent with him. "Trixie tends to get what she wants."

"He's tough as hell in business. His motto is all or nothing. Wins at everything he tries."

Cora scratched her shot. "I hope he's not serious about that idea of his."

Mac nodded and moved behind her. It was a tight fit, and she could feel the heat of him for the second it took for him to come around to the table.

Then he was lining up his shot as Cora tried to catch her breath again.

"Yeah. If it has a dollar bill involved, Royal's golden. He can do no wrong. He risks and wins." Mac sounded bitter, as if there were more underneath his words.

Lightly, she said, "You ever play that game? The investment thing?"

He laughed, once. "Yep. Just as good at it as the rest of my family is with gambling. Bought a house in 2005."

"Yeah? Good for you."

"Bought at the worst time. Foreclosed. I lost every bit of savings I'd ever scraped together."

"Damn."

Rubbing his face, he said, "I don't know why I just told you that. I don't talk about that." He paused. "And Royal there just has to sneeze and someone gives him a hundred dollar bill to blow his nose on."

She glanced again at Royal talking to Trixie. He held his hands out as if he were telling a big fish story.

"And women?" She didn't know if she was asking about Royal or about Mac.

"He does great with the ponies. But women aren't horses, are they?"

No, they weren't. Cora knew that well. Before she could stop herself, she said, "Logan never quite learned that."

Mac froze. Then he shot, and missed the ball almost completely. But it rolled half an inch, and he stepped back. "Your turn."

"Now I know you're going easy on me," said Cora, but the words felt like she was saying something else. What, she couldn't – wouldn't – figure out. "I'm going to get us another beer."

CHAPTER TWENTY

Cables are magic – stability in motion. – E.C.

Mac watched her go, weaving her way through friends and neighbors. She paused to smile and touch a shoulder, then again to give the next woman a hug. It looked like she knew every single person. Heck, he still recognized most of them, and he'd been gone for years. Oh, Cypress Hollow. It felt for a moment like he'd never left.

Cora leaned in at the bar and said something he couldn't hear to Jonas. The low light of the bar lit the top of her head in a red halo, and as she spoke to the man seated on the barstool next to her, Mac felt himself get smacked by a wave of . . . something. Emotion? Lust? Or more?

Oh, man. He was in deep trouble. Staring at the pool table, he waited for the stunned feeling to pass. Took a breath. It was going to pass any minute. Yep. *Any* minute now.

But sixty seconds later, Mac still felt almost dizzy with it. He was so not over Cora Sylvan. Nowhere near it. Never had been, probably never would be, not if she kept playing pool with him, kept sparring with him. All she had to do was breathe near him. *Shit.* Mac wasn't stupid – he'd expected some reaction on his part when he came back to town. A crush was a crush, after all, and a teenaged crush had to be the worst of all.

But damn. You'd think a grown man would have recovered at least a little bit. Mac felt the tips of his ears go hot, and he wondered if anyone else had noticed how she affected him. Royal probably had. Royal saw everything. Trixie, maybe, but she was pretty busy keeping Royal laughing. Now there was a duo he would never have seen coming, but they were looking cozier by the minute. Good. If it kept them both busy, he could keep watching Cora.

At the bar, Cora nodded her thanks at Jonas as he pushed the beers toward her. The round-bellied man next to her on the barstool slid his arm around her, and Mac watched as her back stiffened.

And just like that, he went on full alert. Not caring that his cue stick slid from where he'd leaned it on the table to the ground, he strode across the bar. Royal said something to him – he didn't hear the words.

With her right hand, Cora plucked the man's fingers from her left shoulder. "You think I'd fall for that, Billy?" Neatly sidestepping just far enough away from him that he couldn't touch her, she went on, "Nice trick, but I've seen it before."

Billy Thunker. Holy crap. Yep, those same beady little eyes, same thick neck. He was the same Billy who'd plagued Cora so many years ago in the high school quad. He'd wanted to punch Billy then. And he wanted to punch him now. Even more.

"'S'not a trick, Cora," slurred Billy, poking at three dice cups in front of him. "Just show me where the dollar bill is." He leaned so far in her direction he almost fell off the barstool. "And if you get it right, I'll just schtuff it down your . . ."

Mac took another step closer. He would spin that joker around so fast –

"Nah," said Cora easily, stilling Mac with a single glance. "I got a better one. I bet you can't figure this out."

"You're on." Billy looked to his compatriot at his left. "Ten bucks I can. Whatever it is."

"Don't men ever learn gambling is a waste of money?" she said under her breath. She pulled a handful of change out of her pocket. Mac crossed his arms over his chest and moved so that he could see both of their faces. Whatever she was up to, he was going to enjoy watching her do it.

"What'zat?"

"Nothing." She sifted through the change. Then, holding her closed fist out, she said, "I have two coins equaling thirty-five cents in my hand. However, one of the coins is not a dime."

Billy's face scrunched tight, his lips protruding as he thought. His friend gave up thinking about it almost instantly, going back to his dice game with the man next to him.

"Come on, Billy." Cora put her other hand on her hip as she waited. "You can do it." Her voice was gently mocking. Mac couldn't detect any trace of that girl he'd first seen in the quad – she wasn't shy or scared. She was confident now. Good God, it was hot.

"Gah," Billy said. "It's some kinda trick. I know it is."

"No trick, big guy. Just use your common sense."

Without looking up from his dice cup, his friend nudged him. "Get it? Cents?"

"Shut up, Paul." Billy drummed his thick fingers on the bar, staring at them as if counting. "Impossible. I call bullshit."

"We're not playing that, but okay." Cora opened her fingers and held the two coins up by her fingertips: a quarter and a dime.

"But, but . . . you said . . ."

"I said one was not a dime. I didn't say a thing about the other one, did I?"

"Hey," he sputtered. "You can't – I don't –"

"Just pay Jonas for our beers, and we'll call it even, huh?"

Behind the bar, Jonas laughed and said, "I'll add it to your tab, Billy."

Mac's stomach tightened as Cora caught his eye and flipped him a smile. She wound her way back to him. The beers were full to the brim, and she didn't spill a drop.

He took a glass from her, and foam immediately dripped over the edge and onto his hand. "Pretty roughneck place," he said.

"Hustlers everywhere." Cora winked at him.

Mac had to clear his throat before he spoke again. "Looks like you can handle yourself, though."

She glanced down into her beer. "Guess so."

Too damn true. "Let's finish this game."

"At least we didn't bet anything on it," Cora said.

He couldn't help himself – his gaze dropped to her lips. *They should have bet a kiss.*

As if she could hear his thoughts, her fingers went to her mouth. "I mean," she said, "It's not like I've ever been a gambler."

Nope. She never had. She'd probably never felt the urge to risk it all course through her veins. Mac came by it naturally, he knew that. Luckily, he'd kept himself out of casinos, and only ever went on the back side of the racetrack. The danger of a track was on the front side.

Still. He'd risked it all and lost it all on his house. Just like he'd lost it all so long ago, gambling on Cora. His personal rule was to only gamble when it really, really mattered was a stupid one. He lost anyway. No matter what. No difference between him and the old men with their eyes glued to the horses racing centerfield.

Glancing at the guy slouched at the bar, he shook the beer off his fingers, wishing for one moment that he was shaking out his hand after driving it into Billy's face.

CHAPTER TWENTY-ONE

The man who hand washes the socks you give him is the true king of hearts. – E.C.

Mac had won the game of pool, of course. Cora had skedaddled out afterward, ducking goodbyes, pretending she didn't hear Royal teasing her for running away. The next night, she had spent the whole farmers market in agony, waiting for Mac to bring the dog by the booth for another appearance.

But he hadn't showed. Cora had been grateful. Mostly.

The next morning, Friday, she rose early. For a pair of hand-knit socks, Silas Harrison had agreed to help Cora take down and dispose of the burned out shed. He wore size thirteen shoes, and because his mother, Toots, and sister, Lucy, had drilled into him the value of hand-knits, he knew the worth of such a large pair. The deal was perfect for Cora – she had more yarn floating around than she had dollar bills.

While Silas broke apart pieces of the shed with a mallet and sheer force, she pulled out some gray Romney fiber that had been in a wooden box – it was smoke damaged, but she thought if she soaked it for long enough and then hung it in the sun, it might be redeemed. Almost everything else she'd stored inside was gone. The jams and preserves had burst in the heat. The candles, obviously, had all melted into dirty lumps.

When the state of affairs got to be too much for her, she gave Silas a wave and went to sit in the bomb shelter for a few minutes. Sanity. Peace. Order.

Safety.

Her store of canned food soothed her. The various tools she'd gathered over the years: the hand-cranked radio, the stock of flashlights filled with batteries she changed every year – she wanted to hug them. In the old rucksacks she'd gotten at the Army Navy store, her stores of daily supplies were still good, protected by heavy canvas. Water: she had so much water, also regularly changed out.

It hit her while staring at the paper products that one could pack more toilet paper in a smaller space if the cardboard core was removed and the tissue rewound, like winding yarn off a cone into a ball. It was something she would experiment with later. Brilliant. It might even make a good little video.

"Hello?"

Not recognizing the voice, Cora went up the bomb shelter steps, pushing the heavy door closed behind her. It was *her* spot. No one else's.

"Hello?" she called back.

"Hey, you."

Trixie. Pretty much the last person Cora would have expected to visit. She looked down at her overalls, comparing them to Trixie's perfect skinny-legged jeans. No rhinestones on Cora's ass, that was for sure. A goat would nibble those off in a split second of distraction.

"Royal and I were in the area, and he wanted to see your little place here."

"Mine?" Cora was confused. "Not Mac's next door? Is Mac with you?" She peered behind Trixie and felt a surprising amount of disappointment when Royal shook his head.

"I'm just getting a feel for the land around here," said Royal. He looked delightedly at Trixie. "Turns out I have the best tour guide in the county."

"Maybe if I do a good enough job, he'll give me a horse." Trixie touched his shoulder and smiled.

Royal looked dazed. "Okay," he said.

"Oh, you silly thing. I was teasing. I don't want a horse."

Cora said, "Olivia would like it if you got one, though."

"Olivia?" said Royal.

Trixie turned so that she faced Cora. "What?"

Cora bit her lip. What had she been thinking? "I met your daughter last week at the farmers market."

"Oh." Trixie frowned. "Don't mind her. She's going through a phase."

"Seems like a great kid."

"You talked horses?"

"She didn't want to talk about anything else." Cora wouldn't ask if Olivia had told her mother about the stables. Every teenaged girl needed a few secrets, she remembered that, at least.

But Trixie made the connection. Slowly, she said, "You're the one who took her to ride the other day."

So she did know. "She's a natural."

"*You?*" If Trixie's eyes could shoot lasers – and Cora wouldn't be surprised – she'd be dead on the spot.

"I'm sorry?"

"Damned right you're sorry. You pick up a girl from the high school without her mother's permission –"

She hitchhiked. "I didn't pick her up."

"Even worse! You make a girl you barely know ride the public bus to a place at the back of beyond, and then put her up on a horse. Did she happen to sign a liability waiver by any chance?"

God, Cora hadn't even thought of that. How had that not crossed her mind? She knew the Windward kids were signed off – she'd had to make copies of some of the forms when she'd been helping out a couple of months ago.

What if Olivia had been pitched from the horse and ended up breaking her neck? Stark would have been shut down in a heartbeat. Cora knew Stark was actually the one responsible for that kind of thing, and she was the one who should have thought of it. But it had been so organic – one minute they were looking at the horses, and the next, Olivia had been hiking herself into the saddle. Cora supposed the years of kids running around unsupervised, climbing trees and saddling horses, the years she'd had as a teenager, were over. Now it was about who could sue whom, and she'd been an idiot not to think of it.

"No."

"That's right. Of course she didn't. You know why? Those kinds of waivers require a parent to sign for a minor. And I for sure as hell didn't sign anything." Trixie even looked gorgeous in fury, Cora couldn't help noticing.

"I'm sorry, I truly am. I should have thought of that."

Trixie wasn't listening. "You know, last year I did a piece on that place. What's that woman's name? Stork something?"

"Rebecca Stark. She's good at what she does, I promise you. She's responsible."

"There was something else." Trixie frowned. "That's right. There was a lawsuit against her. Someone sued for negligence after their kid got bucked and broke both legs. That's where you took my daughter?"

"If you reported on it, then you know how it ends. The case was unfounded."

"It means there's an ongoing problem. My child does *not* go back there."

Cora knew, just from the one visit, that Olivia had been hooked. She'd seen it her eyes – horses were going to be Olivia's passion. "You should have seen her, Trixie. She came alive."

"You're telling me my daughter wasn't alive before you took her to a shitty public stable?"

Cora thought about the downcast young woman who had shuffled into her booth at the farmers market last week and contrasted her with the bright-eyed girl who had come into the booth last night, haranguing her about meeting up at the stable on Saturday. "That's not what I'm saying at all. I just mean that when someone finds something that they love, that they didn't see coming – it happens to a lot of us at that age. I found Eliza, and knitting. Spinning. Remember how Mac learned he loved to take care of animals? And Logan's thing was riding?" If the memory of Logan didn't work, then nothing would. Everyone had loved Logan. "And when he got up on a horse, he transformed, remember?"

"If by transformed you mean lobotomized, then yeah, I remember."

That had been exactly Cora's biggest problem with Logan. She had come in second to the horses, always.

Trixie went on, "You think that's what I want? Another one of *them*? You think we don't have enough of those in Cypress Hollow? Idiots who think only of horses and rodeo and racing? She could have *died*."

"There was never any danger of death," said Cora. Crap, crappity, *crap*. How was she supposed to handle this?

How would Eliza have handled it?

Taking a deep breath, Cora took a step forward and placed a hand on Trixie's arm. In her mind she pictured Trixie lying in bed, alone, worrying about her daughter, who as far as Cora knew was the only family she had. "I can't imagine what that's like, to be that scared about a child, since I don't have one of my own." The words brought back that old deep ache. "But I know what it's like to be scared about someone, and there's really nothing worse than that."

"Don't pretend to understand me," said Trixie. But some of the heat had left her voice.

"I wish you would consider it. For Olivia's sake."

"No. I won't." Trixie tightened the brilliant green and blue scarf around her neck. If Cora had worn it, she would have looked like a parakeet. Trixie looked like a wild creature, passionate and full of an electric energy that was spitting sparks at Cora. "And I'll thank you," Trixie went on, "to stay the hell out of my daughter's life. Royal, I'll be at the car."

They watched her stalk away. At least Royal was classy enough not to trot off at her ankles.

"Holy shit, Cora," said Royal, taking a deep breath. "Does that always happen when you two get around each other?"

Cora shrugged, pretending that her insides weren't quaking. "Dunno. We're never around each other."

"You live in the same town."

"We ignore each other."

"Always?"

Cora nodded. "Since high school. If we pass on the sidewalk, she gets out her cell phone or rummages in her purse or something, anything so that she doesn't have to look at me."

"Why?" Royal still looked rapt, as if he were watching a movie.

"Old habits die hard, I guess," said Cora. "I should really get her to get that waiver signed, though. Before Olivia goes riding again this weekend."

"Her daughter really rides that well?" Royal asked.

"She's a natural as my husband Logan was. As Mac is."

"Mac doesn't ride," said Royal.

Cora was so startled she laughed. "Are you kidding? He's the best rider I've ever seen. He's actually better than Logan was, but he decided he liked being under a horse more than on top of one."

Royal pushed back his ball cap. "He told me he got thrown and that he can't ride because of it."

"What?" said Cora. "Yeah, he got thrown. Of course he got thrown. He was a teenage boy, addicted to breaking broncs even then. Both he and Logan got thrown so much they had a word they'd shout as they were going over the pommel. Not a word I'll share with you, either, because it's so dirty it's never come out of my mouth."

Royal said, "So you're telling me Mac didn't have a terrible, life-altering, death-defying moment of clarity when he swore he would never ride again?"

"Nope."

"Wow. I'm gonna bust his chops over this one, for sure."

Maybe she shouldn't have said anything. Maybe Mac had a reason he didn't ride anymore. But Mac had *loved* riding. It was like breathing to the cousins. "Don't say anything to him."

But as she spoke, she got it. She knew what it was – it fit like a thump in her chest. "Oh," she said.

Royal said, "What? What is it?"

"Logan," Cora said. "He doesn't ride because Logan can't." It hurt to think about. It would have been like her giving up spinning when Eliza died. It didn't make sense.

"Well, that would be stupid." Royal scratched his scruffy cheek. "And very Mac."

Royal nodded. "You're right. You know the man, don't you?"

Cora raised a shoulder. "I used to. I thought so, anyway."

Royal gave her a look she couldn't interpret. Then he said, "I'm off to find a high-spirited filly who went round the front, I think. It was nice talking to you, Cora. You have a beautiful piece of land here." With a strange little half-military half-peace-sign salute, he was gone, leaving Cora with the image of Mac in her mind, the time he was thrown so far off a bronc they'd thought for sure he'd broken his back. Instead, they'd found him lying in the weeds, his hat still miraculously clamped to his head, laughing so hard he could barely breathe. She'd been furious with him. Logan, though, had sat down next to him in the foxtails and had laughed just as hard as Mac.

CHAPTER TWENTY-TWO

Pace yourself. Avoid the yarn hangover. Just like you, I've stayed up all night just to see what the yarn does next, but it makes collecting the eggs in the morning a wee bit more difficult. – E.C.

She spent the rest of the afternoon cleaning with Silas, who barely said seven more words to her – he wasn't known for talking. God knew how Whitney and he had managed to have their daughter, but they seemed happy.

As she bathed the day's dirt from her body, Valentine called, inviting her to the house for dinner.

"Just me?"

"Yep, just you, dear heart."

Valentine made her favorite, grilled cheese sandwiches with tater tots on the side. As a child, she'd thought tater tots in various school cafeterias tasted like home.

"There you are, just way you like them, crunchy on the outside, soft inside."

"Where's your sister?"

Valentine pushed two dachshunds that were snuffling at Cora's feet out of the way with one foot and placed a glass of chocolate milk next to her. "She had some board meeting or something. I don't know. Now eat more."

"I brought that fleece. It's on the front porch, in case I forget to tell you," Cora said as she popped another tot into her mouth. She'd loved them as a kid. No matter what school she'd been at, no matter who she'd been sitting near, the crispy potato treat had always tasted the same. Reliable. Predictable.

The fleece she'd brought Valentine was one that had luckily been in the barn after being shorn from Genevieve, the light gray Corriedale, who was Val's favorite of Cora's flock. Valentine was going to prepare it for her – she would wash it in her big top-loader and dry it, and then card and comb it. It would save Cora hours and hours of labor, and she knew as well as Valentine did that her mother-in-law was just being nice to her. But she said she wanted to work with Genevieve's wool, to feel it slipping between her fingers, and Cora allowed the assistance if only for the reason that Cora hadn't *asked* for help, and they both knew it. It wasn't like she had much choice – Valentine was very much like her twin Louisa in her stubbornness, although hers ran to kindness as opposed to Louisa's bitterness.

As if she'd conjured her with the thought, Louisa stepped into the kitchen.

"Meeting done?" asked Valentine lightly.

"Finally. Someday I'll have to stop supporting so many foundations. How can I say no, though? They need me."

Valentine rolled her eyes.

Louisa shuffled her way through the three tiny dogs demanding her attention. "Do we have any wine? Good wine, I mean? Not that stuff you buy at Trader Joe's. We have to talk."

Valentine sighed and got a bottle of white out of the fridge.

Cora said, "Let me." She poured Louisa, and herself, a generous glass. If Louisa was going to talk, she'd need the fortification. "Valentine?"

"No." Valentine shook her head. "Thank you."

"It's about Mac," said Louisa. She took the pansy-covered tea towel that hung from the refrigerator door and brushed off a kitchen chair.

Valentine's voice was tight. "Was it that dirty?"

"You never know."

"You're at home. What on earth do you do when you eat out?"

"They pay people to keep the surfaces clean at restaurants. It's safer to eat out than in most homes. Even ours."

Valentine took a deep breath and leaned against the sink, keeping her back to her sister, but Cora could see her face. She reminded herself that while Louisa drove her crazy, at least she wasn't actually blood-related to her. Poor Valentine.

"What about Mac?" Cora asked.

"I think he's up to something."

Well, for once they agreed. Cora finished washing and drying the silverware and dumped it into the drawer with a clatter that made Louisa wince. Then she sat in the chair opposite Louisa. "What do you mean?"

"He's here. He's home, finally living in Dad's house. He doesn't have a visible job, as far as I can tell, and he told me he's not going to try to start his own practice, nor does he have any interest in buying in with Jim Younger."

"As far as I know, Younger isn't looking for a partner."

"But he could use one, I'm sure." Louisa frowned into her glass. "He has no idea how good Mac is."

Cora decided to share what she knew. It was only fair. "He works privately now. For some rich guy and his thoroughbreds."

"Ooh!" Louisa brightened. "Rich?"

"Drives a Rolls."

Louisa sighed happily.

"So he's not at the track?" asked Valentine. "Imagine that, a Wildwood who left gambling on purpose."

"*My* son has never had a problem with that particular bug," said Louisa.

Oh, crap. Cora wondered if it would be rude to get up and run.

Valentine shut the water off with a ferocious twist. "And what, exactly, does that mean?"

"Nothing." Louisa blinked, her eyes wide.

"You're throwing Logan in my face again. The fact that he had a problem. And you don't realize, do you, how hypocritical –"

"Sister, I'm not saying that at all. I just knew the gambling world was no life for a son of mine."

Valentine cleared her throat and took a deep sip of her wine.

"What?" said Louisa. "Do you have something to say to me?"

"No," said Valentine, keeping her eyes on the far right corner of the kitchen. "Just that any life is a good one."

Her voice dripping with sarcasm, Louisa said, "Oh, right. You're playing the Logan card again."

Cora gasped. The sisters sniped at each other, yes. But not normally like this. It felt as if the air were sucked out of the room, leaving just the sound of Valentine's old clock ticking slowly in time with the dripping faucet. Valentine carefully placed her glass of wine on the kitchen table.

Valentine rarely got mad. Annoyed at her sister occasionally, but Cora had almost never seen her without a cheery expression. She'd smile as she remembered something wonderful about Logan, the corners of her lips turned upward even as tears ran down her cheeks.

But now Valentine took a deep breath. Slowly and very quietly, she said, "The Logan card is the only card I have. You'll excuse me if I play it whenever I want to. My son is dead. My darling boy who loved nothing more than horses, and my sweet almond pie, and this girl – She gestured to Cora. "He's gone. Forever. Your son gets to walk around and smell the night air and look with his eyes up into the heavens and wonder what he did to get lucky, what he did right in some other life that made it so that he lived while Logan died in pain. Mac's alive. Even though he's been gone for years and years, even though he hasn't had the *respect* to care about the family he has left, your Mac is alive. Because of that – and thank God for it – you have no idea what I've gone through."

Louisa opened her mouth and then shut it again. "I'm . . ." Her voice trailed off. Sorry? Was that what she was going to say? It would be an interesting moment if it actually happened. Louisa rubbed at her cheek with three fingers, pushing the skin up as if to test whether it would stay or not. 'I'm sure I have a little bit of an idea. And besides, is it a contest?" Pointing to Cora, Louisa said, "She was his wife. You think she doesn't get to mourn?"

"Don't you drag me into this," said Cora, pushing herself away from the table as far as she could while staying in the chair.

Louisa went on, "I was Logan's only aunt. I knew him from the minute he was born, and I was the second person to hold him, since your idiot man was at the races."

Valentine grimaced. "Your husband with him."

"I never said mine *wasn't* an idiot. We missed them when they died, but nothing, *nothing*, ever got us ready for the loss of Logan."

Valentine nodded her assent.

Louisa's voice was softer. "You know I'd give anything to have him back. You know that, sister. Having Mac back doesn't help with the pain of not having Logan. It might make it worse, actually."

"I'm still so *mad* at Mac," Valentine said.

Her words surprised Cora, but she wasn't sure why. She knew Valentine had been as hurt as she'd been that Mac didn't come to see Logan, that he hadn't been back since his own father's funeral, eight years before. She'd just thought Valentine had been better at getting over it than she had.

"What kind of reason could he have had? He never told us." Valentine eyes looked shadowed. "He just didn't show up. And now your son is back without any real excuse, hale and hearty."

Cora heard what she didn't say, and she knew Louisa did too: *And mine isn't.*

From the other side of the screen door, out in the dark, a shuffle was heard, followed by a crashing sound. Valentine looked at Cora. "Oh!"

As all four small dogs started yapping. Cora had to raise her voice. "It's probably just a possum or a raccoon." It hadn't sounded like either one, actually, but when Valentine and Louisa were together, Cora was left to take care of things.

"Carry the broom," said Louisa. "In case it's a burglar."

"So I can hit the gun out of his hand?" Cora muttered as she took the broom Valentine held out to her.

The screen door swung open silently. "Hello?"

"Who's out there?" Louisa and Valentine stood silhouetted together in the doorway. "What is it, Cora?"

"Shhhh!"

"Should I call 911?" Louisa stage-whispered. "If it's a murderer, we should call them early, not after it's too late."

"Hello?" Cora called. Fog partially obscured the slim sliver of moon, and in the dark yard items loomed black and large. Valentine's old truck looked like something Stephen King would write about – it would probably roar to life at any moment and start chewing yard tools. The old shed looked like somewhere an ogre would live, not a place that merely housed the sisters' gardening shears and trowels.

"Is anyone out here?" She made her voice firm. It was easy, actually; she didn't expect to see anything but a prowling possum. A skunk was her outside guess, and God knew, if she saw white on black she would hightail it back to the house as fast as she could possibly run. One of her goats had been sprayed once, and the barn still sometimes filled with the noxious fumes when the summer sun heated it up.

So when she came around the old Ford and almost ran into the man who stood there, still as stone, arms crossed, hat pulled down obscuring his face, Cora let out a scream that pierced the night air and made the man roar.

CHAPTER TWENTY-THREE

Fear is your body's way of telling you you've cast on too many stitches. –
E.C.

The man's yell frightened her so badly that Cora immediately screamed again, louder, her voice even more piercing the second time.

Mac gave another yell to match. "Goddammit, Cora, what the *hell?* You *scared* me!"

"Who is it? We're calling 911!" yelled Louisa. "Hit him with the broom! The broom!"

"I scared *you?* You're the one lurking out here like a common criminal!" Cora went halfway around the truck so she could see the house. "Don't call! It's just Mac."

"Just Mac," he repeated.

Cora swung back to face him. "What made all that noise?"

"I knocked over the gajillion flower pots at the bottom of their steps."

"If you were on the porch, why didn't you come in?"

He leaned on the truck with a deep sigh, turning his face up to the night sky. An errant moonbeam threw the long, flat planes of his cheekbones into relief, and Cora realized that she was standing too close to him. She took a step back.

"I went to find you first, then I came here. But then I overheard you all talking, and I got the hell off the porch. I can't explain myself to Aunt Val. I mean –"

"Oh, really?" This was suddenly too much for Cora. "Don't you think it's a little late for that?"

"I'm sorry I didn't come when I should have. I wish I could explain why."

"It was good that you apologized to me. But right now you don't say sorry to *me*," Cora said, leaning forward at the waist. She barely controlled herself from shaking her finger like an angry school teacher. "You say you're sorry to *her*. To Valentine. That's all she's needed to hear for years. That's what she's been waiting for, and I didn't know that until tonight, and oh, God, if I'd known, I would have tracked your ass down and made you say it, not because I needed it, but because she looked so damn broken-hearted just now when she brought it up. You don't get to feel sorry for yourself. You get to apologize to her." Her voice broke as she ran out of words and breath at the same time.

Neither of them moved. His eyes were dark, and his chest was rising and falling as if he'd been running. Her breathing matched his.

Was it her anger that made her feel this pull toward him? What put this ridiculous longing in her veins? Why could she do nothing but meet his gaze, battling it back as if it were a challenge that she could meet, could win?

"Jesus, Cora."

And with only those two words as warning, Mac pulled her roughly against his chest, using just one arm, bracing his other against the truck. His mouth came down on hers, and he was kissing her suddenly, and it felt both so right and so far beyond wrong that Cora could do nothing but kiss him back. She kissed him harder than he kissed her, she stroked his tongue with hers, and all the while her brain screamed *Wrong, wrong, wrong!*

But why then couldn't she stop herself? Why was she pulling his head down to her, reveling in the feeling of his fingers jammed through her hair. She sucked for one short sweet second on his lower lip until he gasped and pulled her even closer against him. She could feel him, hard, through his jeans, and the thought of what he would feel like without them made her go hot and wet. She wrapped her leg around his upper thigh and pulled him against her, imagining what he would feel like deep inside her. She was molten, heated and liquid.

Then the guilt hit, landing as heavily as the kiss had. The euca-lyptus above rustled, as if watching. Listening. Anyone could see them out here. Anyone could know.

Cora pulled back. His arm tightened.

She pushed against his chest. "They're right inside. Holy shit, Mac. What did you just do?"

Mac's eyes in the moonlight were languorous now. Unrepentant. "What did *I* just do? You were as much a part of that as I was, sugar. Maybe more."

Cora raked her fingers through her hair pushing down what he had just pulled up. "No. Just – no."

"I wasn't asking for anything. It was a kiss. Nothing more."

He was lying. She'd always been able to tell.

Cora stalked away fast, ignoring the fact that her teeth were chat-tering almost as hard as her hands were shaking. Thank God Louisa and Valentine had gone into the house when they'd heard it was him – if they'd seen that . . .

Cora banged open the screen door and steamed inside and only after she was in the kitchen did she stop to think about what she must look like. She could feel her overheated cheeks blazing. She knew her eyes were as wild as her hair must be. Even her shirt was a few degrees sideways when she looked down at it.

Valentine arched one eyebrow. That was all. Cora wanted to protest, but how could she? Luckily Louisa hadn't seemed to put two and two together yet.

"Where did you leave my son the prowler?" she said, a large bowl in her hands.

"Outside. Where he belongs."

Louisa shook her head. "I don't know what kind of ice cream he wants. We have two, chocolate chip and fudge brownie."

"He wants chocolate chip," said Cora, before biting her lip.

She refused to give Valentine the satisfaction of meeting her eyes, so she got down another bowl for herself. "I want fudge brownie," she said, as if that would make all the difference in the world.

CHAPTER TWENTY-FOUR

*Ask for help. An experienced knitter will have the correct answer; an inex-
perienced one will be so flattered that you came to her that you'll come up
with an even more perfect solution together. – E.C.*

D ammit, he'd put it off too long. It wasn't going to be easy,
asking them. Mac took the bowl of ice cream his mother
handed him with a gratefulness that felt forced. He didn't
want ice cream. He didn't want food, in fact. He didn't want a drink.
What he wanted was another kiss or seventy-three from Cora, but
that was impossible. He had no idea why he'd done it. It was the
worst time, in the worst place. Jesus, practically in front of Logan's
mother, with Logan's *wife*.

If he'd come home to figure out how to forgive himself, he was
shooting himself in the foot. And God help him, he wanted to pull
the trigger again.

"You want more?" Louisa hovered over him, the scooper in her
hand.

"You're dripping ice cream on the floor," said his aunt.

"Hush," said Louisa, but she put the scoop in the sink. "Just tell me if you want anything else, Mac."

He hadn't seen his mother this helpful since . . . he couldn't remember how long. Mac didn't trust it. But maybe it would make this a little easier.

"I have to talk to you. All three of you – that's why I tracked you down tonight. Perfect timing. I mean, with all of you being together like this." He was babbling. Jeez. Mac didn't babble. What was going *on* with him? It didn't help that Cora was looking sideways at him like a racehorse with another coming up fast on its flank. She was ready to hightail it right out of there – he could see it in the skittish look on her face. He took a deep breath.

"So, Royal, the guy who's my boss, wants to buy our land to raise horses on."

Cora stared at him, her eyes wide. "I thought he was just kidding when he said that at the bar."

Mac shook his head. "He's dead serious."

Aunt Valentine laughed. "Why here? There's land up and down the coast."

"None as perfect as here. None with the right drive-time to his other businesses. He can be in Silicon Valley in two hours, and that's important to him. He doesn't want to be inland in the valley. He thinks horses run better in the damp air, and he might be right."

"*Our* land?" said Louisa. "As in yours and mine, Mac?"

Mac shook his head and twisted his mouth. This was the hard part. "All of our land. Yours, Mom. Aunt Valentine, yours. Mine. And yours, Cora. Royal always has big dreams, and he sticks to them. He wants a large parcel of land, here, and that's not available anywhere on the coast right now. But together, our land would be the size he's looking for."

Again Cora didn't hesitate. "The answer is no."

He rubbed at his temple. "That's your knee-jerk automatic answer. And by no means does he expect you to make a decision that's uninformed. There's plenty of time –"

"No," Cora interrupted him. "Never in a million years."

"He'll pay good money."

"How good?" asked Louisa, scooting forward in her chair.

"As good as you want it to be. Over asking price, for sure, for anything on the coast. There's no other location that's this ideal that would be up for sale – I've been scouting it for the last eleven months."

"You've been here and didn't tell us?" Cora's voice was ice.

Shit. Mac ran his finger along the edge of the table that his aunt had always had sitting here, in this very spot, for as long as he could remember. "Only once."

"Mac." Aunt Valentine said his name softly. Sadly.

"I was just checking land records, and I had to go to the local office to pull them in hard copy. Did you know that there isn't another parcel of land that isn't BLM or subdivided into minuscule parcels for twenty miles? Our family, as a block, has the perfect coastal location."

"Where did you stay?" asked his mother.

"What? Oh, I just came down for the day. I didn't even stay a night. That's why . . . That's why I didn't call you." The actual truth was that he'd been in a hurry. Royal had needed him back with the information and had been grateful to him for doing the scouting, but he'd still had his own job to do. One horse had gone lame just that day and while he trusted his vet tech Gomez to do the right thing, he still hadn't been there, at the stables. It had seemed like a good idea, then, that fast zoom down the coast followed by a faster one going north again.

Okay, maybe it hadn't felt like the *right* thing. But it had felt like what he had to do. Dammit, he shouldn't have to justify his actions.

"I don't understand. You came here, but . . . And anyway, our land isn't even for sale." Aunt Valentine shook out the drying towel she was twisting again. Twist, *shake*. Twist, *shake*.

"He wants it to be," said Louisa. "That's obvious."

"Exactly, Mom. We need to discuss selling."

"Maybe you all do." Cora hurriedly stood and took her bowl to the sink. She washed it, using the sponge like a weapon. While her back was still turned, she said, "But I don't have to talk about a damn thing. I'm not selling."

This was what Mac had been worried about. They were jumping to conclusions too fast. "It's not like I'm asking you to abandon hearth and home. With the money Royal's willing to pay, you could hire movers to dig up and move your whole houses and put them back on your new land. Cora, you could still live in the farm house. Aunt Valentine, you don't even live in your house anymore. I've never lived in Granddad's house. Two of the four houses are empty now, and we could just move the other two. You could still sit right here in this exact kitchen, in the same positions, same chairs. Just a different view out the windows.'

Cora turned, pressing her back into the edge of the sink. Behind the anger in her eyes, Mac could see something else, something darker.

He hurried to continue the pitch he'd spent so much time worrying about. "You'd still have your homes. And you'd have land, as well as the money to maintain it. We could even make sure we buy land together, like it is now. Nothing would change but your GPS location and your bank account balance."

Aunt Valentine gave a sharp, humorless laugh. "You say that as if our land doesn't have history. As if we don't love our view. As if the word *home*, itself, can mean whatever you want it to mean. Daddy's buried on this land. My *son* is buried next to him. You'd ask us to leave that?"

"What kind of money?" asked his mother, more quietly.

Aunt Valentine twisted the towel again. "Why do you care, Louisa? It's not like you need the money. If anything, Cora and I would be the ones interested, and we're not."

Louisa clucked her tongue against her teeth, a sound Mac knew that his aunt hated. "At some point in your life, you're going to have stop being foolish about money, sister."

"You have nothing to say to me about my finances. I dug my way out of the hole Skully left me in when he died, and I'm proud of that. And with the pie business, Cora has helped me more than you ever have."

"But *I'm* family," retorted Louisa. "I don't have to –"

"Louisa!" Valentine said.

"I mean, of *course* Cora's family, but I just meant I'm your twin," said Louisa.

But she had meant more. Mac knew it, and what was worse, Cora knew it. She'd wiped the bowl dry and had picked up her keys off the table and put them in her front pocket. He'd forgotten that Cora had always traveled without a purse – just what she could put in her jeans or overalls pockets.

"Well, I guess that's my cue. Thanks for dinner, Valentine." Cora kissed her on the cheek.

Louisa looked miserable, and Mac didn't mind seeing it. His mother could stand to think about someone else every once in a while.

"You're a pain in the ass, Louisa, you know that?" Aunt Valentine snapped the towel again. "Cora, on the other hand, is a delight. Always cheerful, always ready to lend me a hand. And she never, *never*, asks for anything in return."

Cora raised her hands. "Stop this. I hate it."

"No, let her," said Louisa. "Let her get it all off her chest. Let's hear it all, hear how you love Cora more than your own twin."

Aunt Valentine stuttered in what sounded like frustration and failed to complete a full word.

Cora now had tears in her eyes. "Please, both of you, stop."

"I don't love her more, you idiot," Valentine was finally able to say. "But I love her differently. She's easier to love than you are. She's like a puppy dog that's never had a home. Whereas you're a cactus, scaring everyone. And if anyone gets too close, you stab them. That's not easy to love."

Louisa stood. "I won't take this from my own sister."

"If not me, then who?"

Mac didn't know what to do. He should step in, but how? And all he could see was Cora. Couldn't they see what they were doing to her? Her hands were shaking. "Cora," he started.

"No. I'm not talking to you." Cora turned to Valentine. "A puppy dog? Is that how you've always seen me? As a stray? Someone you had to take care of, like all the cats and dogs you take in? Like Lottie there?" She pointed to the dachshund trembling at Valentine's feet. "That makes sense. Now I get it."

Aunt Valentine shook her head. "Don't *you* start on me, Cora. You know how much I love you, and you know why."

"Yeah." Cora's voice trembled like her hands. "I married your son. I took care of your biggest pet."

"That's not the reason. We took *you* in, just like he did."

Cora's eyes widened. She gave a sharp inhalation, and her eyes swam again.

Mac was desperate to tuck her against his side, to lift his thumb and push those tears away . . . It was dangerous to look at her – he didn't know how long he could remain still. In an attempt to lighten the air, he said, "You *do* love a stray, though, Aunt Valentine."

Then Cora looked at him and he wished he could take back every word he'd said in his life, just to get rid of those last few. The pain in her eyes seared him. *No, it was a joke, just a joke.*

She turned and pushed her way out the screen door. In the quietness of the kitchen, they could hear her cowboy boots running, her heels hitting the gravel, and then silence as she turned to cut across the pasture.

No, no, no.

Mac took a breath to regroup. How did it get this hard? He sat with a heavy thump in a chair that creaked under him, ignoring the squawk of the cat he displaced. "Fantastic job, you two. Really impressed."

Aunt Val scowled at him. "I'm sorry. Why did this all come up again? Oh, right, because you want to evict us off our land. Our property. Your grandfather's land."

"Don't be so dramatic. It's not an eviction, merely an offer. All I'm saying is that we should think about it."

Valentine thumped the limp dishtowel into the washing machine at the end of the room. "You've already thought about it, and you want us to think the same way you do. And I'm sorry, Mac, but I don't. And I can't. Maybe your mother will sell to you. Maybe you can use your two properties. Louisa, I know you don't need the money, but I'm sure you'd be thrilled to sock it away."

"Oh," said Louisa, brightening. "Could we sell it in pieces?"

"With Cora's land smack in the middle? No, of course it wouldn't work." Mac stared at his hands, reddened by barn work. Give him that any day. A case of sand crack. A mare with hoof fracture. Not this . . . *emotion*.

Aunt Valentine shrugged. "Then I guess your boss is out of luck." In a voice he'd never heard from her, she continued, "And good job making Cora cry, by the way. I haven't seen her cry since Logan died. Not that you'd know that, Mac."

The air was ice, and Mac's heart froze. He felt more alone sitting in the kitchen with his mother and aunt than any moment he'd ever spent in his single bachelor's condo. The words *I'm sorry* burned inside his mouth. But instead he said, "What? You're the ones who chased her off."

"No," said his mother, shaking her head.

Aunt Valentine made the same motion at the same time.

Then, with their identical eyes trained on him in exactly the same shade of disappointment and with one voice, the twins said, "That was your fault."

Shit.

CHAPTER TWENTY-FIVE

Worrying is like a bad snarl in the ball – sometimes there is nothing to do but to cut it out. – E.C.

This. This right here, was why he hadn't come home after Logan's death. It was too much. Too hard. A goddamn animal told you with his body, with his eyes, what he needed, and you did it, and everything was all right. If you took a risk on an animal, it paid you back with love. Horses, dogs, cats, they were all the same.

People, humans, were too complex. The moon came out as he walked the pathway home. The way was still clear, the weeds beaten down and back. Maybe it was how Cora got to Valentine's, even though you couldn't see the ocean from here – the coast road had a better view, but this one was shorter. He'd run this path a hundred, a million times, with Logan on nights exactly like this one, the sharp coldness of the crisp fall night a reminder of what the coming winter would bring.

As he entered his kitchen, he tried to stop worrying about Cora.

She would be fine. What he'd said about Val taking in strays, she would know that was utter bullshit, right? Just him talking out his ass.

God, his grandfather's old house was so *quiet*. Inside, with the doors and windows closed, he couldn't hear anything but the wooden walls settling around him. He stood in the kitchen for less than a minute, and then barreled back out onto the porch, standing in the one corner where he could just make out the light from Cora's porch.

Was she crying inside? Was she furious? How was it possible that he didn't know the answer to this? Mac kicked the bottom of the porch rail and only succeeded in bruising his toe. Damn old house was sturdier than it looked.

He should have brought that mutt Clementine home with him. Screw Cora. She probably wouldn't know how to take care of a dog anyway. She'd give the animal a job in the barn or something, catching rats or mice, and then probably blame Clementine when she didn't fulfill Cora's deepest desire.

Mac took one step off the porch in her direction. Then he took another, grateful that his jean jacket was lined. The smell of wood smoke mingled with the scent of wet sand as he walked through the easement that adjoined his property to Cora's. For the first time he wondered who took care of this part. For years he'd paid Jack Apfel, a local landscaper, to fireproof his land, keeping the brush short and away from the pool house. But the rest of it, the zones between the properties . . . hadn't crossed his mind. Had Cora been taking care of it all by herself? It was a thin strip only ten feet deep, but it was long, maybe a quarter mile out to the shore road. Mac had to find out if he owed her money for maintenance on it.

And he should probably do it tonight. No time like the present.

It was the excuse he'd been looking for, the one that kept him walking, faster now. Mac knew that no matter what, he'd have found an excuse tonight to go to her.

He had no plan. He expected less than nothing. In fact, he told himself, when he got there, she'd probably slam the door in his face. He wouldn't blame her for being upset. But maybe, just maybe, he could help her think the sale through, right? So, really, this was the best business move, too.

Cora answered the door in a silky looking short red robe designed to kill a man. "Seriously?" she said.

The sight of the robe caused every word he'd thought of on the brief walk over to flee from his mind. As a study in contrast, though, she wore flannel pajamas underneath that were decorated with – were those ducks on skateboards? Yes.

Sexy and utilitarian.

He could look at her all night.

She was staring at him, and Mac realized that she'd said something else while he'd been so busy watching the shape her mouth took, her soft, pliant lips. He hadn't heard one damn word.

"I'm sorry?" he asked.

She formed her words slowly and carefully, as if he were a child. "I said, what . . . are . . . you . . . doing . . . here?"

He racked his brain. There had been something, God, what was it? Then he cursed himself six ways to Sunday for noticing the way her robe curved and folded over her breast.

"Easement!"

"Excuse me?" She pulled the robe tighter at her neck. "Easy what?"

"No, no. Easement."

She stood taller as if she could gain actual height from just straightening her spine. "I have no freaking clue what you're talking about. Did you start drinking in the last twenty minutes? Or are you having a stroke?"

If he was, she didn't look inclined to call him an ambulance. There was no forgiveness in her eyes. He shook his head. "No, I was walking here and I saw the easement. I know someone's had to pay to keep that maintained, and it hasn't been me. I want to know how much I owe you."

"Why were you walking here?"

Bam. Busted. Rapidfire, he thought of several excuses, all of them weak. *Walked home the wrong way, lost my way in the non-existent fog, possible aneurism.*

But he chose honesty instead. "I have no idea, other than the fact that I hated the way we left it at their house. I wanted to see if you were okay."

Cora's hand fluttered again to the neck of her robe. "Fine."

"Really?"

"Mac, I said I'm fine."

"Is it okay if I choose not to believe you?"

She frowned. "What you want to believe is none of my business. And about the easement, I do it myself. So you don't owe me anything."

Mac patted his back pocket as if he were carrying cash or a checkbook, which he wasn't. "I owe you for your time, at least." Then he realized what she'd just said. *"Yourself?* That's a huge job."

Sighing, she stepped out onto the porch and neatly sidled around him. She sat on the top step. "I don't know if you've noticed, but this is all a big job."

Mac chose to take the way she swept her hand out, encompassing her land, as an invitation to sit one step below her. That wasn't what it was, he knew, but she didn't protest.

"You've done all this by yourself."

"For a long time." She gazed out over the front pasture. "Look out there."

Across the road, past the dune that gleamed pale gold in the moonlight, the water glinted. "It's getting choppy," he said. "Windy weather coming in."

"Can you imagine?"

"Wind?" Was it terrible that he wanted her to keep talking? He didn't care about what – Mac just wanted to watch her mouth all night.

"No." But her voice wasn't as angry as it had been at Valentine's. "Not being able to see this. To look out the windows, or sit right here, and hear the waves breaking. To feel that salt in the air, to know the humidity is rising, and the pressure is dropping, to *feel* that against your skin. To be able to walk across the street and swim."

"To swim? Are you insane? It's freezing out there."

"I don't go in for long."

"And it's dangerous." A terrible image of her being swept out by a rogue current, unable – and Jesus, probably unwilling – to call for help, being dashed against rocks or even worse, taken away and never, ever found. "Way too dangerous. You can't do that."

"I don't go far. I just dip." She rubbed her arms, and he saw goosebumps.

"I don't like it. Are you cold?"

"No." Her smile was slow as honey. "I'm thinking about how damn cold it is in that water. You're right about that."

She turned to face him, shifting her body just a few inches but now he could feel the warmth of her legs near his. "I couldn't leave this, Mac. You have to understand that."

He didn't. It was good land with historical and familial attachment. Yeah. So? Other land elsewhere would do just as nicely, wouldn't it? Maybe not with *this* exact view, which was stunning, he had to give it that.

But it wasn't as stunning as the view he had right now, looking at her.

Christ. He felt eighteen again, in love with someone he could never have. One of the worst times in his life, actually. This wasn't good.

"I get what you're saying." He didn't. "I'm just asking you to think about it."

Cora's eyes fell to his lips.

Then she licked her own.

Holy crap. The fact that she could still do this to him, with a single look, frustrated the hell out of him. And it completely, utterly turned him on.

He couldn't.

He shouldn't.

But he did. He leaned forward, drawn to her like a stallion to a mare in season.

Cora swayed, too, her eyes dipping again to his mouth. The heat, the indescribable tension that hung in the breath's space separating them, electrified Mac. He had to kiss her. He *had* to.

Then Cora punched the hell out of his upper arm.

CHAPTER TWENTY-SIX

In meditation, I like to use 'just one more row' as my mantra. Of course,
that's why I knit more than I meditate. – E.C.

The thump was so hard Cora's knuckles hurt immediately. "Ow!" she said. "Damn!"

Mac jumped to his feet, his left hand cradling his right bicep. "*You're* the one saying ow? You punched me!"

"I know," she said, shaking out her fingers. If this put a cramp in her spinning, she'd probably want to punch him again.

"I don't get it," he said, and he sounded more confused than angry. "It would never be okay for a man to hit a woman. Ever. Why is it okay for you to hit me?"

Sudden guilt flooded her. "You're right."

He frowned. "I am?"

"You're completely right. I'm sorry I punched you. I should have pushed you off the porch instead."

"Or you could have done something completely non-violent. Ever hear of using your words? What the hell?"

Cora didn't understand what was happening inside her. She wanted to touch him, and she wanted to push him as far away as she possibly could. "Oh, non-violent? Like a kiss? Is *that* what you expected?"

He crossed his arms then, wincing as he moved his shoulder. "I didn't know what to expect. I never have any idea what to do you with you, Cora Sylvan."

Maybe that was the whole problem, from top to bottom. Maybe Mac had just summed it up. They didn't know what to do with each other. They never had, not from the very first moment they'd seen each other in high school.

She leaned her back against the porch rail and rubbed her knuckles harder. "Do you remember when I met you?"

Even though Mac still frowned, the corner of his mouth twitched. "In the quad with Billy Thunker?" His voice was a low grumble.

"No, you told me that's when you saw me first. No, when *we* met. Officially."

He gave a half-smile. "In Mrs. Gupstern's class. I was throwing spitballs."

"Because even though you were sixteen, you were acting like you were twelve."

"I think that's the job of a teenage boy."

"And one of the spitwads landed in my ear."

He shuffled the dirt at his feet with the toe of his boot. "I felt bad about it."

"You did. You bought me a baked potato at the cafeteria." It had been awful, a soggy mess, loaded with sour cream and ranch dressing and blue cheese. If there was a topping to be had, he'd asked to have it put on for her.

"Which you immediately threw in the trash. Without taking a bite."

"I thought you were teasing me. Like there was a potato joke at the school that I didn't know about." She hadn't known anything at that school yet, hadn't gotten the lay of the land. Every school – and there had been so many – had its own rules and in-jokes, and usually, when she was new, they were all played on her. She'd been a good sport for years, but she'd lost her patience with being laughed at somewhere during the two previous moves, and she'd thought whatever Mac had been pulling on her was probably mean, if not plain cruel.

"It was just a potato. A peace offering."

Cora made a face. "It was still pretty disgusting looking."

"Logan didn't think so," said Mac. "That's the way he always ate his."

Cora pressed her lips together. Would invoking Logan's name change the mood? Should it?

Mac went on as if nothing had changed. "Remember those clouds of seagulls that hung over the quad like a dirty cloud?"

"We held books over our heads as we went between classes. A week without bird poop was like a miracle."

"I bet he never told you about the bird shit in his potato."

She laughed in surprise. "No."

"It must have landed when he wasn't looking, and it blended into all that other ranch and sour cream and he didn't notice until it was too late."

"Oh, God. That's *awful*." She laughed harder. She could just imagine Logan's face. He'd always liked everything precisely so. He'd ironed his Wranglers before he raced.

You're barrel racing. You think anyone's going to see wrinkles in your jeans?

It's the principle. It's my job to look good, baby.

And he had. Logan had always looked great. He was the quintessential cowboy, short and broad-chested with a bowlegged walk, as if he were always on the back of a horse. He was one of the guys in school who had actually needed to shave – it wasn't just an affectation. When he took his cowboy hat off, his head had always looked vulnerable. Delicate, almost. It was one of her favorite parts of him, that softness right where the brim of his hat usually sat. She'd always found it horribly, terribly ironic that it had been a brain tumor that had killed him. He'd protected that noggin of his so carefully, and in the end it had betrayed him.

Mac cleared his throat. "I'll never forget the day he asked you out."

"You? It was the first time anyone had ever expressed any interest in me in my whole life. I mean, the three of us were friends, but going to a dance symbolized being more than friends."

He looked affronted. "I had."

"What?" Cora was confused.

"With a potato."

"What?"

"Okay, so you didn't understand how boys showed interest."

"Ah. The old fool-proof potato trick," she said, and she got the effect she wanted – Mac laughed. Cora reveled in the sound of it, warm and round.

And he'd just said he was interested. Back then, she reminded herself. It was the closest to a confession she'd ever gotten out of him.

"Yeah. Whatever. Logan asked you to the Spring Fling dance."

Cora gazed at the sliver of moon that seemed to hover over Mac's left shoulder. "And I said no. I wanted us to all stay friends. The way we were. People already thought I was after him . . ." Trixie had thought that because Cora had told her so. Cora still regretted that untruth even now.

"You never could do things the normal way."

"No, never."

"What made you change your mind?" he asked, remaining very still.

Cora looked at Mac standing in the moonlight. He was the one in front of her. Logan was in the ground by his grandfather, up on the ridge. She could lie, she could say she'd changed her mind because she'd fallen for Logan. She could make up any kind of lie she wanted – he'd never know the difference.

But Cora had always been a bad liar.

"I didn't think you'd go with me," she said.

Mac blinked. "But . . ."

She waited for it to sink in.

He stopped rubbing his shoulder, his hand falling to his side. "But that means . . ."

Cora knew that if she stood, she would be making one of the biggest choices of her life. Closing her eyes briefly, she told herself to go slowly. To think this through.

But she'd been thinking about being with Mac for fifteen years. She'd thought about it on the worst nights, the darkest ones, the nights she knew she shouldn't *ever* think about him. She'd thought about what his touch would be like, how his lips would taste. She'd thought about losing herself with him.

Mac's eyes darkened, and his broad chest rose with a deep breath.

Cora made the choice.

She stood. She took one step toward him. Then another. His arms stayed at his sides, but she saw his fingers stretch out.

The next step toward him, and then she was in his arms, his mouth against hers, and yes, *yes*, she fit against him like she was made to be there. Like she'd always been next to him.

"Cora," Mac said. "Oh, *Corazón*."

Then it was impossible for either of them to speak.

His lips were hot and his tongue was fire stroking hers, and the flames inside her built, burning down the roadblocks she'd put in place so long ago. Her fingers knotted in his hair and her breasts pushed against his chest in something that was like pain, but better.

She wanted Mac Wildwood in her bed. God help her, but it was all she wanted in the world.

CHAPTER TWENTY-SEVEN

You are the best knitter in the world. This I know with all my heart. – E.C.

Mac knew he had to stop the kiss. But Jesus, the woman lit a bonfire inside him that blazed like the ones he used to start on the beach with gasoline. The heat roared through him, and he couldn't stop his hand from skirting the side of her breast as it skimmed down to her waist. For a glorious second, with her mouth against his, as she bit his lower lip lightly, he had a completely X-rated image of her beneath him, her perfect, round, womanly curves naked under him as he took her.

Logan's wife, Logan's wife.

Cora raked her fingernails against the short hair at the back of his neck, and chills danced down his spine.

She'd just said . . .what was it that she'd said? Something that implied she'd been – interested? In him, so long ago?

As she moved to put her arms around his waist, to pull herself more tightly against him, she tilted her hips into his, and he knew she could feel exactly what she was doing to him. God, he was hard.

He wanted her. Completely. Mac wanted all of her.

This had to be a dream. Didn't it?

Dragging his lips from hers, he straightened his back. "I should," he started. "We have to –"

"Come inside," she said.

She was serious.

"Are you sure?" He had to ask it.

"Yes."

"Totally sure?" Was there anything she could say that would convince him that she hadn't just lost her mind temporarily? That she wouldn't haul off and slug him another time?

Instead of answering, Cora kissed him again. And it was all there in her kiss, everything he needed to hear, every word he didn't know he'd been wishing for. For perhaps his whole life, he'd been waiting for this moment.

He took her hand, noticing how small it felt in his, how soft her skin was even though he knew how hard she worked. She led him inside. At one time, when Valentine and Logan lived here before Val had moved to her own house, he'd known this place almost as well as he'd known his own. Mac knew that Logan and Cora's marriage bed had been in the room Logan had as a boy, something that had delighted Logan as an adult.

Cora led him up the stairs, through the dark, and into the bedroom with the ocean view. Not Logan's old room.

"You moved," Mac said lightly, but his heart soared.

"It's not even the same bed," she said with a calm smile, but her voice shook.

Good. This was affecting her as much as it was him. It shamed him, somehow, how glad he was about that, but he couldn't help it. Bedding his dead cousin's wife was one thing. Doing it in the man's bed, where they'd lain together for years, where he'd probably *died* for Christ's sake, would have been too much.

"Cora." He didn't ask the question, but he knew she read it in his eyes.

She led him to the bed and answered, again, with a kiss. She leaned in to him so that he sat on the edge. Then she straddled him until she was sitting on his lap, her legs hanging over his. Biting her bottom lip softly, she looked at him as if examining his face for the first time. She was thinking something, and she needed time to do it. Even though he strained against her, feeling himself throb with heat, he held himself perfectly still and waited.

Finally she said, "I want you. I nee–" She cut herself off halfway through the word, as if it weren't something she'd meant to say out loud.

"Cora. It's okay. You've gotten used to not needing." He paused, taking her measure. "Is that right?"

Cora shrugged. "I try not to. I try really hard not to." She pulled up on his belt loops and tilted her hips against him. Mac gasped but remained motionless.

"It's okay to need," he repeated.

Cora didn't say anything, just searched his face again. Was she looking for familial resemblance? Mac had never thought he looked much like Logan, but others had mentioned in passing that they shared something in the eyes. Was it this that she was fascinated by? He wanted to ask, but she was so skittish he didn't want to risk spooking her.

"It's okay to ask. To want."

She frowned, and instead of saying anything in response, she bent forward and kissed him again. The heat of it went nuclear, instantly. The way she moved her mouth in rhythm with the rocking of her hips could make him come, just like that, the layers of jeans and flannel still between them, like he was a teenager who didn't know any better. He rode his hands up the robe, over her pajama top, traced the outline of her breast and then over the fabric, thumbed her nipples. She caught a cry in her throat.

He wanted more, more of that from her, more of that noise, and he wanted it now. Mac slipped his fingers under her pajamas until he could hold her breasts, feel the weight of them, the skin that was so soft he could barely feel it. Her nipples tightened into small peaks under his thumbs, and it just made him harder.

Cora slipped off her robe and unbuttoned her pajama top, dropping it onto the floor behind her. Then she took his shirt off, and it followed hers to the hardwood at their feet.

Mac swallowed. He hoped Cora wouldn't mind, but he needed a second to look. Nothing he could have imagined – and he'd imagined her a hell of lot of times – could have prepared him for the sight of her. Her breasts were perfect, full and heavy, tilted up at their tips, her nipples the same flushed pink as her lips and her cheeks.

She started to wriggle against him to go for his belt. He said, "Wait."

"Oh," said Cora. "What's wrong?"

He stifled a moan as she rocked into him again. "Nothing. I just want to look at you. Wait." He looked at each breast, touching the sides as lightly as he could, then tested her nipples with a flick of his fingertip. They rewarded his inspection by tightening even more, and Cora gasped and closed her eyes.

Mac leaned forward, trailing kisses from underneath her jawline to her clavicle, then to the top of her breasts. While one hand teased her right nipple, pinching and twisting lightly, he sucked her left one into his mouth. He was promptly rewarded for his action. Cora ground her hips so hard into his that he saw lights behind his eyes and had to focus again on not losing control. *Slow, take it slow.* He kept his tongue moving, circling the tight skin, sucking her in and then biting gently until her breathing told her she couldn't take much more of this game, either.

Cora lowered her head so that her mouth was next to his ear. "Please," she whispered. "I want you."

Her nipple slipped from his mouth and he licked it, flicking it with his tongue for good measure. "How?" Mac's hand moved to cup her ass, drawing her hard against him. "How do you want me?"

She dipped again, and her lips were warm heat on his earlobe. "In me, Mac. I want you inside me."

A low rumble caught in his throat, Mac stood, Cora's leg's still wrapped around him. "Down, woman! If we don't get these jeans off of us . . ." He ran out of breath and out of thought, as Cora sucked on a sensitive part of his neck. She laughed as her legs released, grabbing at his waist as she stood.

In what felt like seconds, he'd shucked his jeans, and she'd wriggled out of her PJ bottoms. Panties hit the floor, followed by his boxers. They stood naked, a foot apart.

A shadow crossed Cora's expression. "Oh, God. I shouldn't want . . ." she started, and then she folded her arms over her breasts, over those beautiful breasts that he couldn't get enough of.

Mac sat on the bed again, and grabbed her hand, pulling her with him. In one easy motion, he rolled her to her back, and he pressed his length against her. For a moment, none of this need mattered. Only Cora. Only she mattered.

"It's okay to want, Cora."

Her eyes were closed and she shook her head.

"You should want. You should ask. It's okay to ask." He pressed a kiss to a soft, short red lock at her temple.

"You get to ask me what you want. You get to ask me for help or for space, or to be touched, for me to stay, or for me to go. And if you want something, you're allowed to take it." Mac took a measured breath. These words were important. "If you ask me for something, anything, I just want to give it to you."

She opened one eye and looked at him suspiciously.

"I'm not just talking about sex. If you ask me for a jump-start, I'll be there with cables. If you ask me for money, I'll give you my PIN code. We're friends."

Cora nodded, slowly.

"We've been friends since we were kids. You ask friends for help. You can ask me for anything. Anything, Cora."

Both eyes slowly opened, and they were a dark, iridescent blue, a color he'd never seen before.

"I want you to fuck me," she said.

CHAPTER TWENTY-EIGHT

Joy is handspun knitted to gauge. – E.C.

She thought the words might not fit in her mouth, but it turned out that they fit just fine. Mac moved so fast she barely had time to notice that he was gone before he was back.

Cora laughed, looking at the blue packet. "Was that really in your wallet?"

"What? Isn't that where the cool kids keep them?"

"I don't know. Seems awfully prepared."

"You'll remember I was an Eagle Scout." Mac took her hand and assisted her in helping him. Jesus, he was big. Cora had been with two men after Logan died, one a very brief affair to try to get back into the swing of things, and one had been more serious, lasting a few months, but none of the men she'd ever been with compared to Mac's girth. Or, God help her, length. With Mac flat on his back, Cora finished the job of assisting in unrolling the condom, pushed his hand aside and said, "Are you *kidding* me with this?"

His laugh was a dark rumble above her. "Is that okay for you?"

"Honestly?" She ran her fingers down the length of his cock, feeling him jerk in response. "I'm a little intimidated."

"We'll just have to take our time, then."

Cora, though, had other plans. "We could," she said, putting one leg over the breadth of his thighs. She placed her hands on his chest and reveled in the feeling of the muscles that roped from there down to his hips, over his flat stomach. This was a man who used his body to move horses around all day. He was so fit that it made her conscious, for one second, about her curves. Then she looked at his face and saw how he was still transfixed by her breasts, now hanging over him.

"I don't want to take our time," she said. Saying the words out loud made her even wetter than she already was.

"We can go slowly. Just ask me for what you want, *Corazón*." His voice was strained, as if he were standing on the very brink of losing control, and the fact that she was the one who had brought him to this was a heady rush.

"I don't want to ask," she said. She slid up, feeling his length with her body, then opened her legs and drove herself down onto him in one slick thrust.

It was so much pleasure mixed with a too-full feeling of pain that Cora closed her eyes to capture it all – she needed to feel it all at once. Mac inside her was like a sound, a thunderclap she felt instead of heard. It was similar to the time she'd fallen out of a tree onto her back – all her breath was gone, but she wasn't scared. She knew it would come back. For now, though, she held it, and rode up him, slowly this time, until she was at the end of him. And then she drove back down again.

"Velvet," he murmured, his eyes fixed on hers.

"Mmm?" She lifted her body and pushed back onto him again. She was getting the hang of this. Her breath came better now. Less pain and more and more pleasure was making her rock steadily as she moved. He followed her, his hands firmly attached to her hips.

"You're hot, wet velvet. The softest, hottest fucking thing I've ever felt. Don't stop, Cora. *Please* don't stop."

Fire filled her then, a heat that lit from her hair to her toenails. Nothing could cool it, nothing but continuing this motion. After a length of time Cora couldn't begin to measure, Mac's hands lifted from her waist and slid to her shoulders. He drew her down to him so that he could kiss her, and she met him, their mouths a tangle of heated passion that matched their joined thrusting. Losing track of where her body ended and where his began, Cora felt her climax build. She rode it – she rode *him*, and the whole time she knew that she was safe. No matter what, it was Mac that was with her in this, with her in her bed, with her in her home – her *home* – that she hadn't shared with anyone for so long.

Then he clutched her and let out a low roar, and she rode with him over the edge, keeping pace, keeping time, as they tumbled over the cliff they'd raced up, falling into a sweet, sticky heap at the bottom.

It was long minutes before Cora's heart stilled enough to draw a full, complete breath. As she lay on top of him, her fingers laced loosely with his, she felt him breathing the same way, deeply, into his chest. She rose and fell with him in subtle suggestion of how she'd moved with him moments before.

Home. Home, home, home. It was the refrain her heart sang, a ridiculous song, one she never would have guessed she knew the tune to. With Mac, she was home. With Mac, in his arms, she was where she'd always been supposed to be. When Logan had lived here, it was first his home, then theirs. After he died, Cora spent years making it completely hers.

But Jesus, it felt like she'd been making it for *them*, for Mac and herself. As if this was exactly what she'd been waiting for all this time.

"God," he finally said. "I didn't see that coming."

"Yes, you did."

Mac pushed her gently off him, rolling to his side. In the dimness of her room, his eyes glinted. "You're telling me you knew I'd come over here."

If Cora had been asked, even two hours ago, if she'd known it, she would have denied it to her very last breath. But now it seemed as if it had been inevitable, and she'd just never taken the time to notice it, like she'd never taken the time to wonder if the waves would keep rolling to shore. She just knew.

"Not like that," Cora said. Oh, God, what if he thought she'd been planning it? "I didn't ever consciously know it. Or even hope it."

His eyes fell to the pillow she'd propped herself up on.

"You hoped it," she said.

Mac nodded, once.

He was braver than she was. Cora couldn't admit, even to herself that she'd hoped it. "You don't think we should . . . feel guilty?"

With a sigh, he sank back again so that he was looking up at the ceiling. "You kidding me? I keep thinking he's going to walk in here. And if he did, I still wouldn't want to move. I'd want to stay right here." Without looking at her, he reached a strong hand out and rested it on the curve of her hip. "While he went to get his gun."

"Oh, come on."

Mac raised his eyebrows. "You don't think so?"

"I don't think he'd want to kill you."

"Maybe not. But he'd want to wound me. Deeply, with much loss of blood. That much I can say for sure."

Cora smiled – she couldn't help it. "Graze you with the bullet."

"In a place where the sun don't shine, probably."

"Logan was never jealous," Cora said. It struck her, lying there with Mac, that maybe that had been an odd thing. Most people were at least a little jealous, weren't they? But Logan had never acted as if he felt threatened by anyone, not once.

Mac's voice was tender. "Logan was a cocky sonofabitch."

He had been. The cockiest person Cora had ever met. From the moment she'd told him she was pregnant with their child, the one they'd created that single night they'd 'helped' each other lose their virginity, he'd made up his mind that they'd be together, and it never crossed his mind that he needed to ask her, just like it never crossed his mind that wearing spurs during all waking hours wasn't the best idea since sliced peaches.

Cora should have minded. But she felt chosen somehow, even though he'd never actually said the words out loud. *I choose you.*

The slight line of tension that had crept onto Mac's face relaxed. "Remember the way he'd puff up right before he went into the ring to race barrels? He looked like a little rooster, the way he'd stick his chest out."

Cora followed his line of sight to the ceiling which she'd stared at for years, always, until now, alone. The crack that ran from the fan to the edge seemed wider now. One morning, would it just fall on her while she slept? Could it kill her? She didn't have anything in her book about *What If A Ceiling Fan Falls* but she would by tomorrow. That was what the internet was made for.

Mac went on, "And the way he always winked."

Cora had loved Logan's slow dropped eyelid, the assuredness of it. "Yeah."

"I hated that wink. All the girls fell for it."

"Including me," said Cora.

"Yep." Mac rolled to his side again to face her. "I'm sorry. I didn't mean to go right there. To him."

"Most of the time I'm fine about it, but sometimes I miss him so much it feels like a toothache that'll never get fixed," she said. "Sometimes it makes me feel like I'm five again. That was a bad year . . ."

Her voice trailed off.

Mac didn't say anything, but she could feel him listening to her as if every word mattered.

And it did matter. This mattered, deeply. She knew it did, and it made her feel like she was staring out the door of an airplane, the parachute attached to her back but she wasn't confident she knew where the ripcord was located.

She jumped anyway. "When I was five, I had a real family."

CHAPTER TWENTY-NINE

Fixing knitting is like mending a broken heart. It takes time, and belief,
and love, and in the end, the fix will be lost in the beauty of the whole. – E.C.

Mac's gaze was open as if he was really listening to her. "Your first family?"

Cora nodded. She'd jumped and maybe it was going to be okay. "The first one that counted. I know nothing about my original family, and I've made peace with that. I was just two months old when my mother left me on the steps of a fire station in Tehachapi. She left a note saying she was sixteen, and that she was scared of what both her boyfriend and her mother would do to me if I was ever left alone with either of them, and she didn't sign it. That's not the part I remember, though. That's the easy part. Being left by a mother is an easy thing, if you get another mother afterward. And I did."

"Uh-huh." A quiet sound. Encouraging.

Cora sat up, wrapping the top sheet around her body. Sitting cross-legged, carefully draping the cotton over her skin, she laced her fingers in her lap and kept talking. "I got the best mom. In my head, when I think of the word *mother*, I still see her. She had dark black hair with poofy bangs, and she loved bright red lipstick and the smell of baby powder. She would get all the way under my covers to read me books at night, and she told me I was her little girl, that she was my mother. Her husband was nice enough, but looking back, he looks like a paper doll in my imagination. She put suits on him, placed the briefcase in his hand, and shoved him out the door. I sometimes think I remember him wearing a bowler hat, but then I think maybe it was Darrin on *Bewitched* that I'm confusing him with.'

Knitting. That's what she wanted in her hands – her fingers ached from lacing them together so tightly. "Hang on," she said, wrapping the sheet tighter around her body. "I'll be right back." She scooted out of the room and grabbed the lace-paneled sweater on its needles. *Mac is in my bedroom.* This was crazy. Insane. Exactly what she'd wanted to never happen. Her bare feet stalled on the hardwood floor and she took a moment to think very hard about whether she should take that next step into the bedroom.

This was her choice. Hers alone. Just like this was her home, and no one could take it from her, especially not Royal, no matter how much money he threw at her. The last thought bolstered her, and she chose, again, Mac. In this moment, at least – even if it was small, even if it didn't last long – she chose him.

She could choose something else later if she wanted to.

He was still waiting there for her, sitting up, resting against the headboard as if it were what he always did. Cora released a breath she hadn't known she'd been holding.

"Seems like you're better at multi-tasking than you think you are."

"Knitting soothes me." Tucking her legs under herself again, she looked carefully at the needles even though she knew exactly where she was in the pattern.

"That's good. I like watching you knit."

It was astonishing, really, how well he was reading her. He could have reached out and tried to touch her, or take her into his arms. Mac could have tried to tug the sheet off her and lure her back with kisses, but for this very moment, Cora only wanted to sit in place with him and knit and say the words that were stopped behind her teeth, waiting to finally be released.

She knitted her way halfway through a row, the Addi-Turbos *snicking* softly against each other. Mac watched with his arms uncrossed, resting easily at his sides.

Then Cora said, "I thought she was the most magical person ever. She was everything to me. I mean, I was only five, so of course she was everything. But to me, she was better than Christmas. She was my present, every single day. Then she got pregnant."

"Mmmm."

Cora worked a double decrease. "She'd always thought she couldn't. They'd tried for years, and then they'd gotten me out of the system when I was two. They worked to adopt me for two-and-a-half years, but there was always another hoop to jump through, they said, more paperwork. I'd been chosen, so I didn't care."

"Did you remember the time before they chose you?"

She shook her head. "Sometimes it feels as if I remember, but I don't have anything concrete. Just a feeling of motion. I've learned the California system was so difficult back then that kids went in and out of homes by the week. There was always something new, someone else coming to pick the children up and take them someplace. I remember a stuffed blue furry lobster, having it and losing it and crying."

Mac didn't speak but his eyes warmed her.

"So she got pregnant – and I remember this clearly – she started to lose focus on me. Totally natural, I'm sure. A pregnant woman has to think of herself, and what more exciting time is there in your life?" Cora kept her voice light. "But even at five, I felt her drawing back, so I did everything I could to clamp on to her. I turned into a tiny, desperate limpet. I remember reaching for her constantly, and crying when she was too big to pick me up anymore. I threw tantrums when I couldn't sleep in their bed. And then when the baby came, I hated it. I hated how it had taken my mother away from me, and I think I hated myself right out their door. They put me back in the system before the baby was three months old."

Mac tilted his head. "You make it sound like you think it's your fault they couldn't keep you."

"It was." *Obviously.*

"Cora, you were a child."

"I'm aware that I didn't know any better, but that doesn't change the fact that they . . ." *Didn't want me.* Cora dropped the knitting and shook out her hands. "This is ridiculous."

"You can't control everything."

"Oh, I can." She looked around the room and spotted her *What If* book on the nightstand. Scrambling for it, she said, "I mean, obviously not the weather, or the climate, but there are so many things I can control. Anyone can. You should . . . um, you should look at this." Cora opened the book to a random page, her heart racing. Was she really showing him this? She'd never shown anyone but Eliza. Not even Logan had known what she was scribbling. He would have teased her, and she couldn't have borne that.

"'What if America runs out of water?' What do you mean?" Mac's voice was curious. His body language remained relaxed.

"I mean just that. Someday, as a nation, we're going to start running dry. Us, we're lucky." She pointed at the page. "There's a de-sal plant five miles up the road. Right now they're only using it for non-potable water for the strawberry industry, but look, here's the owner's name. I sell his wife wool every winter. She's a huge knitter –"

"Of course."

"– and Ricky knows that if and when that time comes, that I'm a good person to have on his side. I can make clothes. Warmth. From *scratch*. We have an agreement. I can take water if needed, and I'll continue to supply his wife with spun fiber."

Mac raised his eyebrows.

"I know, I know. Five miles is a lot to walk for water. But look, here on the next page, I've drawn a rudimentary sketch for a wagon I could make just for containers. I'd only have to make the trip twice a week, I think, and that includes the animals' water. If I had a horse I could carry more, but then of course, I'd need water for him, too . . ." She trailed off as she realized that Mac's face was incredulous, his eyes wide, his mouth slightly open.

"McGibboney Cross Wildwood. Are you about to laugh at me?"

"I'm not. I'm completely impressed."

"You're not."

He leaned forward and said clearly, "I'm not laughing. I'm surprised. Kind of out of my gourd impressed. You've just blown my mind."

"In a bad way," she said.

"In an amazing way. You're tremendous, Cora."

Naked. She felt more naked than she'd ever been before in her life even though the sheet was still wrapped tightly around her. Slamming the book shut, she threw it in the nightstand drawer. She looked around. "All of this is ridiculous. I can't believe . . ." She stood, taking the sheet with her, not caring that the sweater hit the floor, the metal needles clattering on the wood. Gathering her clothes into her arms, she said, "Look, I think you should just –"

"Cora, it's okay."

Oh, but suddenly it wasn't, not at all. She had a sudden image of Logan in this room, when they thought they might make it into a nursery. He'd been going to paint it yellow but there hadn't been enough time.

"I'll see you tomorrow. Can you clear out?" Her words were an embarrassing tumble of too-fast syllables. "That's rude, isn't it? Oh, God. I know. But if you could just . . . Oh Mac, can you leave?"

Cora ran into the bathroom, cheeks ablaze. She felt better once she was clothed, as if the flannel ducks riding skateboards would protect her in some way. She tied the robe around her waist tightly and brushed her teeth, hoping the peppermint flavor would chase the taste of him away. She brushed her tongue twice, even though if she were honest with herself, she'd admit she wished she could keep the taste a little longer. A lot longer.

No. She placed her toothpaste carefully back exactly where it went on the top of the low white bookcase that held the extra towels. The guest towels. When was the last time she'd had a guest?

Cora stood her toothbrush up in its wooden rack inside the medicine cabinet. One of her favorite things she'd ever carved, she'd made it of walnut from the tree that had fallen in a storm three years ago.

Everything here was hers. Everything had a place. A function.

And Mac was in her bed.

Pressing her ear against the door of the bathroom, she listened hard. Was he gone? Had she given him long enough?

She flossed, and then brushed her teeth one more time, just for good measure. Her tongue felt sore.

Since she hadn't heard anything when she'd listened the first time, she held her rinse glass against the door like they did in old movies. It *did* seem as if she could hear more, and she still heard nothing. No motion. No breathing.

Maybe the coast was clear. She opened the bathroom door and peeked her head around.

Mac was still on the bed, in the same position, his eyes fixed on hers.

Without thinking, Cora pulled her head back in and slammed the door.

"*Shit.*"

CHAPTER THIRTY

Accept your mistakes – all of them – and keep knitting. The feeling of the sweater around your shoulders grants a wonderful absolution to those mis-crossed cables. – E.C.

A moment after Cora surprised Mac by slamming the door, she calmly opened it again and made her way toward him, holding her spine straight. She'd put the robe back over her PJs, and for that he was truly sorry. In so many ways, she was re-minding him of a sorrel Royal had owned years ago, a horse Mac had loved. Rosie had been known for making last-minute decisions on the field and then backtracking, trying to fix them. Not a good quality in a racer, but it had endeared Mac to her.

"Sorry about that," she said.

"Nothing to be sorry for, Cora." He sat up slowly, not wanting to scare her.

"You're still here."

"I wanted to make sure that you really wanted me to leave. Be-cause I don't have to."

"But . . ." She sat and scooted backward so that she was leaning against the headboard.

"And the truth is, I don't want to."

She blinked rapidly, and looked so much like that sorrel after she'd cut across the wrong part of the track that Mac said, "Okay, I'll go. That's not the big deal here. It's totally okay if you want me to leave. What I'm worried about, though, is what you were just saying about your foster mother."

"Oh, crap," Cora said on a sigh. "I'm sorry I said anything at all."

"Before you got placed at Windward, did you have any other families that you thought wanted you?"

"No." The word was clipped.

"Were there any placements where you *wanted* them to want you?"

"Hell, no."

"Was it as awful as it is in movies?" Mac pictured a drunk father wearing greasy clothes, smacking small children as they ran by. He imagined a tired mother, screaming abuse in the din and rubble of a dirty kitchen.

Cora smiled, though there was no humor in her eyes. "That's the funny thing. It's not like on TV. For the most part, foster parents are okay. At worst, they're just looking for money, but in California, the cash doesn't cover what the kids cost anyway, so that's not usually the reason they do it. At best, they're good people trying to do right in a system that makes rewards difficult. And I can't even blame them. How many kids floating through your house like goldfish in a tank can you really care about? The first four or five? After that, is it too many? Maybe they protect their hearts, too, just like the kids do." She folded her arms over her chest, and the next words were spoken low, as if she were reluctant to say them, but they came anyway. "There's only so much heartbreak for everyone. Once you use up your share, you're done. And here, in my home, I'm safe from that." She closed her eyes. "Mostly. That's why I won't sell."

Mac kept his eyes on her face, willing her to look at him. He ignored the last part of her speech and zeroed in on the part that was the most important. "So you're done with heartbreak?"

She gave a bark of laughter. "Are you kidding? I've *been* done. For years. I lost Eliza. I lost Logan. I lost my baby when I was only six and a half months along. A girl."

Mac knew that. It had been one of the only things he'd said to her and Logan when he came home for his grandfather's funeral. *I'm sorry for your loss.* What stupid, lightweight words. But because they were all he had, he said them again now. "I'm so sorry, *Corazón.*"

Her voice broke. "I lost everything."

Including me. You didn't have to lose me. It was a stupid, selfish thing to think, and Mac was furious that the words had run through his head. "I know."

Rubbing her temples, she said, "I think it's best you go."

Standing slowly, Mac reached for his jeans and pulled them on. Then his shirt. He slipped on his socks and his boots and buckled his belt. Her eyes stayed closed.

"Cora."

Rocking her head back and forth against the headboard, she said, "No."

"We both loved him."

Her eyes flew open. "Not in the right way. Neither of us loved him the right way."

"What was the right way?"

Instead of answering, she said, "Tell me why you only came home twice in fifteen years. Tell me why you didn't come home when Logan died."

Shit. He had to tell her. How had he even hoped he might get away with not telling her the complete truth? He should have known better, and he should have told her earlier. Slipping his shirt on, he sat on the edge of the bed. "You know how I told you I foreclosed on that house?"

Cora nodded.

"It wasn't just that house. I'd bought into the whole housing market hype. I took on a second house, thinking I could rent the first one out. The bubble burst, and I spent two years trying to bail myself out, putting everything on my credit cards as I lost one house to a failed short sale, and then the other one."

"So you foreclosed on a couple of stupid houses. And?"

"You're not getting it. I lost everything I'd worked toward for years. That first house was going to be how I retired someday. I was so damn *proud* that I'd made something of myself, that I hadn't turned out like my father, gambling away every dime. I didn't see it coming. I couldn't see that I'd done the exact same thing. I ended up sixty-one thousand dollars in debt, and that was just in credit cards, not including how much I defaulted on. I was behind and upside-down in everything. Creditors calling me constantly, just like they had at my house growing up. I had to get away. I ran." Mac dug his fingers into the edge of the mattress. "I hid. I was still working at the track then, but I took a leave of absence, rented a hunting cabin up near Bishop. I was there for four months."

Mac paused. He could hear Cora's, soft, shallow breathing as she stared at him. "By the time I came off the mountain and checked my voicemail, the funeral was already over. I'd known he was sick, but I thought he'd have a year. Years, maybe. If I'd ever –" He cleared his throat. "If I'd ever imagined I wouldn't get to say goodbye to him, I would have come sooner. Instantly. But I missed my only chance. If you think you can't forgive me for that, believe me, I know the feeling."

"Why didn't you just tell me that? Why didn't you just call when you found out?" Cora's cheeks were pale.

Mac raised his shoulders. "I wish to hell I knew. I'd been running from myself for months by then. Took me a long time to figure anything out. Royal hired me, and I worked my ass off getting out of debt. I got my life back. But Logan lost his, and I . . . I guess I just didn't know the right words to say, to you or anyone."

She made a miserable sound low in her throat. "I guess you still don't."

"I'm not proud of it, Cora. It's probably the worst thing I've ever done."

She nodded. "Kidnapped by pirates, that would have been okay. Or in a coma somewhere, almost dead after being kicked in the head by a horse. But just because you ran away and didn't check your voicemail? Oh, Mac. You should have called. He deserved more than that." She paused, as if considering whether or not to continue speaking.

The only words he could find were simple ones. "Can you forgive me?"

"Yes." A long sigh. "I forgave you when you said you were sorry the first time. I'm glad you told me the truth." She met his gaze and smiled, but her eyes looked bruised, tired. Then she scooted down, turning her back, pulling the covers over her. "Lock the front door as you leave, okay?"

"We have to talk about this −" He hadn't yet told her why he'd come home so rarely in the years before his cousin died. He hadn't told her that she was the reason − that it was just too damn hard for him to see her with Logan. The truth.

"Go." Her voice was so exhausted, so strangled, that Mac went. His staying could only cause her more hurt, and goddamn it, he couldn't do that to her.

So he wouldn't stay with her in the bedroom. But her front porch, well, that would be as good a resting place as any, right? It wasn't like he was going to get any sleep anywhere, either at his house or out here in the foggy moonlight. He grabbed a thick afghan from the back of the couch. As he pulled the front door closed and tested it to make sure it was locked, he realized that he hadn't felt as close to crying in years, not since he'd clutched his cell phone and listened to his mother's message about Logan, not since he'd wept like a child while parked in front of a Dairy Queen on Route 395.

He sat on the porch swing, kicking up his boots, draping the blanket over him. It wasn't long enough, only covering him from the chest down. That was fine. He pulled his cowboy hat low and tugged the blanket a little wider – it would keep most of the morning dew off him. And just for a moment, he let himself remember what Cora's lips had felt like against his, how she'd felt against him, how she'd stretched along him after she came. The image of her back turned, the sorrow in her voice – he wouldn't think of that.

Mac took a breath and settled himself deeper into the porch swing cushions. He'd leave early, before she found him. It just made him feel better, knowing he was there to protect her if . . . hell, she didn't need protecting. It seemed like she'd done a spit-shine job of taking care of herself. But for now, he'd let himself pretend he was watching over her.

CHAPTER THIRTY-ONE

Enjoy the middle part – don't rush so much. Feel each stitch between your fingers. Rub the fabric against your cheek. How lucky we are, to touch every single inch of this beloved sweater! – E.C.

On Saturday morning, Cora's eyes flew open. There was a reason she'd tossed and turned for the last few hours . . . the same reason she was vaguely sore . . .

She'd slept with Mac. Jesus! She'd slept with him!

Screwing her eyes shut tight, Cora groaned and rolled, burying her face in a pillow. A pillow that smelled of him. Of course. She threw herself out of bed.

Saturday. It was Saturday. That meant after chores, she had to meet Olivia at the stables. The girl had been blowing up her phone with texts every day, confirming that they would get together on Saturday to ride – somehow she'd cajoled or bribed her mother to sign the waiver, she said, and Cora looked forward to hearing how Olivia had pulled that one off.

Good. She needed something to do today. Otherwise, she probably would have spent it in the bomb shelter where she would have inventoried the dry stores and rotated the water supply. Again.

Cora took a shower and pulled on her best pair of overalls. She leaned on the bathroom sink, watching her face as she brushed her teeth. Her hair was wild, sticking straight out in a dozen places, and dark circles painted the skin underneath her eyes. Well, crap. It certainly wasn't anything she was going to attack with make-up. If there was indeed something that *could* help, it wasn't anything Cora had in her small make-up kit. What did Mac see when he looked at her? The girls he dated probably had whole drawers full of product instead of her little plastic tackle box, which held one lipstick, one eye shadow she'd bought in the mid-nineties, and a tube of mascara she wasn't sure wouldn't give her an eye infection if she tried to use it. The last time she'd had a full face of war paint on had been her wedding, and she'd hated how the fake eyelashes had held down her eyelids, making her feel sleepy at the reception even though she hadn't been drinking.

Sighing, she gave up. Why should she care what Mac saw when he looked at her? The night was an aberration. It wouldn't happen again. She did the chores and drove to the stables, careful not to glance at herself in the rearview mirror.

When she got there, Olivia was already standing in front, balancing carefully on an old railroad tie. Wearing all black, from the top of the handkerchief that was tied around her head to her worn-out black sweatshirt right down to her ripped black leggings tucked into combat boots, she looked tough. And very, very young.

Olivia hopped off the tie and waved, hard.

"Hi! Stark's already here! She said she'd lend us both horses and we can go out as long as we want. In exchange for some stable cleanup, that is, but I'll do that, you don't have to worry about that part. Isn't that amazing? I wonder what Stark does when she's not here. Do you think she has horses at her house, too?"

Cora got out of the car. "She lives here."

Olivia's eyes went wide. "She *does*? Why didn't I know that? I want to live here someday."

Smiling, Cora led the way to the barn. "Maybe you can someday."

"You think I'm kidding," she said, as she raced to pass Cora and turn around, walking backward in front of her. "But this is what I want to do."

"Which is what, exactly?" If she didn't ask, Trixie was going to, and with a mother like that, Olivia would have to have her answers all lined up.

"I want to work with unprivileged and disabled communities, using horse riding to help participants overcome limitations, attain personal freedom, and better understand themselves in relation to others and the environment."

Cora's mouth dropped open. "Huh?"

Olivia smiled in satisfaction and continued to speak in her knowledgeable voice. "I memorized it from a page on the stable's website. But it's not a unique business model, either. There's precedent for this to do really, really well for the communities they serve."

"You getting ready to fight your mom?"

A brief nod. "How do I sound?"

"You sound great," said Cora. "I think your mom might be a better fighter than you are, though."

"Yeah, but think about it: where did I come from? I've been studying her my whole life. If I can't do it, no one can."

"At least you know you have a battle coming."

She nodded and looked, suddenly, very grown up. "I'll be ready."

Cora remembered the way it had felt when Eliza made tea for her, when they'd sat together knitting. She'd been listened to. Heard.

"You should come to tea at my house sometime," she said spontaneously. "I have the prettiest tea set . . ."

"A tea party?" Olivia stopped just short of rolling her eyes. "For real?"

"It sounds dumb. But it's fun."

Olivia shrugged. "Maybe."

Stark greeted them as warmly as Stark ever did anything. Cora watched, amused, as Olivia followed her every move. As Cora mounted her horse, Stark stood back watching, her legs apart, arms folded, with Olivia next to her, unselfconsciously echoing the pose, every line the same.

"Coming?" said Cora.

Olivia mounted and Stark swung open the back gate.

"Take the hill trail to the west there, and if you take the left fork and go far enough, you'll end up at Moonglass Beach."

"*Really?*" said Olivia. Her voice was pure, unadulterated joy.

"Let's go slow to start," Cora called to Olivia, who nodded.

It was a glorious morning – warm, the scent of leaf fires hanging on the wind, the sun drifting through the branches of the oak trees they rode under. The well-cut trail was quiet and just wide enough for each of them to pass single-file, dust rising lazily behind them. They saw no one else. The fall sky overhead looked like a faded blue sheet hung out to dry.

Ahead of them, the path opened into rolling hills, long brown grass rising in waves, and when the horses came to the left fork, they looked westward to the ocean gleaming dark blue a mile below.

Olivia jerked her head with a smile and Cora followed. She heard her phone beep in her pocket, and even knowing it was like checking it while driving, she pulled it out anyway. She'd gotten more texts this week than she probably had all year.

It was from Stark. *Mac's coming after you. Hope you don't mind.*

What? Oh, God. Mind? Cora minded all right, so much more than Stark would or could ever know.

She nudged her horse and caught up to Olivia. "Let's go a little faster."

No, Mac would be fifteen minutes behind, at least. They should just ride and let the wind blow away this tension. There was nothing she could do about it. And maybe Mac would get lost. There were a lot of trails out here, after all . . .

Mac had never been lost a minute in his life. Never.

As the horses stepped carefully across a slow, almost dry stream, another thing struck Cora.

Mac was riding. A satisfaction filled her, slow and rich. He'd found the reason he needed to get up on a horse again.

She couldn't help hoping that she was part of the reason. An image filled her mind and blotted out the ocean and the white water break at the edge of the pools in front of her: she saw the side of Mac's neck, where the stubble ran down to his jaw and past, and then that soft part just above his collarbone, where she'd pushed her nose . . . Jesus Christ, she'd nuzzled into him, hadn't she? She'd *nuzzled* Mac Wildwood.

Maybe she should have denied what was between them forever. But she hadn't.

Cora cursed herself in low words that blew into the salty wind. She shouldn't think of him, not like that. It wasn't right. Unfair. She needed distraction; that was it. Cora whooped and pushed her horse into a gallop down onto the beach. Olivia laughed behind her.

After tethering the horses to a large piece of driftwood, she and Olivia grabbed a stray plank each and poked them into the tide pools.

"This has always been my favorite thing to do down here," said Cora as they hopped from rock to rock. "I always feel so accomplished, as if I know something about what I'm looking at when I peer into the water."

"Sometimes I pretend I'm a scientist. Just for fun."

"Do you ever really want to do that? Be one, I mean?"

For this, Cora earned an eye-roll. "Sorry," she said. "I deserved that."

Olivia reached down, stretching her arm into the water. She picked up a tiny crab and held it up, watching its legs struggle. "You want to call my mom and tell her I should apply myself more? That I could get to college if I just took a little more time with my homework? Because she's never heard that before from anyone. I'm sure she'd love hearing it, especially from you." She dropped the crab back into the pool and they watched it scrabble away.

Cora admitted, "She's not too fond of me."

"I can't believe you told her that you'd taken me to the stables."

"She guessed! But I confirmed it. I wasn't thinking."

Olivia rolled her eyes again, but it was a softer roll this time. "That's usually *my* line."

"Hey, grownups are just as dumb as kids are."

Olivia laughed. "Nice."

Oops. "Sorry." Cora poked a bit of seaweed that floated into their pool on a gentle swell. "Here, use this driftwood. Move that kelp, right, like that and see? Just under the water?"

Delight lit Olivia's face as she revealed a deep purple starfish glinting in the sunlight. "How did you know it was there?"

"I dunno. I've always been good with tidepools."

"My mom loves them, too."

"I've seen her here before." And she had. They'd never actually *spoken* to each other on the beach, because they didn't do that, but they usually made an awkward wave of acknowledgement. You had to, when you were alone on a mile-long stretch of beach, only one other person in sight.

Olivia cocked her head on the side. "Why does she feel like she does about you, anyway?"

Cora wiped her wet fingers on her overalls. "It's been that way since high school. I dated the guy who turned into my husband, and she dated his cousin. We're just not cut out to be friends, I think. That's all. Sometimes it's like that."

"So, why wouldn't you be friends?" Olivia asked, her face even more curious.

Cora had almost lost track of the conversation. "I don't know why. It was always like that. When I first came to town, I was about your age. There were two sides I could be on, the popular kids, or the not-so-popular ones. With the exception of Logan and Mac, I was in the not-so's."

Olivia stood and balanced on the potholed black rock, hopping to the next pool. "Well, my mom was probably the same even back then. She can be such a challenge."

Cora smiled at the way it sounded like something an adult would say about a child. And the fact that it was true.

Olivia continued, "But it's not like she's mean or anything."

This was where Cora didn't get to say a word in response. She folded her lips tightly and nodded.

"No, really. I know you don't believe me, and when she does that thing where she cuts people down, she's like scary good at it. Once she made the cable guy cry."

Cora's mouth dropped open. "You're *kidding*."

"It was so fucking awesome." Olivia grinned. "He left and sent the manager back to finish the job."

"That's the best story ever."

"So, yeah, I know she can be hard to deal with. But she picks and chooses, and most people in town like her. She has, like, real friends, I swear. Like, besties."

It was true. Abigail MacArthur had told Cora time and time again that she liked Trixie, that she made her laugh. And Naomi Fontaine, who didn't get close to people easily, had had a hard time with Trixie when she'd first moved to town but now they were in same knitting group.

"It's really not a big deal, I promise. Your mom and I are fine. So we're not that close. All adults don't have to be best friends," said

Cora, teetering carefully on a rock that turned out to be sturdier than it looked.

"Hey!" Olivia pointed. "Look! Another rider! No, two. You think it's Stark?"

Cora shook her head and felt her heart start racing. "I don't think she can leave the stables today. But she sent me a text. It's a guy named Mac. Actually, it's that guy I was talking about earlier. My husband's cousin who used to date your mom." She squinted. "He's with his boss, Royal." *Who wants to buy my land.*

"You like them?" Olivia looked at Cora with an open expression. Whatever Cora said was the direction in which Olivia would lean. She could turn her against the men with just a frown, she knew it. How did parents handle this? Knowing they were so powerful? Of course, when it came to a mother like Olivia's, and the situation they were in, it went the other way, too. The fact that Olivia knew Trixie hated her probably made Cora that much more attractive in Olivia's eyes.

"Sure. Mac and I go way back." Oh, God. All the way to back her bed last night.

Together they watched the men approach. Royal was a competent rider, and as a racetrack owner, surrounded by horses, that didn't surprise her.

Mac still rode like he was part of the horse, like his long, muscular legs became one with the animal beneath him. They moved together. If poetry could look like a thing, it would look like that man on a horse, Cora thought, and was immediately overcome with internal embarrassment for even having such a thought.

"In my mom's yearbook, he wrote something like *Our times together were the highlight of our high school years. Love and kisses, Mac.*"

Cora snorted. "Love and kisses doesn't sound like Mac."

"It does kind of look like my mom's handwriting, which is why I always wondered about it. I've asked her about him a couple of times and she always said he was the one that got away."

Which was exactly the kind of thing that caught a teenager's attention. No wonder she was watching him approach like a cat stalking a bird in a birdbath.

Cora tried her best not to watch Mac the same way.

CHAPTER THIRTY-TWO

How fortunate and blessed are we that we are the makers of things. –
E.C.

Mac had been astonished at how good the riding felt that he'd almost forgotten where he was going. Then he saw her, down on the beach, her hair a flame against the grayness of the sand – a touch of color near the brown rocks.

The palomino beneath him reacted to whatever he'd done when he saw Cora – the horse jumped and moved more quickly, breaking into a canter. Mac allowed it. God, what he really wanted was to gallop, to race at Cora like she was the end of the finish line and there were no other horses around.

From behind him, he heard Royal call, "Easy now, big guy. She'll be there when we get there."

Mac inhaled. Royal was right. It was bad enough that he'd gone out to the stables, knowing that Cora had mentioned to Valentine that she'd be there today with Olivia. He hadn't been able to shake

Royal, who had stood next to the Rolls with the door open. "Let's go," said Royal, tapping on the roof of the car. "Let's go get her."

"No."

"We're going to get your girl."

"Not with you. And anyway, that's not what I'm doing," Mac had insisted, but it had fallen on deaf ears. Royal was one persistent little bugger when he wanted to be. When they'd gotten to the stables, Stark had done a good job of deflecting their curiosity until Royal had simply laid it out there.

"Ma'am, my friend has it bad. He's trying to find Cora, and I'm not above bribery, since I'm actually looking to talk to her about business myself. Now, it seems as if a place like you've got here could use a bit more cash in terms of a donation."

Stark, who usually looked as if little surprised her, started like a horse spying a rattler. "You're joking."

Mac, who knew better, said, "He's not."

"If we could borrow a horse or two to go after Cora, I'll make it worth your while. I'm a horse man myself, if that helps."

Stark had narrowed her eyes and gone in for the kill. "Cash is always nice, of course. But this is a non-profit, and I only have one full-time employee in the office. I need more than money. And I read *The Economist* – I know who you are. I just lost a board member."

Royal took a step backward and looked at Mac. "Oh, she's good."

Mac smiled.

"Why'd you lose the board member? Quit? Internal problems?" Royal had gotten his feet back under him again.

"Died. He was old."

"Damn." Royal paused, stared at Mac who tried to look appropriately lovelorn. "Okay, lady. You got a new board member."

"And *you*," Stark had said, waving her hand at the stables, "can pick any horses you like. She said she was going out the west loop to where it breaks to the water."

<<>>

Now they were here, his horse's hooves chopping the dry sand, as impatient as he was to get down to where it was more firmly packed. This was his favorite kind of beach, no fine sand here, just rocky pebbles that got smaller the closer they drew to the water line. The tide was low and a girl and Cora were out peering into tidal pools. When he was a kid, he and Logan could spend hours pulling various things out of the salty water and putting them back, always hoping to find starfish (which they did) and octopi (which they didn't, but they'd lived in hope). An electric eel would have been great, too. They'd loved anything that seemed moderately dangerous.

Cora had seen them – he could tell by the way she'd straightened that she was as nervous as he was. What the hell was he doing out here? God. He'd followed her on horseback to a beach without any kind of plan. To what? Say he was sorry? He wasn't sorry they'd had sex. In fact, he was pretty damn stoked about it. Couldn't stop thinking about it. How she'd looked, how she'd sounded.

What *was* his reason for coming out here? When Royal had asked him, he hadn't had an answer. The real reason lay in the last part of their conversation, the fact that now she knew why he hadn't come home to Logan's funeral. But that wasn't beach talk – he needed to come up with a better reason, a more believable one, and fast.

They drew nearer. Stark's other two horses nickered in greeting.

Cora's face was a question, and all he wanted to do was to slide off the horse and kiss away that worried look .

Instead, he said, "Fancy meeting you here."

"Stark's horses?"

"Yep." He patted the palomino's neck.

"So you had that whole ride here and you couldn't think of anything more original than that to say?"

"Um, yep."

Royal rode alongside him. "Ignore my boy here. We were just trying to track you down. That's all. He's obsessed with you, I think."

Cora blinked in surprise.

"Anyway," Royal went on. He waved at Olivia who had her hands jammed into her sweatshirt pockets, frowning as she examined the men. "You must be the Olivia we've heard is such a good rider. I'm Royal, and that ugly guy over there is Mac."

Olivia tilted her head. "Where'd you hear . . .?"

"We were hanging out with Cora the other night and she mentioned it."

Olivia's face lit in surprise and pleasure. "Oh."

Mac finally figured out what to say. "Wanna race?"

Cora said, "No."

Olivia said, "Yes," and scrambled off the rocks toward the horses.

"Mac, you can't. You should have heard Trixie. She'd be furious if she even knew that she was out here with me right now. I'm probably going to get sued by the paper or something. You can't race."

Royal swung his mare around to follow Olivia. It was just the two of them on the small strip of rocky sand next to where the tide pool began. Mac met Cora's eyes. "Remember?"

"What?" she asked defensively. "What do you mean?"

"No, not last night," he clarified. "Although personally, I can't think of anything else." He cleared his throat. From where he sat atop the horse, he could look down and see the curve of the top of her breast. The bottoms of her overalls were wet as if she'd been surprised by a rogue wave, and her lips were as red as if he'd just been biting them. He felt himself grow hard and checked himself. "Not that," he repeated. "I meant do you remember racing down here?"

Cora stretched her neck as if it hurt, and then looked down the beach. "I can't believe we used to do that."

"Almost daily. You rode Rivet and I'd have Spooner."

"Logan always rode Darkness," Cora said softly, her voice barely reaching him above the dull roar of the waves rolling into the tide pools.

"He loved that horse."

Cora nodded. "More than anything."

Not more than he loved you. "And we'd race. Down here."

"Without any kind of adult supervision."

"We were in high school. We were old enough."

She looked at Olivia, who was chatting to Royal as she got ready to mount her horse from the driftwood. "We were babies. Look at her."

Mac turned. He tried to see Trixie in Olivia but apart from the length of her slim nose, and the set of her jaw, she didn't look anything like her mother. Trixie had always been so proud of her looks, and Mac could imagine she'd have wanted to dress a little girl up just like herself. Olivia, in her ripped black clothing, with the dark eye make-up that looked like raccoon circles around her eyes? That for sure wasn't the reflection Trixie wanted of herself, which probably just killed her. Might be why the girl did it.

"Come on, Cora. Let's do it. For old times' sake."

She shook her head and walked past his horse, giving it a quick nuzzle as she did so. "Not for me. Someone has to stay on the ground to call 911. Go. Just go. You want to."

He wanted to do so many other things he couldn't do – push his fingers into her hair and guide her mouth to his, wrap his arms around her, whisper into her ear, make her laugh until she shook with joy against him, but instead he nodded. "She really as good as you say?"

"Yeah."

"I bet I win."

Cora gave a half smile. "She's good. She might win."

"So make a bet with me."

She turned to face him. He heard her feet crush the rocky sand, and the ocean wind parted her hair, making it dance. "What are we betting?"

"Three dates. Real ones. Dinner. Movies. What people do when they like each other."

"*What?* Three?"

He lifted his hand from the pommel. "That's not that many."

"One. And I pick the date."

"If she beats me," said Mac, "then just one date that you pick. If I beat her, then three, of my choice." Three dates with Cora. Hot damn. He'd win, come hell or high tide.

Her mouth moved but no words came out as a spot of red hit her high on her cheekbones. Good. He affected her then, hopefully as much as she was getting to him.

Finally, she said, "If and when I win, you know that a date means pulling a cleaning shift at the shelter?"

"Hot. Will you wear rubber gloves?"

Cora appeared to be trying to swallow a smile. "Followed by making dinner at Windward for the kids. And then games night."

"Spin the bottle?"

"They favor Wii. And, of course, Twister."

Mac winked at her. "I'll play Twister with you anytime."

Cora laughed, and pleasure rolled through him. God, that was what he wanted to hear, every minute of the day. When had she started affecting him like this again? Like an emotional gut-punch.

He should say something – Cora was staring at him. "So I gotta go win. You know," he stammered. Here he was, throwing his hat in the ring. Again.

"Be careful."

"We will be," he promised.

And they would be. They'd be fine physically. Mac suspected it was kind of too late to save his heart.

CHAPTER THIRTY-THREE

Oh, life is fun! And even more so if you have a pair of socks-in-progress in your bag! Never, ever a dull moment. – E.C.

Cora wasn't left behind on the beach – Royal stayed with her. "Let them go," he said. "I love horses. Obviously. But," he reached behind himself and rubbed his ass, "I own horses. And I hire trainers who hire the jockeys to ride them. I'm used to sitting in a Herman Miller chair, not a rolling block of uncomfortable leather."

She smiled. "Most riders like that feeling."

"Yeah, well, I like computers. And a desk."

Mac and Olivia trotted down the beach, laughing about something Cora couldn't hear. Their words were tossed on the wind, jostled by the waves. The broken sound reminded her so acutely of being with the boys, way back when, that her heart hurt as she looked for Logan behind her. She could almost hear him whoopin' about kicking Mac's ass.

She'd missed something Royal had said to her. "I'm sorry?"

"Ah," he shrugged, and his look was curious. "It doesn't matter."

They turned to watch the riders who had made it to the end of the cove, near the old cave. A quarter mile down the road, where the cliff curved away, perched the lighthouse, an optical illusion making it seem as if it was hovering over Mac and Olivia's heads.

"That's where we always started."

"Where do they ride to? Here?"

Her hands chilled by the salt water, Cora nodded while rubbing her fingers together. "If they do what we used to, they'll ride here, around us to the end, turn and go back again."

"This is pretty broke-down horseflesh we're all on."

"They're not! Don't say that. You're just used to the best. Stark's horses are well-taken care of, even if they're a little bit older."

"A little bit? They all wear bifocals," But he laughed, and Cora couldn't help smiling. He was a friendly guy, and she forgot for a moment that he had enough money to buy God. What she didn't forget was that he wanted to own her part of Cypress Hollow. And he wasn't going to.

Olivia appeared to be adjusting something on her pommel. Sunlight broke through the fog, lighting them both in a pool of watery sunshine at the end of the beach.

"I'm not selling," said Cora. "Did he tell you that?"

Royal sat on the driftwood log and picked up a handful of stones. Just under the surface, they were wet and shiny, and he sorted through them, apparently totally at ease. "He did."

"Are you angry?"

"Of course not. It's your choice to make. But I think I can change your mind."

"I don't think there's any way for you to do that."

"As they say, money talks."

Cora inclined her head. "They do say that. But I like my house more than money."

"We can move the house. And I think if you'll let me show you the plans we've drawn up –"

"You've drawn up plans already?"

"Just to show you what would be possible. I'm thinking green, environmental all the way. The stables would blend into the land-scape so that it would look even wilder from the coast road than it does now. Make it truly coastal and sustainable. You'll love it."

"I like my view more than money."

"That," Royal said, "might present a bigger problem. But I like big problems. They give me something to work on when I can't sleep."

"Why can't you sleep?"

"Big thoughts. Empty bed." He said it matter-of-factly.

"Not to be too crass about it, but it seems like a man with your money could probably find a girlfriend or two."

"Sure. I just don't like the ones who think like that." He picked a deep blue piece of stone-worn glass out of the sea pebbles. "See? I like the unusual ones. They're rare." He paused and seemed to be wondering if he should speak. Then he said, "I still can't believe I'm seeing him on a horse. I've seen him next to them; hell, I've seen his arm all the way up one of 'em more times than I'd liked to have. But you're the one who got him up on that horse. Mac's a lucky man."

Frowning, Cora ignored the last part of his speech and said light-ly, "I'm glad I have small thoughts. I usually sleep pretty well."

"Yeah. Money can't buy that. You're lucky, too. Look, they're starting."

At the cave's opening, Mac's arm was raised. It dropped, and they started. Mac, obviously, was better seated than the girl from the be-ginning. He knew how to hold the horse with his legs, how to lift his weight and move with the animal.

"Like riding a bike," Cora murmured. The rolling, thunderous sound got closer and closer as they galloped.

Mac was ahead, of course, but then, improbably, Olivia began to catch up.

A date. With Mac. In every moment she'd ever spent trying to turn off her feelings – any feelings – she'd never accidentally pictured that. Out with Mac. Would he hold her hand? They could go into the Book Spire together and chat with Lucy about new releases, followed by ice cream at Tad's. The image twisted at her heart. It wasn't fair to think like this. Not for any of them.

"Damn," said Royal.

It was as if they were watching time-lapsed photography. Olivia was hurtling up the learning curve before their eyes. Even head on, Cora could see her think about her positioning, changing her seat, and then, in mid-flight, the horse and she became one. By the time the horses were upon them, splitting and going around where Royal and Cora stood, then charging to the end of the beach and turning, hard, Olivia was next to Mac. When they passed by again, Olivia whooped, a sound matched by Mac.

She heard it then.

She *saw* it then.

Olivia drew ahead, her body perfectly positioned on the horse as if she'd been born to do nothing more than ride, forever, to the ends of the earth.

Just like Mac.

Mac was Olivia's father.

Cora sat on the log with a thump as the realization pounded through her body as firmly as she'd just felt the hoof beats pounding the sand around them.

"Oh, help," she whispered so quietly that she knew the wind took the words away from her even before they left her mouth.

CHAPTER THIRTY-FOUR

Breathe into the difficult bits. They aren't a hurdle to be gotten over in one great leap – they are to be leaned into just as sweetly as the long stretches of stockinette. – E.C.

The ride back to the stables wasn't what Mac hoped it would be. Olivia was so excited about her win, and he hoped that Cora would buy into it, just a little bit. They'd been safe, couldn't she see that? No one had been thrown, no one was hurt, and more than that, it was obvious that Olivia had proven to herself that she really could ride, that this really was her thing.

And Mac had lost the bet, which meant that he'd still won, of course. That had been the goal. One date with Cora was one more than he'd had this morning. He couldn't keep the grin off his face. Hot damn.

Why, then, was Cora staying a hundred yards ahead of them the whole ride to the stables? Her back was stiff and every time Mac hurried his horse to try to catch up with her, she sensed it and rode faster. Once she broke into a gallop, as if she were running from him, and after that he stayed back, feeling rejected even though she hadn't said a word. Was she that upset about the date? Mac wouldn't hold her to it, not if she felt like that.

He wasn't a monster.

Finally, he gave up entirely and fell all the way back, listening to Olivia chatter to Royal. She spoke as quickly as the words could tumble out of her mouth, and Royal laughed at her, encouraging her.

Mac wondered if Trixie had ever said anything to her about him. Did mothers talk about their old boyfriends to their kids? He had no idea. Olivia had given him a strange look down there on the beach, but the strangeness between them had gone away as they'd raced.

God, Mac hadn't felt that sensation of flying in so long that he was still drunk with it.

At the stables, Cora mumbled some excuse about stopping by Windward on her way home, and she talked Olivia – who hadn't needed much convincing – into currying her horse and putting her away along with the one Olivia had been riding. "Stark can give you a ride home so you don't have to ride the bus."

Mac said, "Cora, about tonight –"

"Stop."

"Can I pick you up?"

"No. You can't."

"But the date –" Although he tried not to let the emotion reach his voice, Mac felt eight years old, promised a gift that was snatched away before he could touch it.

"You have *got* to be kidding me," she muttered. Then she said more loudly, "If you're still serious about that, then meet me at the shelter at five, when they close."

"I don't mind picking you up –"

She held up her hand without turning to look at him, and then she'd slammed her car door so hard Stark's dog barked in protest.

"Jeez, Mac," said Royal as he dismounted awkwardly. "What burr did you put under her saddle?"

"No freakin' idea."

"How'd you leave it with her last night?"

Twisting his head quickly to stare at Royal, Mac said, "How did you know?"

With a satisfied look, Royal said, "I didn't. But I do now."

"Oh, for cripe's sake. You're a piece of work. And no. We didn't leave it well."

"Figured. Otherwise you might have just called her on the phone rather than tracking her down here, over hill and dale. Literally."

Mac looked to make sure Olivia and Stark were occupied and safely out of earshot. Stark was showing the teenager something in the office before they started currying. "She kicked me out."

"Before or after?"

Mac felt his mouth twist. "After."

Royal hooted. "Oh, burn, brother."

"Shut it."

"The girl of your dreams kicks you out of bed? You ever *been* tossed after the deed before?"

"No," Mac said. "Have *you*?"

"So many times I can't even count."

"Seriously?"

"Well, not since I made all the money, no. Women don't do that to me now." He looked wistful for a moment. "It was kind of nicer when I didn't know what they wanted. Now I do. And it's not my body." He patted his beer belly. "What are you going to do?"

"I don't know." Mac finished putting his saddle on the hanging rack. "I blew it. I'm not sure how, but I did."

"And you're giving up?"

"No." Mac scowled.

"Because it kind of sounds like you are."

"You're just worried about your new land."

"True," Royal acknowledged. "But you're my friend."

"And the one who's supposed to get the deal done for you."

"I like to hedge my bets."

Mac shook his head. "I'm going to finish this and then we're out of here."

"Royal?" Olivia approached, brushing her dirty hands on her black pants, leaving a dusty trail on the fabric. "Can you guys give me a ride home? Stark said she would, but she's all stressed out about a group that's coming tomorrow."

Royal agreed, and they waved goodbye to Stark. Palming the wheel of the giant car, Royal guided the Rolls smoothly over the dirt road, down the hill, gliding into town.

As Royal made the turn onto Chestnut, a woman getting her mail out of her mailbox spun in place as they slowly drove past. Two teenagers leaning against a Honda, both texting, did a double take, their thumbs slowing as they followed the Rolls with their eyes. Phyllis Gill, who'd been ancient when Mac had lived in town and who was doubly ancient now, almost fell right over into the rosebush she was pruning.

"I told you we should have taken my truck out here," Mac muttered.

"It's a good thing she's wearing her glasses, because I think her eyes would be popping out of her head right now," said Olivia with a delighted laugh.

Royal shrugged. "It's just a car."

"For *you*," Mac said. "For you, this is a way to get from point A to point B. For people who live in this town, this is a rolling symbol of more than they'll ever have in their bank account. Ever."

"Oh," said Royal in a smaller voice as he slowed.

"No way," said Olivia, sliding from one side of the leather bucket seat to the other. "I feel like I'm in a movie. I want to drive past the houses of all of my enemies and let them see me."

Royal grinned. "Wanna? We can. Dude! We could toilet paper! I was too square in high school to ever do it, but I feel like I missed out on something important. Do you have a house you wanna TP?"

"Hmmm. A couple." Olivia's voice was satisfied as she thought about it. "Oh, this is *awesome*."

Even Mac, grumpy as he was with the day and with himself, couldn't fault her. He'd have felt the same way if he'd been chauffeured home in a sweet ride at her age.

"But I gotta get home before Mom does," continued Olivia. "If she sees me looking like this, she'll know. She'll sniff it out of me. She can smell a horse at a hundred paces. I found that out last week the hard way. She has the nose of a bloodhound. Speaking of bloodhounds, did you know there's a couple of dogs in California specially trained to sniff out suspects who've left crime scenes in *cars*? I think my mom could do that if I ever ran away. She could just point her nose out of the car and follow my scent. That is, if I'd left the window down. Right? If I'd left in a car, then there wouldn't be a scent trail to follow." She took a quick breath and popped forward between the front seats. "Right?"

Mac shook his head. "*What?*"

"There," she pointed the house out to Royal. "The little blue one."

"I can't believe she's still in the same house."

Olivia looked at him curiously. "You came here when she lived with my grandparents, right? Before they died?"

Crap. Mac nodded, wishing he hadn't said anything.

"You dated?"

"Um . . ."

"Oh, *shit*," said Olivia, clutching the headrest of Royal's seat. "Keep going! Keep driving!"

The front door of the blue house opened.

"Nope," said Royal, pulling over to the curb. "We've been made already."

Trixie walked toward them, determination in her step. For one brief moment, Mac was transported back. He was pulling up in front on a Friday night, and Trixie was darting out of the house, yelling something at her parents as she flew down the walkway. In a second she'd be in the car, seated next to him, scooting over to kiss him, and then pulling back immediately to complain about something – that she could smell cigarette smoke on him if he'd smoked with Logan behind the barn, that he smelled like sweat if he'd worked at the barn before coming to get her. Even his deodorant sometimes bothered her. Hell, half of everything he'd ever done had bothered Trixie. They hadn't dated long, but apparently, it had been long enough for her.

Now her hair was still as red, but again, it struck him how bottled, how artificial the color looked, especially outside. She still had the same body style, but she moved differently now. Less bounce, maybe. More sway.

And she could still throw him that same I'm-beyond-pissed-at-you look. Ouch.

Olivia threw open the car door. "I'm fine, Mom."

"You're fine? What does that mean? What were you out doing that you have to tell me you're fine for? Why are you with *them*?"

"Yow. I've got so much homework." She lugged the backpack up to her shoulder. Mac hadn't even noticed her carrying one before, but she lifted it now as if it weighed a thousand pounds. "And I'm tired" She drew the last word out so that it was three or four syllables.

"Where were you?"

"They just gave me a ride home. I asked."

"From *where*?"

If someone didn't tell Trixie, her head was going to explode. But before Mac could say anything, Royal had already stepped forward. "I am so sorry. I told her I would call you and tell you where we all were, but then I forgot to get your number from her, and we just got carried away."

Trixie's eyebrows couldn't go any higher and still be attached to her forehead.

"We were riding. Mac and I were. We stumbled over your daughter at the beach, and then we rode back with her. Just to make sure she was safe."

Trixie whirled on Olivia. "You went to the beach alone?"

Worse and worse. Mac didn't want to be the one to break it to her. But someone had to –

Olivia, though, spoke. "Mom. No biggie. I was with Cora Sylvan. She met me out there and we went to the beach."

Trixie said nothing, appearing flabbergasted. Then she managed, "Her? I thought I told you . . ."

"You did. But I can make my own friends."

"She's not your friend." Trixie's voice was dangerous. Mac remembered that tone – it came right before all hell broke loose. Back then, everything was always his fault. Years later, he was still in the path, and worse, so was her daughter. Trixie stepped forward and took a deep breath. Mac thought of the big bad wolf, and steeled himself to stand in the face of the wind.

But again, Olivia surprised him. In a casual voice she said, "Yes, she is. She's just like you, actually. I keep being surprised by how much you have in common. It's nice. You might like her, if you gave her a chance. Anyway," she smiled at the men. "Thanks for the ride. See you around." And with that, Olivia walked easily into the house, as if there was nothing wrong.

Maybe that was the whole point. There wasn't.

Trixie's shoulders fell. "That's it?" she asked. "That's all the answer I get?"

But the heat was gone from her voice and she lifted her eyes to Royal, who was somehow at her side, hand poised to place below her elbow. He guided her to the Rolls and opened the broad rear door. "There," he said. "Just sit."

"Are you going to offer me champagne or something now?" She pushed the hair from her forehead. "Isn't that what people with cars like this do?"

"Nah," said Royal. "But I have bottled water. Sparkly. I like the bubbles. Want one?"

Trixie shook her head. "I've done something wrong. I'm not sure what it is, but she won't talk to me. That's the most I've heard her say in weeks, and she only said it because she's happy she's spent the day with someone I . . ."

"Have a bubbly water," insisted Royal, but Trixie fixed him with a look, and Mac felt his pain. That look used to be able to stop the entire football team from ruining a pep squad with a pre-planned group full moon.

"She's really okay, Trix. She seems like a good girl. A lot like you were at that age." Mac squatted to sit on the curb so that he was below her. Couldn't hurt. "She knows what she likes."

"What do you mean?"

"You loved writing. That's what you wanted to do. And now you write professionally. You did that for yourself."

Trixie laughed, and for the first time, Mac saw age in her face. Tiny lines at the corners of her eyes crinkled, and it made her look more human. Mac remembered the girl that she'd used to be, the fun one, the one that he'd wanted to hang out with back then.

"I have a shitty job at a tiny podunk newspaper. Approximately sixteen people, if that, read my paper, and on any given day the biggest news story is what bluegrass band is playing that night at the VFW. On a good week, I get a car crash to report on. Bad weeks, I write about how honey production is down again." She pushed the heels of her hands against her temples. "This wasn't what I went to school for. This isn't what I pictured my life to be like."

Royal said, "Are you kidding? You have a family. You know what I got?" He jerked a thumb at Mac. "Him."

"And . . ." Trixie looked around the inside of the Rolls. "You have enough."

Royal's voice became serious. "Enough is just something you work on getting while you're waiting to find your family."

Trixie looked as surprised as Mac felt.

Royal went on, "You already have that. Do me a favor and don't lose sight of that."

Mac expected Trixie to come back with a smart-assed answer. She'd cut him down, and that would be that. Or she'd flirt outrageously in the hopes of turning the tables just to upset the balance, using her wiles. And she had 'em, Mac knew that. They didn't work on him anymore. If they ever really had.

Instead, though, Trixie stood and turned to face Royal. She seemed to be deciding something. Then she said, "Would you like to have dinner with me tonight?"

Royal's eyes widened. He poked his chest with his forefinger and glanced over his shoulder before looking back at her. "Me?"

"You."

"Yes." He grinned.

"Good," she said, and Mac heard relief tinge the word.

"I'll need that phone number I mentioned, the one I don't have for you." Royal had a smile for when he closed big deals, when he was on top. And he had a smile for when he ordered the biggest ice cream sundae with extra bananas and hot fudge. This was the latter. Royal was smiling his joyful ice cream smile, and even though it was strange as hell that it was Trixie who was putting that smile on his face, Mac was glad.

"You don't mind, do you, Mac?" Trixie asked as she scribbled her number on the back of one of Royal's business card. "With our history and all."

"You kids knock yourselves out," said Mac. "Just don't go to the animal shelter, because I've got a hot date planned scooping poop."

CHAPTER THIRTY-FIVE

Every once in a while, your colors will clash. The yarn won't show the cables. The lace will be muddied. Go for a walk. Play chess. Make a kite with a child. Do something else. The knitting will wait. – E.C.

Cora sent Cindi home with the promise that she'd take care of the rest of the closing chores. "I know how to feed everyone, and you've marked the runs that need cleaning. I know where to file these papers, don't worry."

"Are you sure?" asked Cindi. "I mean, don't get me wrong. If you're serious, I'd be thrilled to get out of here. Richard went home this afternoon with the flu and I told him I'd bring him wonton soup. It'll be nice to get home earlier than normal."

"Everything," said Cora. "We'll do it all. I have a helper coming, and I'm going to make him work."

Cindi escaped gratefully, and Cora did a quick tour through the shelter. Apart from the normal poop-scooping, the last three dog kennels needed to be hosed down, the floors and walls scrubbed.

"Good," Cora said as she jotted notes on a Post-it. "Let's see if he can hack it." She sat at the front desk and did the filing Cindi had left in a pile so she could keep an eye on the front door. With great effort, she kept from resting her head on the desk and bursting into tears. It was hitting her hard – this revelation that Mac wasn't the man she'd thought he was. Even though he'd disappointed her by not coming home when Logan was dying, she'd always felt – believed – that deep down Mac was a good man.

But a good man didn't knock up a small-town girl and flee.

A good man didn't turn his back on his responsibilities.

A good man didn't leave a baby behind, to grow up alone, without a father. A girl *needed* a father, goddammit.

When she accidentally shut the filing cabinet on her thumb, she just stared at it, watching the thumbnail slowly turn blue. It should have hurt, and somewhere in her body she knew that it did. But she couldn't register the pain. It didn't exist, and that fact, while interesting, couldn't stop her from raging at Mac inside her mind.

He'd abandoned her.

Olivia, she meant. Mac had abandoned his *child*.

There had been gossip, of course, about whose baby Trixie was carrying, she remembered that. But by then, Trixie and Mac had broken up. Cora, pregnant herself, had thought it was sad that the father of Trixie's baby, a rodeo rider that Logan knew from the circuit, had left no forwarding address or phone number for Trixie.

"Pathetic. Men are weak," she remembered saying to Logan late at night as he talked to her baby bump. She would never, *ever* have guessed that there was no rodeo rider. That Trixie's pregnancy was why Mac had hightailed it out of town. And why he hadn't come back.

If Cora hadn't lost the baby, she and Trixie might have actually ended up being friends. Isn't that what pregnant women did? They bonded over booties and the difficulty of opening umbrella strollers, spending time at the same playgrounds, working in the same co-op pre-schools. Olivia and her little girl – Cora's heart ached, as it always did – could have been friends.

The animal shelter phone rang, startling her back to the present. She answered it, hoping it was Mac calling to cancel. It wasn't, just someone about a dog license. "Call tomorrow after eight," she said, injecting false cheer into her voice. "Thanks, you too." Releasing a long breath, she collapsed against the desk, resting her forehead on the calendar blotter.

She and Logan had laughed about their shotgun wedding, but in the most important respect, it really had been one – if Eliza Carpenter had been the shotgun-wielding type, which she wasn't. Instead, Eliza had just said rather sadly, "Oh." She'd clicked her needles a little harder than normal. "Are you in love with him?"

"Of course. I mean, I love him . . . He's *Logan*. Everyone loves him."

Eliza had given her a sharp look. "Well, I'll miss you being here, my girl." Cora's heart had broken a little bit then – in her mind she'd halfway imagined continuing to live in Eliza's cupola room in the cottage, dating Logan, raising her child on Eliza's sheep farm.

But instead they'd married and moved into the farm house. Cora had planted flowers and had said, 'Home, home, home,' under her breath as she rattled around the rooms, her hands placed protectively over her stomach.

Then she'd lost the baby. Just one of those things, they said. It happened. She was young. She'd barely been married a month. She'd have more chances. Cora could barely find the strength to get out of bed, to stop the stupid tears that kept coming even after she swore she was finally done crying.

And during her grief, in the few snatched seconds that she wasn't thinking only about her lost daughter, she thought of that moment. With Mac. When he didn't kiss her.

Her life had been divided – Cora realized that now – into before that moment and after it. Even though she hadn't ever *had* Mac, after that non-kiss, she knew she'd lost him. By staying in place, standing her ground, she'd chosen to lose him forever. And lord, she'd already been so experienced in losing the things that mattered most. Friendship. Families. Love.

After watching Mac walk away from her as she stood frozen in her wedding dress, she knew that what she had with Logan was good. Sweet. Going forward, they were kind to each other, and she knew Logan loved her in the way he could love anything that wasn't a horse. She'd thought she could lean on him but what had turned out to be true was that she'd had to learn to be even stronger. For him. Logan wasn't strong. But he was real, and he loved her.

And she knew she didn't love Logan the right way, the way he'd deserved to be loved. She didn't exactly know what the right way *was*, which was the worst part. She didn't know how to fix it. So Cora had done everything in her power to make that up to him every minute of every day. She made them a home, and she made it the best, brightest, happiest home that was in her power to make. He loved apple muffins – Cora made the best in the county. She planned for emergencies. She went to bed with her *What If* book and made lists. She'd *made* herself strong.

Ironically, she'd even had a list for what to do if one of them got sick. She'd listed their insurance information, and where to find their advanced directives. She hadn't expected Logan to actually go and do it, to get sick. As he got worse, Cora's lists got longer. She even made a *What If* list just for him, what to do if *she* died. "Look, this page that I've marked. Right here. If I kick it, just make these phone calls, okay? I've planned everything."

He'd laughed at her. "You're crazy. You think too much. We're both going to be fine."

But he wasn't. Her lists *had* come in handy afterward. She called the coroner. The pastor. She knew how to get copies of the death certificate and why she needed them, because she'd researched it. She knew where to mail them, and after the land deed was transferred to her name alone, after she'd received the life insurance, she'd made Logan's home – her home – better. Stronger. She yearned for the child she'd lost, imagining the little girl clambering the ladder in the barn, playing with the baby sheep. She ached every moment for years. But she took care of herself and her land.

And the whole time, Mac had been gone. Living his own life, while ignoring the most important thing – his child. His flesh and blood.

Cora shook her hand. She finally felt the throbbing in her thumb from slamming it in the drawer, and the pain came as a kind of relief.

A knock at the front door made her jump. Mac looked in at her.

Instead of moving, she stared at him through the glass.

Was it remotely possible he didn't know? That was really the only thing that could explain his absence, right? Had Trixie never told him? He must have heard she'd had a child – even though he wasn't in town, gossip still travelled. He would have wondered if it was his, right? Hadn't he asked her? There was no way Mac could look at Olivia, could see those eyes, and the way they were shaped, wide and expressive, and not recognize himself. No way in hell.

Well, damn. Cora hadn't seen it herself until today. Until she'd seen Olivia ride.

Mac knocked again, his smile still in place.

Slowly, she got up to let him in. Without preamble, she said, "I'll have you start in the back kennel. The German Shepherd's had the trots, and it's pretty bad."

He frowned. "Is the dog okay?"

Sometimes Cora forgot he was a vet. "Cindi says yeah. The kennel just needs cleaning."

He looked surprised but was amenable. "Okay. Whatever you want, I'll do it."

She took dull pleasure in his words before showing Mac where the supplies were and pointing him to the run. "Once you're done with that, there are about a million dishes that need to be washed. The sanitizer's down again, so we have to do it by hand."

"Of course." He smiled. Cora's thumb throbbed.

Cora kept him busy for two hours, until sweat dripped from his nose as he stood rinsing at the hot sink. He was so cheerful about it that her determination swayed. "Anything else you need help with?" he asked.

Cora shrugged.

"You know Clementine has a mild case of kennel cough, right?"

Shaking her head, Cora said, "The other day Cindi said a couple had it, but she didn't say anything today."

"You should take your dog home."

Cora shook her head, hard. "Not my dog."

Mac's tone was light. "She's your dog. She needs you. And there are a couple of kittens I want to get a closer look at." He put away the last bowl and threw the drying towel into the laundry bin. She followed him to the cage. She'd only glanced into it earlier, and the three tiny cats had appeared peacefully asleep but now she could see that they were worse than they'd been the other day. Their eyes were red and runny, and two were wheezing.

"Rhinotracheitis. And this one has stopped drinking." Mac pinched the tiny tabby's neck softly. "Probably pneumonia by now. If we get some fluid in them, they'll be okay, although they'll always be carriers. If I don't, they die. Most likely tonight."

Cora was horrified. "Cindi said the other day they'd gotten the medicine they needed."

"She was wrong."

"You honestly think they didn't treat them?"

"I don't care what she told you, and maybe they did treat them. But I'm doing this."

"I can't let you," she said. "You're not authorized."

Mac ignored her, rummaging in the cupboards and then in the drawer next to the sink. "You think I give a shit?"

"You can't, Mac."

"Why? Someone will sue? They're suffering. I'll give them subcu-taneous fluids – here, this is what I need." He pulled a box down to the counter with a thump. "Then they'll just need to sleep and eat some more, and they'll be fine. Hopefully." He pulled out another box.

"Mac."

He held the kitten against his chest with one hand and with the other prepared the needle. "Leave, Cora." His voice was firm. Some-how the power balance had shifted. He would allow her to boss him around and make him clean, but now Mac the veterinarian was in charge. "They're not going to like this, but you don't have to watch. I'll meet you in the front."

She paused in the doorway, looking back at him. The cat was so small in his large hands, barely moving.

"I mean it, Cora. Go. *Now.*"

She went.

CHAPTER THIRTY-SIX

Know the function and life of your yarn. A sturdy three-ply is good for an Aran, but not as good for a lace shawl. Take time to learn the yarn's personality and you'll be rewarded, richly. —E.C.

When Mac came out with his hands still red from scrubbing, Cora sat in the reception area, her head down. When he took her hands in his, she let him.

"I'm sorry,' she said. "I never meant for you to have to – that wasn't why I . . . Will they live?"

"Probably. I hope so. It's no one's fault, you know," he said, tucking a red lock of hair behind her ear. God, she was sexy, even now, covered in sweat from cleaning, wearing the same overalls that she'd worn riding. She smelled of horse and antiseptic and something sweet, just under the surface . . . Honey, that was it. She smelled like honey.

"It's just something that happens in a kennel. You can't save all of them. Cora," he said, putting his other hand on her knee lightly, not wanting to startle her. "What are you punishing me for? Is it for last night?"

Making a noise that was almost a whimper, Cora bit her bottom lip. Then she stood abruptly, pulling her hand out of his. Her voice was cool. "Don't be ridiculous."

"Is this still about Logan?" Jesus, he had whiplash. How could they move forward if she kept going backward like this? He'd thought – naively, perhaps – that they were past this part, that he'd apologized enough, but hell, he'd keep saying he was sorry as long as it took. He *would* always be sorry, so that part was easy enough.

"I wish," she said. "Look, this was a stupid idea. Thanks for helping me tonight. It was kind of you." She leaned on the counter, her hand on top of a pile of blue file folders, and for a moment Mac had the idea that if she hadn't been holding herself up, she would have swayed, a thought that made him want to gather Cora to him, to hold her, to be strong for her.

On second thought, she looked as if she wanted to punch him, not be held by him.

"What about our date?" he asked.

She laughed but there was no humor in her voice. "It was a stupid bet."

"Most bets are."

"Yeah, well, I agree. That's what gambling gets you." Her tone was bitter.

If she wouldn't tell him what this was about, how was he supposed to fix it? Mac felt a knot of solid frustration in the middle of his stomach. "Yeah, I have as much experience with gamblers as you do. More. Is that what this is about? Logan losing your money?"

"No matter what, your family held on to the land." Cora straightened the files under her fingers for the fourth time and didn't raise her eyes to his.

"And Logan blew it all. Including your savings. And that makes you furious."

Cora took a deep breath and paced across the small room. She stood at the glass door and for a moment they were both quiet as an older couple walked past the windows. The old man held his wife's elbow and she smiled at something he said. How long, Mac wondered, had they been walking together like that?

She turned to him, and in the way she stood, he could see her strength. She'd been standing alone for so long. How could he hope that she would ever accept help?

"That's just it, Mac. I'm not furious. I'm not even upset. I came to terms long ago with the fact that I either keep my little farm running or I don't. If I fail, I have no one to blame but myself. I can't fail. So I won't. You come to town, you just roar in, guns blazing, aiming at everything I love, everything your family holds dear. And that's not even the worst thing, not even *close* –"

"What?" Mac was beyond confused. It was like she was speaking a different language, one he knew only a few useless words of. "Tell me what you mean."

"Nothing." Pressing her fingers to the back of her neck. "Just...nothing." She twisted the key in the deadbolt. "Let's just close up. Thanks for helping."

"What about Windward?"

"What about it?" Cora still didn't meet his eyes, even though he desperately wanted her to.

"The rest of our date? Dinner and games night?"

"I'm still going to Windward. The kids are waiting for me. But you're no longer invited. I don't know what I was thinking." She shook a set of keys in her fingers as if she was trying to determine the right one by its sound. "It's a place where kids who've been *abandoned* live. It's their last chance, just like this place is Clementine's last chance. If she or the kittens don't get adopted, they die. Can you possibly understand that?"

He opened his hands toward her. She was saying something he just wasn't getting – he could feel it. "Maybe not. But I know you get that better than anyone else, and I want to help. I want to learn. If you want to take me to Windward and assign me the shitty tasks, I'll do those there too. I'll wash their plates or clean the toilets, or . . . I don't know what I'd do in a place like that because besides picking you up when we were in high school before you moved to Eliza's, I've never been inside a group home. You always waited for us outside."

She glared up at the ceiling. He wasn't getting through to her – he knew he wasn't.

"But I'm willing to try anything to make you see that I'm not an asshole, which is what you obviously think of me."

"I waited outside because I didn't want either of you coming in."

Mac made his voice soft. "Was it that bad inside? I never knew."

"It wasn't bad at all. It was all the home I had. I protected it." She did that head-tilt thing again, and Mac stood straighter under her gaze.

Finally, as if to herself, she said, "Is it possible you don't know?"

"Know *what*?" Jesus, he was desperate. He *had* to figure this out.

"Never mind." She shook her head. "If you honestly don't, then I have no idea how to tell you."

"God, Cora. Why are you being like this?" His patience, held thinly in check, snapped. "I don't get it. This cryptic push-pull bullshit is making me dizzy. If it's because you don't want to be around me, tell me. If it's about the land, then let me know. Give me *something* to work with."

"I don't want you around the kids."

Mac took a step backward, his boot striking the window seat. The smell of bleach was suddenly harsh in his nose. "Are you serious?"

"Completely. Kids need stability. They need people they can count on."

"What about you? You don't count on anyone. You used to. But not anymore, is that right?"

She went on as if he hadn't spoken. "And you, Mac, are not that kind of person. You are, in fact, the opposite of reliable as you've proven repeatedly, and if you don't know that already then you're a bigger idiot than I thought.'

As he stood, stupefied, she pushed past him and held open the door for him. She waited until he'd passed through, and then locked it behind them. Outside, the last of the evening's light was departing in a burst of yellow and red radiance over the water. A trio of screaming little girls trailed by their tired-looking father raced down the sidewalk toward the gazebo.

And without another word to ease what she'd just said to him, Cora strode away, her back stiff as she held her head high. Mac ached to run to her, to *make* her tell him the truth, to explain what was underneath her words, but he knew that would be the worst thing he could do.

He had to let her go.

Jesus Christ. Sometimes it felt like that was all he'd ever been good at.

CHAPTER THIRTY-SEVEN

The perfect cup of tea seems as much of a mystery as knitting lace, but re-
ally, they're very simple. Tea is just hot water, poured over leaves. Lace is just
knits and purls, with pauses in between. – E.C.

Four days later, Mac had the dog. Clementine. He wasn't sure yet exactly *what* he was going to do with her, since he hadn't been able to talk to Cora yet, but keeping the dog made him feel like he was at least doing something. He saw Cora's face when she looked at the dog – the two of them were made for each other. She cared for it. Clementine adored her. She could rescue something for no other reason but to love it. Mac knew he was right about this, about them needing each other. At the shelter, Cindi hadn't even blinked when he'd asked to borrow Clementine again, and told him he could finish the paperwork another time. Then she'd offered him a job, saying their sometimes-vet had extended his vacation again. He'd laughed, thinking she was joking, then when she hadn't smiled, he'd told her thanks, he had a job. She said to keep Clementine and to rethink his answer.

Small town life. Sheesh.

Cora hadn't returned even one of Mac's five phone calls. She hadn't responded to any of his texts. He'd gone and knocked on her door, but when he'd seen the parlor curtain twitch, pride had driven him away without knocking twice.

Maybe it was because they'd had sex? It had to be that.

But it had been incredible sex. Wild, hot, passionate. Possibly the best sex he'd ever had. No, scratch that. Completely, *indubitably*, the best sex he'd ever had, bar none.

The sex he'd been waiting for his whole life.

Royal had drafted up the official offer, and later today Mac would take it to his mother and Valentine. If he could just talk them into it, he'd be that much closer to getting it done. If the sisters could leave the land their father left to them, then Cora would have to consider going along with them. Without her land, the deal was moot anyway. Royal didn't want three parcels with a hole out of the middle.

Letting Clementine bound over a low dune ahead of him, he rubbed his eyes.

Cora had called him an idiot. And she was right. He'd fallen for her the first moment he saw her, and he'd never recovered. Maybe, he now realized, that was why he had dated women that were so diametrically opposed to Cora. Maybe that was why he'd never fallen in love, not truly. The women he'd fallen in like with had never been a threat to his comfortable bachelor existence. Somehow, he'd kind of thought he might be above all that. He didn't need it. While his friends – Royal excluded – fell in love and got married and had children, he'd watched, half amused, half confused. Why couldn't he have that with any one of his girlfriends who gave him so much and demanded so little? For God's sake, his last girlfriend Samantha hadn't even gotten mad at him when he didn't return her text messages for days. She *should* have been angry. He'd been callous. Never concerned enough. He'd felt numbed to his girlfriends, somehow. He'd thought he just didn't get it.

But he'd never felt numbed when it came to Cora.

And here he was, about to pull off another stupid stunt.

Mac stood on the dirt road in front of her house while Clementine dug at something underneath the oleander. Part of him wanted desperately to march the dog up her driveway, to bang on her door. And then what? Doorbell ditch, leaving the dog tied to the porch rail?

Clementine snuffled and scratched at the dirt, obviously interested in something that was alive and hiding from her. Mac said, "Leave it, girl."

The trouble was, he was having a hard time picturing Cora anywhere else. Since being in her room, seeing her in the home that she'd created around herself, he understood. She'd built herself the ultimate shell, the safe haven she'd always wanted. The one she'd thought Logan would give her. When he'd watched her move through the rooms, it was as if the house was breathing around her. He'd never seen anything like it. Mac himself was still treating his grandfather's house as a hotel room. He hadn't even fully unpacked his suitcase. It was propped up on the chair outside the bathroom. He parked his boots under it at night, and he hadn't hung a single shirt, preferring to lay them back on top of the suitcase after they came out of the dryer.

If he was honest, he'd never even fully moved into his condo. He'd meant to put up framed art at some point, but the walls were still blank and white. His pantry didn't even have the staples for pancakes, something a woman had once told him in obvious shock. "*Everyone* has the makings for pancakes. But you don't even have the makings for rice," she'd said as she put her earrings back in. He remembered those earrings, oblong, wrapped with silver thread, better than he remembered the woman's face.

Not like Cora. He knelt to scratch Clementine and pictured Cora. He could see her eyes, the way they crinkled at the edges when she smiled. They were so light blue they reminded him of the edge of the sky at dawn, when the blue wasn't quite sure of itself yet.

Fuck it. He couldn't just stand out here, considering the lines of her house, the peak of her roof, without seeing her body in his mind's eye. The way her house fit against the stand of eucalyptus behind it echoed the way her body had fit his.

So what if she hadn't answered his phone calls? Maybe her cell phone was dead. That would explain why she hadn't picked up, right?

Clementine tromped ahead of him, appearing glad they were moving toward the house. Could the dog sense her there? Smell her? Barreling up the steps of her house, Clementine skidded across the porch, stopping just short of the door. She gave one sharp bark, as if announcing herself.

"Clementine!" Mac bounded up the stairs. "We knock. We don't sit in the car and honk, dog." He took a deep breath to steady himself. Even now he wasn't sure what he actually wanted to say to her.

What if he just put one hand behind her neck and pulled her to him? If he kissed her, what would she do? Would she melt against him? Would she press those perfect breasts – which would probably be encased in overalls, sexier than they should be on anyone – against him?

No, she'd tell him what for, probably. She'd never, ever had any trouble telling him exactly where she stood on an issue, which was why the other day was so confusing to him. There was something big – huge – that she was hiding.

Kissing her probably wasn't the best way to go. Dammit.

He raised his hand to knock, but instead, the door swung inward. "I saw you come up the driveway."

It was Olivia, the girl from the beach. She looked frankly curious as she pushed open the screen. "I bet she doesn't know you're coming, huh?"

"Nope."

"Uh-oh. I'll go get her."

"No need," said Cora from behind her. "I'm right here."

She was, in fact, *not* wearing overalls – she wore a green dress decorated with small yellow flowers. She held a teacup delicately balanced on a saucer. Her feet were bare, and her cheeks were pink. There wasn't anything or anyone prettier in the whole world. Mac knew this for an absolute damn fact.

"I came to give you a dog," he said, cursing the slight hesitation in his speech. "But it looks like it's not a good time. I'll come back."

"It won't be a good time then, either." Her voice was cool.

"Oh, damn. I'm fuckin' outta here," said Olivia. "Thanks for the tea thing."

Cora held out her hand and Olivia slipped past Mac and down the front steps. "Don't go. Not without the yarn you made, at least."

"I'll come back for it. You two have fun," said Olivia, picking up a bike Mac hadn't noticed lying on the front lawn. She rode away with a crunch of gravel, Clementine following her to the fence line before doubling back.

Cora carefully placed the teacup on the small metal table that stood next to the porch swing.

"Did I interrupt a tea party?"

"Yes."

"Oh." He'd been kidding.

Sighing, Cora crossed her arms and sank into the swing. It creaked as she rocked her legs. She didn't invite him to join her. Clementine didn't wait to be asked – she jumped up and leaned against Cora.

A half-smile crossed her face as she looked down at the dog. Slowly, she said, "Eliza Carpenter used to have tea parties with me."

He remembered that, now that she said it. Tea and knitting. He'd teased Cora back then about it. "Right," he said. "We teased you for being such a grandma."

"I loved it."

"I know. So what, you're trying to be Olivia's Eliza?"

The sadness in her eyes made him wish he could take back the words. When would he get this right?

"I guess. Yeah."

"You could pull that off."

Her mouth twisted, and Mac wanted nothing more than to sit next to her and take her hand. But he steeled himself to stand still. And wait.

"I thought so," said Cora. "But it's not like it was then. I swear, Cypress Hollow when we were growing up was like some throwback to Mayberry. Sure, kids were probably having sex in the backs of cars, but I couldn't think about anything but knitting. And riding horses with you two. I was naive, young. Heck, I loved Eliza's tea set so much that she gave it to me when I married Logan." She touched the gold rim of the cup. "She made me feel normal. Like everything was going to be all right. And I needed that so much back then . . ."

She needed it now. Mac could see that, and he ached, unable to help. "It's not like that with Olivia?"

Cora laughed. "No. It's not."

"But you said she made yarn?"

Inclining her head, she said, "True. We did spin a little. She mocked it like crazy and swore every time it hit the floor. And man, I thought I could swear but a drunk Irish bartender couldn't keep up with that girl's mouth."

"Spinning? That's Mayberry, right?"

"She didn't like the tea, and she wouldn't finish her scone, citing too many carbs. She told me I should keep my glycemic index lower by eating more protein with my sugar."

"So . . . she's concerned about you?"

Cora shook her head. "They were Trixie's words, coming out of her mouth. Then she said –" She broke off and jammed her fingers into her hair.

"What?"

"Why are you here again? I was going to ignore you till you left."

"You can't. You won't," he said, hoping against hope he was right. "What were you going to say? About Olivia?"

Cora seemed to be making a decision. She sighed, deeply. Then she said, "She asked if we were . . . fucking."

The word was startling. And at the same time, it was decidedly sexy. Goddamn, she was so hot. He blinked to try to clear his mind of the image of Cora – naked and arching, reaching for him – that raced through it. "She did?"

Cora frowned. "How did she even know to ask that? She's not even quite sixteen."

"You ever seen any of those CW TV shows? *Vampire Gossip Girls*, whatever. She's not six. They know this stuff now. They have computers in their pockets, porn on demand in grammar school. Like you said, this isn't Mayberry. Nowhere is. Not anymore."

"She was around us for what, an hour? Is it that obvious?" Cora rubbed Clementine's forehead with her fingers and the swing creaked harder.

"I don't know. Maybe." If he'd given off one hundredth of what he felt, yeah, it would be obvious from the moon.

"Why can't you see the truth, then?" she asked.

His heart sped up. Whatever it was, they could fix it. Together. "What truth?"

To his surprise, tears filled her eyes.

"Cora –"

"I'm not *crying* – oh, crap. It's only because I'm so *mad* at you." Cora stood abruptly, the back of the swing hitting the wall, and spun around. Then with one motion, she threw her teacup at the end of the porch where it smashed into a porcelain cloud.

"Oh!" Her hands flew to her mouth. Now they were real tears. "Jesus!"

"What is going *on*?"

She crumpled to her knees and started picking up the biggest pieces. Seemingly to herself, she said, "I've never thrown anything. In my life. And look, this is why. You throw something, you just have to clean it up. Oh, *Eliza.*" Her chin dropped toward her chest, and her eyes screwed shut. Despair radiated from her, from the slope of her shoulders to the way her hands cradled the shards as tears dripped down her cheeks.

"Let me help."

She met his eyes then. "I can't believe I broke this. Eliza gave me this, entrusted me with the set, her favorite set – and then I . . . Oh, I knew I shouldn't use it – I should have kept saving it for best –"

"Would Eliza have thrown the teacup?"

It was the right question. She hiccupped as her eyes searched his face. "Yes. She believed in using things she loved. Only she might have thrown it at your head. Once, she threw a whole cooked ham at Joshua because he teased her about making yet another garter stitch sweater."

"You're going to have to talk to me." Mac took the pieces of porcelain from her and laid them carefully on the small table next to the swing, then he sat. "Sit next to me and Clementine. Come on."

She did, and then groaned, leaning forward, her elbows on her knees, her face hidden in her hands. A low-flying airplane droned over the breakers, a sleepy afternoon sound.

Disentangling her left hand, he threaded his fingers with hers. "Is it about the sale? I was going to talk to Mom and Valentine some more about it later . . ."

"No," she said, pulling her hand away sharply. "Of course it's not about that."

"Then what is it, Cora?"

She closed her eyes and opened them slowly, keeping her gaze focused far out on the dunes. "About her."

He gave it his best guess. "Aunt Valentine?"

"Olivia."

He couldn't have been more surprised. "What about her?"

"She's your *daughter*, Mac."

"No." Nothing Cora could have said would have shocked him more. "No, she's not."

"I know you think that, but . . ."

"She's not. Trust me." Mac head felt fuzzy.

"No, *you* trust me. You couldn't see her yesterday, racing next to you. No one moves like you two. You were exactly the same up there. You matched. She holds her body, even tilts her head the same way you do. I know you and Trixie were broken up by the time she got pregnant, and she told people in town that it was some circuit rider's baby. Everyone believed her. Because they knew if the baby was yours, you'd have taken care of her, of them, and you never came back, so I think people forgot to wonder after a while. But in that moment when you were racing toward Royal and me, your faces were almost identical in their expression and focus."

"You're saying you think she's . . . my *daughter*?"

"Yes." Cora lifted a hand and touched the back of his wrist so lightly it felt like a hummingbird landing.

He stood. Speed was what he needed. No time to waste. "I have to go. I mean, I have to do something . . ."

"That's fine. I have to go to the bank, anyway." Cora stood, also, coming up to his shoulder. "But she's yours, Mac. You can still find her. *You can still make it up to her.*"

Mac heard the longing in her voice, the echo of her own grief that no one had found *her*.

He had. Mac had found Cora, even if she'd never been able to believe it.

But he had to take care of this first. "I'll be back." He leaned forward and pressed a kiss to her mouth. She gasped, but didn't pull away. For one brief, electric second, they were together – he felt it. When he broke the contact, she swayed, her eyes closed.

"Dammit," she whispered. "That's not fair. Oh! What about your dog?"

Mac put everything he had into the words. "Will you please keep her?"

"And that's *really* unfair." But Cora's hand fell to the top of Clementine's head. "Shit."

"I'll be back," he said again. It was a promise.

CHAPTER THIRTY-EIGHT

You already know what to do. The answer is closer than you think. — E.C.

Cora tied Clementine up in front of the bank with no idea how the little dog would do. It was possible she had separation anxiety and would bark the whole time. Or she might, God forbid, bite some passing dog, or worse, person.

And whose fault would that be? Mac's. Fairly, squarely his. She crouched and pulled on Clementine's orange ears. "Be good. Can you do that?" A tongue swipe on the cheek was her answer. "Good enough for me."

In line inside, Cora held her envelope tightly against her chest. She should be thinking about her balance. She should be making plans. That's what she was good at. She *loved* making plans, and if there were ever time for a planned Hail Mary pass, it might be now. But instead of her fingers itching for a pencil to scratch out a new *What If* list, they drifted up to her lips, the lips that Mac had just kissed.

Jesus. She rolled her eyes at herself. Mac had a daughter with the one woman in town Cora didn't get along with. He'd somehow saddled her with a dog – oh! Cora gasped, startling Zonker, the town pharmacist who stood in front of her wearing his perennial Grateful Dead tie-dyed T-shirt. "I'm okay," she said, waving her hands.

"Cool," said Zonker.

Was it actually possible that she had let Mac leave her with a female to take care of?

Was that just what he *did*? Cora felt sick.

But it was time to think of herself, of her little farm. Not time to think about McGibboney Cross Wildwood. So she whistled quietly along with the Muzak version of 'Paperback Writer' playing on the speakers overhead. The Bank of Cypress Hollow was small and never had more than two tellers on shift. Today it was just one. Mary Platte was known for gossiping with every customer she came into contact with. It had always made Cora nervous, and she needed absolutely no extra nerves of any kind. And of all people, Valentine and Louisa were ahead of her by four customers. That means that Mary would get to gossip with *both* sisters. Cora was in for a long wait. Valentine caught sight of her and beamed, leaning around Zonker.

"Sugar! Hi!"

Cora waved. Valentine blew her a kiss and Louisa smiled thinly.

Fiddling with the slim envelope, Cora shuffled forward slowly with the line as Valentine and Louisa stormed Mary's window. She kept her eyes on the windows above the side desks. Nothing but blue out there today, not a cloud in the sky, not a whisper of fog. It was as clear out there as she was stormy inside.

Ahead of her Valentine tittered at something Mary said. Louisa's back was ramrod stiff. What were they doing? Valentine had been selling pies pretty steadily, both through Cora's booth and on a side table at the church. But what if she needed money? What if she was borrowing from Louisa? It was something that she hadn't thought of – that Valentine might be as hard up as she herself was.

A heavy ball of sadness sunk inside her stomach. It was one thing if Cora herself was poor. It was worse, somehow, if Valentine was so broke she was borrowing from her sister. How bad off was she? Did Valentine really *need* to sell her land? By refusing to talk about it with Mac, was Cora hurting Valentine?

A peal of laughter rang, and Mary waggled her fingers at Valentine and Louisa, her signature goodbye. The sisters passed Cora, Valentine pressing a kiss to her cheek. "Darling, pop over tomorrow. Apple pies coming out my ears."

Cora nodded. "All right," she managed.

Louisa walked past without saying a word.

"Is she okay?" Cora asked. "She usually takes the time to diss me at least a little bit."

"Oh, her," Valentine flapped her hand. "She's fine. A bit angry, maybe, but that would be at me, not you. Sugar, we need to talk about that thing Mac was asking us about."

"I know. We . . . are you . . ." Cora didn't know how to ask, and Mrs. Luby was leaning forward behind her, trying to listen in. Good thing she was so hard of hearing. "Are you okay? You know . . ." She cut her eyes to Mary and back and then glanced at the envelope Valentine was holding.

"Oh, this? Honey, I'm fine. Don't you worry. I'll see you tomorrow?"

She and her sister left. The line moved faster then, and within minutes, Cora was presenting her few checks to Mary.

"Nine dollars and forty cents," said Mary, her fingers flying over the ten-key calculator. "Four dollars thirty-two, and twelve seventy-one. Oh, you folded this one up a coupla times, huh?" She uncrinkled the check from Abigail for three pots of jam that Cora had carried in her back pocket for a day or two. "Twenty-one even."

Did Mary have to read the amounts out loud? Cora was dying. Mrs. Luby was still too close. Wasn't she supposed to stand behind that white line? Just because she used a walker didn't mean she got special eavesdropping privileges.

While Mary flipped through the checks, hitting them with stamps, Cora wondered about Mac.

He hadn't known. That was obvious. For a second on the porch, she'd felt a wave of sympathy for him. It hurt to learn the truth too late to do anything about it. Was he at Trixie's now, confronting her? Was he somewhere panicking? Freaking out?

For a moment, Cora felt a hot, ugly twinge – Mac had a daughter. If she'd managed to keep her own baby, if her body had done what it was supposed to do instead of rejecting the life inside her, what would her daughter have been like? Would she have had Logan's ears? Would she be drawn to gambling, or was that a male familial trait? Would she have been a knitter? Or would she reject what Cora loved in order to make a point? Would she refuse to garden in favor of learning computer programming? Would she wear clothes like Olivia's or would she be a girly girl and beg Cora to buy her fingernail polish and lip gloss?

The revelation of his daughter's existence couldn't fail to change Mac.

Would it make him stay? Jesus, what if it did?

"Any more, hon?"

Cora wished. "That's all of them."

"Okay." Mary peered over the top of her glasses at the screen. "That brings you almost out of the hole, sugar. Now you're just negative twenty-two dollars and thirteen cents."

"What?" Cora's hands jerked involuntarily.

"Didn't you know you'd bounced a couple –" Mary squinted at the screen again "– no, four checks?"

"No!"

"Don't you get the email notifications? Or the postcards?"

"No." Cora hadn't ever set all the email stuff up, and she usually threw her bills into a pile and paid them all once a month, the same time she balanced her checkbook – that was what she'd always done. It was her system, and it worked for her. Until now.

"Oh," said Mary, sounding disappointed.

Cora leaned on the counter and glanced over her shoulder. Mrs. Luby looked like she was practically taking notes. Turning back, she whispered, "Doesn't it pull against my savings account?"

"Your savings?"

"I have a savings account, too. I don't think it has too much in it, but there's probably something. Can you check?"

"Sure, hon." Mary punched at the keyboard, her fingers striking with force. "Nope. There's no savings account."

Cora dug her fingernails into the wood. "But I have one."

"If an account stays at a zero balance for more than six months, it's automatically closed."

"You closed my account without *telling* me?"

"You should have gotten an email about that, too."

Cora sighed. "I can't believe – this is impossible. I don't do this kind of thing. Ever."

"Only by twenty-two thirteen. Looks like, yeah, right here, it dipped under when your fall property taxes got withdrawn automatically."

"Automatically? Oh, *shit*." She *had* set that up, last year, when the state had offered a five percent rebate for automatic bank withdrawals. Saving money was good. But not having it? That was crappy. And there was still the second half of the year's property taxes, which would be due after the new year. "Well, it's not like I would have had it anyway, right? That one slipped by me." It was painful to admit. "Guess it's better that it's paid."

Mary glanced over her shoulder and lowered her voice. "I love those rosemary candles of yours. I could buy twenty-three dollars' worth in advance. If you want me to."

Charity. *Awesome.*

No, Cora would sell her clothes, her furniture, hell, she'd sell her own bed before she'd take charity. "No one needs twenty-three dollars' worth of candles. Stop by the booth tomorrow and I'll give you a couple, okay?" Charity, take *that.* "I'll bring cash in to settle up." Surely the change jar at home held at least that much. "You have a good day, Mary."

"Oh, you too, hon." Mary waggled her fingers at Cora. "This too shall pass, I promise. I've seen lots worse, I can tell you that."

Mrs. Luby looked like she'd won the eavesdropping lottery. Cora only just prevented herself from hissing like a furious cat as she pushed open the door of the bank.

Clementine was being perfect, still tied to the light pole, her wide orange head perched on top of her front two crossed paws. She jumped to her feet when she spotted Cora, her wiry tail beating the metal post rhythmically. Oh, she was a sweet dog, wasn't she? Cora could get used to being welcomed so enthusiastically.

"No, no, don't look at me like that," pleaded Cora. "I can't even afford to feed you, dog-whose-name-is-obviously-not-Salt-anymore. I can't keep you. There's no *reason* to keep you."

Clementine didn't care what Cora said. She leaned with abandon on Cora's shins, panting in happiness.

Cora was failing. Her business was failing. "And crap. I have a dog."

She straightened, holding the leash lightly between her fingers.

No, it was possible that she'd failed. Already.

Completely.

CHAPTER THIRTY-NINE

The person who mocks you for knitting deserves all the acrylic they get. –
E.C.

The sign on the door of the *Independent* read 'Closed', but Mac
didn't pay it any heed. Trixie's car was parked in front – she
had to be in there, and goddamn it, this couldn't wait.

"Trixie?" he roared.

From deep inside a cluster of empty offices, he heard her call,
"Who is it?"

"It's Mac. I need to talk to you *now*."

"Mac!" Trixie came around the corner, straightening her hair
with her fingers. Passing a small wall mirror, she took a second to
check herself. She pressed her lips together as if she'd just applied
lipstick. "Fancy you both being here."

"Both?"

Royal hurried around the same corner Trixie just had. He used
the same mirror to adjust his hair.

"Really?" said Mac. "At work?"

"Well, it's practically home to me," said Trixie, no trace of apology in her voice. "What's up?"

"Who is Olivia's father?"

Trixie stumbled on her way to kiss his cheek and aborted the move at the last minute. "Shit," she said.

"I can't believe you never told me," said Mac. He sat in a swivel chair that sunk under his weight, and pushed the one next to it for her to sit in.

"I couldn't." She sat, carefully crossing her legs at the knee.

"You told me it was over. Did he ever know?"

Royal leaned over the low cubicle wall. "You're Olivia's *father*?"

Mac and Trixie both stared at him.

"No," said Mac.

"Of course not," said Trixie. "You think I'd let Mac get away with that? No way in hell."

"I'm confused," said Royal. "But I'm thinking this sounds like none of my damn business, so I'm gonna go to the Rite Spot and see if I can make some money on pool. Find me there afterward, buddy?" He tapped Mac on the shoulder, and then surprised Mac by kissing Trixie on the lips. "Call me later."

"You're later," she said with a smile.

Royal left, the 'Closed' sign flapping against the door behind him.

"But you let him get away with no child support." It wasn't a question.

She straightened a pile of papers on the desk. "Logan was always different from you."

"Did he ever know?" repeated Mac.

"He suspected," said Trixie. "He asked me point blank once if she was his." A pause. "Or if she was yours."

"You and I never even slept together."

"He didn't know that. He just assumed like everyone else did. And I told him no, she wasn't either of yours. I thought for a long time he believed me."

"How long were you together?"

"Not long." Trixie rubbed her eyes. "A few weeks, just before Cora found out she was pregnant. I thought for a little while I was just trying to get back at you for leaving, but then I realized that Logan was the right one for me, that he always had been. I fell in stupid, stupid love. I'd probably been halfway there a long time." Her voice cracked and she coughed to clear it. "I broke it off as soon as he said she was pregnant, that they were getting married. I think I was the only one in town who didn't come to the wedding, but I couldn't watch that, especially because by then I knew *I* was pregnant, too. God, he was stupid about some things. But then once, at Tillie's, I saw him looking at Olivia. You know how when we played poker, we teased you about that tell where you tilt your head and pull on your earlobe? You remember Logan's tell?"

"Where he blinks twice and then looks to the right?" It had allowed Mac to win more teenaged hands of penny poker than he could remember. He remembered Cora and Trixie had played with them, too.

"He caught me staring at him as he looked at her, that weird look on his face. Then he blinked twice and looked out the window. The next week a bike with a red bow showed up on the porch with her name on it. She broke her wrist falling off it. We were uninsured. It took me three years to pay off the emergency room bill."

"Goddamn him." Mac had to consciously uncurl his fingers. "How could you keep it up? Keep it going?"

She shrugged, and for the first time Mac saw the person underneath her perfectly made-up eyes and freshened lipstick. The girl he'd known was still there, the girl who had argued with her father about staying out late, the girl he'd had rock-skipping competitions with late into the nights when everyone in town thought they were doing something else.

He'd just never suspected that she was getting her rocks off with other guys. Other guys like his cousin. Mac had been too hung up on Cora to even notice.

But then again, Trixie had always been tough. Strong. A fighter. She went for what she wanted. He'd admired that about her, and still did.

She laced her fingers together. "Do you think Cora knows? The only thing I could give her out of this whole stupid mess was the gift of keeping it a secret. We just messed up, Logan and I, him by screwing me, and me by falling in love with a man who could never be mine. I never wanted her to know, and then when I heard about her miscarriage after they got married, I knew I'd been right to keep it a secret from everyone. I could never, *ever* have done that to her."

"She thinks I'm the father," said Mac.

Closing her eyes, she said, "Oh, crap."

Mac told the truth. "I have no idea what to do now."

He waited for her to say something, anything, and when she didn't, he realized that she was waiting for him. To what? To say he understood? He didn't. He couldn't even come close to understanding the way her brain must have been working for so many years.

"She'll find out," he said.

"You can't tell her," said Trixie. "Don't leave it to Logan to screw up, again. Please."

"But he *did* screw up. That's the shitty part of this. Yet another of Logan's fuck-ups. I covered for him in school when he hadn't studied, letting him copy off my exams. I even covered some of his debts a couple of times. Cora doesn't know that. He'd call, looking for money and I'd wire it to him. That was to help Cora. If he'd been on his own, I never would have done it. Yeah, I loved him. But he was a jackass way too many times in his life."

"Well, hell," said Trixie lightly. "I should have called you asking for money."

He leaned back in his chair. "You know I would have given it to you. You wouldn't have had to give me a reason. I can't believe I never suspected, this long . . . Goddamn it, I *should* have."

She smiled thinly. "I was fine, though. I've always been fine."

"Does anyone else know?"

"I don't know how they don't. She looks so much like him. But no one's ever said a word. Not to me, anyway."

Mac could see it now, how both Olivia and Logan were short, thin and compact, yet put together with that wiry strength that seemed to emanate from just under their skin. That long nose. That stubborn way of scowling.

"You did everything all by yourself."

Trixie shrugged. "Whatever. You do what you have to do." She paused. "It wasn't fair that I was pregnant at the same time. By the same man. And my child made it, while hers didn't. I warned Logan if she found out, I'd kill him. It wasn't *fair*. It wasn't right. I hated him for that." Trixie's voice broke on the last word, and her eyes filled with tears. "Oh, Mac, what are we going to do?"

Mac reached forward and took her hand. His fury melted into something different, something softer with a ragged edge of pity. Trixie's hand was cold, her fingers long. Holding her hand felt nothing like holding Cora's warm, soft one. "I don't know, Trix. But I think Pandora might be lifting the lid on this box at some point. All those demons are fixing to get loose. We have to tell her."

She clutched his hand, her grip almost painful. "I can't. I've spent almost sixteen years not telling her. It would destroy her."

Cora? Destroyed?

"She loved him, I always knew she did. God, the first time we ever really talked, she said she was interested in him, and that was at the beginning of our senior year, before anything started for any of us. All Cora ever wanted was someone to lean on. A real home. A family of her own."

Mac pinched the bridge of his nose tightly. Then he said, "How did you know that?"

"Mac. Come on. Everyone knew that. She gave up college to stay home and take care of Logan. Could she have *been* any more Anne of Green Gables?"

"I don't even know what that means."

"Orphan finds a home? Never mind. The girl needed a place of her own. She made one. It was good for her. Good for them both. Logan's the type of guy who couldn't handle getting his own car insurance. You think he could have handled the complication of trying to balance an out-of-wedlock kid that made his wife a step-mother?"

"No," said Mac. It was true. Logan would have frayed at the seams of his western shirts, taking everyone else apart with him.

"It was the only respectful thing he ever did for her."

"After you, when they were married, did he . . . ?"

Trixie pulled her hand away from his and pushed her hair behind her ear. She folded her lips tightly, and then said, "I don't know. But I think he did. With a couple of others. But maybe I was wrong."

Mac spun on his boot, headed for the door, then turned around again. He had to *go* somewhere, *do* something, but he had no clue what. What he really wanted to do, he knew, was punch Logan so hard that he had cartoon birds spinning around his head for days. But Logan wasn't here to give him that satisfaction, was he?

The fury wrenched in his gut was hot. Pure pain.

"Trixie –" He shoved his thumbs through his belt loops and then pulled them out again.

"She can't know," Trixie said softly.

Yeah. He'd figured that out. That was the worst part of this whole fucked-up mess – where it placed Cora. Right in harm's way. Again. "Yeah." He took a deep breath. "No matter what, though, I'm going to start sending you money every month."

Trixie laughed, a peal of delighted laughter that startled him. "Honey. You're always the savior, but in this case, you don't need to be. I don't need your money. I'm just fine. I've been doing it this long. But you're sweet to even mention it."

"If things had gone . . . another way, Logan would have been giving you money. I'm his kin. It's my responsibility."

"Oh, Mac. If things had gone another way, the way they should have, you and Cora would have been together, the way you always wanted. But we can't change the past, can we?"

"No," he said impatiently. "That's not –"

She interrupted him. "It's true. We all knew it, Mac."

It was a soft hit to his solar plexus. He lost his breath.

Fine. But the only thing that mattered now was cushioning the blow for Cora. He wouldn't let Logan hurt her again. If that meant letting her think Mac was Olivia's father, well, he'd cleaned up Logan's messes before. This one would just be harder.

Okay. Exponentially harder.

CHAPTER FORTY

*Some people keep their handknits wrapped in plastic, stored in bins, safe
from moths and all other disaster. But knitting is like skin: it breathes. It's
prone to wrinkles and blemishes and tears. Scars are just proof of survival. –
E.C.*

The next day, Cora sold her ass off at the farmers market. If
she could have shilled her own blue boots, she would have,
but they were pretty beaten up. She made the money she
needed first for booth rental, then to get out of the hole, then for
the dog food she needed – Clemmy could only eat chicken and rice
for so long. She even made a hundred dollars extra, which was
astonishing given the state of her product level. It helped that she'd
raided her personal stores, selling the canned green beans she'd put
up last fall and the cashmere she'd been saving for knitting into a
heavy lap blanket someday. It was a luxury she didn't need. She had
blankets already. And the two tourists she'd sold the cashmere to,
Jeremy and Leon from Ohio, had been over-the-moon in love with

the fact that she told them the names of the goats the fiber came from.

She sold all Valentine's pies, too, which made her happy. However, when she called to tell Valentine she had money for her, Valentine had said, "You keep it, honey."

"No way. I'm bringing it over tomorrow night."

"I'll still insist you keep the cash. But yes, come over. We'll have dinner. We need to . . . talk. Can you come over?"

"Let's get together somewhere else," she'd said. She'd heard, in Val's halting tone, what she wanted them to talk about that night. Money. Selling the land. No, she couldn't have that conversation, not in the house, not on the family land. Not near the property they wanted her to give up. "What about Tillie's?"

A pause. "We should be somewhere private, honey."

"The beach?"

"It's getting cold at night." In the background, she heard Louisa squawk.

"A bonfire, then."

"Oooh," said Valentine. "We haven't done a bonfire in a long time. No, hush, Louisa, you'll be fine. Wear a coat." It sounded as if Valentine had covered the mouthpiece of the phone – Cora heard garbled whispering. Finally, Val came back on, hissing, "You can wear mine, then. Okay, sugar. We'll be there. You'll build it, right? What time?"

Now, on the beach as the sun finished setting, Cora set the last pieces of driftwood on top of her carefully built pile. It was perfect. Because if there was one thing she knew how to do, it was how to build a damn fire. It was on the second or third page of her book, in fact, and she had Eliza Carpenter to thank for it. After the knit and the purl stitch, beach bonfire building was the next task that Eliza had taught her. She had obtained the rarely granted permission for Cora to leave Windward after dark and had led her to Thousand Steps beach by the light of a real, old-fashioned oil-powered lantern, which Cora had coveted, instantly. Imagine, even if the power went out for a week – more – you'd still have a perfect light, indoors or out, banishing the dark, pushing it back by force.

That night, Eliza had showed her where to look for the right kind of driftwood – high, at the edges of the ice plant. Anything on the sand was too wet, having just come in on the last tide or two. Small pieces, the kindling, then the larger ones. "They'll spark different colors. That's the gift of the seawater. The fire will burn as if sunlight is bouncing off the surface of the ocean," said Eliza. Cora had felt almost overcome with joy, stumbling over half an old fishing float she hadn't noticed. "Then you use the newspaper you've brought with you" – Eliza pulled the paper out of her knitted bag – "and you start to ball up the pieces that you don't like. I, personally, love the obituaries because I like thinking about peoples' lives, and I like the opinion section because I never agree with any of them, and it pleases me to argue at them over breakfast. But the news? Let's burn it! Tomorrow, who will care about today's troubles? Small, tight twists, and then make some bigger, looser balls for the base. Remember, Cora, everything good needs to breathe. You, me, my favorite sheep, the lavender bush in front of my house, those two cousins who follow you everywhere, this fire."

Cora had blushed in the dark. Eliza, though, had pulled back her long gray hair with one hand and had crouched in the sand, blowing on the faint glow. "Sometimes," she said, "the wind on the beach makes this easy. Tonight, our breath will make the magic." After another long deep breath blown outward, Eliza said, "You give it a try." So Cora had knelt and had blown into the fire, laughing as it grew brighter. The glow gathered, growing large and noisy, and the fire had begun to leap, dancing the same way Cora's heart had, that night so long ago on this very same beach.

<<>>

In the wind tonight, as Cora stacked her wood, she could smell something under the salt water and seaweed – the light scent of lav-

ender Eliza had carried with her. And even with everything else –
her betrayal of Logan, Mac's own betrayal of Trixie and Olivia, Royal
with his damn land dreams, and the aching knowledge that she'd
gone beyond poor right into broke – Cora felt, for one moment,
buoyed. Loved. She closed her eyes and imagined Eliza was next to
her.

And she was. Cora knew it. Joy, even through everything else,
lifted her heart and she sat, hands folded, perfectly still as she let the
feeling fill her. The last line of orange color at the horizon was fad-
ing into the deep blue of the sky above and the sea below. Soon the
only light would come from the fire and the regular flash from the
light house a mile down the shore. Clementine ran the shoreline,
rapturous, darting into the surf to bite at the waves, then dodging
out again with small happy *woofs*.

The fire grew, and the lovely smell of charred creosote and tim-
ber filled her nose. Such a heady scent – tomorrow it would still be
in her hair and in her sweater. She'd worn her old sheep-feeding
Aran for this very purpose. Bonfire smoke was Cora's favorite per-
fume.

"You look like you're calling on the four winds or something.
Shouldn't you be stirring a cauldron?" Mac's voice came from behind
her. She'd been so focused on the fire, she hadn't heard him coming.
For one second, from the base of joy that had settled into her stomach, she let herself feel warmed as she looked at him. That same red
flannel shirt – did he have ten of them? – over a thin black tee, his
broad chest, oh, those Wranglers . . . Her Mac. He filled her eyes
just right.

Then reality slammed back into her.

"I can't believe you just called me a witch," she said and poked
the fire with a longer piece of oak she'd brought with her from the
house for this purpose. "Didn't know you'd be coming." She should
have, though. If Valentine and Louisa wanted to talk about the property, Mac would be in on the conversation. He, after all, would have

to sell his land, too, to get what he wanted. "Where's your partner in crime?"

"Royal's out with Trixie. Again." Mac dropped into a cross-legged seat next to her on the sand. "Fire looks good."

"You don't mind your boss dating your baby's mama? Don't think that's kind of confusing?"

Mac leaned back on his hands easily. "Fine by me. I think they really dig each other."

His voice was so casual – how could he be that easy with this new truth? Had he and Trixie talked?

"Besides," he continued, "this should be just family. He's the investor. This meeting is none of his business."

Meeting. Business. Cora had to keep that in the forefront of her mind – that's all this was. The fact that the last time they'd talked – fought – he'd kissed her as he left, as much as she hadn't – or had – wanted it, this was business.

Money.

"Where are the sisters?"

He gestured with his chin up the road. "A minute or two behind me."

"Ah." Cora forced her gaze away from his lips back to the fire. She was so *furious* with Mac. So angry that he'd let everyone down the way he had. She couldn't, wouldn't ever, think about those kisses. She wouldn't think of all that had happened so ill-advisedly in her bedroom. All that heat, all that passion . . . his mouth, his hands, the way she had wrapped her fingers around the muscles where his biceps joined his shoulder, the way his sweat had tasted against the tip of her tongue . . . Jesus.

"Cute dog you got there." He gestured at Clementine who was dragging a piece of driftwood across the damp sand.

"Humph." The dog had snuggled cozily against Cora last night, keeping her warm. Mac didn't need to know that, though.

Mac had abandoned Trixie. Worse, Olivia. With Cora, he'd betrayed Logan. And the ways in which he'd let Cora down didn't even come into play. She just had to keep Olivia's face in her mind. Just fatherless Olivia.

"Cora –" he started.

"No." Cora was quick to stop him. "Do we have to talk? Shouldn't we wait for them?"

He moved sideways so that he was facing her, still cross-legged, and put his hand on her thigh, heavy and warm. "This isn't about them. This is about –"

"No," she said again, standing quickly, brushing the sand off her backside, not caring that the wind carried it directly into his face. "There is no us."

He blinked and wiped off his eyelashes and nose. "But –"

"There's only you, Mac. You and your life, which isn't here, and that's the whole problem I have with it, actually."

"You want me here?" he asked in a low voice.

"No! What I want is for you to take some responsibility for what you left behind here. Even if Trixie kept it from you, you should have guessed. You should have had some kind of idea. Jesus, Mac."

He opened his mouth as if to say something, but a light bobbed behind him on the path.

"Yoohoo!" called Valentine.

Thank God, their arrival would let her avoid whatever he was trying to say until he was gone again. She waved at the women, feeling both grateful and disappointed. "There you two are," she called back, with a cheer that made her teeth ache. "I have cold roast chicken and sweet potatoes. We'll eat with our fingers."

"And wipe them on our pants," said Valentine happily. "We brought s'mores! And wine!"

As she trudged through the cold sand to meet the women, Clementine racing to greet the four tiny dachshunds, Cora thought the idea of s'mores should cheer her up more, but it didn't. That, in itself, was enough to break a heart. Good thing hers was already broken.

CHAPTER FORTY-ONE

I'll never tell you outright that knitting makes things easier. (But it does.)
– E.C.

"Tarthis is delicious," said Mac's mother grudgingly, taking a second helping of chicken. Mac liked seeing how eating with her fingers made her uncomfortable, and that she did it anyway. Maybe his mother *was* coming along.

"How did you roast this?"

"Like I normally do, with that German red garlic I grew," said Cora, taking a bite. Around chewing, she added, "And lemons and rosemary."

"Everything from your own garden!" said Aunt Valentine in delight. She raised her plastic cup of wine toward Cora, who sighed, as if something about that thought bothered her.

Louisa continued, "The chicken *is* a little tough, though. Did you cook it too quick? Maybe you should have brined it."

"Well, it was quick, all right. Scrappy little sucker. Miss Honey was brave right up to the last minute."

Mac gaped at her. "This is one of your chickens?"

She nodded and appeared to swallow hard.

"I thought you said . . ." Cora had said she'd only kill a chicken if she was flat broke.

"The Gilroy pickle gig really and truly fell through. They closed in the middle of the night, leaving only bills behind. I bet my pickles are still sitting on their bankrupt shelves." She waved a bone at him. "I'm sure you're pleased that I'm at the chicken-killing stage. The procedure was worse than I thought it would be, by the way. Do you like that too?"

She looked like she might cry, her eyes glittering in the light from the fire. God, Mac wanted to *take care* of her. It was all he wanted.

And she'd never let him. There was just one way he could help.

"I hate it," he said. "But since we're on the topic, we should deal with it. Mom and Aunt Valentine want to sell."

Valentine glanced at Cora as she pushed two tiny dogs off her lap. "I don't really *want* to, dear child. But Louisa needs the money."

"Wait, Louisa does? Not you?" said Cora.

"Mom?" said Mac. What was she talking about? Wasn't Aunt Valentine the perennially broke one?

His mother wiped her fingers carefully on a tissue she'd pulled from her Coach handbag. "It's something I wasn't comfortable talking about."

"But the life insurance from Dad. We invested it. My half's doing just fine. You said you needed money, but I thought that was just you wanting another tummy tuck or something. What happened to your half of the insurance money?"

His mother craned her neck, looking up at the stars that had blinked on overhead. "I don't have it."

"It was a lot of money, Mom."

"Don't blame her, dear," said Aunt Val. "It's a disease. We all know that."

"What are you talking about?" This was getting weirder, fast. Only one disease had ever cost his family money. And yeah, his mother used to gamble, but she'd only ever done that with his father.

Lifting her hands, his mother said, "Don't be mad. It was just a little bit for a long time. I had it under control. But last winter, when I bought the new car, I didn't have quite enough to pay cash for it. So I played a little extra up at the Indian casino. I've had trouble with the payments ever since even though one was such a *sure* shot . . ." Her voice trailed off and for a terrible moment, Mac wondered if his mother was going to cry. He had never seen tears in her eyes. His mother was too tough, too strong for that.

Jesus. Should he be angry at her? He was too upset for that right now. He was so . . . *disappointed* in her.

"I've been helping as much as I can," said Valentine apologetically. "But I try just to live on the interest of what Skully left me in that piddly old will of his. We were just lucky he hit it big right before he died, and I put it away in the coffee can. And those pies that Cora sells for me actually bring quite a bit more than you'd guess. My pin money, I call it. But I'm out of pin money. And interest."

"We'll *all* be happier if we sell," said his mother, still sounding stubborn though she kept her eyes down. "All of us. God knows Cora needs the money, and we could still find a place inland, stay together, stay close." Her voice turned surprisingly fierce. "I want to stay close."

"But . . ." Cora started, her voice slow. She clutched the long piece of wood like she would wield it as a weapon if she had to. "I'm sorry to have to ask this. But why would I *want* to be close to you anymore, Louisa? You've treated me like less-than for so long, and I've let you, because you were Logan's aunt. My family. But you want me to give up my home, my perfect home, the one that I love just so *you* can live a better life? Because you gambled yours away?"

"Darling," said Valentine, her voice soft, "you had to kill a chicken. Wouldn't this help you?"

"Sure. Sure it would," said Cora. "But so would me getting a job waitressing at Tillie's."

"Waitressing?" said Mac. She wasn't serious.

"Shirley said the job was mine if I ever wanted it. And I'd be good at it, too."

She would. He could imagine her, serving coffee and pieces of pie with a smile that would knock the tourists' socks off. If she was ever his waitress, he'd leave her a huge tip. Maybe he'd flirt with her, hoping for her phone number.

And she would shut him down like a puppy mill.

"So you're going to relegate me to poverty?" His mother's voice shook.

Cora poked the fire again with the stick. "I didn't put you there."

Clementine barked upward at the shower of green and blue sparks that flew into the night air and then leaned against Mac's legs. The warmth was welcome.

"Darling," said Valentine gently. "Think about what you're doing."

"Are you kidding me? I've thought about almost nothing else since this all came up," Cora said, sounded choked. "I want to make you happy, Valentine. For Logan's sake. And Louisa, no, of course I don't want you to struggle. You've never been easy on me, but that's fine. Whatever. I just want to take care of the one thing that I love. The one thing that was entrusted to me." She closed her eyes and leaned forward. "How do I make you understand this?"

Mac longed to reach out, to touch her, but he couldn't. So he balled his fists and shoved them into his pockets.

"My home is . . . It's not just the shell I keep around me. You've always thought that's what I was doing: protecting myself. But it's more than that. My home is my soul. I've invested everything I have in it, every piece of energy, every scrap of love. It's where I grew up, for real." She looked down at her hands folded in her lap. "The walls breathe around me and the house goes to sleep at night when I do."

Aunt Valentine made a strangled noise in the back of her throat.

"I'm sorry,' Cora said quickly. "But doesn't that mean anything to you? The place your son lived? The home he rebuilt with his own hands?" She turned to Valentine. "Your home, where you held him as a baby. Where he took his first steps."

Then her glance took in both his mother and himself. "Louisa, your home where the boys played. Those stairs. Logan told me he could ride down the banister in less than three seconds if you'd recently polished it."

"It's just wood," said Louisa, but her voice still trembled.

"It *isn't*," Cora said. "That's what I mean. It's memory. It's life. It's our life."

Mac thought of something, an idea that might carry weight with Cora. "So what if The Big One hits?"

"What?" A single tear streaked her face, breaking his heart as it slipped its way down in the firelight.

It would hurt more, but he needed to try. "What if the earth opened up? A big nine point oh? All the buildings fall, and those that don't fall, burn. We're left with nothing, and it's not your fault."

He could almost see her mentally flipping the pages of her *What If* book. Before she could decide on the right answer, he said, "Or what if we suddenly, right now, hear the water being sucked out. We sit here on the beach, and watch the tide be drawn back half a mile or more."

Cora blinked and she picked up the stick again, holding it tightly. "Tsunami," she whispered.

"Half an hour later, the water comes back in and keeps coming. Where's the only safe place, Cora?" Mac knew she must know.

"Top of Mount Selina. Or anywhere on 35, at the highest points."

He nodded. "Everything down here will be lost. Everything."

His mother and Aunt Valentine stared at him. Val said in a warning voice, "Mac. She doesn't do well with –"

"With random worries? Free-floating anxiety about nothing she can do anything about?"

Cora shook her head but kept her mouth shut.

Mac went on. "Say the coast starts to burn. It's the hottest summer on record, and everything from the manzanita on down catches fire. It spreads from Big Sur to Mendocino. Thousands of firefighters from all over the country can't put it out – it's the burn of the century."

He could almost see the images of devastation forming in her mind. "Yeah, you'd stand on your roof with a water hose, keeping the building wet until when? Until those eucalyptus behind the house exploded? Because they do that in high heat, did you know that?"

She gave a slight nod. Of course she did.

He went on, mercilessly. Jesus Christ, he was an asshole. "And then the pump on the well goes out, because the power won't stay on, you know that. You have to evacuate. Leave the house to burn."

"No."

"You wouldn't leave? To save yourself?"

"I mean, no. Stop this."

"Why? It's everything you worry about."

"Mac . . ." She rubbed her hand over her eyes, and when she took it away, her face looked hollow. Haunted. "I can't be sure of hanging on to anything. Ever."

"That's not what I –"

"So when I can, when I have any say in the matter, I make the choice to hold on. That's why I have those plans. You think I don't know I could lose everything in a second? That I haven't spent countless nights worried about exactly that? I have. Too many nights. Which is why, when I have a choice, I'll hang on. God can take this away from me. I know that. The natural world, the universe can smack me down and leave me with nothing. But you? And Royal? You two can't take away the life, the *soul*, that I've built for myself."

Cora stood and looked down at the fire, her bare foot digging into the small hole she'd dug. "I'm sorry that I can't please you three. You can sell your plots, and I'll give Royal right of passage through my land if he needs it. But even if my house needs to back up to a parking lot, at least it will still be *my* house."

"Cora –" Mac didn't know what to say next, but there had to be something that would stop her, that would change her mind.

"I'm sorry to leave you with the fire. Just dump the wet sand on top when you leave. Make sure nothing sparks. I've got my basket – you can have any leftovers. Clementine . . ." She paused, looking between the dog and Mac, pausing as if making a decision. "Clementine, come." She snapped and Clementine ran obediently to her side.

She held her canvas shoes with one hand, her basket in her other, cutting her way through the ice plant path with that absolutely determined walk of hers, the dog leaping in and over the plants next to her. Mac didn't think, didn't stop his feet from following her. It was difficult running over the dune, but he pushed, hard. At the top of the path, where the sand dipped back toward the road, he caught up with her and took her hand.

"Cora," he started.

"Oh, God," she said, and there was a plea in her voice he didn't know how to answer. But she didn't pull her hand away.

He would try his damnedest. "I can't change what I did. When Logan was dying, I should have been here. And I'm sorry for my actions. I can't change the past, though. God, Cora, if I could, I'd change everything about it, don't you know that? I wouldn't have gone with Trixie to that stupid dance. I would have decked Logan when he decided to ask you out. Our lives would be so different that it's completely unimaginable. Logan still would have died, and I bet he would have been married to some nice woman who'd still be grieving him, too. But it wouldn't be you. *Because you'd be with me.* That's what I would change if I could only change one thing. It's the only thing that matters."

The look in her eyes – he'd attended a mare once during a difficult foaling, and right before she passed out, she'd looked like that. Nothing but panic. The sheer, unadulterated need to get out of the worst situation she'd ever been in.

He'd caused that. Mac hated himself for it.

"That's all. I thought you needed to know that."

"But Olivia – and . . . But –"

"We can talk later," he said, and he drew her hand to his mouth. He pressed his lips against the back of her knuckles, breathing warmth onto their coolness. "I've always loved you."

CHAPTER FORTY-TWO

*No matter how clever you are, at some point, you will fail. That's where
the real fun begins. – E.C.*

It was all right that she pulled her hand from his, turned and
walked away, leaving him there, his boots sinking into the soft
sand of the dune. Dammit, Mac felt like running too, and not
back to the beach where his mother and aunt waited. How could
Cora possibly accept him, thinking what she did about him? That
he'd abandoned a child. He wanted to run, and keep going, past the
pier, past the lighthouse, over the rocks, and to the southern part of
the sand that stretched for miles, the part of beach that only the
fishermen went to. He wanted to run all night until he was nothing
but pain and heat and exhaustion.

But instead, he went back to the fire. His mother was holding her
hands up to the flames, and Valentine was pulling a raw marshmallow apart and then pushing it back together until it turned into taffy
in her fingers. Then she threw the marshmallow into the fire and

wiped her fingers on the sand. "I'm going to get the wet sand. Come on, wee dogs."

His mother sat in place, looking stunned.

"You know we were right to try," she said to him. He heard the unspoken question in her voice. "If we sell, we should all sell."

"I don't know. Maybe we weren't right. Maybe nothing was right about it," he said.

"But we have to take care of ourselves."

"Yeah, Ma. That's exactly what Cora's doing."

Louisa's gaze dropped to the sand. "You won't believe me, and I don't blame you, but that girl is my family, too. I've loved her almost as long as you have."

Mac started.

"Just because I don't show it, doesn't mean it's not real. If your father were alive, he'd tell you that was true." Louisa rubbed her hands together in front of the fire. "I don't have to tell people I love them. They should just know. Family just knows."

"You should say it, Ma.' Mac felt exhausted. "Every once in a while. Might do you good." Maybe that had been the problem all along with his mother. Maybe if, as a family, they'd been more demonstrative, he'd have pulled it together earlier in his life. Gone after Cora when he should have. Instead of running away.

"I love you," his mother said. The words sounded gravelly, as if she had a cold. Her trembling fingers reached tentatively toward him.

Mac took his mother's hand for the first time since he was eight years old. Funny, it felt just the same. A little thinner, but still tough. Strong. As if she'd fight for anything, anyone. Maybe fighting was all she'd ever known. "I love you too, Ma. No matter what, okay?"

He saw relief on her face, starkly outlined in the light of the leaping flames.

Fuck Royal, anyway. Fuck him sideways for starting all this, for being all or nothing, for wanting more than he could have. Mac stood, taking a deep lungful of smoke and immediately started coughing.

If he was going to pretend to be a father, he was going to have to stay in town. Period. Maybe he should rethink this sale thing.

"Son?" Louisa's voice was querulous and he realized she'd gotten older since he'd been gone. But he'd think about the ramifications of that later.

He needed to be near Cora.

Shit. Just being near her wouldn't do.

No way in hell would it do. He needed her, and goddamn it, she needed him too. He knew she did. Mac felt a throb, a pulse of blood at the base of his wrists. The only other time he'd ever felt that was when he'd been about to make his first surgical cut on a live, breathing horse. The scalpel had shaken in his hand, until he'd finally drawn breath and held it, high at the top of his lungs.

The adrenaline spiked in his blood, sending a shot of electricity through his body. He breathed in slowly, holding the oxygen now like he had then.

Mac turned and met his mother's eyes. "She's not going to sell," he told her. "And you know what? I might not, either."

Louisa, to her credit, didn't look surprised. "Will he take a smaller amount of land?"

"Not likely. I wouldn't be able to talk him into it. He's a stubborn cuss."

She poured one more plastic tumbler of wine. "Go on then, son."

"Do you understand me? I'll make sure you're taken care of. That you get the help you need somehow. But it won't go the way you wanted it to go."

His mother raised the glass to him. "Even if you think I don't, I *do* understand. We'll work it out." She sighed. "Love conquers, and all that crap. Both you boys loved her. Now, go get her."

Yes.

Mac started up the dune.

CHAPTER FORTY-THREE

Always be brave. – E.C.

An hour later, the barn – a place that could usually soothe her through any anger, any sadness – was doing nothing for Cora. Every chore was a burden. Lifting the latch that led into the goat pen gave her a splinter the size of a two-by-four. She pulled it out with her teeth, and immediately felt nauseated. While she was moving hay, chaff flew into her eye. And she missed Miss Honey, the chicken they'd had for dinner at the beach.

Chickens were for eating. In case of emergency. She had three whole pages in her book, written out by hand – directions for killing and plucking a chicken with the least amount of trauma for all involved. Miss Honey, a Golden Laced Wyandotte, had never been one of Cora's favorites, but she'd had a personality that couldn't be denied – when Cora fed them, the hen would fly up to the roosting bar and make a sound that sounded suspiciously like a rooster crowing. From the bar, she attempted to boss all the others. They'd always ignored her, gobbling the grain as Miss Honey crow-gulped above them.

Tonight, when she stood still and listened to them roosting, making the rare sleepy cluck, there were no annoying noises coming from above.

Stupid chickens. And Clementine! What was she thinking, keeping the damn dog? Every time they went to the barn, she showed signs of having a strong prey drive. She'd have to keep her on leash when they were near the chickens. What kind of life was that for a dog? A farm dog locked in the house. It wasn't right.

She sat on the bench she'd made and rested her hands on the wood, smoothing it with her fingers. Wood had seemed so foreign when she'd built it, a substance that wouldn't bend or stretch like the fiber she was so used to. Cora could knit a sweater, spend weeks on it, and when she held it up after grafting the underarms, it could either fit her perfectly or seem suited for a giant. And that was *after* doing a gauge swatch.

Wood, though. Wood was solid. Long-lasting. Measuring mattered. If she measured a board right, it fit. There was no guesswork in wood. Things didn't crop up and surprise a person. It was trustworthy, like the wood that framed her home.

Home.

That moment after she and Mac had made love – before she'd bolted to the bathroom – her house had been more a home in that moment than it had ever been. That was the feeling she'd been after without knowing it, the one she'd been actively looking for this whole time. Maybe her whole life.

If she slept with him again, just once before he left, would she feel it? Strictly sexually, the orgasm he'd given her had been mindblowing. She could imagine women lining up to feel that way. He could sell tickets. Expensive ones.

But that was only part of it. That connection they'd had, that feeling of warmth, of . . . love? Cora sat on the bench and stared at Mavis, who bleated comfortably back at her. It had felt like . . .

Love.

No. That feeling of home that had imbued her soul with that radiance and warmth, wasn't that just the afterglow? Every woman he'd ever been with had probably felt that way afterward. They'd all wanted to get up and make him muffins and give him a place to put his boots just inside the kitchen door, right? He'd probably fit like that in every woman's bed. In every woman's home.

Cora pressed her fingertips against her lips and smelled the dust of the corn on them. She held her hands out and looked at her cracked nails, at the fine line of dirt under them that no amount of scrubbing ever completely took away. She held up her feet. Old mud was still caked up the sides of the canvas shoes from when she'd thrown them on late one night during a freak summer storm. Mac couldn't want her. Not like *this*.

But she knew he did. She felt it in her very bones – that with her, he was where he'd always wanted to be, too.

Home.

She stood, and finished the chores, willing herself to think only about them.

Then she went to the bomb shelter. Ostensibly, she was checking the preserve stores. She'd had to sell more of them than she would have liked, but that was just something she would have to do to hang on. To make it. It was fine. She'd put in another couple of vegetable beds this next week and start some late tomatoes. If the weather held, there would be winter sauce.

But instead of doing the inventory on the canned goods, Cora sat. She'd made the bench in here, too. It had been her second wooden project, and she'd been more confident about the sawing and sanding. She'd been proud of the gleam she'd brought out of the rough aspect of it, proud of the way the stain had brought out the personality of the wood.

She'd left the flap of the shelter door open and now flipped off the interior light so she could look out and up at the stars. The night breeze sighed through the oaks, and the acrid scent of eucalyptus filled the small room. She pulled the afghan she'd knitted years ago over her knees – the orange one with the yellow fringe that always smelled of the trees, even though she'd washed it three or four times since she'd moved it out here.

The orderly rows of bottles of water, none of them past their expiration date, comforted her. She could just make out the glass jars of pickles and beans she'd put up last summer.

Cora wrapped the blanket tighter. She breathed.

Then she let herself think about Mac.

He'd abandoned a child. But true, it didn't seem as if he'd known about Olivia. Could he be blamed for that? And what if he stepped up now, and did the right thing? A thin trail of something that felt suspiciously too much like jealousy threaded through her. Would he, then, spend more time with Trixie? Wouldn't that be natural? What if they started up what they'd had before?

Before that happened, before she lost Mac again, what if she let herself feel that way one more time, feel that sense of falling-into-home? Just once, before he left. Was it too awful, too crazy to consider? Maybe this was what addiction felt like, telling yourself you only needed one more hit, and that would be the last. Would giving in to it only make the addiction that much worse?

Did she care?

There was a crunch of gravel from the driveway and the low growl of an engine before it shut off.

It was all the answer Cora needed. She shivered even though she wasn't cold.

Waiting, she listened as Mac went up on the porch of the house and knocked. From inside, Clementine barked, but the lights were all off. He would check the barn next.

She heard his boots crunching that direction.

Cora stood. She took a deep breath and pulled the string on the overhead bulb of the bomb shelter. From where he was in the yard, it would attract his attention immediately . . .

The footsteps stalled.

Then she heard him start to run toward her, and her heart took up the sound, the rhythm. She heard him as he ran through the yard, then he raced down the steps.

"Cora," he started, immediately. "I don't have to sell, either. We can stay –"

Cora launched herself at him. Heaven help her, she didn't know if this was right. Maybe it was the worst idea she'd ever had. She didn't care. Mac was the last man on the earth she should be kissing. She was outraged with him, personally and morally affronted by what he'd left undone in his life.

And he was her home. Goddamn him, he was her heart.

When he'd said he should have been with her all this time, she'd unraveled inside. She knew he was right. She should have said yes back then. She should have run away with him.

His mouth dragged heavily against hers, and his lips told her that he wanted her in the same way. Possession, now. He tasted her lower lip, and drew her tongue into his mouth. When she groaned against him, he moved his kisses down her neck, and the way his stubble scraped her sensitive skin made her sides shake with need.

Cora reached down, and pressed her hand to him. He was hard, and ready. There was nothing in the world as important as having him inside her.

"Here?" he asked, in answer to her unspoken question.

In a moment – a second – of clarity, she tore herself away from him. "Oh, God . . ." Then, again, as she leaned against his chest, she felt it again. *Home.*

There was nowhere else she wanted to be. Consequences: they'd still be there in the morning. When the sun came up, it would be a new day, and she'd deal with it then. But now, she just wanted him. Mac. The man she'd loved since she was a teenager, since she saw the look of frustration on his face that he wasn't the one dealing with Billy Thunker.

That same frustrated look was on his face now, and it made her want to laugh with the joy of it.

"Cora." Mac's hand was still on the small of her back and he pulled her against him, as if they were dancing. Cora could feel the length of him pressing against her stomach, and she turned liquid with need. She couldn't wait – he was like a drug she'd had a taste of and needed more, as much as she could have. Unbuckling his belt, she unsnapped his jeans and slid her hand inside. She could hear the tension in him, feel it in the silk-covered strength she held in her fist.

"This is what I want," she said against his mouth.

He blinked, hard. He moved fast, twisting away from her, reaching for the leg of the cot with his foot and dragging it closer. "Might need this," he said, and then he was kissing her again, his mouth heavy on her lips. He was strong when he needed to be, and Cora felt how it was that he could move a thousand pounds of horse – he acted as if she weighed nothing as he lifted her and placed her on the cot.

Leaning over her, his voice was barely controlled, as he said, "If you tell me to stop now, I'll stop."

"Don't," Cora said. She took hold of the open fronts of his flannel shirt and pulled as hard as she could. Mac toppled onto her, and his weight, though it took away her breath, was exactly what she needed. "Don't stop," she said.

The words made him move faster, and Cora was so overheated she could only be thankful for his speed. The snaps of her overalls were undone in a second.

"Have I ever mentioned how sexy you look in this getup? No one should look this good in farm wear." He slipped off the straps and then undid the buttons at the side of her waist. "It's a little more work to get into, but hot damn, Cora . . ." He ran his hand up her side, under her shirt, tracing the outline of her breast before he traced the vee between her breasts. "Jesus."

She wriggled until the overalls were off as he pushed down his jeans to just below his hips. His cock was so hard, so ready. He pulled her panties down until she could kick her way out of them.

"Mac –" Cora wanted to tell him, had to . . .

But he got there first. "I love you," he said.

Cora laughed with unadulterated joy. They were the best words in the whole world. "Yes," she said. She lifted her leg and wrapped it around his hip.

Mac reached down and grabbed her other leg behind the thigh. He lifted her, pressing her into the afghan below them, and held her there, for just a moment, an agony of seconds, before sinking himself – hard – into her.

Cora kept her arms around his neck, kept her mouth on his, drawing his tongue deep into her mouth as the rocked against each other. With each thrust, she felt him climb, and she moved against him more frantically, needing her own release. "Yes," she said again. "Love. Don't stop. My love."

The word felt almost as good in her mouth as he did deep inside her, and as she came around him, she wanted to laugh again from the happiness that bubbled up, so she did. He came with a deep, guttural roar, and then he joined her in the laughter. His chest shook, and as he pressed his face against hers, she felt her tears against his cheek.

"Love," she said again, and her body shuddered.

"Love," he repeated, running one finger from the corner of her eye down her jawline and then to her mouth. He kissed her again, and instead of hot, it was soft. Instead of need, it was sweetness.

"When I'm with you . . ." Mac's voice was tentative. She could feel the words inside him, building on the breath in his lungs before he spoke. "I feel like . . . I feel like I've come home." He paused. "Does that make any sense at all? Do you know what I mean?"

Through the open door at the top of the stairs, she could see just one star between the branches of the eucalyptus. It winked at her as the tree swayed in the wind.

She pressed the shape of a kiss to his temple. "I do."

CHAPTER FORTY-FOUR

*The right combination of needles and wool is like a good marriage –
comfortable, familiar, and surprisingly exciting. – E.C.*

After lying in the bomb shelter until they were cold, they'd run naked into the house, tumbling up the stairs to the bedroom where they'd found each other all over again. Cora knew there was so much to say, so much to talk about.

But talking would probably ruin everything, and she just wanted one night. One full night with him. It was selfish. Weak. And it was what she wanted. They slept entwined, face to face, and instead of feeling as if she couldn't breathe, she felt perfectly fitted to his body. His knee between hers, his arm slung over her, her hand on his waist. She fell into a sleep as deep as she'd ever known, and woke hours after daybreak.

Mac was already awake, propped up, watching her with sleepy eyes. "Good morning."

"Chores," she mumbled. "Late."

"They can wait a few more minutes." He kissed her sweet and lazily.

"Mmm. Good morning," Cora said. And it was.

"I told them I wouldn't sell either."

The sated, pliant feeling left her body. She felt as if he'd suddenly slipped an ice cube behind her shoulder blades. She sat up, bringing the top of the sheet with her. Sure, he'd just seen everything she had to offer last night in the bomb shelter and afterward, but a conversation about the land, about her home, required some kind of clothing. The sheet would have to do. "What?"

"They can do their own thing. Maybe Royal can make it work."

"But Louisa's and Val's properties are separated by ours in the middle. He won't want the outside bits. That doesn't make a lick of sense, and you know it."

Mac shrugged, his shoulder lifting and falling. "Then Royal's fucked."

Cora tore her eyes away from the ropy muscle delineation. "He's your boss."

Inclining his head, Mac said, "And my friend. But he'll get over it. Money is money, and he can find more land. If Mom needs the cash that damn bad, maybe she can sell to someone else, someone who wants a house on the coast. It's more important to me that I'm close to you."

Big words. Cora felt them reverberate in her chest, thumping around, and then she felt the fear again. "So you're what, staying?"

"If you'll have me."

Have him? She wanted nothing more.

And it could never happen. Not with what was unspoken between them. "We still have to talk." Famous last words. She wound the corner of the sheet around her fingers and pulled.

"About Olivia," he said, agreeing with her. He slid his leg further out under the sheet so that it pressed against hers. The weight and warmth of it felt like something she could rely on. Something real.

Cora took a breath and tried to bring the oxygen through her blood, slowing it down.

"Yeah."

"I didn't know about her, Cora." He was telling the truth. She could see it. He'd never been able to lie to her.

Mac went on, "But I'm going to take care of her."

Shaking her head, she said, "Good. But before you start saying –"

"It doesn't excuse the fact that she didn't have a father all these years. I know how you feel about that, that she was left behind with no one but her mother."

Yeah, that. That was it.

"But Trixie isn't as bad as you make her out to be, Cora. I promise you that."

There it was then. The start of what he and Trixie would have together. Sudden exhaustion hit, a rough crash-landing as the wind was knocked out of her. The happiness that had filled her moments ago left her body with a *whoosh*.

"Fine, Mac. That's fine. I'm glad you'll be doing the right thing." She swallowed, hard. "I just can't believe I never saw it before. Never suspected. Now that I know, it's so *obvious*." Her voice broke, and she regretted what he must hear in her words. "What I can't figure out is how you didn't know. That you didn't ever guess, or wonder."

He lifted his shoulders and didn't meet her eyes. "Just an idiot."

"You couldn't do simple math? When did you first hear Trixie'd had a baby?"

"I didn't know. Not for a long time, until years after the fact. And then, it just . . ."

"It just what?"

"It just didn't cross my mind."

"But now that you know that you're her . . ." She waited for him to fill in the blank. He could acknowledge it here, with her, at least. "Come on, Mac. Fill in the blank. I want to hear you say it. Now that you know you're her . . ."

"Stop it, Cora."

"Say it. You're her . . ."

"I'm her father." Mac tilted his head and tugged his earlobe. Cora felt a chill run through her. No, this didn't make sense. It was his tell. From their teenaged penny poker days.

"I'm her father," Mac said again, his eyes wide. He knew he'd done it. Mac was *lying*. What the hell was he lying about?

Cora felt the rest of the world melt away. There was only the space between them. And then that, too, fell away from her, and there was nothing underneath. Nothing to support her. She couldn't feel the bed, couldn't sense the air in the room, couldn't even see Mac's face, even though he was right in front of her.

"You're not her father."

"Cora –" He reached for her, and she scrambled backward off the bed as if he were wielding a knife.

"Then who is?" But she knew. The knowledge fell into place, dropped into the nothingness that surrounded her. It filled the space, and it was so much worse than anything else could have ever been.

"No," she breathed and shook her head. "It couldn't be. Logan and she never – they weren't . . . That's insane."

"Damn it to fucking hell." Mac spoke to himself, not to her. It was all the confirmation she needed.

CHAPTER FORTY-FIVE

Knit through everything. – E.C.

"Y ou've got to be kidding me." Cora felt a laugh rise, completely and totally inappropriate. "Oh my God, Mac. Tell me I'm
wrong."

Mac kept quiet, which, as it turned out, was even more painful
than anything he could have said.

No. It was not only crazy, it was impossible.

Yanking her hand out of his, she stood, hating the fact that she
was naked, that the sheet stayed underneath him. But she could
move fast when she had to, which was *now*. With one hand, she
wrangled her overalls up, and with the other she pulled her T-shirt
over her head. The shirt tangled, turned the wrong way and she had
to use her other hand to make sure she pushed her head through
the neck hole and not the arm, as she'd been trying to, and the overalls, meanwhile, dropped back to the floor.

"*Shit*. Goddamn it, Mac! Turn around!" It was a ridiculous request but she made it anyway, even though it was too late for modesty. Way too late.

But he obliged, turning his gaze to the wall. "He never admitted knowing, not to Trixie, anyway. Not out loud."

"But she was with *you*."

"We never slept together."

Cora could only gasp as she jerked the strap and clicked the clasp over the metal button. "Do *not* lie to me, Mac Wildwood. If you have any respect for me at all, which I'm beginning to doubt, don't lie."

"I'm not lying," he said. "But I don't expect you to believe it."

"You were dating *Trixie*. For months. You're telling me you never slept together?"

"She wanted to have sex. I didn't. People just assumed."

"You're telling me that an eighteen-year-old red-blooded American male wouldn't jump Trixie's bones when she threw herself at him? Why the hell would I believe that, Mac?" She pulled on her socks, and over them her blue cowboy boots. The more dressed she was, the stronger she'd feel.

"I was only ever in love with one girl." Mac's voice was clear. Steady. He pushed himself backward in her bed until he was leaning against the headboard again. "It wasn't Trixie. You know that, Cora. In your heart, you know it's the truth."

The words, though. Cora had to hear the words out loud, to weigh how they fit into her bedroom. "You're telling me that Logan had a baby with Trixie. And that baby is Olivia."

Softly, Mac said, "Yes."

"You were going to keep it from me? With her? So what, you were both in cahoots?"

Mac shifted on the bed as if to go to her.

"Don't. Don't touch me. Don't move." She sucked in another hot, sharp breath. "Please just give me a minute."

Olivia, Logan's child. She pictured Olivia and Mac racing the horses on the beach. Yes, it was there. Olivia's seat had been so natural. She'd held on to the horse with her legs like Logan always had, with full confidence she was going nowhere but the finish line. Mac had always been a strong rider, but he'd respected limits. Cora had seen in Olivia's shining eyes that there *were* no limits. Just like Logan.

Then the worst thought hit her, the thought she might not live through. Suddenly nauseated, her knees felt unsteady, as if they were made of unspun fiber instead of knitted bone, and she sank to sit on the cedar chest. She leaned forward, putting both hands to her waist, and breathed out heavily, sucking in her next breath as the new realization walloped her harder than anything else.

She met Mac's eyes, and saw in them that he'd been waiting for her to get to this place. Even though she held up her hand in warning, he was beside her, wrapping the blanket around her shoulders, moving her gently back to the bed, where he let her curl into the tiniest ball she could get her body into. He tucked the blanket over her, pulling it tight, even over her boots, and then he lay down beside her, also on his side, face to face, waiting.

"We were pregnant at the same time."

Mac nodded and touched the side of her cheek. "You were, love."

Tears came then, and Cora let him hold her. It didn't help – the strength of Mac's arms, the length and warmth of his body, nothing could eliminate the sudden, bitter cold.

That first winter after Logan died, the furnace had gone out. The life insurance hadn't come through yet, and there wasn't enough in the bank account to cover the repair. Then, on winter solstice, the longest night of the year, the chimney flue's handle had broken off in her hand. There would be no fire that night. Cora had put on three sweaters and two hats; then she'd wrapped four hand-knit blankets around herself. She'd sat on the floor in the living room on the old Persian rug she and Logan had found at an estate sale, the rug she'd scrubbed with a stiff brush and baking soda. She waited for the cold to come. And it had, but it had come in a different way – instead of the kind that made a body shiver, she'd felt something sharper and icy sink into her bones. The grief that night had been more chilling than anything else she'd ever felt. Knowing the sun was so far away from the earth that she'd have to wait – maybe forever – for it to come out again, knowing she'd be alone tomorrow, and the tomorrow after that, and the all the tomorrows of the future. No one to share home with. No one to *be* home with. Logan, his cheeky smile, his warmth that she'd taken for granted, gone forever.

And then selfishly, she'd cried herself to sleep, knowing it was selfish even at the time. She should have been crying because she hurt for Logan – that he'd never see the fruition of his dreams. But she'd cried for that so many times already. That longest winter night, she'd cried for herself. For the baby she'd lost, for the child she'd never hold. For her imminent and never-ending loneliness.

She'd frozen over so hard that she hadn't ever felt the frost of the room she'd been dreading so much.

Now that same coldness was back.

Olivia.

Olivia would have been her step-daughter. Cora ignored the obvious fact that had she known the truth, she and Logan probably wouldn't have made it as a couple. Oh, who was she kidding? They never would have made it. For her to have had to accept the child who lived, who wasn't hers, but who was her husband's – could she have been that advanced at that age? She'd been so young. They all had. And Logan would have handled it badly. That was a given. It was almost guaranteed they would have left each other, leaving nothing behind but bitter regret.

Cora would have been alone then, too, and she wouldn't have had this home. Her safety blanket, the one she'd knitted together herself.

Plunging her fists forward, Cora twisted her fingers into the yarn of the afghan Mac had wrapped her in. The thick yarn, a tough

Romney two-ply she'd spun two years before, didn't give, and neither did Mac, whose arms tightened around her. He pressed a kiss to the side of her temple. She was reminded of the moment in her market stall, when Olivia had held the fiber in her hand, surprised by the warmth it generated. Cora could feel it now – her body heat trapped by the blanket, by Mac returning to her. She didn't need it though. She *craved* the chill.

Then Mac said, "I can't swear what I'm guessing is right or wrong, but I think if Logan knew, he pushed it so far out of his mind that he didn't actually *know* anything."

Cora nodded against his chest, feeling a button graze her eyebrow. "That sounds like him." Logan could bet on a horse and watch it falter on the way out of the gate, watch it hit the dirt with a sickening crunch, and his fists would still be balled up in hope as he whispered. *Get up, girl, get up. I know you can get up. Show 'em all, girl. Show 'em what you're made of.* He'd been an optimist to the point of idiocy.

When Logan had gone down, he'd never believed it was for good, either.

"I hate him so much," she said. Her voice was muffled against the yarn, against Mac's chest.

"Only because you loved him so much."

It cut to the bone. "I did. You know I did. I loved him in my way. In our way. We made this life together. He let me take care of him. Logan needed me."

"And you were amazing for him." The words cost him, Cora could feel it. He went on, "Who took care of you, though?"

"I didn't need that."

"You did, *mí Corazón*. You did." Mac paused before continuing. "You made a home for him. Somewhere safe. He'd never have gambled that away."

"But he did, didn't he?"

"You can't bet on the risk of cancer. No one can bet on that, sweetheart."

Cora pushed against him, gaining only inches. Mac was strong, his arms thick. But she was stronger. "He gambled our whole life away. What, he thought I'd never see it? He thought Trixie would never tell? Would never change her mind?"

"He always liked the long shot."

Cora sat up, still resisting him. "He broke it all."

"No, he didn't –"

"Yes." Cora cut Mac off. He knew a lot about his cousin, but not everything. And Mac didn't know everything about her. He barely knew *anything*. He didn't know what she was capable of. How strong she was. And when she made up her mind, how determined. "Logan's ruined everything. Every bit of everything I've ever worked for, he's ruined it now."

"Cora –"

"I made a *home* for him."

"You made it for both of you. You needed it as much as he did."

"But it was for him, at first. It only became mine later. And now – oh, God. Do I have to give her the house?"

"No –"

She couldn't let him speak, couldn't let him finish whatever he thought he understood. "But . . . this would all . . . wouldn't it belong to his daughter? After he died?"

"Cora! It's yours. You were Logan's wife. There's nothing wrong with keeping your house. I understand the impulse, but . . ." Mac looked stunned as he too pushed himself into a sitting position.

"Olivia never had a father, even though he was around for the first . . ." Cora paused and did the math. "The first ten years of her life. Do you have *any* idea how much a father can mean to a little girl?"

Mac started, "But –"

"And he never even gave her money? He gave her nothing."

"He gave her a bike once. That's what Trixie said."

"Jesus Christ! Are you serious? He gave her a *bicycle*. That's worse than nothing at all. So you're saying he acknowledged her once, and that was it. *God*. So completely Logan." Cora slid to the edge of the bed. "I need to find Royal."

Mac looked stricken. "You can't just jump into a decision like this – oh Christ, I'm sorry. I've screwed this all up."

"It doesn't matter," she said, as she grabbed her wallet from her bureau and stuffed it into her back pocket. "Let the dog out," she muttered. "Then chores. Then I'll find him."

"What are you doing?"

"One guess." Cora said, her heart lower than the floorboards. Lower than the hole that still gaped under the kitchen table. "I have to figure out how to give Olivia and Trixie the money that Logan owes them."

"Give it a day or two, love. It's a lot to take in."

Cora threw the word back in his face. "*Love*. So you were ready to lie to me for how long?"

Mac scrubbed at his face, rubbing the sides of his cheeks. "That wasn't how it was."

"And you would have built everything on that lie. Is that right? If we'd – I can't even believe I'm saying this – if we'd ended up together, you would have kept that lie going? You and Trixie? For how long? Oh, God, would you have let *Olivia* believe it too? Would you have acted like her *father*?"

Again, as before, silence was her answer.

He could have fixed it, Cora realized. She loved him so much that if he'd told her she was wrong, if he'd been able to convince her that she was crazy, she would have forgiven him. But he couldn't lie to her. For one long painful second, Cora regretted that. But then she did what she had to do.

"I'm leaving. We're done, Mac. Whatever . . . *this* . . . was, is over. Take your time getting out of my house," she said.

"I'm –"

Her heart shattered into powdered porcelain, just like Eliza's teacup had. "But then get out."

CHAPTER FORTY-SIX

*Gauge is as deceptive as a gambler. It will lie, whisper to you exactly what
you want to hear, and you'll run out of yarn six inches before you finish bind-
ing off. Always, always buy that extra ball of yarn. – E.C.*

The newspaper office was closed when Mac squealed into the
parking lot. He banged on the glass, but no one answered.
Punching Royal's number again, he threw the truck into
drive and roared the short distance to Trixie's house.

He had to beat Cora. He *had* to.

If he beat her, he could tell Royal the deal was off. Hell, it had
never been on. And wasn't that mostly his own fault when it came
down to that? He'd encouraged Royal as much as he could, spurring
him on like a drunk jockey, telling him this would be the best place
for horses – it was true, sure. It was fine horse land, but so was a
whole hell of a lot of other inland California real estate without
ocean views. When Mac looked back on it, he knew he'd been the
driving force behind the whole thing.

Mac had wanted to come home.

He'd wanted a reason, instead of just going home, instead of taking the risk on seeing Cora on her own merit. Instead of just showing up, open handed, no ulterior motive. Then he could have helped her through this honestly. Openly.

He was a goddamned idiot.

Braking so hard the tires squealed, he slid the truck into park crookedly in front of Trixie's low-slung bungalow. And yep, Royal's Rolls was parked neatly in the driveway. Cora's car was nowhere to be seen. Thank God.

"Royal?" Mac yelled as he banged on the front door. He gave it a minute, and then pushed it open, praying that they weren't draped naked over the living room couch. There were some things he knew he could never un-see, and Royal's bare ass would probably fall into that category. "Trixie?" he said loudly. "We have an emergency!"

Through the kitchen, the back screen door slammed as someone entered.

"What the hell, Mac?"

Trixie was dressed, and for that Mac was truly grateful. "She knows."

Trixie stopped moving, placing the flat of her hand carefully on the counter. "We're in the backyard."

Mac's heart thumped.

"Just me and Royal. We're having breakfast out back."

Royal was in a hammock slung underneath two young acacia trees. His eyes were closed, the bottoms of his feet dirty as if he'd been padding about in the dirt. A cup of coffee rested on the ground next to him. In Royal's own home, everything that surrounded him had been picked by an interior decorator who'd had ultimate designs on the man himself. Same with Royal's offices. Even his car didn't really fit him. The only thing that had ever seemed truly Royal were his old, beloved, ratty T-shirts and the way he could make money on horses. But on Trixie's hammock? He looked more relaxed than Mac had seen him in years. Damn. Everything was so frikkin complicated.

"Hey."

"Wha?" Royal scooted to sitting. He rubbed his face. "I fell asleep."

Without preamble, Trixie said, "She knows."

Royal stretched. "Saw that one coming."

"You what?" said Mac.

"Didn't think you two could keep that kind of lie going for as long as you seemed to want to."

Trixie frowned at him. "Because you're the expert on this situation?"

Royal shrugged and scooted onto a sunnier section of the hammock. "I'm an expert on Mac, yeah. He's my best friend. And honey, I plan to be an expert on you by a week from Tuesday."

"Good luck," she said, but they exchanged a glance that left Mac, just for a second, feeling very left out.

Turning back to Mac, Trixie said, "I can't believe you told her."

Mac sunk onto a low wooden bench and leaned forward, propping his elbows on his knees. "That's the thing. I didn't."

"Shit. I *knew* you couldn't lie to her."

Royal laughed. "And that was the part of the plan I figured would fall through first. Just didn't think it would only take five minutes. You're a terrible liar, Mac. It's good you don't actually gamble, 'cause you'd be fleeced on a paycheck-to-paycheck basis."

Yeah, well, at heart, when it had the highest risk possible, Mac had played against the odds – again – and he'd lost. Just like everyone in his family always did, eventually.

"She's coming to find you, Royal," he said. "And you have to tell her no."

"Oh, it gets even better," Royal said. "What part do I play in this?"

"You're not playing a *part*. You don't belong here. I'm going to tell you what you can and can't do, and because, as you say, you're my best friend, you're going to go along with it."

"What if it's in my best financial interest to ignore you?" Royal's voice was still teasing, even though it was growing obvious that neither Trixie nor Mac appreciated any levity in the situation.

"Don't buy from her."

"Mac. I want the land."

"So take less. Take my mother's. Take my aunt's."

"I'm an all –"

"All or nothing kind of guy," said Mac. "I know. Shit, Royal, help a brother out here. Listen. She thinks she wants to sell and give the money to Olivia."

"Oh, God," said Trixie.

"And you can't do that, Royal. You can't sell to her. Because then Olivia would have to learn the truth."

Royal frowned. "It sounds like the deal we came up with is off. So dude, and I mean this in the nicest way, you know you're being an ass, right?"

Mac drew taller. "Don't buy her land."

"You tell me what to do with my horses all the time, so I'm going to pretend you're not the jerkwad you sound like right now. But, brother, you act like this around her? You'll lose her. You don't tell an adult what they can and can't do."

Trixie touched Royal's leg. "Sometimes compromise is better than loss." Her voice was so serious that both men stared at her. "Sometimes you'd give anything just to have things work out some of the time instead of none of it."

Yeah. It was too late. Mac had already lost Cora. At least he could help avert this disaster, if only Royal would listen. "If you buy her land, and she tells Olivia . . ."

"Well," said Royal, "you *were* both going to tell her someday that Mac was her daddy, wasn't that the plan? That's just changed a little, right?"

From inside the screen door in the kitchen came the sound of a glass smashing to the floor.

"*Shit*," said Trixie. "Honey?"

The door slapped open and Olivia tumbled out, shaking liquid off her hand.

Trixie stood and took a step forward. "Was that a glass?"

"Fuck, Mom. Who cares? Mac is my father?"

"No, honey," she started. "But it's complicated."

Olivia's face clouded into an angry mask, and Mac couldn't blame her. "There's been some confusion about that . . ." he started.

"For almost sixteen years I haven't known who my dad is. Yeah, I'd call that confusion, all right. I just didn't know Mom was still confused about it. I just thought she was keeping it a stupid secret for some stupid reason." She crossed her arms awkwardly over her black hoodie. "Someone tell me what the hell is going on, right *now*. Is Mac my dad or not?"

Mac opened his mouth and then closed it again. Was this his place? Wasn't it Trixie's story to tell? But Trixie had tears running down her face, something that shocked him more than if she'd passed out.

Royal leaned forward. "I guess that your mom and Mac here were going to try to make things easy on you. That was their plan, anyway."

Trixie nodded and Mac felt something in his chest tighten.

Royal went on as Olivia, pale, listened with her eyes glued to his. "The truth of what happened is complex. Mac and your mom were dating back then, yeah. But as your mom told me, she was in love with someone else, and he wasn't exactly free to be with her. She had to keep it a secret from everyone for a very long time. Now that everything's kind of coming out into the open, it's hard for both of them."

"Do I look like I give a shit about who it's hard for?" No tears for Olivia. Just pure, frustrated rage shone from her eyes. "Coming out into the open, my ass."

"Language," Trixie said weakly.

"Mom! Tell me the goddamn truth! I'm not going to break. Don't you know that by now? I'm so much stronger than you think I am. You always think of me as a little doll who should be in dresses, but I'm a real person, almost an adult."

Mac's heart twisted at the pure longing in the girl's voice. If Trixie didn't tell her, then by God, he would. The kid deserved that.

But Trixie took a tentative, shaky step toward her daughter. "His name was Logan."

A furrow appeared between Olivia's brows. "Was?"

"He died five years ago."

Now it was Olivia's turn to sit. She crossed her ankles and dropped into a cross-legged seat on the edge of the porch. "You didn't tell me in time."

A pause. "No, I didn't," said Trixie.

"Did he know?"

"I think he might have."

"Think?"

Mac heard raw pain in the kid's voice, and he longed to do something, anything, to help, but he was powerless, watching a runaway horse bolt.

"I denied it when he asked me."

"Mom." Olivia's eyes begged her mother to help her understand. She was teetering on the edge of panic, and a comforting lie might balance her. But a lie wouldn't last, and Trixie knew it.

"Honey, I thought it was the only thing I could do. He was married by then."

"To who?"

Trixie hit at the tears that were now streaming freely down her face. "Oh, lovey."

Olivia's spine straightened. She would give no quarter to her mother, not now. Mac could see that plainly.

And so, apparently, could Trixie. "Cora. He was married to Cora."

"Oh," breathed Olivia.

Silence fell in the back yard, broken only by an incongruously cheerful bird that chirped three happy tones, over and over. A small plane buzzed overhead, probably on a sight-seeing trip over Half-Moon Bay. Could the occupants in the plane see what was taking place down here? Mac looked up, envying them the ease of their flight, their unawareness of the tectonic shifts that were occurring below.

"Honey," Trixie started, "I always wanted to tell you. But it wasn't my secret to tell."

Olivia sucked in a stuttered breath. "That's total crap. You were ashamed of me, and I've always known that. I just didn't know why. Now I do."

"I have *never* been ashamed of you."

"Seriously, Mom?" Olivia pulled at her sweatshirt and then stuck out her combat boot. "This is the daughter you wanted? You're seriously trying to tell me that? You wanted something perfect, and I've never been able to be that for you. Does Cora know? Does *everyone* know?"

"No, she doesn't," said Trixie quickly.

Mac cleared his throat.

"I mean, she didn't. Not until today, apparently." Trixie reached her hand toward her daughter, but Olivia scuttled backwards like a startled crab.

"So you ruined Cora's life, too. That's what you do. You ruin people's lives, completely, and you think that's okay."

"All I ever wanted to do was to take care of you. I just didn't . . ."

"You didn't think. You didn't care. You didn't love me enough."

"No." Trixie's voice rang clearly through the yard. "I have *always* loved you more than anything else in the whole wide world. I messed up, Olivia. I didn't do it the right way."

"Neither did I, Mom. And that's what you've always gotten upset with me for. You always say I do things the wrong way. That I'm screwing up."

"No, baby."

"I'm never good enough. I could always do better, *be* better. God, were you trying to fix yourself or something?"

Trixie shook her head. "No, I just wanted –"

"To screw up as many people as possible?"

"I know you're not going to understand this, Olivia, but I've just been trying to hold things together. For you. That's all I've ever tried to do."

Olivia stood, brushing off the back of her jeans. "Good job, Mom. You sure fucked that up."

And she was gone, the screen door banging one last time.

Royal stayed put on the hammock. "Why don't you sit on over here with me for a while, huh?"

Mac expected Trixie to lash out, to shout at him, at both of them. To blame them, which, really, he wouldn't fault her for doing. She'd just had her world turned upside down, and it was due, partially, to Mac coming back to town in the first place.

Instead, she moved in a slow sleepwalker's shuffle to sit next to Royal. She accepted the arm he put around her shoulders, but Mac could tell she was seeing neither of them.

"My biggest fear was losing her," she said in a voice so low he almost couldn't hear her. "And it's so much worse than I ever thought it would be."

Mac knew it was possible that Trixie had lost her daughter. Just like he was pretty damn sure Cora would never look him in the eye again. They'd both gambled on the longest shot of all, that love would hold them together, that it would be enough.

It wasn't.

CHAPTER FORTY-SEVEN

A true friend always carries an extra stitch counter. – E.C.

Cora had heard Mac roar down the driveway, and knew she'd never beat him to Royal. That was fine, actually. She had to figure out what to say, how to talk him into buying her land even if Mac disapproved. She'd gone over it again and again in her mind – there didn't seem to be another option. She had no money to offer Olivia, nothing but her tiny farm to give. The chores took her longer than they normally did – every motion seemed weighted with meaning. She touched Mavis as she went into the pasture – how many more times would she feel that lovely lanolin, deep in the sheep's wool? In the barn, she sat on the first bench she'd made, then shifted to lying on her back looking upward. Her rafters, dusty and beautiful, hung above her, the sun streaming through a knothole just below the roofline. How much longer would all this belong to her?

Royal owed loyalty to Mac, sure. But maybe he'd see her side of the argument, and buy her land and house anyway. And if he didn't, well, she could always put it on the open market. Prices were just turning around, and while she'd never get what it was worth ten years ago, at least it would be a nest egg for Olivia – she could sit on the money until college and then do whatever she wanted.

As Cora filled the sheep's troughs, she smiled, thinking of Olivia having a couple of her own horses. Maybe the girl would even buy a little piece of property close by. It pleased her to think of Olivia continuing to ride.

Wheels crunched outside, and Cora held her breath until she could see that while it was a truck, it wasn't his. She pushed aside the disappointment and felt relief disguised as a vague dizziness.

Abigail MacArthur climbed out of the truck. "Hey, you! I came to check on the neckline of that pattern. I'm not sure if it's going to work . . ."

Cora pushed through the pasture gate, brushing off her hands, leaning in for a hug. But instead of a quick squeeze, their standard greeting, Cora shocked herself by holding on. She leaned into Abigail, who said, surprised, "Oh! Oh, sugar."

The hug was long and tight. The awful, painful tears that Cora felt start didn't seem to want to stop. Abigail's hand rubbed small circles in the middle of her back. Eliza used to do that when she cried. The thought only made Cora cry harder until hiccups made her nose run and her head hurt.

Finally the gasping tears slowed to a trickle. Cora snuffled and didn't know where to look.

"Come here," Abigail led her by the hand to a bale of hay that Cora had tossed near the pasture gate yesterday. "Sit. Talk to me."

"I finished the sweater," Cora choked out. "It's gorgeous. I want to keep it . . . but I can't afford to . . ."

"No. Not knitting. Tell me what broke your heart."

The words made the hot tears well again, but Cora gulped them back and scrubbed her face with her dirty hands, knowing she'd probably only just added mud and God knew what else to her cheeks.

"Okay," said Abigail. "Is it Mac? That tall drink of hotness I met two weeks ago at the booth? He's already made you feel like this? Honey, that was fast."

Cora shook her head. "It's taken almost twenty years to make me feel this awful."

"Ahhh, yes. The torch. It still burned."

Even though she didn't want to, even though she tried to keep them back, Cora said the words that would not stay behind her teeth. "I've always loved him."

"Then why on earth –"

"He lied in just about the worst way imaginable."

"Oh. Well, that sucks. But everyone lies, right?"

"Not about being the father of a child."

"Oh!" Abigail was quiet for a moment. She pulled out three long pieces of alfalfa and began to twist them. "No, I guess not. So he's a dad? And you didn't know?"

"No. He's not a father."

Abigail's brows came together. "You've lost me."

Cora crossed her legs and turned to face Abigail. "Can you keep a secret?"

"I'd love to."

"Logan was Olivia Fletcher's father."

Abigail dropped the braided hay. "Whoa. *That* I did not expect."

"Are you horrified?"

"For you, sure. But I wasn't married to him, and God knows I've learned that everyone has skeletons."

"The dead man's skeleton is almost sixteen."

Abigail tilted her head to the side in the same way Clementine did.

"What is it?" asked Cora.

Abigail started braiding a new section of hay. "You realize that you've never told me a secret, and in the last few weeks you've confided in me twice?"

"I'm sorry?"

"No, it's just that . . . I always tell *you* secrets. I come blab when I'm pissed off at Cade, and I run to your farm when my own is about to make me crazy. Good grief, you've helped me unsnarl yarn that had me in fits, which is above and beyond the call of friendship, truly. But in the four years that I've known you, you've never once come to me for anything. Not one thing. Not even knitting questions! Everyone comes to me at one point or another, but you just keep knitting industrially away, getting your work done. You help me all the time, with the pattern testing and bringing me vegetables that you won't let me pay for, but I never get to help *you*."

Cora didn't know how to answer. Should she be proud of that fact? Embarrassed? Apologetic?

Abigail went on, "It's just nice, that's all. I like it when you talk to me. And I'll hug you all day if you need it. But I'm sorry you're hurting, sweetheart. Do you want me to go kick his ass?"

"Oh, God. No."

"Does he deserve it?"

Cora thought. "He lied."

"We all lie."

It was a surprising thought. "What do you mean?"

"It's something I've learned with little kids. They lie just because it's fun, to see what they can get away with. I lie at the store because women who look awful in green love it more than any other color and they would be sad if I told them the truth. I lie at home when Cade asks me if I'm okay, and I'm fighting a migraine and the kids have been screaming all day but what I really want is just to lie on the couch with him, so I say I'm fine. And soon, most of the time, I actually *am* fine."

"You don't plan to lie to children about their parenthood." Cora shoved her hands under her thighs, not minding the scratch of hay against her palms. "Or to the woman you say you love."

"Did you call him on it?"

"Yes."

"Did he apologize?"

"Yes. Badly."

Abigail shrugged. "You love him. So forgive him."

The ground seemed to sway under Cora, and she felt dizzy again. It couldn't be that easy. Nothing was that easy. "I –" she started, but Abigail gasped.

The earth wasn't only seeming to sway anymore. It was bucking, rolling underneath them.

"Earthquake," Abigail said, a delighted thrill in her voice. "Here we go."

Cora's dizziness intensified, made stronger by the sudden frisson of fear that chilled her heart. The swaying grew, and the land at her feet dropped and lurched. Abigail stood and tried to move toward the house, but Cora caught her by the hand. At the next violent jolt, both lost their balance, falling to their knees on the grass. "Safest – here – outside, no power lines. Stay. Here."

It was by far the biggest earthquake that Cora had ever felt. It grew, rocking in a sickening rhythm. By now, any other temblor would have played itself out, but this one went on and on, ripping, jolting, thudding underneath them.

Sand. Liquefaction. First motion. Focal depth, and hypocenter. The words she'd studied scrolled through Cora's mind as Clementine gave a short bark of alarm from where she'd been tied on the porch while Cora did the chores.

"The Big One," she breathed.

"What?" Abigail dug her fingers into the dirt, holding on.

"Nothing." Cora's only experience during earthquakes had been to run through the house, trying to get out. They were always so quick she'd never gotten outside before the rocking stopped – during this one, she could only sit still. Literally ride it out.

The checklist of her *What If the Big One Hits* page opened in her mind's eye. She knew what to do. This was it. This was when all her training would come in to play. She'd make sure the animals here were safe, that her outside gas main was turned off. If the house was safe to enter, she'd fill the bathtub and all the sinks with water if it still flowed, then she'd go into town to check who needed the most help, stopping at the fire house first to see if they needed her in a particular spot.

Mac. Oh, God, where was Mac?

The swaying was lessening, and the jolts slowed. She looked up at her house, waiting for it to slide to the ground. What would go first? The old mudroom on the north side of the house? Would it simply topple? Or would it crack and open like she'd seen in old earthquake footage?

"Whew," said Abigail, standing. "That was a *good* one."

"Wait, don't get up yet."

"It's over, Cora. It's okay."

Cora looked back at the house and then at the barn. Both building stood, cheerily undaunted, nothing moving but the porch swing, which swayed as if a strong breeze were pushing it.

"It's okay," said Abigail again, giving her a hand up. "Are you all right?"

"That wasn't the big one."

Abigail shrugged. "Depends. If it was centered here, nope. If that was an L.A. quake we just felt, then yeah, Los Angeles is floating out to Hawaii by now."

"Jesus."

"I'm kidding. It felt local. If it were far away, it would have rolled more gently instead of jerking like that. We're all right. Hey, Cora, *are* you all right?"

Cora folded her lips and nodded.

"You sure?"

Cora nodded more assertively. "Go home. Check the kids."

"Okay. Yeah. If you're sure."

She forced a smile. "Go. Thank you."

"And Cora?"

"Yeah?"

"Forgive him."

Another hard hug and Abigail left, waving one hand out the truck's window as she went.

Checking the barn, Cora found no damage. In the bomb shelter, four jars of pickles had slid from the shelf and broken on the concrete floor, filling the space with the sharp scent of dill and vinegar. In the house, one mirror in the spare room had fallen.

Seven years of bad luck? Seven more? That was all she got?

<<>>

Outside again, standing between the barn and the house, she paused. She toed off her blue boots and stripped off her hand-knit socks. Digging her toes into the grass, she . . . waited, deeply ashamed of the disappointed feeling that flowed through her.

She knew how to deal with an earthquake, the Big One. Checklists. Plans. She was ready.

This life? She had no freaking idea what to do next.

Right here, below her feet, was the space she'd planned on putting in four more raised planting beds for more tomatoes, cucumbers, and late spinach. More to come? meant more money coming in. More chances to save herself. Glancing at the barn, she thought about the two Targhee lambs she'd thought about adding to the flock next spring. Spinners were *crazy* about the bounce and crimp of Targhee. She'd have paid for the sheep in two seasons.

She could have saved all this. She could have turned it around. Again.

And dear lord, she didn't care.

Didn't care about any of it. She looked at the house – it could have fallen, crumbled into pieces, and it wouldn't have mattered as long as Clementine was out of it. The barn could burn to the ground, and as long as she got her beloved animals – she loved them! – out of there first, she couldn't care less.

As long as Valentine and Louisa were okay. As long as Abigail and her family were safe.

As long as Mac was safe.

Mac.

She dug her toes deeper into the grass and waited for the aftershock. For whatever it was that was coming that was worse.

But nothing happened. The sky above stayed blue. In the field, the goats bleated, a familiar call.

Maybe there was nothing worse than this – the realization that the things she'd been keeping safe didn't matter. Just the heart mattered. Love. She had no idea what to do next, and she'd never felt so desperate for a bulleted list before in her life.

"Cora!"

She was never going to get out of here to find Mac. No, first she had to find Royal and make sure that this girl, the one skidding up to her on her bike, was taken care of.

"Did you feel that?" Olivia was breathing hard, sweat dripping down the sides of her face.

"Yeah. You okay?"

"That was awesome!"

"Well, we don't know how much damage it's done." That was true, Cora realized. There might still be people in town who needed help. Pipes might have blown – a gas main break could be catastrophic. And Cora knew what to do about all that, how to help . . .

"Nah, I was in the middle of Main Street when it rolled through. Tillie's has a broken window, but Old Bill was on the sidewalk and he said it broke a while back when Phil Dougall hit it with his wheelchair one night when he was drunk."

"Nothing else?"

"Three tiles fell from the gazebo and took out the new bougain-villea, and Toots Harrison is ticked about *that*. Oh, and one of Mrs. Luby's little rat-dogs bit someone in the ankle, but I don't think that was related."

"Oh."

Olivia dumped the bike on the grass and stood with her, looking down at Cora's bare feet. "What are you doing?"

Cora looked up at a robin that wheeled past. The bird probably didn't have a clue that the earth had almost just swallowed them all. Didn't have any idea how close death had come. "Being grateful."

"Yeah? Know what I am?"

"What?"

"Pissed as hell at my mom. And Mac. And your dead dang hus-band." Olivia kicked the wheel of her bike and then dropped to the grass. "The only one I'm not mad at is you 'cause they said you didn't know, either."

She knew about Logan.

Cora had planned on Olivia knowing, learning the truth at some point. She had planned on giving her the money from the house sale. But she hadn't taken any time thinking about what it would actually do to Olivia.

"Crap."

Olivia nodded. "Yep."

"What are you going to do?"

"Move in with you?"

Cora looked at the girl sharply.

"I guess I'm stuck with my mother. *God.*" Olivia pulled a clump of grass out by its roots and then realized what she held. "Oh. Sorry."

"It's bermuda grass, anyway. Pull as much as you want." Cora sat with her, cross-legged. She was spending a lot of time on the ground today.

"So now what?" asked Olivia.

Cora took a deep breath. The worst hadn't happened. The world hadn't fallen apart. The earth hadn't swallowed the land, whole cities weren't in flames.

No one needed her. No one needed her checklists, her organization, her preparedness.

And it hit her then. Cora lost her breath as the realization sunk in, deep behind her sternum.

The worst had already happened. "Oh," Cora said.

"What?"

The worst had already happened.

When she was born and given away. Again at five, when she lost her second family. When Eliza died. When she lost the baby. When Logan died.

When Mac left because Cora chose the wrong life.

And this morning, when she sent Mac away the second, final time.

The worst had happened, and she'd lived through it without even *noticing*. There was no page for *What If The Thing That Matters Most Isn't Noticed*.

But she'd lived through it. That was the amazing part. She'd made it through. What if . . . what if, in the future, she made different decisions? Better ones?

Olivia's voice was worried. "What, Cora? What's wrong?"

"Nothing. Everything."

"You're scaring me."

"Oh, honey. I'm sorry." Cora reached out to touch Olivia's knee. "I think I screwed up."

"You? No, please don't tell me that."

"I think maybe we all screwed up."

Olivia shook her head emphatically. "I didn't."

"No. You didn't. You're probably the only exception. You want to come with me? I have to talk to Royal. And your mom." *And make sure Mac is okay. Safe.*

Olivia sighed and flopped backward on the grass. "Are you serious? Right now?"

"Dead serious."

"Jeez."

"Coming?" Cora stood and held out her hand.

"If I have to." But Olivia allowed herself to be pulled up and held on to Cora's hand a little longer than was necessary.

CHAPTER FORTY-EIGHT

Sometimes we must knit a new sweater because we lost the one we loved best. This can feel like a terrible betrayal, but really, it's paying the best kind of homage to our devotion. – E.C.

By late afternoon, Mac had found what he was looking for. It had taken all day and he'd flipped more than a hundred miles on his truck's odometer to find it, but it was the one thing he could think of to give Cora, the one thing that might show her how he felt.

Even though she knew. Mac knew she felt the same way he did – he could see it in her eyes. Or he *had* seen it in her eyes. Maybe he'd never see it again. That was something he should start thinking about. How to live his life – now that he knew he'd always been right to dream of her – without her in it.

Yeah. He'd get right on that.

His old man used to get this certain look right when the last of his paycheck was almost gone. No matter what denomination bill was in his hand, be it a fifty or a five, he'd look down at Mac in the bleacher seat next to him and show him the line the horse was running. *This one, Mackie. This is the one that takes us all the way.*

Mac had never asked where exactly all the way lived. He'd known, even then, that *all the way* meant all the way back to the house where Louisa would scold his father, not for gambling, but for picking the wrong horse. Again.

But in that moment of hope, as his father led him by the hand to the betting window, the belief that sparkled in his father's eyes was like the tiny diamond chip in his grandmother's wedding ring, and when Mac accidentally caught sight of himself in the rearview mirror as he backed out of the parking lot in front of the store where he'd finally had success, he saw the same glint of light in his eyes.

All hope.

Only bet on a sure thing, son.

That's all Mac had ever done, which was why he rarely betted. He'd lost every time. But he'd never bet on anything he didn't believe in with all his damn heart.

As he turned up Cora's driveway, Mac reached out to touch the small box on the passenger seat next to him. It all depended on this, whether she'd accept it. Whether it was right.

Dammit, if it wasn't right, he had no idea what he would do.

Even though her car wasn't there, hope still filled him like helium. A ridiculous emotion, he scolded himself, as he walked up her steps, but it didn't make him stop feeling like he was floating a good foot off the ground. Maybe he was feeling aftershocks? He wondered how she'd done during the earthquake. Had she been terrified? It was a good 6.8, more than respectable. They were lucky it hadn't done more damage than it did. She'd probably run right for her *What If* book afterward. He knew, to Cora, that book proved that no one needed to take care of her.

No, Cora didn't need him. But goddamn, he hoped she would want him again.

There was no answer at the door.

She wasn't in the bomb shelter, which smelled like pickles and reminded him of the way she'd looked underneath him, her mouth wet, arms around his neck, eyes fixed on his as she came.

Lord.

She wasn't in the barn, either. Okay, then, she'd probably gone to find Royal. Whatever they worked out, Mac would be fine with it. Back in the truck, bouncing down the rutted road toward town, Mac reminded himself that Royal had been right. Mac couldn't tell Cora what to do. He'd never been able to do that. Didn't want to. If she wanted to sell her house, if that's what she thought was the right thing, then by God, he'd back her to the fullest. Maybe, just maybe she'd need a place to stay, and she'd move her things into his grandfather's old house . . .

Idiot. Get a hold of yourself. One step at a damn time. But how was he supposed to slow his heart which was beating as loud as a freight train inside his ribcage?

He drove slowly past Tillie's. No sign of her car or the Rolls.

What if she just left after this was all over? Got the hell out of Dodge? Started a new life, far, far away? What if she said the hell with him and moved to San Francisco and got a waitressing job? He could see her living in the Mission, a tiny apartment with an even smaller yard where she'd somehow raise chickens and make all the neighbors notice how sexy she looked in those overalls. She'd sell basil and fresh eggs to the restaurant where she worked and she'd date some tall writer-hipster named Yves.

Mac clutched the steering wheel. That would *not* happen. God, please don't let that happen.

No one was home at Trixie's, either.

Shit. He was out of ideas. No one was answering when he called their cell phones. Where else would they all be? Somewhere out of range?

The stables at the end of Mines Road.

His tires kicked up dust as he threw the truck into gear. He held the box on his lap. It was too precious to risk letting it slide around anymore.

Jackpot. In the stable parking he found all their cars – Cora's, Royal's, and Trixie's.

Stark saw him first. She was at the front paddock, combing the mane of a horse so old it might have been part of the Pony Express. She looked at what he was holding. "You sure about that?"

Mac's fingers tightened on the box. "Yep."

With a jerk of her head, Stark motioned to the smallest barn. "Everyone's *talking* in there. I had to get out. Tell them to work it out, okay? The horses don't like the drama and I'm worried about Olivia."

Mac nodded. Olivia was here. That upped the stakes even higher. Deep breath. Keep moving.

They were at the back of the barn in an empty stall. No one was shouting. That was something, at least.

Cora. She filled his eyes like sunlight and Mac realized he was more nervous than he'd ever been in his whole life, even more terrified than the moment he'd asked her to run away with him so long ago. Back then he didn't know you could lose everything in the space of a second, in the moment it took to look in a woman's eyes and see she wasn't going to leave with you after all.

They were older now. Wiser.

Mac wondered if he were going to have a heart attack.

"Mac!" Royal's voice was warm. That was something. "You're here just in time."

Cora blushed as red as her hair, and she turned away to hang a rope on the far wall.

Olivia said, "Guess what?"

"What?" He wasn't sure he wanted to know.

"My mom's gonna let me have a horse!"

Mac looked at Trixie. That was one hell of a way of getting back in a daughter's good graces, he supposed. Not that he knew anything about parenting.

Trixie shrugged sheepishly, pushing her long hair over her shoulder. "It's not a bribe. I swear. It's something I've been thinking about . . ."

"And I'm going to get to know Valentine, too. I have a grandmother!" Olivia was even more amped than she'd been after their race on the beach.

"Yeah, you do," Mac said. "You couldn't have a better one, I can tell you that much. And you have a second cousin, too."

"I do?"

He poked himself in the chest with his thumb. "This guy."

Olivia's mouth formed a circle of perfect surprise. "That's right! Wow! Can I borrow twenty bucks, cuz?"

"Olivia!" said Trixie.

The girl grinned. "Just kidding. But dude, that was funny. Know what else?"

"Hoo boy. What?"

"Cora's giving me half her house. I mean, the money from the sale of half her house. And I'm going to help Royal with the horses he's going to keep in the back."

Mac sat on the small bench, careful to keep the box tight against his thigh. "Wow. So a lot's gone on since I saw you all, huh?"

Trixie grimaced at him and glanced at Cora, whose back was still stubbornly turned. "We met with your mom, too. Royal's buying her house and land."

"Whoa. What about all or nothing?"

Sheepishly, Royal said, "Maybe my eyes were bigger than my stomach. Trixie pointed out I don't have to move *all* the horses here, after all. Louisa and Valentine are both moving into Val's vacant house. Louisa's land, along with five of Cora's ten acres will be more than enough for the horses I want here."

"Trixie convinced you of all this?"

Trixie shrugged almost shyly. "I want this guy to stick around a while."

"You know." Royal grinned. "Compromise. Like grown-ups do. And I'm paying Cora a stipend to stay on as stable manager."

"You can't do that," muttered Cora. "I won't take it."

"She's giving me the money from the sale," said Olivia in a voice of wonder. "For college. She wanted to give the whole house to me but mom said no. And I agree. That's just dumb."

Cora turned at that. Her eyes avoided Mac's. Was she still furious? Stupid question. Of course she was.

She said, "It's not dumb. You're Logan's daughter."

Trixie put her hand on Cora's wrist. "And you were his wife."

Mac watched as the two women looked at each other. Something real passed between them, something he wouldn't have ever predicted.

And still, his heartbeat hadn't slowed a single iota since walking into the barn. "You guys? Can I have a moment with Cora? Alone?" His voice shook, and he knew they heard it.

Royal gave a pointed glance at the box. "Yeah. Come on, ladies. Let's go see what Stark is up to."

They filed out, leaving Cora twisting the rope into a quick release knot. She pulled it, and made it again. And again.

"Cora."

"No," she said, her voice small. "I'm not ready for this."

She wasn't mad, then. It was fear Mac felt coming off her in waves. That was okay, he was terrified, too. "Not ready for what?"

Cora pulled the rope tauter. It must be burning her hands by now, and Mac barely prevented himself from reaching out to stop her. "For you apologizing. For you leaving. Again. Can you just go, and we'll skip all that? I'm glad you came – I needed to see you and make sure you were all right. I can't quite –" her voice choked and she took a deep breath "– I can't quite take you leaving again, so I wish you'd leave quickly. I'm sorry I let you down."

"Let me down? Cora . . ."

"Don't, please. I didn't see that you were trying to do the right thing. I know that now. It took a literal act of God to see that I've already had my earthquake, the one that mattered, anyway. So if you'd just hurry up and go back to your life and your job, I'll be fine. I promise. I'm always fine."

Was she crying? Oh, God. "*Corazón.* I don't want to go back –"

"Don't *call* me that."

"But you're my heart."

Her eyes met his, and for the first time, the hope Mac felt took on color and shape and weight. But he said it again, in case she hadn't heard him right, in case she didn't feel the same hope building. "You've always been my heart."

"Oh." The word was small and floated between them. Mac wanted to take her in his arms, but he remembered what he'd brought her.

"Here," he said. "Take this." He handed her the box.

"Mac," she started.

"Don't say anything. It's for you. Just open it."

A soft *snick* as Cora opened the thin piece of cardboard. She unfolded the tissue paper. "What on earth?"

She pulled out the teacup. The exact match to the one she'd regretted breaking the very second she'd thrown it.

CHAPTER FORTY-NINE

Even though on some days everyone looks like they're better at knitting than you are, it's not true. You are perfect. You are good. You are doing it all exactly right. Knit on, my friend. – E.C.

C ora didn't understand at first. How had he glued it so perfectly back together? Where were the cracks? She'd thrown the pieces out, so . . .

"You should be able to use your favorite china whenever you want. Every day. Not just for special occasions."

"But how . . ."

"I stole the biggest piece when you weren't looking. I went up the coast this morning. Went to about four thousand antique shops – I can tell you they didn't like the roller we had today. I hit paydirt at a place that was getting ready to close for the day."

She held the teacup so that it caught the light from the open door. "Oh, Mac. It's a perfect match."

"Sometimes broken things are."

Cora felt another aftershock and looked up at the bare bulb that hung over the stall. It didn't move at all. It was just her, then.

"I need to sit down."

Clementine, who'd been snuffling around the far wall, bounded in and greeted Mac with a nose pressed to his palm before leaning against Cora with a happy groan.

"She loves you," said Mac.

"She's a ridiculous dog," said Cora, still examining the teacup's pansies. It had made her ill that she'd been so stupid, hurling away something that she loved so much. And here it was again, perfect in her hands. He'd done this for her. Mac had known exactly what mattered the most to her.

Mac shook his head. "She's not. She's just right."

Cora felt the corners of her mouth start to tilt. "What's she good for, though? She tried to catch a mouse earlier, but she scared herself almost half to death when it squeaked at her."

"She'll get braver as she goes. I know people like that, too."

"Yeah? She scared of mice, but she's a chicken-killer."

Mac raised an eyebrow. "That dog?"

"Okay, she would be. If she could."

"If you let her get at the chickens. Which you won't."

"When my friend Abigail came to the house earlier, she didn't even bark."

"She must have known she was your friend, then." Mac knelt on the clean straw at Cora's feet and took Clementine's square head in his hands. "What a smart girl you are, knowing the difference between friend and foe."

Cora was running out of ideas. "And look at the way she leans. Why does she *do* that?"

"It's the way she shows love."

That word, again. Coming from Mac's mouth. His eyes met hers, and Cora's breath evaporated.

"Love," Cora said weakly. "Love isn't shown by leaning on someone else."

"Why not?"

"It just isn't."

"You think this dog can't take care of herself? She's what, two
years old? Probably been on her own a long time. That doesn't stop
her from knowing who to trust." Mac took Cora's hand. "Doesn't
stop her from knowing who to love. She chooses to lean on you,
Cora."

"Mac . . ."

"I'm sorry I lied to you. I'm even more sorry we came up with the
cockamamie idea of lying to Olivia. But we thought . . ."

"It was for my own good."

Mac nodded. "Trixie . . ."

"Feels awful about the pregnant-at-the-same-time thing. She told
me."

Mac's hand was cool and wide. Strong. Trustworthy. "And you
forgave her?"

Cora shrugged. "Yeah. Strangely, I would have done the same
thing, I think." She looked into the teacup. Who had drunk out of it
in the past? What had the leaves at the bottom foretold? "Oh, Logan," she said to herself.

"Logan," Mac agreed. "Next time I see that guy . . ."

She shook her head and looked directly into Mac's eyes. He
needed to hear this next part clearly. "I loved him."

"I know," Mac said, the smile falling from his face. "I know you
did. I did too."

"I didn't know the difference until you came back, but I was never
in love with him."

Mac's eyes had never looked more intense than this moment. His
hand tightened on hers.

Cora went on, "Because I was always in love with you. And I told
you. I'm not good at multi-tasking."

Mac didn't wait. He was kissing her before she could take another breath, before her heart started beating again. "I love you," he said between kisses. "*Corazón.* My heart."

Cora leaned her forehead against his.

It felt more right than anything had ever felt before.

And on that short, splintered bench in Stark's smallest barn, love was felt in both a kiss and in a lean, and a single teacup was big enough to hold all the love that threatened to overflow Cora's heart.

EPILOGUE

Love through everything. – E.C.

The next summer, nothing was going according to plan.

Cora finished filling the clear glass jar with the crunchy granola that she'd gotten out of bed early to make, first stirring the oats, nuts, sunflower seeds and honey over the stove, then carefully checking while it cooked in the oven. It was healthy for both of them. Mac's triglycerides had been a little on the high side when he'd seen Dr. Keller last month. He'd started running again every morning, and sometimes she joined him in a jog down the beach. He always ran faster than her, turning around and jogging backwards, teasing her until she ran harder, faster, until she tackled him from behind and they tumbled to the sand.

She poured a refill of tea into her favorite teacup. Her everyday teacup, now.

Mac came in the back door, still breathing heavily, the sweat dark on his tank top. Clementine raced for the water bowl, and then did a lap of the kitchen, forgetting, as always, to close her mouth so that the water dribbled all over Cora's clean floor.

Holding a white bag aloft triumphantly, Mac said. "Look what followed me home!"

"Don't even tell me –"

"I'm just thinking about your needs. You love Whitney's morning buns. Still steaming when I bought 'em."

"Oh . . ." Cora did love those light pastries filled with a heavenly brown sugar trail. "But I made granola."

"On purpose?" But he grinned and pulled her in for a kiss.

She supposed she should mind that he smelled of wet dog, salt air, and sweat, but she didn't. His lips on hers made her shiver all the way to her toes and she wondered how much time they had before he had to get to work.

He pulled back and said, "I'll eat that later. For lunch."

"You can't have granola for lunch."

"Says who? It's gonna be busy today – I got a message from Cindi that the pregnant Rottweiler was in labor when she got in this morning. And at eleven we're getting a tour from Mrs. Boonstomple's second grade class. If all the puppies are out by that point, I expect to recruit at least five or six of them as potential homes." He grinned. "Their parents aren't gonna be happy they toured the shelter today of all days."

"Still, you should have protein or something . . ." Cora's voice trailed off as Mac leaned in to gently nip the side of her neck. "*Oh.*"

"I'll have milk with the granola. That's protein."

"But not whole milk. At least use non-fat."

"You worry too much. Think about last week."

Cora turned to grab a Ziplock bag and started packing what she knew would be three or four times as much granola as Mac would be able to eat. "That was different."

"You loved it."

"I did not," she protested weakly.

Mac leaned on the edge of the old kitchen table and stretched his lower back. "You said it was one of the most fun things in the whole world."

"Okay. Yeah. But you tricked me. And since then I've decided that skydiving is the most foolhardy thing I've ever done."

"Besides falling in love with me, that is."

She raised an eyebrow and watched with approval as he stripped off his tank top and threw it in the washing machine. "True."

Mac turned and pulled an ankle up behind him. "You couldn't control a minute of it."

"The skydiving? That was the problem." Mac hadn't told her where they were going. He'd just pulled up to the Half-Moon Bay airstrip and took her inside where he'd smooth-talked her into signing on the dotted line that she was taking the class and waiving all liability.

"And you couldn't do a lick of research."

"That's what the internet was *made* for. All the scare stories and grisly pictures, right there for the googling. All for me."

Mac grinned, and her heart tugged. Lord, she loved his grin. She'd always loved it.

"And instead," he said, "you strapped yourself to a man you'd never met before . . ."

"Well, that *was* kind of thrilling."

Pointedly ignoring her, he continued, "And hurled yourself out of an airplane at eleven thousand feet."

"If that guy hadn't been dragging me down to earth, I could have climbed the air right back into the plane. I know I could have."

"I don't doubt that, darlin'." Sitting, he opened the bag. "Yep, they're still warm."

"Terrible man. Gimme one."

He handed it to her. "Royal coming by today?"

Cora nodded, her mouth full. Around the morning bun, she said. "Yesh, later. He's bringing in a new filly this afternoon."

"Good. She's supposed to be a good one."

"And NBC is sending a follow-up crew on the jam story – the producer said they want a whole series on canning."

"Linked to your videos?"

Smiling, Cora said, "Yup."

"Hot damn. You should wear this sweater." Mac touched the lace at her shoulder. "It's sexy as hell. You'll inspire a canning revolution across the nation." He took a sip of her tea. "Are Olivia and Esteban working on roping?"

She nodded and swallowed. "She's coming this morning. Every time I mention the rodeo to her, she goes totally green."

Mac didn't look worried. "She's gonna love it."

"She's scared of falling off the horse, of getting bucked, of getting her hand caught. She's scared of everything."

"And yet she's doing it anyway. Huh."

"What's that look for?"

He leaned back in his chair, tossing the last bit of the bun into his mouth. "She just reminds me of someone."

"Logan was never scared."

Mac looked at her pointedly. "I was talking about you, Cora. She reminds me of you at that age."

"Always nervous? Planning too much?" She stood, balling up the bag and moving toward the stove.

But Mac grabbed her around the waist and turned her, pulling her down into his lap. "Always brave. Scared and doing it anyway. Plans or no plans. Like this one here." He touched her nose lightly.

She shook her head and tugged at the hem of the lace-sided sweater she'd knitted for Abigail. It was her favorite, and she wore it at least once a week. Mac said it was his favorite, too, but she knew it was just because he could touch her skin through the lace. "Not very brave. That's the whole problem."

"You keep telling yourself that. Keep making your lists –"

"I will."

"And I'll keep watching you do things that scare you. Because it's one of the hottest things about you." He touched the side of her face and leaned in to kiss her neck, right at the place he knew made her crazy.

"How much time do you have?"

"For you? All the time in the world." He stood, bringing Cora to her feet as he went. "I need a shower, though. Care to join me?"

"You don't mind being late to the shelter?"

"Sometimes you have to break the rules, *Corazón*."

He was right. Damn right. He usually – though not always – was about these things. She hadn't planned this. Any of it. And it was perfect.

Cora lifted herself to her toes and kissed him, hard. "I've got some rules for you to break, big guy. Last one in the water's a rotten egg."

Cora turned and fled, racing through the house, letting her love pursue her.

And as it did so often now, their laughter floated throughout their home, drifting out the open windows into the yard and across the dunes, where the waves caught the sound and threw it joyfully back to them.

ABOUT THE AUTHOR

Rachael Herron is the internationally bestselling author of the Cypress Hollow series (HarperCollins/Random House Australia) and of the memoir, A Life in Stitches (Chronicle). Her newest novel, Pack Up The Moon, will be available in March 2014 from Penguin (USA) and Random House Australia (NZ/AUST). Rachael received her MFA in writing from Mills College and is a 911 fire/medical dispatcher when she's not scribbling. She lives with her wife, Lala, in Oakland, California, where they have more animals and instruments than are probably advisable. Rachael is struggling to learn the accordion and can probably play along with you on the ukulele. She's proud of her dual citizenship (New Zealand and United States), and she's been known to knit.

Email Rachael at yarnagogo@gmail.com for a copy of Cora's Side Impact Sweater (by KiraK Designs).

Website: Yarnagogo.com
Twitter: twitter.com/rachaelherron

28946498R00196

Made in the USA
Lexington, KY
07 January 2014